Elizabeth Wilson is a res[illegible] r bo[illegible] *it* [illegible] and *The Girl in Berlin* are also published by Serpent's Tail.

Praise for *The Girl in Berlin*

'The picture of an earlier era of austerity Britain has a confident sweep and truthfulness that establishes *The Girl in Berlin* as something rather special in the espionage genre' *Independent*

'This is a clever, well-written and carefully plotted novel in which class, hypocrisy, moral corruption, treachery and taboos ancient and modern are cunningly interwoven. It's a thoughtful, clever read with a twist at the end that makes you want to turn back the pages to wonder how you missed the clues' *The Times*

'Wilson's third novel has all the strengths of her others. She's great on style; atmosphere (the foul taste of smog in your throat); and how the covertly interlinked milieus that ran the country operated' *Guardian*

'Quite splendid' *Shots Magazine*

Praise for *The Twilight Hour*

'This is an atmospheric book in which foggy, half-ruined London is as much a character as the artists and good-time girls who wander through its pages. It would be selfish to hope for more thrillers from Wilson, who has other intellectual fish to fry, but *The Twilight Hour* is so good that such selfishness is inevitab

'A vivid portrait of bohemian life in Fitzrovia during the austerity of 1947 and the coldest winter of the twentieth century' *Literary Review*

'Fantastically atmospheric ... The cinematic quality of the novel, written as if it were a black and white film with the sort of breathy dialogue that reminds you of *Brief Encounter*, is its trump card' *Sunday Express*

'An elegantly nostalgic, noir thriller; brilliantly conjures up the rackety confusion of Cold War London' *Daily Mail*

Praise for *War Damage*

'[A] first class whodunit ... The portrait of Austerity Britain is masterfully done ... the most fascinating character in this impressive work is the exhausted capital itself' Julia Handford, *Sunday Telegraph*

'[Wilson] evokes louche, bohemian NW3 with skill and relish' John O'Connell, *Guardian*

'The era of austerity after the Second World War makes an entertaining and convincing backdrop to Elizabeth Wilson's fine second novel ... A delight to read' Marcel Berlins, *The Times*

'*War Damage* captures the murky, exhausted feel of post-war London. Buildings and lives are being reconstructed and shady pasts covered over. The atmosphere of secrecy and claustrophobia is as thick as the swirling dust of recently bombed buildings. Wilson excels at a good story set in exquisite period detail' Jane Cholmeley

SHE DIED YOUNG

ELIZABETH WILSON

A complete catalogue record for this book can be obtained from the British Library on request

First published in the UK in 2016 by Serpent's Tail,
an imprint of Profile Books Ltd
3 Holford Yard
Bevin Way
London
WC1X 9HD
www.serpentstail.com

ISBN 978 1 78125 484 4
eISBN 978 1 78283 177 8

Designed and typeset by sue@lambledesign.demon.co.uk

Printed and bound by CPI Group (UK) Ltd, Croydon, CR0 4YY

10 9 8 7 6 5 4 3 2 1

Cover her face; mine eyes dazzle. She died young.

John Webster: *The Duchess of Malfi*

part one

chapter 1

THE QUEEN'S HEAD WAS well away from Fleet Street. You didn't find journalists there. Nor policemen. Faced with tiles the colour of brown ale, it stood on the corner of a street that wandered away towards Soho. Its shabby *moderne* decor, unchanged since before the war, hardly welcomed visitors; the locals avoided it. It resembled a railway waiting room, home to no-one in particular. It was the ideal anonymous meeting place: a pub without regulars – and that was the very reason Gerry Blackstone liked it.

He kept a low profile in a raincoat or tweed jacket and trilby, neither smart nor shabby. There was an air about him – louche and slightly running to seed, weary, yet purposeful and alert – that could have marked him out as a reporter, but passers-by seldom looked closely enough to make a guess.

He paused in the doorway and glanced round the saloon bar. None of the three lone drinkers looked like the man he was to meet. He fetched a pint and sat down in a corner, lounging against the cracked American cloth of the banquette. He ground out a cigarette on the floor and at once lit another. With it stuck to his lip he pretended to be studying the racing tips in his copy of the *Evening News*, midday edition, but he was actually thinking about the coming meeting. It was tricky, because DCI Jack McGovern had a reputation. Not bent, like the rest of them. Once he'd been the coming man, but then he'd fallen foul of MI6. He was still with Special Branch, but there'd been one or two rumours of a new role.

Blackstone hoped he'd picked the right man. Because what he really wanted was to find out more about the girl.

What a turn it had given him to see her like that. His heart had skipped a beat when Rob Crowther at the mortuary had opened the drawer. Horrified, Blackstone had recognised the almost childish face, the little scar between the nostrils and the upper lip. The skin had a horrible fishy glaze to it, but she was still beautiful. Valerie, that was her name.

Crowther hadn't expected Blackstone to recognise the corpse. The girl was of interest because no-one had claimed the body. Sheer coincidence.

Blackstone had felt upset for days. Now he was here to talk about the Soho stabbing, but to him it was only an excuse.

And there was the man himself: a tallish copper in a subtle tweed suit. With that thick, dark hair and olive skin he looked more like an Italian than a Scot. They shook hands.

'What'll you have?'

'Thanks. Half of bitter.'

Abstemious then. Blackstone brought the drinks to the table.

An observer might have taken McGovern for a toff and Blackstone for a man of humble origins. In fact, the Scot was the son of a Clydeside shipyard worker, while Blackstone's father was a well-off undertaker. The journalist's roving life was part of an effort, never successful, to escape the smell of formaldehyde, for his job continually brought him back to corpses and death. But along the way he'd got rid of his cut-glass accent and developed a careless appearance more in keeping with the villains alongside whom he lived.

He watched as the policeman took out a silver case, eased a cigarette from under its elastic band and tapped it against the lid. Expensive, that case; so McGovern thought he was classy, did he. Wasn't that what they held against him? Thought he was different, better than the others, above the fray. That was why Blackstone had chosen him.

'I knew Superintendent Gorch from way back. Sad to see him go.' He hoped it was the right opening gambit. And he meant it. Gorch had always cosied up to the press and he'd be missed by the journalists who thronged the press room at Scotland Yard. You'd see him in the pubs round Scotland Yard, too, hobnobbing with them all. Crime reporters and coppers: they needed one another; like a tree and its ivy or a rhinoceros and the ticks it housed in its crumpled skin.

Jack McGovern nodded, non-committal. Chilly Scots bastard. Blackstone pressed on. 'Hope he's enjoying his retirement. He deserves it. He and I—'

McGovern cut him short. 'You're right. He was a good policeman.'

'Aren't many like that now.'

They gave Gorch a moment's silence, as if he'd passed away, although in fact at this moment he was sunning himself in Cape Town.

It was no use being nostalgic about Gorch. He'd gone and Moules, the new man, was an altogether different kettle of fish. A new relationship had to be formed. It was all unknown territory, uncharted waters.

'So, Mr Blackstone ...?' The Scot waited. He wasn't going to make it easy. And that accent – hint of Scots, not pronounced, but enough to give the impression of reserve, that he was canny, that you wouldn't get much change out of him.

'The *Chronicle*'s keen to help Scotland Yard in any way we can.'

'The right sort of cooperation's always welcome. Not much in evidence just now.'

'I think you'll agree the *Chronicle*'s assistance has been

crucial in the past – Burgess and Maclean, just one example ...' Then he wondered if it was a bit too risky to have mentioned the defection of the famous spies, five years ago. McGovern hadn't been involved directly, but he'd got caught up in a related scandal, exposing the crimes of a top British agent. The spooks hadn't liked it. They hadn't been able to discredit the Scot completely, but they'd done some damage.

Well, he'd said it now. He hurried on. 'And of course we realise the importance of sharing information – it's a two-way system. Superintendent Gorch understood that too.'

'He'd not have appreciated the way you've hammered us over the Soho case.'

'The public's worried. Can't understand why there hasn't been an arrest.' The Met had egg on its face and the *Chronicle* was running a big anti-lawlessness campaign, amplifying a single Soho murder into a major crime wave.

'I'm not involved – I'm sure you know I'm with the Branch. Inspector Slater's following up a number of leads, I believe,' said McGovern cagily, about as forthcoming as Ben Nevis. He stubbed out his cigarette, then added: 'The point is, Superintendent Moules feels the press have not exactly helped in this case. Quite the opposite. If Gorch had asked you to lay off for a few weeks, you'd have listened, would you not?'

'But as we said, Superintendent Gorch ain't here. '

The policeman looked away across the room as if for help from Gorch's ghostly presence.

'How many weeks since Tony Marx was murdered?' persisted Blackstone.

'They need more time. No-one's talking.'

McGovern sat there and waited. Blackstone had to engage his interest, aware that the Scot wasn't going to make it easy, and wasn't prepared to wait indefinitely.

'Inspector Slater's case, you say,' he ventured.

'As you know.'

'Inspector Slater is quite efficient, or so I thought, at getting villains to talk.'

Silence.

Blackstone moved on. 'It's not so much the Marx case in itself that interests me.'

'So what does interest you, Mr Blackstone?'

'All sorts of rumours going around ... the new Super ... heard he's a bit of a bureaucrat. Very keen on cracking down on irregularities, as it were.'

McGovern said nothing.

'CID's got a bit of a reputation these days, hasn't it, and not least Inspector Slater. His time in the flying squad was full of incident.'

'Well, now he's at West End Central, Division C.'

'Plenty of opportunities there for Inspector Slater's special methods.'

McGovern stood up. 'If you brought me here to talk about my colleagues, you're wasting your time.' Blackstone half rose too, started to put out a hand. McGovern mustn't leave, not yet.

But McGovern merely said: 'Same again?'

That must be a good sign – unless the policeman's move had been to stop the conversation getting into choppy waters.

With the refilled glasses on the table in front of them, Blackstone pursued his point. 'Rumour has it your new guvnor is piloting a little sort of unofficial enquiry into what's going on and it occurred to me that he might think you're just the man.'

McGovern stared into the distance. A young woman appeared in the doorway, silhouetted against the white November chill outside, hesitated and left again. 'Who did you hear that from?' he said with apparent indifference.

'No-one mentioned your name. I worked it out for myself.'

'Remind me – you're the big-time crime reporter? Bigger

fish to fry than ill-founded gossip about police corruption, I'd have thought.'

'The crimes of the powerful, Chief Inspector. Aren't they the biggest crimes of all?'

Silence again. Blackstone feared McGovern's reputation for discretion was going to outweigh his alleged dislike of corruption; however before the silence had become too uncomfortable, the Scot said: 'Superintendent Moules has been in post – how long – less than a month? And already you're hounding him over the Soho case. That'll not help if it's cooperation you're after.'

'Say we go easy for a couple of weeks ...'

'That would be welcome. As for the rumour – like every new super, Moules thinks he's a new broom. He wants everything all neat and tidy. You're aware of his reputation in Birmingham. He'll not tolerate irregularities any more than Superintendent Gorch. But you've picked the wrong man if you think I'm involved. In the Branch, we lead a life apart, a charmed life, some think. You surely know that.'

'That's the very reason—' Blackstone was surprised that the Scot had said even this much. Because as Blackstone read it, the denial was a kind of admission. So perhaps the stony Glaswegian was going to cooperate. He must have played it right after all. On the other hand, if McGovern's remit had been to get the *Chronicle* to cool down, he'd achieved his mission – or at least done what he could, which wasn't much, to stem the flood of bad publicity.

McGovern was finishing his drink. Blackstone had to act, to mention the thing that really mattered to him.

'What about the girl in the hotel?'

'Girl?'

'The one they found in some knocking shop at the back of Bloomsbury.'

McGovern frowned. 'I don't recall the case.'

'Hotel in Argyle Street. Well ... call it a hotel ...' He pulled out a crumpled packet of fags and without offering it to his companion, lit a tired-looking cigarette straight off the previous stub. 'An accident. Girl fell down the stairs. Barely a mention in the local rag. Funny, that. When I was on the *St Pancras Gazette*, a death like that would have been all over the front page. Used to be my territory, you see. Now I'm with the *Chronicle* – fair enough, it's not a story for the nationals. Not yet anyway.'

'An accidental death'll not hit the headlines.'

'That's just the point. She was supposed to have tripped – fell down the stairs and broke her neck. High heels can be dangerous.'

'No doubt they can.' Finally McGovern smiled. 'But you know, those hotels might be sordid, that doesna turn an accident into a crime.'

'The coroner had doubts. Opted for an accident in the end, but it was very iffy. And no-one's claimed the body. There was a doctor very conveniently on the scene. Signed the death certificate there and then. The police weren't even called. It wasn't properly investigated and I can't help wondering why not.' Blackstone raised his hands to indicate huge areas of uncertainty and suspicion. He hoped he'd sown a little seed of curiosity. He wasn't going to let this Itie-looking Hibernian, this block of effing North British granite defeat him; and glancing sideways, Blackstone thought he had aroused the detective's interest, because a faint frown had replaced McGovern's studied neutrality.

Finally the policeman looked up and straight at him. 'You say the coroner returned a verdict of accidental death. But you don't believe it was an accident. And yet there was no police involvement.'

'Let's just say there's more to it than meets the eye. And I reckoned Superintendent Moules wouldn't like to think a death like that hadn't been dealt with properly.'

McGovern drank the rest of his beer and stood up. 'I'm sure he would not. I have to be on my way.' He looked down at Blackstone. 'I'll look into it, but I doubt I'll be much help to you in the short run, I'll be away from London, checking up on Hungarian refugees in Oxford.'

'Poor sods. What a bleeding mess.' But there was no time to chat about the failed revolution in Hungary, so Blackstone also stood up. 'I'll be in touch, Chief Inspector. Perhaps you'll have some news for me.'

McGovern merely smiled and said: 'Good to meet you, Mr Blackstone.'

Blackstone watched the policeman walk away. He moved quietly, inconspicuously, not one of those coppers that swelled to fill the space. Not self-important, as many of them were. Though of course you could prick their balloon double quick when you got to know what they were up to.

Gerry Blackstone hadn't had high hopes of the meeting, but he had a feeling it had turned out all right after all. McGovern hadn't actually denied that something was going on with the CID. And by drawing McGovern's attention to the Argyle Street affair, he had possibly given him a little help – if he was involved in some sort of internal investigation. Personally, Blackstone thought there was little chance of any superintendent successfully ending police corruption, but he wished the new man all the luck in the world.

That McGovern was involved in the attempt to clean up the force was just a hunch, based on rumours he'd gleaned from Johnnie Hay. Johnnie had told him some disgruntled copper or other had come into his club one evening and had been grumbling about the new man, Moules, cracking down on all the methods that made police work possible and talking about how McGovern was the blue-eyed boy again. Could have all been spite and jealousy, but Blackstone sensed there must be something in it.

More important than all that, though, and very personal, was – he had to know how Valerie had died.

The saloon was almost empty. He made a phone call from the booth in the corridor that led to the lavatories and then took a taxi to Bayswater. He'd chalk it up to expenses, as he always did. He took a lot of taxis. The editor – the Little Man as they called him, but he terrified them all – never objected. Blackstone was tired (he was always tired) and he felt he deserved the ride.

chapter 2

'TA, MATE.' THE TAXI DRIVER rang up the little 'for hire' flag and drove away. Blackstone surveyed the neo-Georgian mansion block he was facing: Balmoral Mansions. It was situated in a dull, conservative district near Marble Arch. He took the lift to the second floor, avoiding the sight of himself in its mirrors.

The maid opened the door. 'We haven't seen you for a while, Mr Blackstone.'

He held his cigarette between two nicotine-stained fingers. 'You're looking well, Mrs Smith.' He wondered fleetingly about her past. She reminded him disturbingly of his former nanny; similar grey bun and air of homely efficiency.

He waited for Sonia in her drawing room, seated cautiously on the Louis XVI gilded sofa. It was fake, of course, and the peach velvet curtains and pale Chinese carpet were all very Hollywood, as was the radiogram that doubled as a cocktail cabinet. Still, it was classy enough for what it was – although exactly *what* it was would have been hard to define. You couldn't call it a brothel. He supposed it might have been described as a place where you came to have a good time.

'Gerry! How nice to see you.'

Sonia wore a close-fitting grey dress and high-heeled black court shoes. Since he'd last seen her she'd had her dark hair cut short in a sleek gamine style. He didn't like short hair on any woman and it made Sonia look more untouchable than ever. But when she sat down, her legs were something else, slung sideways in the smooth perfection of her nylons.

'Madge will bring us something in a minute.' She raised her winged eyebrows slightly, friendly and a little mocking, but it was as if all men were the object of her mockery, Blackstone being merely the current representative.

He didn't mind. He took people as they came and she came in useful from time to time, as much for the information she slyly passed on as for the girls she provided.

'You didn't want an introduction today, Gerry? If you'd given me a bit of notice – there's a new girl, lovely young thing, definitely your type, up from the country ... '

Blackstone shook his head. 'Just thought I'd look in and say hello.'

The maid brought drinks on a tray: whisky for Blackstone and tea for his hostess.

'Don't you ever drink, Sonia?'

Sonia poured two fingers of whisky for her guest. 'You know I don't.'

Blackstone edged himself further up the sloping sofa. 'All work and no play, you know, makes Jill a dull girl.'

'I like being dull, darling. It's much more profitable. Let other girls have the fun.' She dropped a slice of lemon into the cup of pale tea. Its steam wafted the tarry scent of Lapsang Souchong.

'Things going well?' he asked and they chatted for a while until he felt it looked natural enough to say: 'I wondered if you'd heard about that girl in a King's Cross hotel, broke her neck falling down the stairs. Apparently.'

Sonia lifted the lid off the lacquer box that contained cigarettes, delicately picked one out, pushed the box in his direction and lit up with a gold lighter, which she then set down carefully, so that it made no noise against the glass table top. Every gesture was careful and precise. There was nothing unpremeditated about Sonia.

'Really? Poor girl. No – I hadn't heard. Should I have? Was it in the papers?'

'She wasn't just some scrubber hanging round the stations. The thing is – it gave me a shock, I can tell you – I knew her. In fact, you introduced us. I met her through you. Just the once. She was nice. Quiet, quite well bred. And a looker. We were meant to meet up again, but somehow we didn't ... it was a while ago.'

'You could have asked me at the time if you'd wanted to see her again. If you'd lost touch with her.'

'It wasn't a big thing. You know how it is. I meant to follow it up, anyway, that's not the point. It was just ... I got to wondering what had happened ... I thought you might know something about where she went to – not *now*, but ... I suppose it was about eighteen months ... maybe two years ago. Yes, couple of years, must be. Valerie ... that was the name ...'

'You going soft, Gerry? Not like you to be sentimental.' She stared quizzically at the reporter and shook her head. 'I don't recall ... I've known quite a few Valeries,' she said vaguely.

Gerry shifted about on the slippery sofa, impatient. 'Blonde, with lovely big brown eyes.' The lids had been closed over them, of course.

'They don't work for me, Gerry. You know better than that. I'm just a go-between, I put people in touch.'

'You know what I mean.' He leaned forward. 'Lovely body. Voluptuous. Bit like Marilyn Monroe. And yet she was quite shy and ... naive I suppose. Didn't seem to realise she was God's gift to man.'

Sonia frowned. 'Oh, *that* Valerie. Yes ... I do vaguely remember. Came from the south coast somewhere ... Portsmouth, I think ...? You're a shrewd one, aren't you? You're right. She had no idea.' She took a drag, inhaled deeply and blew out a plume of smoke. 'Of what could be achieved with a body like hers. So ... she fell down the stairs, you said. But that's terrible,' said Sonia, with a solemn expression in recognition of the awful reality that anyone, however young and beautiful, could die at any time. 'And yet I suppose in a way I'm not altogether surprised that ...' Her voice faded away. Then: 'I hadn't heard anything of her for a long while.'

'How long?'

'Oh ... I really can't remember. I mean, they come and go, you know. I'm not a jailer, the silly bitches do what they want and often it's something stupid.' She shrugged, but then leaned forward and smiled in a change of mood. 'But I might have known you weren't here just to pass the time of day. You're very naughty, Gerry, always out for information, never off duty, are you – talk about me being all work and no play, but look at you. Always got your nose to the ground, always on the lookout for a story!'

It was more than a story to him, but 'You know me,' he said with a shrug and a guilty grin. 'Thing is, looks like the Bill might take an interest. Falling down stairs – always seems a bit fishy, don't it. There's a new man ... one of those "I'm going to clean up the Met" types, y'know, he's interested so ...' He wasn't interested yet, of course, but Blackstone hoped McGovern would pass on the message and that something would come of it; although it was already late in the day, weeks since the accident.

'It all sounds rather sordid, darling. Sad, of course, but so many of those girls, they don't seem to know how to look after themselves. I try to warn them, but ... most of them are too flighty or too stupid to listen, I'm afraid.'

Her shrug told Blackstone she'd said all she was going to say. He had to contain his frustration; and he didn't like the way she dismissed the girls with a sneer. She was a cold bitch, but that was part of what made her useful. They chatted for a while – about whether Princess Margaret had got over not marrying Peter Townsend. It was an old story and bored Blackstone rigid. He was sorry for the princess in a way, but she was just an over-privileged rich tart, after all, with nothing to worry about, compared to Valerie.

'All those stuffy old archbishops and their cant about Christian marriage,' Sonia smiled. 'And then they come here and want a good time with my girls.'

For a moment Blackstone thought this might be something big. 'Not the Archbishop of Canterbury?'

Sonia laughed out loud – a rare event. 'Good God, no, Gerry. And d'you think I'd tell you if—'

'No – course not. You're the soul of discretion. We all know that.'

'I just meant priests in general. They're human like everyone else, I suppose.'

'Are they? What sort of human things do they get up to then?'

Sonia leaned forward slightly. 'Well, I mustn't be indiscreet, darling, but there's one old gentleman ... an archdeacon, I think that's what he calls himself ...'

It was quite amusing, as gossip, but it wasn't big enough to interest him. He knew he wouldn't get the information he'd hoped for about Valerie, so as soon as he decently could, he heaved himself to his feet, and said: 'I must be off. Thanks for the whisky, Sonia.'

'So soon? It's lovely to see you. And you haven't been to one of my little parties for ever such a long time. I'm having another one soon – I'll let you know.'

'Oh, I'm just an old square, Sonia, too old for that sort of thing.'

'Nonsense, darling, everyone needs a bit of fun every once in a while. Do you good. You're looking tired.'

She saw him into the corridor and then, just as he turned

to say goodbye, she said: 'You know, I think I do remember – I think ... Valerie, that *was* her name, wasn't it, I think she went off to live with someone in Paddington somewhere, some West Indian, I believe.'

That was a bit of a shock. Gerry prided himself on being open-minded and he had useful contacts in that community, but the way some of them treated white girls ...

Sonia continued: 'It was only a rumour. But why don't you ask Sonny Marsden or someone you know down there?'

'Sonny Marsden?'

'Of course it was a while ago, quite a long while, actually.'

'Thanks, Sonia. I'll think about it. Good idea.'

They didn't kiss or even shake hands as they parted. She never touched him.

chapter 3

THE PORTOBELLO ROAD MEANDERED downhill away from Notting Hill Gate past the ramshackle antiques rooms and junk stalls and the fruit and vegetable market. Only twenty minutes away from Balmoral Mansions, this was a different London. The further you went the more West Indians passed along the pavements. On this dingy November afternoon their faces looked pinched and grey. Gerry Blackstone thought if you came from a Caribbean island you'd never get used to the cold. He walked on – he spent a lot of his time walking, when he wasn't in taxis – until he reached Golborne Road and turned right. He found the house he was looking for in a cul-de-sac, cut off by a wall that plunged cliff-like to the railway line far below.

A train rattled past. He stared up at the sooty façade in the twilight. The terrace was slowly dying. A stringy buddleia had seeded itself in the pediment above the windows. Weeds pushed up between cracks in the pavement and around the area railings.

It was hard to believe that this whole area had once been fields, so completely had the land been buried by bricks and paving and mortar and streets, streets, nothing but streets. Yet as stone decayed, nature returned, crept up from the railway sidings and bomb sites, its fingers unsettling the foundations, dislodging the pointing between crumbling bricks and sending spidery cracks up the flaking stucco.

Near here, John Christie had hidden the decaying corpses of women he'd strangled under the floorboards of his kitchen, and the seedy necrophile still seemed to haunt the solitude. Blackstone had a lot to thank Christie for. The case had made his name.

He approached the end house, squeezed up against the railway wall. The scumble stain on the door was worn away in places. There was neither knocker nor bell and only a raw slit where a letter box had once been. He banged on the panel. Getting no response, he banged again, though with diminishing expectations, but he heard footsteps inside and the door was opened.

A tall West Indian stared at him. The look wasn't so much suspicious as simply blank, closed off, as if the man had long since ceased to expect favours from anyone.

'Sonny Marsden at home?'

'Who want him?' The accent was Jamaican.

Blackstone produced a card from his inner pocket. The Jamaican looked at it. Then he shook his head. 'Ain't here.'

'Know where I can find him?'.

The taller man stared at Blackstone as if seeing him from some far-distant location or down the wrong end of a telescope, as if Blackstone were a minute speck of dust in the gritty air.

'I'm a friend of his,' ventured Blackstone.

'At his club. Powis Square. You find him there most likely,' said the stranger. Blackstone found his deadpan manner strange and oppressive. Dressed in a suit too loose for his gaunt frame, the negro wore a royal blue tie and a clean white shirt, as if ready to go out himself, but spoke as if he came from another planet, and also as if some nameless mental burden afflicted him.

'Thanks mate. I'll try there.'

Blackstone had been to the club – more like a shebeen – at 6 Powis Square before, but then he had been escorted by Sonny Marsden himself. 'Tell him I called, anyway, will you? Give him my card. He knows me.'

He turned to walk away.

'Wait, I'm goin' that way myself.' And now the Jamaican spoke with more animation. He strode along so that Blackstone had difficulty keeping up with him.

'Any special reason you wanting to see him?'

'I'm looking for someone – a girl. Valerie. Name ring a bell?'

The man from Jamaica made a strangled coughing sound, which Blackstone realised stood in for a laugh; it was meant to convey that there were many girls around the area, that quite a few of them might well be called Valerie, and that he couldn't be expected to remember them or even distinguish one from another.

The near-darkness veiled the dereliction of Powis Square. Blackstone followed his companion down the shaky metal stairs to Sonny Marsden's basement club.

A West Indian opened the door, but not the whole way. 'Who's that with you, man?'

'Says he a friend of Sonny's.'

'Gerry Blackstone.' Blackstone spoke with confidence.

The man disappeared into the darkness. They waited. When he returned he gestured silently for them to follow him.

Sonny Marsden was as short as Blackstone's companion was tall.

'Gerry, man! Good to see you. You met Alfie, then.'

The proprietor escorted the arrivals along a dark passage. He pushed aside the curtain at the end and opened a door onto a large, ill-lit room. The smell of ganja hit Blackstone at once and indeed the air was thick with smoke. Blackstone made out a pool table in the middle of the room. Two black men and a white man were using it to play cards. He also glimpsed through the fog a black man and a white woman seated, smoking, on a sagging Victorian sofa against the wall to his left. The atmosphere was relaxed.

Beers were brought. Something a good deal stronger was Sonny's forte, but Blackstone had to get back to the office in a while.

'There was this girl ...' he began and retold the Argyle Street story. 'I heard she'd moved down this way a year or more ago. And you know everyone, Sonny, you know what's going on round here ...'

'This a while ago, though, I ain't remember every damn bird come down this way, Jeez, there's so many ...' and Sonny Marsden started to laugh, but it was an angry laugh. 'I ain't never heard nor seen of this Valerie, man.'

And indeed, the more Blackstone thought about it, the less likely it seemed that Sonny would remember Valerie. She might or might not have drifted down to Paddington, but there was no reason Marsden would have remembered her among all the others; except for her looks, that is. Or unless she'd been one of his girls. Had that been what Sonia had been hinting? 'Lovely girl,' he said, 'looked like Marilyn Monroe.'

'What she doing then got to do with what happened to her now?'

'Just background stuff.'

Yes – she might well have passed through Notting Dale, but few would remember her now and if Marsden remembered he'd as like as not keep quiet about it. Blackstone decided to let the matter drop for the time being, just pump Sonny a bit generally to see if there was any other useful information in the offing.

He never smoked ganja himself, but the air was so thickly laden with the smoke that he began to feel its effects. It wasn't difficult to get Marsden talking and soon Blackstone was hearing lurid tales of life in Paddington. There was a tasty story about a gambling den in Blenheim Crescent, on Church Commissioners' premises too, but Blackstone didn't think he could use it. The Little Man had the greatest respect for the Church. Unlike other established institutions, the C of E was safe from the *Chronicle*. Yet he might try to follow it up, or get someone else to.

On the other hand when Sonny boasted about all the society folk and film stars who'd come to Powis Square, you had to take it with a pinch of salt. 'A man come in here the other night, looks the boys up and down, pick one out. You know for why? His wife want a bit of rough. Looking for a stud. And that's not the first time. These rich white women, they got the money, but their husbands, they don't give them no satisfaction.'

That was also not the sort of thing that could go in a family paper – if for no other reason than that it would be an insult to the white male readership. It could only inflame prejudice and increase the resentment, because it was already a powerful myth, that the newcomers took all the white women thanks to their possession of some magical and mysterious sexual power.

'Film stars! In here, eh!' Blackstone looked round the shabby room. 'Give us some names, Sonny.'

Sonny just grinned.

'And what does your brother think of all this?'

'He telling me to get a job. Make like it's a good job, London Transport, but … ' Sonny shrugged. 'Don't sound like a lot of money to me. And he get lip from passengers, lotta lip. All the time.'

'I'd like to meet your brother. I'd like to hear his story.' Two lives, two brothers, the contrast between the two: that wouldn't do for the *Chronicle* either, but he might get it placed in a magazine … *Picture Post*, even, they'd done sympathetic stuff on West Indians from time to time, but *Picture Post* had gone downhill.

'He don't bother me and I don't bother him. Ain't seen him for a while anyway. Last I heard he was in Warwick Road. Number 81, if you're interested.'

It was gone seven by the time Blackstone roused himself. He had to get back to the paper to file a report on the Soho stabbing. Not that there was anything to say about it.

Sonny accompanied him along the passage. By the door he suddenly and unexpectedly gripped Blackstone's arm. 'What's it all about, man, you coming down here with this story about the girl? Who told you come and see me? Ain't got nothing to do with me, man.' Suddenly he was angry and suspicious.

Blackstone did not point out that his host was more or less a pimp, nor that his reputation was not exactly for treating women with kid gloves. 'Just a general enquiry, old cock,' he murmured soothingly.

'It better be. And don't you go putting stuff about me in your paper. I sued the *Graphic* and won. Remember that.' His eyes glittered in the darkness of the corridor.

'Who could forget that, Sonny?' Indeed, it was a miracle. You had to tip your hat to a West Indian who'd taken on the might of the great British press and come out on top. No wonder the press now treated Sonny Marsden with kid gloves.

The smell hit him before he reached the glass-partitioned rooms: printer's ink and cigarette smoke, metallic as the tannin in the dark brown tea they drank.

Four of his colleagues, shirtsleeves rolled up, sat deep in page proofs. The floor was littered with torn-up sheets of paper and the spikes were piled high. Orders were shouted at the messengers.

'You're bloody late, Gerry. Where the hell – the Little Man's on the warpath.'

Against the cacophony of clattering typewriters, telephones ringing, shouts for tea and general curses, he wrote fast and well. It was basically an anti-police story, but he toned it down a bit as he wanted to keep on the right side of McGovern. His fingers pressed eagerly down on the keys – he loved the feel of it as you touched the keys like buttons, it was a sensual, almost sexual sensation, like pressing a woman's nipples. He shifted the article towards more of a mood piece, less about mobsters outwitting Sergeant Plod and more about Soho, that colourful community of exotic workers, with Italian waiters as the chorus in a romance of bohemian entrepreneurs, battling to save their unique way of life from the porn shops that were threatening to move in. He wanted them to put a splash on his piece, but there was still too much stuff on the fallout from Suez and Hungary.

He was hoping against hope to avoid the Little Man. But his nemesis caught up with him. 'This doctor in Eastbourne. You'd better get down there. Find out what's going on.' The proprietor's hoarse voice was the sort to give bronchitis a bad name, and it always suggested menace. 'You should have been on to it weeks ago. Rumours been swilling around since ... if it hadn't been for Suez ...'

The genteel south coast resort was rocked with the speculation engulfing Dr John Bodkin Adams, a benevolent general practitioner suspected of hastening the end of the many elderly ladies who'd left him large sums in their wills. It was shaping up to be a huge scandal. Blackstone knew he'd have to get down there. But it didn't interest him. He could think about nothing but the girl in the hotel, and after he had finished his Soho piece he made sure Valerie's death finally made it to NIBS. Normally the short pieces in News in Brief were written by stringers trying to get a toe-hold, but he had a feeling about the girl and wrote it himself. And the mini-headline: 'HIGH HEELS ARE DANGEROUS'. That had the ring of the American writers he admired – Dashiell Hammett, Micky Spillane, Jim Thompson and Raymond Chandler. Chandler was originally English, of course. He'd even been to the same school as Blackstone: Dulwich College.

chapter 4

'I OVERHEARD A *HILARIOUS* conversation in Blackwell's.' They were seated at the back of the Cadena Café on the corner of Cornmarket and the Broad. 'There was this woman in the languages section – obviously a don's wife – and she was asking for a *Hungarian phrase book*! "We've got a *wonderful* young freedom fighter staying with us,"' mimicked Charles Hallam in his campest falsetto. '"A refugee from the revolution! *So* brave and so handsome!" God!'

Penny Brookfield squinted at Charles through the smoke from her cigarette. She looked puzzled, and didn't seem to see why it was funny.

'Don't you see how pretentious it is? All that rot about freedom fighters. Half of them are just petty criminals trying to evade justice back home.'

'Oh – *are* they?' Penny looked terribly disappointed.

'Well – not all of them I suppose.'

It was Fergus, his communist friend, who had told Charles that. But that was before Fergus had left the Party, disgusted by the Soviet invasion. Charles, like almost everyone, sided with the rebels, yet was cynical about the Cold War propaganda that daily flooded the papers.

'D'you think there'll be another war?'

'I shouldn't think so.'

The excitement of the past weeks grew ever more feverish. There was bad news every day. Even the undergraduates talked about nothing else. It seemed as if he alone was bored now, sick of the photos of Anthony Eden, a broken prime minister, with his toothbrush moustache and weak chin, sick of pictures of fighting around the Suez Canal, and equally sick of the Hungarian uprising and the anti-communist hysteria in its wake.

'You're not in a very good mood, are you,' said Penny.

Charles resented Penny for having noticed. Not that it was a mood. These days it was a settled disposition. 'I'm fine.' He looked away across the crowded café, through the swirls of smoke. At the front, W.H. Auden, the famous Professor of Poetry, could be seen silhouetted against the light as he held court amid an admiring circle of acolytes. That annoyed Charles too: the jockeying for position, the fawning on celebrity – and Fergus, for all his revolutionary views, was as bad as the rest of them. In fact he was sitting there now, gazing with rapt attention at the poet's craggy face.

'Are you going to Julian's party?'

Charles made an effort to smile. 'Not sure. Probably not. I was surprised he even invited me.'

'Alistair said he'll see me there. Oh, do come.'

She stirred the foam around in her coffee. She was pretty, he supposed, her face still rather unformed, with big eyes and mouth and thick eyebrows; her short curly hair was mousy brown and hadn't been brushed; and she shouldn't be so desperately earnest.

'I don't go to undergraduate parties any more,' he said. 'I'm no longer in circulation. In fact my life is a social wasteland.'

She laughed, astonished. 'What on earth do you mean?'

They had, after all, met at a party. Long ago, it seemed, on the New Building lawn at Magdalen. Alistair's party. The funny thing was, he'd had his eye on Alistair and then the truth had dawned – that Penny was Alistair's girlfriend. So he'd chatted to her, flattered her, found out which college she was at (St Hilda's) and later sent a note round inviting her to tea. He'd never got anywhere with Alistair, but he and Penny became friends, which was ironic, really.

He didn't know quite why he liked her. He just liked having a girl friend, someone to chat and giggle and talk about clothes with, but that was another irony, because Penny wasn't the chattering or giggling type. She'd rather talk about Simone de Beauvoir.

'It's different, being a postgraduate,' he said. 'It's a different world.'

'I should've thought it'd be rather exciting.'

'It isn't.'

'But last year – and this summer even – you were enjoying it, you seemed to be ... '

'It was still new then, it was still a novelty. And that was before I got lumbered with Professor Quinault.'

She looked at him with wide-eyed anxiety. 'So what are you going to do? You're not going to chuck it up, are you?'

Silly idiot. She always took everything so literally. At face value. Face value was everything where Penny was concerned.

'Of course not. I might if I could think of anything else to do. You know I did the Russian course for National Service.'

'I'm not sure what that is.'

'It seemed like a cushy option for intellectuals, miles better than going to Cyprus or Germany. We just did all this Russian. But one gradually realised it was really for recruiting spies. I might have joined the secret services.'

'Might you really? How exciting!'

'It didn't appeal.'

'Anyway, your research is so interesting. The first Roman emperors. You mustn't lose heart.'

Both of them were utterly unaware of it, but as Penny

spoke she looked just as her mother used to when making conversation with Indian dignitaries: head slightly on one side, an encouraging smile, hands locked together on her lap. The difference was, Penny's interest and concern were genuine.

He longed to write a really shocking book about the early Roman Empire; but it was already too late. The Romans – Tacitus, Suetonius, Juvenal – had started the scandalmongering themselves and it had gone on from there, right up to the eighteenth century and Edward Gibbon's enormous history, *Decline and Fall*. There was no shocking revelation you could unearth that had not already been reported by all those historians and writers, and as if that wasn't bad enough, Charles had been pipped to the post by Robert Graves' much more recent novel, *I Claudius*.

Anyway, that sort of thing was not what Oxford wanted at all. A study of Roman farming practices in the Latium with a discussion of the slave economy would be far more appropriate; an article in the *Journal of Roman Studies*, not some lurid bestseller. Even were he capable of writing such a book, it would only create a sensation if it was totally counter-intuitive, if those bloodthirsty pagan murderers could be presented as heroes: a revisionist account of the Emperor Caligula, tragically thwarted transvestite, the Oscar Wilde of his day. Now that the *fin de siècle*, Aubrey Beardsley and the *Yellow Book* were coming back into fashion, of course, all things were possible. Charles rather liked the idea of spearheading a revival of decadence, something to shake up the stodgy tedium of the mid-twentieth century.

'What you don't understand, Penny, is that undergraduates are here to have fun. It's a children's tea party. But fun is an entirely foreign concept to the world of the postgraduate. As postgraduates the troglodytes, the cave dwellers, come into their own. It's a world of dreary grammar-school types.'

'I'm sure that's nonsense,' said Penny firmly – again, it

was her mother speaking. 'You're being awfully cynical. And snobbish. Janey – you know my friend Janey – she went to a grammar school and she's much cleverer than me. She wants to go into the civil service.'

'I thought girls were here to get husbands.' This was deliberately provocative, all part of Charles' bad mood.

'Don't be like that. That's just nasty. Mind you, that's what the Principal told us. We're being educated to be diplomats' wives.'

'Really?' Charles thought fleetingly of the only girl in his seminar, a dreary young woman with glasses. 'How depressing.'

'You just find everything depressing at the moment. You need cheering up. Come to the party later. Please come. Alistair won't be able to take me. He has to be there early. He's one of the hosts. And I won't know many people. Most of Julian's friends are rather grand. I was only invited because of Alistair. He and Julian see a lot of each other these days. You know – that Christ Church set.'

Charles could see she was anxious, so he said: 'We'll meet up beforehand and go together, shall we?'

'Oh, *can* we? Yes, let's.' On this, she stood up, knocking her cup over so that the dregs of coffee dribbled onto the table. 'I've got a lecture.'

He stood up when she did. 'I have to see Quinault. But I'll meet you outside St Hilda's at six.'

Charles was not in fact due to see Professor Quinault until four in the afternoon. He went back to Blackwell's bookshop and loitered there for a while, then biked to the Bodleian in search of the learned paper a fellow doctoral student had recommended.

At three-thirty he left the library and set off on foot for Corpus Christi College. He'd collect his bike later. He hadn't eaten, but wasn't hungry.

The mauve November afternoon suited his mood. A mist rolling up from the river further softened the faded old buildings of Cotswold stone. The dank cobbled lanes along which he paced lived in perpetual dusk. Tattered yellow leaves clung to branches but most of the foliage was underfoot, rustling in the gutters like torn brown paper. He could imagine he was walking through some impressionistic painting – Whistler, Corot, Piper even.

But how wearisome it was to experience life through the veil of art instead of directly. As he wandered along, a pair of rugger players in muddy shirts and shorts jogged past him. He envied them. To experience life directly, physically, was so much more authentic than to be a pallid aesthete.

He walked slowly, reluctantly. He didn't enjoy his sessions with Professor Quinault and was only too glad they were few and far between. It wasn't even as if it'd be a proper discussion of his work. There'd be other people invited to tea.

On this occasion, however, there was, after all, no-one else. A fire spat and glowed in the stone grate, providing more illumination than the foggy light bulbs. Everything in the room was ancient and shabby, like the Professor himself. Like Oxford itself. Oxford wore its ancient shabbiness to disguise the ambitions of members such as Professor Quinault. Indeed, the Professor himself had once said: 'Patina, my dear Hallam, patina, is so important in creating the right impression.'

Certainly the room created the impression of a scholarship and a culture with a pedigree so long and precious as to take any foreigner's breath away (but particularly any American's). Patina, however, was hazardous and the room full of booby traps. The ancient Turkish carpet, for example, was frayed at the edge so that the unwary visitor was in danger of tripping up on its unravelling strings; an ancient book sent up a cloud of dust if removed from its shelf; and the springs of the visitor's leather armchair had long ago collapsed, so that sitting down involved an undignified bump.

Professor Quinault himself, shrunken and mummified inside the stiff tweed three-piece suit he always wore, matched the room. Sparse strands of tallow-coloured hair straggled across his scalp and hung over his forehead to meet eyebrows as unruly and sprouting as his locks were scant. His lizard skin was dry and cracked and he had cultivated (Charles felt sure it was cultivated) a shuffling, wavering walk. His voice sounded equally uncertain; but – and that was the trick – he managed to infuse his utterances, no matter how banal, with vague significance.

They faced each other, seated either side of the chimney piece. The rosy firelight contrasted with the darkness of the rest of the room, making it even more shadowy. An ancient electric kettle came fitfully to the boil and Professor Quinault poured water into the teapot, which stood prepared with the cups and saucers on a tray. Charles had rather hoped for sherry.

'How are you getting along, dear boy? Making progress, I hope.'

'I'm doing a lot of reading at the moment,' Charles began cautiously. He'd actually done very little work since the summer. The heat of the fire was stupefying, and made him feel dull and sleepy. He began to rehearse the tedious argument of the article he'd just read, but to his relief a knock on the door was followed immediately by the appearance of a stranger.

'Ah – I'm interrupting.' The hesitation of the new arrival was formal rather than sincere.

'Turbeville! Not at all. Not at all. Come in. An unexpected pleasure.'

Charles scrambled to his feet from the depths of the armchair. He recognised Rodney Turbeville at once, for as a junior minister at the Home Office he'd been in the front line of the Hungarian crisis, dealing with refugees, and so had featured recently in the press. Seen close to, Turbeville was shorter than expected, but still had the slightly larger-than-life quality that politicians tended to acquire: he was bald and rather untidy, his torso filled out by good tailoring and a personality projected by his professional smile.

'I'm on my way back to London after constituency business – a minor emergency. At a time like this – the crisis. I managed to sort it out, I'm thankful to say – the constituency stuff, that is. Now back to the general turmoil.'

There was a moment of uncertainty as Quinault dragged a chair into the vicinity of the fireplace, nearly overturning the tea tray. 'Sit ye down, a cup of tea for the weary traveller.'

Almost as an afterthought, as if wishing to minimise Charles' presence, he mumbled an introduction. But the new visitor thrust out his hand.

'Delighted to meet you. How I envy you. What an oasis of calm even in the midst of these testing times – wonderful to get away from Westminster, no matter how briefly.' Unable to reach the tiny table on which the tea tray was perched, Turbeville held his cup and saucer perilously on his knee.

That was the trouble with patina. It usually involved discomfort. Patina indicated a world where things didn't run smoothly in the modern way. Patina was quite different from Turbeville's energy. That was as modern as you please.

Turbeville sprayed the patina with crisp platitudes about the crisis, giving away nothing, as Charles noticed. It was a polished performance, with, in fact, a patina – or patter – all its own, but Charles couldn't help wondering what made it worthwhile for this up-and-coming politician to visit his former tutor. He watched and listened and soon detected – not from anything said – that his own presence was inhibiting the two older men. There was a hint of something withheld. Rodney

Turbeville had not just casually dropped in out of friendliness, good manners or respect for a distinguished scholar.

'All prepared for the onslaught of Hungarians?' Turbeville leaned forward and Charles guessed that this was what the politician had come to talk about – although he couldn't imagine why Quinault would be interested in them.

He rose languidly. 'I have to be off, I'm afraid, sir.'

'Oh ... must you ... but we haven't discussed ... ' The protest was purely formal.

'Good luck with your endeavours,' said Turbeville. This came with another hearty handshake.

A black Austin Princess limousine stood parked outside the college in the narrow lane, impeding the passage of any vehicle other than a bike that might wish to pass.

The party was in full swing when they arrived. Penny had been late meeting Charles, presumably because she'd taken great trouble with her appearance. It hadn't quite worked. The black top and full taffeta skirt didn't flatter her rather chunky body and although she'd washed and tried to set her hair, the effect was still formless and untidy.

Charles himself felt ill at ease. This would have been quite his scene in undergraduate days. Then he'd flitted from one party to the next on waves of sherry and champagne, drunk Benedictine till dawn while arguing about Wittgenstein's philosophy and flirted as much with Bullingdon types as with the communists who rose from their beds to leaflet the Cowley motor works just as he was off to his, preferably with a new conquest.

This evening his black polo-neck sweater looked out of place among the coloured brocade waistcoats of the poseurs and the paisley cravats and twill trousers of the desert boots brigade.

He found the girls too bright and hard and they already looked like their mothers with their stiff perms and cocktail dresses.

As soon as they'd arrived Penny, in spite of her pleas to him not to leave her side, had dashed off into the crowd in search of Alistair. She must have found him, for he hadn't seen her since.

He joined a little group around one of the stars of the theatre set, a cadaverous actor with a horrible little goatee beard. An undergraduate with a flop of blond hair was enthusing over Tolkien's recently published *Lord of the Rings*. After listening to this drivel for a while, Charles couldn't help himself.

'I can't understand why anyone of even average intelligence could possibly want to read novels about elves and goblins. Wouldn't it be just a little more grown up to learn about the real Middle Ages?'

There was a shocked silence in the midst of the hubbub all around. Then the blond spoke in tones of the utmost disdain.

'I don't think – I don't think I could *ever again* trust the judgement of someone who didn't recognise Tolkien's genius.'

'Really?' Charles attempted to return the disdain with interest, but he felt humiliated. He shouldn't have put himself in the position of being patronised by some little shit of an undergraduate. In the old days he'd been a personality on the scene himself, but now he was forgotten and invisible to a new generation. Fleeting fame.

To them he appeared simply as some troglodyte in a sweater. He was about to withdraw, clinging on to what dignity he could muster, when Penny appeared at his side, clutching his arm. She seemed distraught.

'Alistair's not here. Someone said he was here, but he's – he's gone.'

chapter 5

McGOVERN SAT IN THE battered leather chair that was the only remaining piece of furniture from the Gorch epoch and observed his new boss. For a start, the desk was much neater than in Gorch's day; and in choosing rimless spectacles and a smart charcoal grey suit, Superintendent Moules perhaps consciously intended to present an image of the policeman as civil servant, one of the new breed, a moderniser, efficiency his watchword. McGovern, however, did not jump to conclusions. He reserved judgement, watched and waited.

'So you've met Gerry Blackstone of the *Chronicle*,' said Moules in a tone that suggested suspicion of so unorthodox a move. He leaned forward slightly as he spoke. 'That's the one who's been giving us a hard time over the Soho affair.'

'That's not what he was interested in.'

'Not interested? The *Chronicle*'s been down on us like a ton of bricks.'

'It's not what *he's* interested in.'

'Personally I don't believe in hobnobbing with the press,' said Moules primly. 'I don't trust journalists. Hyenas. Out for information.'

Gorch had said the trick was to make the press believe they were using you, when in fact you were using them. McGovern had had mixed feelings about his old boss' cosy relationship with journalists, but the outright hostility expressed by the new man did not please him either. All he said, however, was: 'Well, sir, I suppose that is their job. And Blackstone is influential.'

'Influential?' Moules cleared his throat. 'We cannot allow the gutter press to set the agenda for policing.'

'No, sir. But he's put two and two together and worked out that things'll not be carrying on the way they were, now you're in charge.'

Moules fidgeted with the stationery tray on his desk, aligning it more neatly with the blotter. 'My results in Birmingham are well known.'

'Exactly, sir.'

'Ever since my arrival I've been concerned at what one might call the general atmosphere. I don't like what's going on. Something has to be done about it. Policing cannot be carried out by nods and winks, you scratch my back and I'll scratch yours. There must be standards and there must be procedures.'

McGovern agreed, but wondered at Moules' tactics in making his intentions so clear at such an early stage. 'He also guessed that I'm the man you have in mind.'

Moules raised his eyebrows slightly and moved the pen tray a little further to the left. For a moment the square rimless lenses caught the light, concealing his eyes.

'You didn't drop any hints—'

'On the basis of one conversation with you? No. In fact, in no circumstances would I—'

'Of course not ... As you say, you and I have had a discussion, that's all. It's hard to see how anyone could have heard—'

'It's probably naught but gossip.'

Moules looked affronted, as if the very idea of gossip concerning such an important issue was a form of insubordination. 'That's rather cynical, McGovern. And how could anyone have given him the idea that I want you—'

'He's not a stupid man. He worked it out.'

'You haven't given me an answer. You haven't told me what you think of the idea.'

'Not much' was the truth, but McGovern wanted to avoid getting off on the wrong foot with his new boss. 'I'm not best placed – CID don't trust the Branch and—'

'But that's the point. You're apart, a detached observer.'

'It's exactly that that could be the problem. It's the opposite of a detached observer you want, sir. You need an insider, you need someone they trust. And they'll not trust me. They'll think I'm a spy. So I doubt it will work.'

Everyone knew there was a lot going on in the CID, but McGovern's solution was to stay clear. He minded his own business.

'I wouldn't put it quite like that. You'd be putting out feelers, a preliminary reconnaissance to see if a full-blown inquiry is required – or could be avoided with a quiet word here and there, tightening up procedures, a little more discipline. It worked in Birmingham.'

'I'm not popular. And I don't come into contact much. Our work does not overlap.' He'd thought about his next words. 'If it's an inside picture you're wanting you'd be better with my former Sergeant, Jarrell. He's working with the crime squad now. And he gets along with them.'

It was true. Manfred Jarrell, who should have been the butt of all their jokes, a teetotal boffin, an egghead intellectual, in short a laughing stock, was on excellent terms with his colleagues.

'You think so?' Moules was silent. He again straightened the already straight blotter, aligning it with knife-like precision to the letter rack and rearranging the paper knife and pens. 'You could then liaise with Sergeant Jarrell. Is that what you're suggesting?'

It wasn't, but McGovern didn't contradict him.

Moules cleared his throat. 'It was clear to me as soon as I arrived that we're not making full use of your talents.'

'With respect, I'm not exactly in agreement with you there, sir. I was responsible for security during the Soviet leaders' visit earlier this year.'

Again Moules looked displeased, but McGovern was beginning to realise that his sour expression was habitual. 'Well,' said the Superintendent, 'we'll talk of this again later, but in the meantime, as it happens, we've been rather overtaken by events. Now you are off to Oxford. We need to talk about that. Hundreds of refugees are about to descend on us, McGovern, indeed have already arrived. I daresay some riff-raff is managing to get across the border as we speak. Petty criminals, some of them, all sorts of undesirables. But we can cope with that. In any case, most of the students are perfectly genuine and they've been more or less vetted. They were assessed by British academics in Austria, where they'd first sought asylum, as you know. Most have been found places at British or Canadian universities.'

The Hungarian uprising, crushed by the Soviet army, had gripped the headlines for weeks, but McGovern had already discovered that Moules had a habit of rehearsing in detail information everyone already knew.

'There will also be others. Subversive elements.'

'Because they come from a communist country? Do we not trust any of them?'

'It's not the disillusioned ones, McGovern. But the genuine refugees make the perfect cover for the others – who aren't disillusioned.'

'Spying on their own dissidents and on us as well.'

'Exactly. This is, as you must have realised, a considerable emergency. An unknown mass of arrivals from a Soviet Bloc country – we have to take it very seriously. *They*' (and by *they* Moules meant MI5) 'worry that an agent could quite easily be brought in under the cover of the general refugee crisis. There are rumours – but it's rather vague. Or perhaps they're just keeping more definite intelligence to themselves.'

It made sense. There was bound to be someone stirring up trouble. On the other hand his years in the Branch had convinced McGovern that the spies exaggerated everything, talking up the slightest bit of information in order to increase their importance and, perhaps more importantly, be given enhanced powers to spy on their own fellow countrymen. McGovern might have rejected his father's radicalism, but some remnant of indignation persisted at the anti-democratic nature of the secret services.

'I have been briefed, sir.' But as Moules conceded, the information hadn't been at all specific, little better than gossip. Then again, gossip could often be important.

'There's a detective up there will help you. I've got his name here.' He lifted a piece of paper from his in-tray. 'Venables. But they're a bit out of their depth, I suspect.'

McGovern had known from the moment it all started that he'd be involved. The poor bloody Hungarians. Their fate interested him far more than Moules' doomed plan to clean up the CID. He was looking forward to his trip to Oxford.

'*Have* you been fully briefed?' Now Moules spoke sharply. 'Because there's something else. I'm told you should contact a Professor Quinault. There are some questions about his activities.'

McGovern's heart sank. He hadn't been briefed about *that*.

'In fact it's a rather delicate matter. He was with them during the war, you know, involved in operations in that part of the world. Hungary, that is. And they say he still has his ear to the ground. You know how it is – some of those scholars and intellectuals – they returned to academic life, their adventures in spying officially over, but still wanting to be involved

– anyway, it seems as if Quinault has retained links of one kind or another.' Moules fidgeted with the paper knife. 'This rumour about a spy may even have emanated from him. And in fact it seems there have also been doubts ... suspicions as to what he might be up to.' He leaned forward slightly. 'This is not my area, McGovern. You're aware of that. But ever since the Burgess and Maclean affair ... the possibility of a third man—'

'They think this Professor might be the *third man*?' McGovern couldn't keep the astonishment out of his voice.

'No, no, no. Nothing like that. A cloud of suspicion hung over Kim Philby, but those rumours have been dissipated, put to rest. Philby is in the clear. So now they are grasping at straws. They know there is a traitor somewhere and I got the impression they think this Professor Quinault may know – there are friendship networks, you know, Quinault knows everyone ...'

The Burgess and Maclean affair had been a disaster. The Americans would never trust the British secret services again. But there was still a double agent out there somewhere, so they were charging around in the dark in their desperate search for whoever he might be.

'Quinault has ongoing contacts with Hungarians he knew in the war, I'm told. He may have information he's keeping to himself, suspicions, perhaps. He's being monitored. He's been travelling up and down to London a lot recently. And there've been a lot of rather odd phone calls abroad.'

So they'd been tapping the Professor's telephone. 'There's no possibility I'll be able to get any information out of him. That's not a sensible way to go about it. I was told Quinault has never forgiven me for what happened in Berlin.'

'What happened in Berlin ... ah, yes.' Moules paused. 'They seem to think that for that very reason – well, it was put to me like this. Professor Quinault won't expect you to be the one who's poking about in his affairs.'

'I don't see it.' McGovern shook his head.

'They just want to know if he's up to something. All this travelling he's been doing lately. Not just going up and down to London. Travelling abroad as well.'

'Is that suspicious? Surely not! His work must take him abroad.'

'Hardly, McGovern. He's a classical scholar, I'm given to understand, a specialist in ancient Rome.'

'Might he not need to visit ancient sites?'

Moules brushed that aside. 'He's not an archaeologist. In any case I gather he's also been causing them problems, ringing them up and trying to stir up trouble about Hungarian infiltrators. I suspect they're being over-sensitive. My impression is they see conspiracies everywhere, but as I said, I'm no expert. And with regard to the Professor it seems to be more just a question of giving him the once-over. Possibly your appearance is meant to act as a kind of mild warning.'

'I see.' McGovern let this sink in, with all its unpleasant implications. 'I'm the last person he'd take any notice of.'

'On the contrary, you will remind him of bungles in the past. That he supported a friend who turned out to be a criminal. Supported him up to the hilt, I'm told.'

For someone who claimed to know nothing of the secret services, Moules appeared quite well-informed. 'Just do your best, McGovern,' said the Superintendent.

'Sir.' McGovern stood up.

Moules put up his hand and said: 'We haven't finished our discussion about the newspaper man, Blackstone. My fault – we got sidetracked – the Hungarian business has driven everything else off the agenda, but we can't lose sight of other objectives. Is Blackstone going to be a problem? Is he going to put a spanner in the works?'

McGovern sat down again. In the discussion about the Hungarians and Quinault, he'd forgotten about the girl in the hotel and his promise to the journalist. 'He can do a lot of damage if he wants to, but he can help us too. The reason he wanted to see me – that's how I read it – was he thinks he's onto something and he's thinking we might help him.'

McGovern paused. He wanted to put it in the most palatable way he could. 'He mentioned an accidental death. A girl fell down a flight of stairs in a hotel. I felt he had some kind of personal stake in it. But whether that's the case or no, he feels there's more to it than meets the eye. The post-mortem was inconclusive. The coroner returned a verdict of accidental death, but he wasn't happy. And there was no proper police investigation. Another look at the case might lead to ... to matters related to your own concerns, sir. He's interested in police methods and so is the *Chronicle*.' McGovern watched Moules as he spoke. 'It could lead to something that might be helpful in any changes you may hope to make.'

'I see.' Moules paused.

'If that's all, sir ...' McGovern stood up again.

But Moules still hadn't finished. 'So there might be something questionable about this King's Cross affair. Allegations of incompetence – we have to take them seriously.'

'Or more than incompetence.'

'I see.'

'His reputation's not for nothing, sir, as the top crime reporter. He does have an instinct.'

'I don't believe in instinct, McGovern. Police work deploys reason, not instinct to establish facts. And, as I said, I don't trust journalists.'

'You can trust Blackstone to milk the Tony Marx affair.'

Moules was silent, presumably thinking about that.

'If we followed up the girl's death he might ...' McGovern had been about to say 'do us a favour in return', but guessed that Moules was suspicious of favours, so instead changed it to '... he'd be pleased. And it might be a useful lead in any procedural inquiry.'

'So he was suggesting the investigation of this girl's death wasn't all it should have been?'

'He suggested there was something not right about it, sir.'

Moules now leaned forward and put the tips of his fingers together, in a gesture McGovern found annoying. 'The publicity over the Soho stabbing has been terrible. We need to assist the press to see things from our point of view.'

'I don't know how much the *Chronicle* knows. He did hint there might be a reason there's been no arrest in the Soho murder case.'

'I think we know that, don't we? Unbreakable alibi. Slater questioned the suspect on – three occasions, wasn't it – but he couldn't be budged. He stuck to his story. Slater's team checked out his alibi. It's rock solid.'

'I know, sir. There's a wall of silence. Hell has frozen over. But that's not what Blackstone meant.'

Moules stared at McGovern. 'That makes it all the more remarkable that in this case ...' He didn't complete the sentence.

'It's possible Blackstone could be helpful – if we gave him something to expose.'

'No, no.' Moules stood up and walked over to the window. 'We can do without that sort of help. That would never do. It must be dealt with on a strictly internal basis.' After another long silence he said: 'But we'll make a few enquiries about this girl in the hotel. Low-key. Jarrell's working in that division now – King's Cross. We'll proceed cautiously.'

At that moment there was a commotion in the corridor. Slater's unmistakable voice was heard shouting, 'Then effing well lock him up.'

A bang on the door, and Slater flung it open without waiting for an invitation. Seeing McGovern, he did a fake double take. 'Apologies, sir. Am I interrupting something?'

'What is it, Slater?' Moules stared at the intruder. For

Slater's presence did intrude. He seemed louder, larger than other men as he stood in the doorway. He was the image of the glaring American eagle, his domed forehead sloping into a great beaked nose, with piercing eyes on either side, the head supported by a massive neck.

'Need a search warrant, sir. There's a fence down Old Street way—'

'Calm down, Slater. And another time, wait till I answer before entering the room.'

McGovern would have been interested to see how the encounter developed, but Moules dismissed him. Reaching his own office, he sat down at his desk and looked out of the window. During the brief interregnum following Gorch's departure he'd made sure he got moved to a better room. But he'd lost his Sergeant, Jarrell, who'd had enough of the Branch.

He missed Jarrell; and in a way he missed Gorch. He didn't think Moules understood the personal significance to him of Professor Quinault.

What had happened in Berlin ... what had happened was that McGovern had brought about the downfall of Hegley Quinault's great friend, the MI6 agent Miles Kingdom. While working for Kingdom, McGovern had discovered his past crimes against children. Kingdom had committed suicide. The spies had not forgiven McGovern for exposing their best interrogator. If there was one thing they didn't like, it was having their dirty secrets aired in public. Worse, in their eyes, McGovern was responsible for Kingdom's death. Quinault had taken his friend's death particularly badly; it was said he'd blamed Special Branch in general and McGovern in particular.

Gorch had protected McGovern in spite of the spies' hostility and made sure he got promoted after this defining episode. Yet the scandal had clung to McGovern, defining him as a man who put highfalutin notions of truth and personal integrity above the more weighty matters of state security.

More damaging, even, than the distrust of the secret services, had been McGovern's own personal sense of doubt. For Kingdom had tricked him. McGovern had fallen for the disgraced agent's surface charm and cynicism. He thought the less of himself as a result. His confidence was undermined.

That he was now surreptitiously to investigate Quinault, the man who had most resented his part in the Kingdom affair – and at the request of the very organisation whose favourite son Kingdom had been – was more than surprising. It was totally unexpected and therefore disturbing: ironic, but above all, sinister.

He even suspected it might be a trap they had set him for some devious purpose of their own. They might want revenge for Kingdom's disgrace. Or perhaps they were using him to advance some private vendetta against the distinguished historian of ancient Rome. It was an unpleasant thought.

chapter 6

NIGHT HAD FALLEN BY the time McGovern left the railway station. Mist blurred the trees that stretched tall and bleak along one side of the suburban road. The golden squares of light from the neat, uniform houses on the opposite side seemed the more welcoming by contrast with the vague darkness of the park.

Towards the end of the road the houses changed, with curved windows, portholes and flat roofs. The eccentricity of the ocean-liner style had delighted Lily.

As soon as he opened the front door he heard voices and laughter. Lily and her friends Mike and Eveline from the art school sat in the sitting room. They looked up at him as he stood in the doorway. He wondered what brilliant discussion he'd interrupted.

Lily swept her long hair back from her face in that lovely familiar gesture of hers.

'You're early, darling. D'you want some tea?' She lifted the teapot. 'Oh, there's none left. Sorry.'

'I'll get a beer.' Although it was tea he wanted. He sat down on the sofa.

Mike grinned. 'Solved any crimes today?' The jocularity was awkward. 'Murder and mayhem as per usual? The Soho stabbing ...'

Eveline laughed. 'Poor Jack. He's only just got in. You don't want to talk shop the minute you get home, do you?'

'Nothing to report, I'm afraid. Not my case, anyway.'

'I'll make some fresh tea,' said Lily.

With his wife out of the room, her guests valiantly kept the conversation going. 'We were talking about having an exhibition,' said Eveline. 'Our new work.'

'Sounds exciting,' said McGovern, but he was still thinking about Professor Quinault.

'It's great Lily's been made head of the art department at the school,' said Eveline. 'We're lucky – of course it's hard work at the college, but teaching art students is a lot easier than a horde of school kids who probably don't even want to be there.'

'I think they like her classes.'

Mike laughed. 'A rest from maths and geography.'

'And she still finds time to do her own work. I do admire her,' added Eveline. 'I don't know how she has the energy. And with you working such odd hours. Away, here and there. All over the place.'

'Well, that gives her more time, doesn't it?' said McGovern drily, aware too late that it sounded ungracious, but the whole conversation felt awkward and he was too tired and preoccupied to try to be charming. If only Lily's arty friends could accept him as he was, as normal, but they seemed to view policemen as an exotic species, slightly alarming and at the same time a bit comical.

'We'd better be off, I think,' said Eveline. 'Jack wants to relax, don't you?'

'No – please,' he protested. But he never felt at ease with the couple, especially Eveline, a dark, thin woman, who advertised her artistic identity by wearing colourful peasant skirts, black polo-neck sweaters and gay peasant scarves. Her husband dressed to match in his black shirts and red ties. McGovern told himself they were perfectly pleasant and friendly, but he was beginning to fear they were drawing his wife away from him and into their world of suburban bohemia, a world he hadn't expected to find in this far south-east corner of greater London. He tried not to dislike the self-conscious way they paraded their unconventional credentials, setting themselves against the conservatism of their neighbours and railing against 'keeping up with the Joneses'. Mike was fond of expressing supposedly shocking opinions, with the follow-up: 'It's the anarchist in me, you know.' But he wasn't an anarchist, McGovern thought, irritated. He held a perfectly ordinary middle-class job as a teacher at an art college. He was state-employed; effectively he was a bureaucrat.

'Please stay,' said McGovern politely. 'I've had a rather busy day, that's all. You'll forgive me if I don't bore you with the details.'

But they left. 'We'll see ourselves out,' they shouted from the hall.

Lily brought in the new pot of tea. 'I hope you didn't frighten them away.'

He leaned back in the big, old-fashioned armchair, soothed by the familiarity of the room and its objects, assembled gradually, mostly by Lily, over the four years they'd lived here, an eclectic mixture of the exotic and the banal: the odd bits of Victorian china, the soapstone Ganesh, the framed photographs she'd taken in Scotland, the old, velvet-covered sofa and the oriental screen. But Mike and Eveline had left a little ripple of disturbance in their wake and as McGovern sipped the tea his wife had poured, he felt for a moment lonely and ill at ease.

He knew he should have encouraged Lily to talk about the proposed art exhibition, but he was too worried about his dubious assignment in Oxford. 'I'm to go to Oxford next week. Have a look at the Hungarian refugees.'

'The poor things.'

'At least, that was what it was supposed to be about. But now it turns out it's more about some suspect professor. One of their own, or used to be – only it seems they've turned against him. He was a close friend of Kingdom; he blamed me for what happened.'

'Oh ... That's not good.' She said no more, when he'd been hoping for her most intense sympathy. Now he felt she wasn't really listening.

'It's bloody difficult. Nigh on impossible situation, to be honest.'

'Oh dear.' She had folded her legs under her on the sofa and looked up at him, softly smiling as he turned up and down the little room.

She wasn't taking it seriously enough, but he suppressed his resentment and continued: 'The new Super wants me to keep an eye on CID as well.'

'What d'you mean?'

'Things have got lax. He seems to think if I cultivate them, which means spend time drinking with them, I'll pick up information about what's going on, their wee schemes. That's not my idea of what I should be doing. They'll not trust me, so it's pointless anyway.'

'That all sounds rather difficult.'

'If I get to hear of something and he can crack down on them as a result he'll get the credit. If it all goes wrong, which it will, then I'll get the blame. But I think I persuaded him that Jarrell would be better suited. And I'll be going to Oxford next week, so it's not imminent.'

'Oh, darling – it's such a difficult job. I sometimes wish ...'

He knew what she wished. She wanted him to retrain as a lawyer. It's not too late, she would say, you're only thirty-five.

Sometimes he felt a hell of a lot older. He couldn't help resenting the way she didn't want to talk about his work. But perhaps he was neglectful, insensitive. Hers was important too. He sighed and changed the subject. 'Mike and Eveline were telling me more about this exhibition you're planning.'

'Isn't it exciting? It was Eveline's idea. An exhibition at the art college. We'll show our work. Have a grand municipal opening. Show Chelsea and the Royal Academy what the suburbs can do.'

'Sounds like a good idea.'

'Or we might have it at the public library. They don't really do things like that, but we might get more of the general public in then. It's the new movement, you know – Pop Art.'

'Pop Art!'

'It'll shock Bromley! We hope!'

'It does not take much to shock Bromley.'

'Mike and Eveline are very keen. So are the Bradleys.'

In other words, her little coterie of arty people; there were so few of them, which made them rather too embattled, unnecessarily he felt, for the citizens of Bromley were indifferent to great new movements in the art world rather than actively hostile. It was a live-and-let-live sort of suburb, where people 'kept themselves to themselves' – to him an alien and coldly English concept. Yet because of his work, so much of it confidential, it suited him well enough.

After supper they sat on the sofa and listened to the Third Programme. She curled up comfortably against him and he put his arm round her. He stroked her hair, loving its sweet, clean, shampoo smell. After a while he said what he'd been thinking, off and on, for a long time now.

'We're not getting any younger. Isn't it time we started a family? More than time. You'll be thirty-two next birthday and—'

But she'd stiffened within the circle of his arm.

'What's the matter?'

Her head down: 'Nothing.' And after a while: 'What's the

hurry? There's plenty of time.'

'Don't you want to have kids while we're still young enough to enjoy them?'

'Oh, Jack,' and she moved a little away. 'Don't be tiresome.'

He was tired and didn't want an argument, but he couldn't understand why she wasn't more enthusiastic, so he persisted obstinately. 'I know you said when we first moved here, you didn't want kids *yet* – we were moving house – you were starting your new job – then your mother was ill ...'

'I suppose I'm not as – I mean it's really you who's so keen on children, isn't it?'

'Aren't you? Don't all women want bairns?' In his agitation he'd slipped back into an old way of talking.

She laughed. 'What d'you know about all women?'

He tried to stay calm. 'Well, *I* want children. You know that. I always have. I've always *assumed—*'

'Yes. *You*. You just assume.'

'Jesus Christ, Lily – what are you talking about?' He could no longer sit still. He stood up, roughly switched off the wireless, looked down at her, angry, baffled. 'Is it your job? You can go on working, I won't stop you.'

'I wouldn't have time. Eveline says children eat up your life.'

'She hasn't got any. Didn't you say they couldn't have children? Envy, that's what that is. Sour grapes.'

'You hardly know her.'

'You pay far too much attention to them. You'd have more time. You could give up the teaching and devote yourself to your painting. I can support you. And that's no way to talk about children. Eat up your life! They're what keeps life going!'

'You don't care about my painting. You're not even interested in the exhibition. Why do we have to talk about this now?'

Startled, he stood over her. She shrank back in the sofa as if afraid of his anger. He was angry, but more than angry, he was shocked, baffled. How had this all blown up out of nowhere?

'We're happy as we are, aren't we? Aren't you happy?'

'That's not the point. You never said ...' He walked up and down the room. It seemed too small to contain him and this huge shock. The fire sparked merrily in mockery at his wrath. She'd completely winded him. And how long had this been festering in silence? It was a silent lie. She'd lied by omission. What it amounted to was that she really didn't want children at all. It was as bad as if she'd been unfaithful to him: a betrayal. 'What are you saying?'

'I'm not saying anything. I just wish you wouldn't go on. You can't leave things alone.'

He could see she was almost afraid of him and that affronted him too. A cocktail of rage and guilt and incomprehension surged through him. 'It's selfish not to have children.'

That was his mother speaking. He'd heard her say that of the childless couple in their tenements. And it was true, although in that case it had turned out they couldn't have kids.

'Please don't shout, Jack. I didn't say we wouldn't. I just said there's no hurry. And please turn the wireless back on. I was listening to that programme.'

He left the room and walked through the kitchen into the garden, leaving the back door open. He smoked, pacing up and down. The trouble was, she was spoilt, a spoilt only child. She'd come from a privileged family. She was too used to having her own way. His princess – but she was too much of a princess. She was haughty, wilful. His bitter thoughts fed on the disagreement, so that it swelled into a denial of him, of what he was. Why had she married him if she didn't want children?

But all he said when he returned was: 'We might as well

have stayed in central London. If we hadn't moved you'd not have got friendly with those poseurs who've filled you up with all their rubbish about art and artists.'

chapter 7

ARGYLE STREET LED AWAY from King's Cross towards a neglected region of narrow back streets still scarred from the war. Explosions had shaken the terraces and left them cracked and fragile. The forbidding Victorian tenements had withstood the Blitz better, Blackstone thought, but their dark inner courtyards were like prisons.

Halfway along Argyle Street two houses had been combined into a hotel. A notice propped against the window advertised 'Vacancies'. The flimsy glass front door was unlocked.

Blackstone stepped cautiously across the threshold into the narrow passage. There was no reception desk. He was about to call out when a middle-aged woman appeared from the back regions. She looked at him with troubled dark eyes, as if she saw an intruder rather than a potential guest.

'I wondered if you had a room. A single room. For one night.'

'You want room?' She seemed to find this a surprising, even a suspicious request. She pushed back her black curls.

'It says you have vacancies – on the door.' He smiled encouragingly.

'Yes. We have room. This way.' She gestured towards a door to the right and led the way into a reception room with a counter, a sofa and some chairs. The furnishings were plain and shabby, but not obviously dirty. On the wall hung a reproduction of an Impressionist landscape Blackstone vaguely recognised: Monet? Manet?

The dark-eyed woman slipped behind the counter and reached for a key from the pigeon-holes behind her.

Blackstone leaned on the counter. 'Nice place you've got here.'

She looked at him doubtfully.

'Good position. Near the stations. Matter of fact, a friend recommended it.'

'Yes?' She looked a little less wary, but her smile was hesitant, reluctant, as if she expected the worst, as if she suspected some nasty twist behind his words. 'You see the room?'

'Please. The name's Hunt,' he said. 'I travel quite a bit myself. Haven't seen many hotels as smart as this.'

She nodded uneasily.

'I'm a travelling salesman, you see.' He somehow had to gain her confidence and in order to do so embarked on a rambling story of mishaps and misunderstandings at other hotels he'd stayed in. He wanted her to think of him as harmless. At first she fidgeted, but quite soon he'd lulled her into a state of passive acquiescence. He smiled winningly as he told her about his wandering life and after a while he felt it safe to move on to personal territory.

'I come from up north, myself. Yorkshire – they say we're the salt of the earth, y'know. Don't know about that. Ever been to Yorkshire? It's a great place. Cold, though. I bet you come from the south, the sunny Mediterranean, the glorious Med. With those lovely eyes you must be Italian, right?'

'Malta.'

'Malta! Lovely place, I believe. Never been there myself. Romantic, I should imagine. I expect your name's just as romantic. Ariadne? Dolores?'

'Maria – Maria Camenzuli.' She had definitely relaxed a bit.

'Manage this place on your own?'

She shook her head. 'My husband ...'

The very mention of her husband seemed to revive her anxiety.

'Mmm. That's nice,' he said soothingly. 'You meet some interesting people, I dare say.'

She shrugged, cagey again now.

'It must be hard work, though, looking after this place ... guests not always as tidy as they might be ... leaving things behind ...'

'They are like pigs sometimes.' She spoke with sudden venom.

'Maria – if I may – a lovely woman like you – doesn't seem right you should be clearing up after people who haven't the decency—'

'Is very hard life.' With a look of self-pity she warmed to the subject. 'Cleaners – they don't stay. I am working all day – my husband has other work, is not here – people come. Are sometimes rude ...'

'Not the best type of guest sometimes ... I imagine – you must get all sorts so near to the stations ...'

'Riff-raff! Girls ...' and she made a sweeping, ambiguous gesture with her hand.

'And you such a lovely woman. It doesn't seem right. I tell you what, Maria – this weary traveller is badly in need of a drink and I don't suppose you could see your way ... the pubs are all shut at this hour of the afternoon, but a hotel ... something a little stronger than tea, you know ... we've so much to talk about – I want to hear all about you – you must see all sorts here.'

She hesitated. Then, having weighed up the proposition, she nodded and left the room. She was quickly back with a bottle and two glasses on a tray. 'Is special Maltese liqueur.'

It tasted like slivovitz, the horrible stuff he'd drunk in

Yugoslavia in the war, but it had a strong after-kick.

'So tell me about running a hotel? It must be worrying at times. Strangers day after day ... and you on your own? Husband out all day, is he?'

'Yes – of course. He never help. And people are rude. Argue about money, not want to pay.' Then for the first time came a genuine smile. 'And then there are nice ones like you.'

He raised his glass to her and smiled. He complimented her some more. He sympathised expansively. 'Shocking. They don't appreciate all your hard work ...' and after a while he said carelessly: 'Things can go wrong too, I suppose. I mean, I read something in the local paper about an accident in one of these hotels.'

She stared. 'Accident?' She put her hand up to her mouth. At the very mention of the word she seemed to unravel before his eyes, her hair more obviously uncombed, her blouse sagging open to reveal a sliver of bra.

'Oh – I've upset you. Forgive me. It wasn't in this hotel, was it?' He sounded convincingly shocked and concerned. 'I'm sorry. I didn't mean to upset you. So very upsetting,' he murmured.

She was actually shaking. She clasped her hands together. 'Was awful. Horrible.'

'A lady fell down the stairs or something? Something like that? A young woman ...? It must have been terrible. A terrible shock.'

Maria Camenzuli nodded speechlessly. Now she seemed mesmerised.

'I suppose you had to call the police—'

'No police. Accident, just doctor—'

'Mmm ...' He nodded and leaned forward to pat her hand. 'You called a doctor?'

'My husband. He call doctor. Doctor friend. Dr Swann. Very nice doctor.'

'Dr *Swann*?' Amazing! She'd given him a name! What luck! He was on the qui vive now, all right, but he must try not to show too much interest.

'Why you ask?' She'd caught the excitement in his voice and seemed to withdraw into her earlier mute suspicion. She stood up. 'You want room? I show you room. Very nice room.'

He followed her upstairs, annoyed to have given the game away. Yet perhaps he'd got as much as he'd needed. No point, really, in asking more questions, about the police, the doctor, the girl. Too many questions and she'd clam up completely.

She flung the door open onto the first-floor front room. 'Best room,' she said, with something closer to defiance than pride. If it was the best room he hated to think what the others were like.

He thanked her and turned away to the window. He pulled aside the lace curtain. It was slightly greasy to the touch with the invisible grime of London. He looked out at the quiet street, catching a glimpse of King's Cross station at its end.

'I'll take it,' he said.

She still loitered in the doorway.

'If you don't mind – I need to rest – lie down for a while. I'll come down shortly – I expect you'll want me to pay in advance. Just give me a few moments.'

As soon as he judged her safely downstairs he made a quick search of the room. He didn't know what he was looking for, though. He left the room and looked around the landing and the corridor leading off it. He tried to imagine the scene. If she fell down the stairs ... he knelt down and examined the landing carpet. The staircase was typical for a nineteenth-century house of this type, narrow with a twist at the top onto the first-floor landing. The carpet was thin and at the very top there was a bit of loose weave. Blackstone pulled at the torn threads. They were not frayed. They looked as though they'd been deliberately cut, perhaps to make the story that she'd tripped more plausible. He also wondered whether the girl would have fallen all the way down from the top step, or whether she would have just landed up against the wall at the bend.

He stepped back into the shadowy depths of the landing and its corridor. He tried another door, but it was locked. Then he heard a man's angry voice. At the head of the stairs he stared down to the hallway. The individual who now stood behind Mrs Camenzuli was smaller than she, but there was something that would make you think twice before taking him on: the furrowed face, the small, angry black eyes, perhaps, or the way he stood alert, behind his wife, like a dog ever ready for the signal to attack.

'Who are you? What you doing?'

The woman said something in an unfamiliar language.

'I've just booked one of your delightful rooms.'

'Why you were moving about up there?'

Blackstone ignored this. As he descended the stairs, as casually as he could, he glanced at the banisters, but they showed no signs of damage such as a body ricocheting past them might have caused.

The man snarled something in their language at his wife. She shrank away from him a little. Blackstone edged towards the door. Camenzuli stared at him. You wouldn't want to meet him on a dark night in the back streets.

'I have to go out for a while,' murmured Blackstone, as he placed his hat on his head and made for the front door. 'Thank you. I'll be back shortly.'

Outside he stood still for a moment and looked up and down the street. From within the hotel he heard Camenzuli shouting. He looked back through the glass door, but there was nothing to see. He wondered if he should go to the woman's aid, but he was not a physically brave man and Camenzuli would be the sort to have a knife.

A cold wind had got up. He wasn't wearing a coat, so he made for the station. There were telephone kiosks there and a tea room. He needed a cuppa. After that, there'd be another taxi.

Two days later, on the Friday, he met McGovern in the same pub as before. The policeman looked lined and older in the sallow light of the saloon bar with its grimed windows and its ceiling treacly from the smoke of a thousand cigarettes.

McGovern had brought with him a pallid carrot-head, a loose-limbed young man, whose over-large raincoat drooped from his shoulders.

'Detective Sergeant Jarrell,' said McGovern and then: 'Can we make this brief? I'm off to Oxford on Monday and I have to get ready. I spoke to Moules, he agreed to have a look at the case you mentioned – the girl in the hotel. I've brought Jarrell along because he'll be dealing with it.'

Blackstone didn't want to let on quite how pleased he was, but gratitude was certainly in order. 'Thanks. I'm glad you persuaded him. I think you'll find it's worth a look. I went round to the hotel. Just to have a dekko. Maltese chap, the manager. Shifty bastard. Very cagey. *And* he's got form.'

Blackstone had done his homework. He'd trawled through his exhaustive archive of newspapers, police reports and notes collected over a decade.

'He was a hanger-on to one of the Maltese gangs. Got a couple of convictions, but recently he's been clean. You could find out more about him at your end, I'm sure. I sweet-talked his wife a bit. And she told me something I found interesting – the name of the doctor at the scene. Swann. I vaguely remember the name. Rang a bell. I haven't had time to follow it up. But I think you should. And there was something else. I looked at the carpet at the top of the stairs. It had been tampered with. Cut to make it look as if she could have tripped, you see. Camenzuli caught me at it, nosing around. He was very suspicious. Didn't like it at all.'

The Scot stood up. 'I'm not surprised,' he said drily. 'Moules has said he will have it followed up. But there's no guarantee he'll make it a priority or consider reopening the case. At this stage he just wants Jarrell to have a look at it. He has other things on his mind. If we don't turn up something quickly, it may get forgotten again.' He added rather coldly: 'So I hope you're right in thinking there's something worth the investigation.'

Left alone with Jarrell, Blackstone eyed the young man and pulled out his packet of fags.

'I don't smoke.'

'Your superior officer didn't seem in the best of moods.'

Jarrell smiled. 'He's upset about something, got things on his mind. Trip to Oxford, I shouldn't wonder.'

Slyly, Blackstone took his chance. 'Could it have anything to do with his new role?'

Jarrell's pale, watery eyes gave nothing away.

'No point in stonewalling about it. He told me himself.'

'We're going to see some changes,' said Jarrell and smiled.

chapter 8

MRS WILLIAM DROWNES, Regine Drownes, formerly Mrs Neville Milner, before that Mrs Smith (at least, that's what her first husband had called himself), earlier still, Roisin and originally – but never, never mentioned – Kathleen O'Kelly: in other words the London hostess familiarly known to her friends as Reggie, took Charles' arm as they paced the length of Longwall. She liked to be seen in the company of a good-looking man and Charles, only slightly taller than she, fulfilled the role perfectly. He no longer resembled a Caravaggio boy. These days the classical planes of his face reminded her more of a marble statue looking impenetrably into – what?

They turned left into the High towards the Botanical Gardens. 'William says the climate isn't bracing here. Unlike Cambridge. He was at New College. It's because Oxford's in a valley. Damp and slightly depressive, he says.'

'That more or less sums up how I feel.'

'Darling! I thought you were having such a good time …'

'It's different now – it's nothing really – I suppose I'm feeling a bit glum – not exactly looking forward to Christmas.'

Of course – Regine remembered now. It had been at Christmas a year ago that his mother had killed herself. And six months later his father had married again – his secretary or something.

Regine squeezed his arm, but conventional platitudes were not her way. She excelled in the art of silent sympathy. If her companion didn't choose to unburden himself (and it was usually a he) then things could go on in a perfectly companionable absence of words, but if he wanted to talk she'd listen with total understanding, conveyed with her body rather than with words: a tender bend of the head, the turn of a shoulder, a hand tactfully placed, in this case her linked arm. Yet while she had the reputation of being a sympathetic listener and believed her own myth, as often as not she listened for her personal ends, which were ever at the centre of her thoughts.

'You're looking marvellous, anyway,' said Charles. 'Very Pre-Raphaelite, this coat really suits you. So good with red hair – marvellous scent, too. Chanel Gardenia, isn't it?'

'How clever of you, darling.' Few men noticed such things the way he did. They'd say you smelled lovely or looked beautiful, but they weren't interested in the creation of the illusion. That was actually just as well. Yet it was amusing to *parler chiffons* with a man who had taste. 'I'm so glad you like the coat. I simply had to have a mauve coat – not purple, you know, *violet* – and I couldn't find one anywhere. I had it made specially in the end. William was furious. Such extravagance! And do you like the scarf?' She pulled it forward over her collar. 'From Liberty's. They've reintroduced all the old William Morris designs.' It was a leaf pattern in strange tones of spinach and moss and mauve. 'We're thinking of having the drawing room done in one of the Morris wallpapers. A lighter pattern than this, of course.'

'How glamorous. I can't wait to see it.'

They walked on. Oxford was colourless in the still air. No wonder Charles was depressed and undergraduates attempted suicide; a whole ward was reserved for them at the asylum, William had told her.

As if reading her thoughts, Charles said: 'I'm not as gloomy as I sound. I'm doing a bit of tutoring this year, as well as slogging away at ancient Rome. I do enjoy the subject. The early Roman Empire was so fantastically *modern*.'

'All those wicked emperors; rather like Stalin, I suppose. William says if there's a book at the end of it – well, you will think of Drownes', won't you?'

She acted as a scout for her husband's publishing firm, keeping up equally with the *Times Literary Supplement* and the little magazines, prowling through literary parties, listening out for all the gossip.

'Nice of him to say that. But I've hardly started writing – and my research isn't meant to be about that side of it. Lurid perversions not the thing at all. And even if it were, Drownes' isn't that sort of publisher, is it?' He smiled sideways at her. 'And what I'm working on ... it's more about political change in the early Empire and its relation to the economy. Which is a problem as what I'm really interested in is not the economy, but all their religions.'

'Religion? That might be interesting. And you know Drownes' isn't as fuddy-duddy as it used to be. I'm making sure of that.' To the horror of that dreadful old gorgon, Edith Blake, once the power behind the throne, now reduced to fuming impotence on the sidelines. If only she'd leave ... she was dangerous. A frustrated lesbian, what else could you expect? Regine was sure Edith guessed something was going on – and if she found out, if *anyone* found out – but it was better not to think about that.

They turned through the gate of the Botanical Gardens and walked along the gravel paths between neat box-edged beds. 'We might be in another century,' she said.

'Actually, we are. That's part of the problem.'

'Let's sit down, shall we?' She gestured to a convenient bench. 'It's a little chilly, but ... a short rest.'

She settled herself, her legs crossed, the coat pulled richly round her. She turned towards him, pale, thin face and great green eyes so closely focused on him that he could not help, she was sure, being flattered. He might not desire her; there might be that dead space between them where erotic attraction should have pulsed, but young men like him always lapped up the attention of an older woman, a woman of the world. She was, after all, in her own small way a figure of sorts on the literary scene, with her parties and dinners for her husband's distinguished authors and the gallery owners and artists and critics who were also of their world. Lately, however, had come a new turn, so that now she understood that her world could stretch wider still and that she could gain a foothold in thrilling regions of real power: the murky world of politics.

'D'you mind if I smoke?' He took a packet of Sobranie Turkish from his pocket. She couldn't help smiling at the affectation. He was still so young, after all, half her age. He lit the oval, untipped cigarette and blew out scented smoke. 'My social life's taken the most tremendous dive.'

There was a purpose to her visit. The cloudy afternoon wrapped them in a kind of companionable melancholy, but she must break the comfortable silence to introduce the vital subject. It was stupid to be so nervous. 'I met your supervisor the other day. Hegley Quinault, isn't it? He thinks very highly of you.'

'You met Professor Quinault?'

'He published a book with Drownes', you know. He's supposed to be tremendously clever. You're lucky to have him, I imagine.'

Charles looked at the tip of his cigarette. 'He said he thought highly of me? He was just being polite. I don't think I interest him at all, actually. He has bigger fish to fry.'

'He came to one of our parties ... a funny little man ... He was in intelligence during the war, wasn't he? His book for us was about Julius Caesar, but it's his adventures in Eastern

Europe that really interest William. Since the spring, when Burgess and Maclean reappeared in Moscow, everyone's so interested in all that again.'

'Really?' He murmured the word between almost closed lips, too blasé to speak aloud.

'But I daresay he's rather out of touch now. Isn't he very old? He looked old. Is he interested in politics at all?'

'I hardly ever see him. Don't be taken in by him, though. He pretends to be a moth-eaten old don, slowly turning to dust in the library, and doddering around College, but that's just a smokescreen. The other day, when I was having a supervision with him, some Tory MP turned up.'

Her heart jumped against her ribs beneath the violet coat and she squeezed and kneaded the dark blue gloves she'd taken off when they sat down. Tory MP? It must be! What amazing luck he'd raised the subject himself! She played with the empty glove fingers, pulling and smoothing them flat. That made it easier to say what she had to say, what she was dying to say, even though it was so difficult.

'Rodney Turbeville.'

A faint tremor of surprise disturbed Charles' marble pallor. 'How did you guess? Untidy but energetic. Bald but forceful. He came to talk to Quinault about the Hungarians. At least I suppose it was about that. So I pushed off. They clearly didn't want me around.'

'Darling – can I tell you a terrific secret? You absolutely mustn't breathe a word.' She took a deep breath. 'I'm having an affair with him.'

'With Turbeville? Really?' Again the murmur from between his lips. As if it were ... nothing. That again must be his youth, the self-absorption of the young, and he couldn't be expected to understand. University life, said William, not to mention public school, could easily lead to arrested development. Well, he should know. Of course Charles couldn't understand, he knew nothing of the great public world. Yet she leaned forward, inflamed by the insane desire to talk. 'You mustn't tell anyone. You won't, will you?'

'Who would I tell? But what a coincidence. That he should have turned up during my supervision.'

'You mustn't think – I mean I do love William, I do love my husband, it's just that ...' and she looked away into the distance, squeezing and crushing her poor, limp kid gloves. 'You know when you fall in love ... and you're right, he's a very forceful man. He makes me feel ten times more alive. But of course it's frightfully difficult.'

Her marriage, the humiliation for William, her twin girls, Lucy and Sarah, Drownes' ... but all that was nothing compared with the risks to Rodney's career and his wife and family. He risked far more than she did, oh *far* more. She already had a reputation – a divorcée, a woman with a past, but Rodney – as a politician he must be purer than pure. The difficulties were so vast and complex. The hugeness of it all, weighing on her, suffocating, silenced her. Eventually she said: 'He knows your Professor Quinault. They were together in the war for a bit. Rodney said he absolutely found himself in the war, found out what he was good at. Before that he didn't have a clue. When he was up here, and afterwards, he was basically a gambler, international bridge player, absolutely lived at Crockfords – or else living the high life on the Riviera – and look at him now, he's the most promising politician in the Party – he may well be prime minister before long.'

'All sounds a bit reckless, Reggie. He must be very keen.'

She laughed, pretending to be offended. 'Reckless? What makes you say a thing like that?'

Could Charles really understand the madness of love? The jolt of electricity? How could he understand, a young man of twenty-two, how could he understand that longing to submit, to be carried away? 'It's the chemistry,' she said. Chemistry gave adultery a kind of scientific determinism. You couldn't fight against chemistry.

Charles flicked his ash away. Now he consented to smile. 'Freddie used to say you were an adventuress in Shanghai before the war. It must have been fun out there.'

Freddie. Their dead friend, dead eight years ago. Their friend ... well, *her* friend; but Charles? Freddie had seduced Charles, hadn't he, he'd been mad about the boy, as she was mad about Rodney, but of course that wasn't the same ...

'Did Freddie say that?' And she wondered if Charles fully understood the doubtful implications of the word 'adventuress'. 'Did he really?' It was a shock, an unexpected insult shot out of the past. That Freddie, her greatest friend, whom she'd always trusted, could have said ...

'Why are you telling *me*, Reggie, about your affair? I'm hardly a substitute for Freddie, I'm afraid.'

It was true. If only Freddie had still been here she could have talked to him. He'd have understood, he'd have known what to do. And perhaps, coming from him, 'adventuress' had been a compliment. 'Do you miss Freddie?' she asked.

Charles frowned and stared at the tip of his cigarette. 'I suppose I do. From time to time.'

'I miss him. Still, after all this time; eight years. He was the only person who knew me before the war ... He'd have known what to do – how to carry it off. But I have to talk to someone. I can't talk to my married women friends; all the good little wives.'

And Charles was queer, after all, so he must know something about forbidden love. Although – if Freddie had been typical – the way they went about it seemed so very different from love between a woman and a man. So perhaps Charles was a stranger to passion. Freddie had been in love with *him*, of course, but that didn't mean ...

'I feel I can talk to you, Charles. Perhaps Freddie does have something to do with that. Does that sound silly? But the thing is, you know Hegley Quinault. I only met him briefly at that one party of ours. I didn't get much of an idea of him. I just wonder why he seems *quite* so important to Rodney. Rodney seems to set great store by him.' She'd jealously wondered if it was an excuse, if he had another mistress in the university city. Now at least Charles had confirmed that Rodney wasn't lying to her. Not about Quinault, at least. 'What's he like?' she asked.

Charles shrugged. 'As I said, I don't really *know* him. He's very keen on promoting the study of the classics ... and he writes articles denouncing commercial television. According to him it'll destroy western civilisation. But you know, I'm in this kind of – well, almost a sort of limbo. Once you're a graduate it does sort of begin to dawn that there's a whole world of Oxford politics the undergraduates are completely oblivious to. But one's not part of it. Though some of us might be one day ... I suppose,' he ended doubtfully, as if thinking of a rather unattractive future for himself.

She stared ahead. She wasn't quite sure Charles had got the message. Did he understand her urgency? She *had* to know about Quinault. She suspected it had something to do with the war or MI5, something Rodney was not telling her, something that might threaten their relationship, and nothing must be allowed to do that. There was also Quinault's relationship to Drownes', of course, but that was of less importance.

The whole thing was a minefield. She sighed and twisted her emerald engagement ring. Charles looked down at it, but said nothing.

Then he squeezed her arm and she knew he had after all got the message when he said: 'I'll spy for you, Reggie. You can rely on me. In fact, it might be quite amusing to dig up some dirt on old Quinault.' But his tone of voice was laden with irony. Did he really mean it? Of course, he always sounded like that – as if nothing in this world really mattered.

At least she now knew Rodney was telling the truth about

Oxford. She gathered herself together to rise in her magnificent coat. 'It's a little cold, don't you think? I'll stand you a sherry at the Mitre. If you have time, that is.'

'That would be awfully nice,' he said, and she had no idea whether his reply was just good manners or genuine enthusiasm.

'But we haven't talked about you.' If he'd been a normal young man she'd have joked about romance, asked if he had a girl, but you couldn't do that with Charles.

Perhaps, however, he intuited the unasked question, for he replied: 'The most exciting thing that's happened to me since the summer is some frightful old pervert at All Souls compared me to the *Mona Lisa*.'

'The *Mona Lisa*? What an insult! She's so frumpy and unattractive. I've never understood all the fuss.'

'There's a famous essay by some Victorian aesthete who really preferred boys.'

'Oh?' she said vaguely, still pondering the mystery of Rodney's association with Quinault.

'He seemed to think quoting great chunks of it at me was the best way to get me into his scrofulous little bed. Passages so purple they'd make your coat pale by comparison. "The eyelids are a little weary … like the vampire, she has been dead many times." Like her, I have an unfathomable, sinister smile, it appears. I nearly died of embarrassment.'

It was the closest he'd come to animation all afternoon.

'Darling, how horrid. Are all Oxford dons that peculiar?'

Privately she thought that his eyelids *did* look a little weary. And – she tried to suppress the giggle that unexpectedly bubbled up – there *was* something ever so slightly vampiric about him.

'Why are you laughing? It was ghastly.'

'Hardly the best seduction line, I can see that. But I suppose they're all in love with you.'

'Unfortunately, I'm not in love with them.'

chapter 9

ON HIS RETURN FROM Eastbourne, Blackstone had the evening to spare, so he treated himself to oysters at Wheeler's in Old Compton Street. Afterwards he thought he might as well look in at Johnnie Hay's Premier Club in Little Compton Street nearby.

At first glance this was a drinking club like any other in Soho. The basement room was uninspiring. The walls had been painted pink a long time ago and the bar with its zigzag wood veneer must date from well before the Festival of Britain. A jukebox had recently been installed, but no-one played it. The tables and chairs had been assembled from junk shops. Yet perhaps that was the point: that it looked so ordinary, so shabby and unimportant, when in fact it had established itself as information exchange extraordinary for all the villains, bent coppers, bookies, hangers-on and newshounds of central London. This was largely due to Johnnie Hay himself.

From behind the bar in the corner he kept a benevolent eye on his guests. His spotted bow tie, hunting green waistcoat and the pork pie hat he wore indoors vaguely referenced the racing fraternity and at the same time made a shaky claim to dandy status, but his manner belied the image, for his was a motherly presence, quiet and unobtrusive, an invitation to confidences. He had a reputation as a keeper of secrets. However,

Blackstone had discovered that it was often useful to get him into conversation.

Blackstone chatted with him for a bit, gradually working his way round to the subject of Valerie.

Johnnie Hay already knew about the accident in the hotel. 'Nice girl, tragic, an accident like that. Absolutely tragic.'

'You knew her! How come?'

'Last I heard of her she was looked after by Sonia.'

Blackstone leaned across the bar towards Johnnie. 'That was a while ago. Not any more. I heard she'd been knocking around with Sonny Marsden.'

Hay puffed on his cheroot, pup – pup – pup. He shook his head. 'She wasn't Sonny Marsden's type.'

'Does he have a type? I thought all women were grist to his mill ... so to speak.' It wasn't the happiest metaphor.

Johnnie Hay repeated firmly: 'Not Sonny's type. Not his scene.'

'She wasn't just an ordinary tart,' agreed Blackstone, but as soon as he'd spoken, the nostalgic note he'd struck embarrassed him. It was probably meaningless, a sentimental falsity. He hadn't cared for her, hadn't even really known her, he was just casting a romantic glow in retrospect on what had been a squalid little one-night stand.

'Sweet on her, were you? Well, you weren't the only one.'

Blackstone savoured the pure, stinging bite of his whisky. It went down very smoothly, but then there came the fieriness in the throat. 'Same again, Johnnie. And have one on me.'

'Thanks, old cock.'

'Sweet on her – no ... just ships that pass in the night. Who else, though?'

But Johnnie Hay wouldn't be drawn. 'I'm just speaking generally.' Girls like that, he philosophised – well, it was true, a girl like that was not 'just' or not exactly a prostitute. And ruminatively Hay implied she inhabited that uncertain moral area between a straightforward tart and the sort of 'kept' woman who lived off men, rather than them living off her, and retained at least a degree of independence. Or seeming independence. Of course it was all based on looks and sex appeal. The future would be uncertain, once the allure faded, if some permanent arrangement hadn't been achieved by then.

'You seem to know a lot about her.' Blackstone felt frustrated and irritated now.

'I know a lot about *them*,' corrected Johnnie Hay. 'Women with the God-given gift of a beautiful body.'

'But …' Blackstone had been going to say that Valerie's charm for him had been precisely that she seemed not to be a woman of the world, to be on the contrary a waif shipwrecked on an uncertain sea. That was probably an illusion too. 'There was a doctor at the scene. Name of Swann. It rang a bell. Couldn't remember why, though.'

Johnnie Hay relit his cheroot, squinting down at the tip. Tiny bursts of smoke came popping out. 'Wasn't that the doctor Vince Mallory used to use? He'd got struck off, of course, but that didn't worry Mallory. On the contrary.'

Vince Mallory! Blackstone had first heard of Mallory as a small-time boxing promoter in the East End. Boxing was a grey area where the perfectly legal strayed into criminal activity. Nothing wrong with it. In fact, you could argue that the sport was a good way of keeping lads off the street and away from crime. It also sometimes led to fame and fortune, even if by the end of it the pugilist's brains had turned to pulp – and as for that Labour MP, Edith Summerskill, who wanted to ban the sport, wasn't that just simple proof that she understood nothing – *nothing* – about the working class she claimed to represent? When had she last been to the East End?

Those were the arguments Blackstone had heard many times in the early days when he'd worked around Bethnal Green. That was where the name of Vince Mallory used to crop up. He hadn't started out as a boxing promoter and the question always was what he'd been doing before that. It was known he organised illegal fights, bare-knuckle contests. He'd been at the murky, rough end of things at the very least. And there were rumours about what else he was up to. Prostitution rackets were a good way, in some respects a relatively easy way, of raising funds to finance other kinds of crime. Or it could have been the black market. Or possibly both. Mallory could never quite be described as a gangster, but he'd certainly been a spiv; and something about the man – whether it was the uncertainty surrounding his activities and where he got his money from, or the rumours about his sexual tastes, or simply his intimidating physical presence – generated a wary respect that bordered on fear.

'I don't think Mallory needs the doctor any more,' mused Hay. 'Gone legit, ain't he, gone up in the world a long time ago. You know he opened that poncey club in Soho last year? Well, of course you do. The Vice Squad don't like it at all, I've heard. West End Central isn't best pleased. And now he's trying to get into the property racket, ain't he? There are rumours, at any rate.' Hay's smile was sadder than ever. 'The doctor on the other hand – I believe he's fallen on hard times. Of course there's still abortion, and villains wanting their faces altered a bit, but they say the doctor's lost his touch, hands a bit trembly these days.'

'He's not working for Mallory any more, then?'

'In the old days if one of Mallory's boxers got injured in a fight in some back-alley venue, derelict factory, you name it, he didn't want them ending up in hospital, did he? All sorts of questions asked. But it isn't like that any more. You know that.'

'So nothing to do with Mallory?'

Johnnie Hay lifted his shoulders to indicate how little he knew, how mysterious it all was. 'Who knows? Shouldn't think so, though.' He swilled his whisky round in its glass. 'As regards poor Valerie's accident, though, I'm a bit surprised the doctor was involved. Sounds fishy to me.'

'D'you have an address?'

'I might have.' Johnnie Hay looked vaguely round. 'Might have it somewhere. Come in the back a minute.' He stood up, cheroot still in play. Blackstone followed him into his tiny back office. There, Hay approached the battered filing cabinet in the corner. He rattled a drawer open and looked through the files it contained.

Blackstone slid a note from his wallet. Hay still had his back to the journalist, but whether he heard a faint rustle or whether he simply sensed the appearance of the money, he said: 'I've remembered it. Somewhere off Gray's Inn Road ... Cubitt Street, number ten. Basement. Henry Swann.'

'Thanks. I'll look him up.' He tried to speak casually, but the information excited him – in an unpleasant way. He felt nervous, tense, sweaty.

'You're taking a special interest in the case.'

Blackstone shook his head. 'I hardly knew her. It's just that it doesn't add up.'

Hay finally let his cheroot die. 'Talking of doctors,' he said, 'what's the latest on Bodkin Adams? Are they finally going to nail him? After all, there've been rumours for years ... '

chapter 10

THE NEXT DAY BLACKSTONE made a detour on his way to Eastbourne for a second time. He deposited his suitcase in the left luggage at Victoria station and then doubled back to King's Cross to visit Dr Swann.

The doctor's residence was approached down a flight of steps to the basement area of a terraced house. It was similar to so many others in this part of King's Cross – not unlike the hotel in which Valerie had come to a sticky end. A clean net curtain veiled the window onto the basement 'area'.

Blackstone paused before ringing the bell. He wasn't too sure of his story. He might get the door shut in his face. Perhaps he cared too much. Adrenalin was speeding his pulse rate. He took a deep breath and pressed the bell.

The man who opened the door must be, Blackstone thought, well over seventy. Sprucely dressed: a cardigan, neatly pressed trousers, a spotted bow tie. Blue eyes sparkled behind glasses and beneath flaring white eyebrows. He had a good head of white hair, too.

'Yes?' The look was enquiring, benign, in no way suspicious.

'Dr Swann? I – I've come to see you about a friend of mine. In need of a bit of help.' He hoped this was vague, yet suggestive enough to get him through the door.

The elderly gentleman gazed at Blackstone with benign speculation. 'Ah – yes – and what makes you think I'm your man?'

'D'you mind if I come in? It's rather personal.'

'And I hope *you* won't mind if I ask you who recommended me?'

Blackstone hesitated, then: 'Johnnie Hay.' He wasn't sure that was the right answer, but it did the trick, for Dr Swann stepped aside with an: 'Ah, yes. Johnnie Hay. I haven't seen him for some time.'

The corridor passed the front room and appeared to lead to gloomy regions at the back; but Dr Swann ushered the journalist into the parlour, a room that seemed to Blackstone like a cross between a consulting room and a waiting room, with shabby leather chairs, a desk, a calendar and reproductions of hunting prints on the darkly papered walls, together with old advertisement posters for various medical remedies. The desk was almost excessively furnished with penholders, letter racks, a blotter and in and out trays, suggestive of a busy practice. There was also a lamp with an oblong green glass shade. In a way, Blackstone thought, the room was a parody.

Blackstone sat on one of the leather chairs, noticing as he did so a copy of the *Chronicle* on the floor beside it. Rather to his surprise, the doctor seated himself on the adjacent one, which stood at a receptive, confidential angle, rather than behind his desk. As if to still the tremor of his papery hands, he gripped the chair's arms.

Blackstone decided to plunge in straight away. He didn't want to miss too many trains to Eastbourne. 'There's a hotel near here,' he began. 'A girl had an accident. They say she fell down the stairs.'

'Yes?'

'A doctor was called. Certified her dead. Made all the arrangements.' Blackstone pulled out his cigarettes and lit one.

'If you don't mind my saying, old chap, those things are turning out to be a bit lethal.'

Blackstone took a deep pull. 'Scaremongering, if you ask me.' He wasn't to be deflected. 'I wondered ... were you by any chance the doctor ... ?'

The doctor sat up. Now he looked alert. Blackstone was finding the room oppressively hot, but it wasn't clear where the warmth was coming from. He looked round, but there was no sign of a fire. Central heating seemed unlikely.

'Why is this of interest to you, if I may ask?'

'I was – she was my girl, you see. I was away at the time.'

'Ah ... ' The doctor gazed sharply at Blackstone with his twinkling blue eyes.

'You were the doctor they called? It's important to me, you see, to know just what happened.'

'I'm not sure how I may be of help to you.' The doctor spoke blandly, but Blackstone knew he would be very much on his guard.

'You were present when she died – or were you called to the scene afterwards?'

The doctor crossed and then recrossed his legs. Eventually he said: 'I signed the death certificate.'

'There was an inquest. The verdict was accidental death. But there seemed to be some doubts about it. You must know what actually happened.'

The doctor gazed speculatively at Blackstone. 'She was your sweetheart, was she? And yet you've only just got interested.'

'I told you. I've been away.'

'You said you hoped I could help a friend of yours. I don't quite see what this line of questioning has to do with any friend.'

Blackstone thought he might have blown it. Impatience had been his downfall. 'I meant the girl. I meant Valerie.'

'She's beyond anyone's help, old chap.'

Blackstone decided he might as well take a risk, shock the old crook. 'You see, I wondered if she really did fall down the stairs.'

The doctor stood up. Blackstone thought he was about to be shown the door, so he added: 'I thought you might like to know the police have got interested.'

Swann said: 'If you'll just excuse me for a moment …' and left the room.

He was gone for rather a long time. When he returned, he took his seat again. His eyes had darkened a little; his mottled hands no longer trembled like moths. 'I signed the death certificate, always ready to do a favour for an old friend. Could cause me some trouble, but then …' He didn't finish the sentence, but looked dreamily away into the corner.

'Are you implying – was there a reason you shouldn't have signed the certificate?' Well, of course there was. He'd been struck off. But was that what the old man was hinting at? 'Did she really fall down the stairs? You can't help wondering … an accident like that … ' The doctor didn't lose his composure. If anything, he looked slightly glazed. Blackstone remembered: drugs. That's what had got him knocked off the register. All those years ago. Where did he get the stuff, these days, that kept him going? That was a question for later, for another day.

'Implying? You're the one implying, it seems to me. Implications – implications – there are always implications, don't you agree?' He spoke with dreamy composure. 'In my reduced circumstances, I can't afford to be choosy.'

Blackstone took out his wallet, an act not lost on the doctor, even if he now seemed becalmed on a drug-induced dead sea.

'I trust the boys in blue aren't going to get involved,' said the doctor. But he no longer seemed at all worried about it. His papery hand slid the banknotes into an inner pocket.

'I don't think it was an accident, was it?'

The doctor smiled dreamily. 'Dead on arrival, poor girl.'

'At the hospital?'

'At the hotel. A foregone conclusion. Her fate was sealed. I didn't go with her to the hospital, my dear. That would never have done. With my reputation!' He laughed gently.

'On arrival. At the hotel. Are you saying that—'

'Reputation – reputation's gone. Othello, y'know.' The doctor stood up. 'I'm afraid I'm going to have to ask you to leave now. I'm feeling rather tired ... Will you see yourself out?'

'She was already dead when she got to the hotel?'

But the doctor was on his feet and with a protective arm steered Blackstone very firmly towards the front door. On the doorstep Blackstone turned. 'What does that mean – dead on arrival?'

But the doctor only winked and patted his finger against his nose.

Blackstone walked slowly away down the quiet street. God, these streets were small and crabbed and dark. They were like another kind of indoors. That's what London is really like, he thought, an enormous indoors without end, a labyrinth of endless passages.

From a public telephone at King's Cross station he made a call to DS Jarrell.

chapter 11

OXFORD WAS FAMILIAR TERRITORY to McGovern. He saw the spires rising across the meadows as the train approached the station and for some reason remembered that other Oxford down by the motor works at Cowley, visited a few years ago, on the lookout for trade union subversives. No ancient buildings there; it had been very different from the quads and colleges and ancient back streets of what the world thought of as 'Oxford'.

More significantly, as a senior Branch officer he'd covered the visit of the Soviet leaders, Khrushchev and Bulganin, the previous April. That was the sort of work he did well, minutely precise and therefore tedious, but work where one failed detail might spell disaster. He had taken charge of the meticulous pinpoint examinations of hotel rooms, proposed routes and locations of official visits. Every paving stone trodden on by Field Marshal Bulganin and Chief Secretary Khrushchev had to have been sterilised, so to speak, the slightest possibility of assassination by bomb, revolver or any other means eradicated. At first the Russians had even insisted on having their own special agents to taste everything in the kitchens at Claridges Hotel, where the Soviet leaders were to stay. There were fingertip searches of Portsmouth harbour, where their Russian cruiser was to land them, and of Westminster pier, where the Russians would arrive in London. There were Branch personnel crawling round under the stage at Covent Garden before the gala performance and others guarding every port and aerodrome in the country. His silver cigarette case was his thank-you gift from the delegation.

Communication had been via interpreters, which slowed things down and caused tension. It was also frustrating, as McGovern, good at languages, had added Russian to the German and French in which he was already fluent. He could have talked to them in their own language, but this was not permitted, because his remit was partly to overhear the Russians speaking among themselves. That had revealed disappointingly little, except that they seemed bedazzled by what they glimpsed in the shops in London and elsewhere.

It was at Oxford that the worst demonstrations were expected, but the students hadn't managed anything more confrontational than a chant of 'Poor Old Joe' as the visitors approached the Sheldonian Theatre. This was a mocking reference to the convulsions in the communist world since Khrushchev had denounced Joseph Stalin at the Twentieth Party Congress. Normally the Congress was a celebration of Soviet triumph and progress, but in 1956 Khrushchev had acknowledged the purges and murders committed at the behest of the late great Uncle Joe.

As the cortege had moved along the Broad the strange thing was that, on hearing the chants, Khrushchev had raised his arms and clenched his hands together above his head like a victorious boxer in a gesture of apparent approval. Whether he believed the students were simply welcoming him, or whether he agreed with their jeers about Stalin – good-humoured enough after all – was unclear.

The most interesting part of the assignment, however, had been McGovern's interviews with every supposed dissident and enemy of Soviet Socialism. Each had been paid a visit. He had met cranks, fascists, embittered exiles, thwarted priests and idealistic socialists. None of them had appeared as a genuine threat. The only real trouble, and it didn't amount to much, had come from the League of Empire Loyalists, a diehard, far-right group.

That was all in the past. The team had achieved the result for which they hoped: nothing had happened. By contrast, he thought, as he waited by the desk at Oxford police station, there was no possible satisfactory outcome for his current mission. There were those who hoped he'd find some kind of evidence that Quinault was up to no good. There were those who hoped the opposite. Probably all of them were united in hoping he'd come to grief himself. In his paranoid moments he suspected some sort of trap. Whatever the outcome, he'd fall foul of someone. It wasn't a good sign, either, that they'd communicated with him only through Moules.

A stout, middle-aged detective emerged from the back regions to greet him. 'Pleased to meet you, sir. Detective Sergeant Venables.' McGovern's hand was clasped warmly in the Sergeant's moist one. 'The Superintendent sends his apologies. He's been called away.'

McGovern followed him through to a back office.

'Have a seat.' There were papers everywhere. Venables moved some off a chair so that his visitor could sit down. He sat down himself and looked expectantly at McGovern.

As if it hadn't all been explained – discreetly – to the missing Superintendent over the telephone. 'I'm just here to check over some of the new arrivals,' said McGovern blandly. He hoped his detachment reflected a courteous implication that the police in Oxford were perfectly capable of identifying any security risk without intervention from London. 'It's just a formality.'

Venables looked puzzled. 'There hasn't been any trouble to speak of. '

McGovern smiled reassuringly and added: 'I'm sure you've

done extremely well. The sudden influx must have been difficult to handle.'

'You can say that again. We've had our hands full. But the social workers and the WVS have worked like Trojans. It's been all hands to the pump and we've got most of them settled now. We're expecting more, though. Tragic, really. You have to feel sorry for them.'

The expression of concern on Sergeant Venables' pale, round face seemed genuine. His dishevelled appearance – suit crumpled, shirt strained against his belly, a few hairs drawn lankly across his bald patch – suggested either that it had all been very stressful or that his wife didn't look after him properly.

'Sounds as if you've done excellent work and it's gone to plan.'

'More or less. There was a certain amount of grumbling at the hostel in Jack Straw's Lane – some of them are very keen to get to Canada and feel we're not dealing with it quickly enough. But the first priority has to be to get them all out of Austria. And I think they understand that, really. Simon Holt – the man in charge up there, the social welfare chap – he's done an excellent job. They had a terrible time, some of them. Some don't know what's happened to their folks. You can understand why they get a bit heated. Hungarian temperament's a bit fiery, you know.'

McGovern offered Venables a cigarette. 'Is that so?'

'All the universities are making arrangements for students to be allocated places to study. The Warden of St Antony's College went to Vienna himself with two other high-ups to interview students who might be eligible to continue their education here. It was done very thoroughly.'

McGovern knew all this. 'I hope I'll not be treading on your toes. I'm just here to get an overview of the arrivals. I'll need to look at their papers.'

Sergeant Venables blinked. He pulled out a handkerchief and blew his nose. 'We thought it best – the records are kept with the welfare people. Mr Holt knows you're coming. He seemed to think he could accommodate you there. I can take you up there now, sir, if it's convenient.'

So he was being shot out of the police station as quickly as possible. McGovern wondered if he could be bothered to feel offended that no-one higher ranked than a sergeant had been deputed to look after him, to meet him, even. Well, no doubt there was ill feeling that anyone from the Met should have been sent up to teach them how to do their job, as it must seem to them. 'Yes,' he said, 'we might as well get going.' There was no point in making a fuss, in insisting on a room at the police HQ. In any case, if he was to be based at the hostel he'd have more opportunities to observe what was going on.

The first item that caught McGovern's eye as he entered the hostel was the poster.

RALLY!
PROTEST AGAINST
THE SOVIETS IN HUNGARY AND
TROOPS OUT OF SUEZ!

'I'll tell them you're here.' And Venables, who'd driven him in a police car, bustled off out of sight.

McGovern looked round the cream-painted hall. A hard bench, its wood splintered and scarred, was the only furniture apart from a notice board. The place had an institutional feel. He heard voices. A door to the right opened and two young men burst out. They were arguing in Hungarian.

Sergeant Venables reappeared and ushered McGovern through a door on the left. 'Mr Holt's out of the office at the moment, but Mrs Mabledon will be able to help you.'

The woman who came forward to greet him from behind

her desk was dressed in the WVS uniform, grey-green, piped with maroon. She held out her hand.

'Sally Mabledon. So you've come to give us the once-over, have you?'

Venables hovered uncertainly. Then: 'Well – I'll leave you in Sally's capable hands.'

'Thanks,' said McGovern, 'I'll be in touch.'

'Let's go into the back office. It's more comfortable there.'

They passed three more desks piled with papers as they eased their way through to the second room, which was separated from the front office by a frosted-glass partition. Here there were two easy chairs, as well as another desk and some filing cabinets.

'So how can we best help you, Inspector? Simon Holt, the liaison officer, is out at present. You'll want to speak to him. He'll be back tomorrow. '

'Yes, I'll need to meet him. I'll be here for a few days. In the meantime I'm sure you're very busy and I don't want to take up too much of your time, but it would be helpful if you could just take me through the way it's organised here – I'll need to look at your records. I hope that won't be too much of an intrusion.'

'I think you'll find it's all quite properly organised.'

McGovern hastened to reassure her. 'There's no suggestion otherwise. It's simply a routine check on the refugees.'

'They've been very patient,' said Mrs Mabledon. 'They are volatile. But they have a genuine grievance in a way. So much energy has gone into bringing them all over here from Austria that plans for sending them further on have lagged behind rather, I'm afraid.' She stood up again. 'Perhaps you'd like a cup of tea?'

'No thank you.' Then he thought she'd probably like one herself. 'Unless you're having one.' It turned out she was, so five minutes was wasted while she made it.

When she'd poured and offered him broken biscuits from a tin, she continued: 'Mind you, they're a good lot, quite patient on the whole. It's true there have been one or two instances of arrivals who turned out to be – well ... there was an unpleasant incident with the head of one of the colleges. They kindly offered hospitality to two of the young men and then found some silver had disappeared. It was all very unfortunate. And then one of the Hungarian girls became rather too friendly with the son of the family in another case. Some of these continentals seem to have a rather different idea of morals. But the Oxford police have dealt with the case of theft. I don't understand why Scotland Yard should be involved.'

'It's a matter of security. Purely routine.' There was no question of him mentioning the rumours emanating from M15. Possibly they'd picked up something from their dogged surveillance of the British Communist Party; or perhaps they'd received suspect intelligence from some dubious informer in Budapest, even a malicious invention emanating from East Germany. Or possibly Quinault himself was the author of the stories. Little better than gossip, probably. But: 'We can't be too careful.'

'Security?'

He watched as comprehension slowly dawned. And then he recognised her look as one of suppressed excitement. This was the most thrilling time she'd had since the Blitz and the evacuees. 'Oh, of course. Yes. Naturally. But they are such very nice lads, most of them. And they've had a terrible time.'

'I'm sure you're doing all you can to help them. Perhaps – if you've time, that is – you could explain the filing system to me now. Then I'll leave you in peace.'

'That would suit very well. And of course I can show you our system. It's quite simple.'

The recording system did indeed seem straightforward and well organised. Mrs Mabledon took him through it briskly and added: 'You'll be able to work in here. It's only used for interviews.'

McGovern looked at his watch. It was after midday. 'I wonder – is there a copy of the list of the refugees staying with families? I could start going through that in the hotel.'

'I think so – let me have a look ...'

'How were they allocated? Was there any special system? Or any special reason why some have gone to families and some are in the hostels?'

Sally Mabledon hesitated. 'Not really. Those that spoke the best English, I suppose we thought they'd more easily fit in to a family. And I think ... there were one or two special requests. You see, some of them come from families out there, academics, you know. One or two of the dons actually know the parents, from before the war, even. I can't remember off hand, but when you're here tomorrow I can look out some more information. I can let you have the list now, though.'

'Thank you. That would be most helpful.'

McGovern was staying at a hotel – more of a pub, really – near Magdalen Bridge. The empty lounge was warm and cosy, almost too warm, in fact, and there was a lot of panelling and red upholstery. He asked for sandwiches, which were reluctantly brought by a dishevelled young woman. While he ate, he read through the flimsy carbon-copy list of families who had offered a Hungarian student hospitality. He'd asked for it out of instinct and only afterwards realised that a half-conscious supposition lay behind the request: that if an agent of some kind had been sent under cover of the refugees, it was likely he'd speak fluent English. But he wasn't sure even of that. Only by working methodically through all the information available on each student might he find something that didn't fit, some clue to suggest a hidden purpose. Besides, he wasn't even sure he was meant to be looking for an infiltrator. His gloomy mood was hardening into cynicism. His visit seemed like a waste of time.

Some distinguished names stood out from the list. Among them was that of Professor Quinault.

And McGovern was deputed unofficially to investigate Quinault, Quinault who regarded him as his enemy. Dismayed as he'd been by the unwelcome assignment, he now thought he saw how it was meant to unfold. In a twisted way it was understandable. That didn't make it any more palatable. Quinault wouldn't cooperate with him; he wouldn't get anywhere; Quinault's supporters would then be able to say that any rumours were groundless. The whole thing would be batted into the long grass (as they, no doubt, would put it). Quinault's enemies, on the other hand, might hope that the very presence of McGovern would indicate that they were serious, that they were gunning for him in their own subtle way. The mere presence of the representative of Special Branch would warn Quinault that he'd better take care. Still, because the Professor had a Hungarian staying with him, McGovern had an excuse for a visit.

McGovern sat still in the quiet lounge. To an observer he might have seemed comatose. The dullness that had overcome him acted as protection against the gnawing memory of the argument with Lily. It was some days ago now, but he was still, perhaps, in a state of shock, had not yet fully realised how bruised and angry he felt. Yet his drowsiness contained the seed of an impulse: to take the bull by the horns, to get Quinault over with, or at least to confront his own misgivings about the whole enterprise.

It was now pouring with rain, so he borrowed an umbrella from the reception desk and walked out into the deluge. At this hour, mid-afternoon, there were few people about and the liquid vistas of bleakly rain-washed streets harmonised with his sense of the futility of his task.

He paused in the shelter of a doorway to get his bearings and then set off in the direction of Corpus Christi. He asked at the porter's lodge for the Professor without showing his identity card. Directed to a staircase at the far end of the little quad, he marvelled at how quiet it was in the unrelenting rain. It was hard to believe that these ancient, crumbling buildings housed students, full-blooded young men with National Service behind them, no longer schoolboys wet behind the ears.

The place was like a monastery, he thought, as he mounted the dark, curving stone staircase, its steps hollowed by the feet that had trodden them for five or six hundred years. Once, of course, it *had* been akin to a monastery. He'd often passed Glasgow University on his way to visit Lily in Hillhead, but that impressive edifice was pompous and thrusting in a Victorian Gothic way. Here, the worn steps, twisting upwards into medieval obscurity, suggested a superiority so ancient it need not be stated at all.

McGovern knocked on Professor Quinault's wooden door. He waited. Silence. Then, just as he was about to turn away, a reedy voice sounded: 'Come.'

It was almost as dark in the room as on the stairs, save for the glow from the coal fire and another from the standard lamp beneath which an incredibly old man was seated in a high-backed chair. Yet he stood up with surprising agility.

'I'm sorry to disturb you, sir.'

McGovern advanced, nearly tripping over the carpet, and this time he did hold out his identity card.

Quinault peered at it. 'Can't see a damn thing ...'

'Detective Chief Inspector McGovern, sir.'

There was a silence. Then Quinault's high-pitched laugh was followed by his cracked voice. 'This is an unexpected visitation. Pray be seated.'

McGovern lowered himself into the armchair opposite the old man. The seat was nearer the ground than he'd expected and he landed with a painful bump.

McGovern had never met the man seated opposite him, knew only of his war history and reputed anger at Kingdom's death. He risked a direct approach. 'You'll probably not welcome a visit from me, sir.'

The old man peered forward. 'McGovern, eh.'

In the silence that followed, McGovern began to regret his impulse, but he had no alternative than to press on. His voice was hoarse as he said: 'I know you feel I was to blame for what happened ...'

Quinault seemed sunk in thought. His chair creaked as he bent even further forward. His silence was oppressive.

'... to Miles Kingdom.'

'Kingdom.' Quinault dredged up the word as if from a depth of memory, some sump of forgotten and decaying residue from a long-banished past. Another long silence followed. McGovern felt increasingly uncomfortable.

Finally: 'Kingdom was a fool,' murmured the old man. 'And now you've come to ... what? Apologise? Justify your actions?' His voice died away, then revived. 'All in the past now, dear boy, all in the past.'

McGovern was so surprised that he didn't know what to say, but simply let the old man's words sink in, and it was Quinault's creaking voice that broke the silence.

'No, that's not it, is it? You're here because of the Hungarians.'

This further startled and unnerved McGovern, although he knew he should have expected Quinault to work it out.

Another creaking laugh. 'They were bound to send someone, weren't they?'

It was hard to decipher the Professor's expression, but McGovern caught a sense of alertness and anticipation, as if long-dormant instincts for conspiracy were suddenly revived, as if the old hunting dog sniffed the air and heard the distant sound of the tally ho.

'That's correct, I'm here to check up on the new arrivals.' Yet now he was here, he hardly knew what to say. He hadn't got over Quinault's disconcertingly benign welcome. 'I thought you might possibly, well, tell me your general impression. Inevitably there are rumours, the possibility that unfriendly individuals might slip in under cover of the general influx of the refugees.'

Even Quinault's laugh was wizened. 'It's highly likely, isn't it? But sending you charging up here is rather a case of shutting the stable doors, don't you think ... Are we really so feeble that we couldn't pick up on any problems back in Vienna? Well ... in any case my days in intelligence are long since over, as you know, Chief Inspector.'

'I know, sir. But you have one of the students staying with you and that might have given you some idea ... '

'Gyorgy Meszarov? I felt we should do our bit. Many university families have opened their doors, offered hospitality. My wife wasn't keen, but ... in any case we never see him, he spends all his time at the hostel with his friends ... I knew his parents, you see ... '

McGovern waited for more. He fidgeted, trying to find a comfortable position.

'Gyorgy is an interesting boy.' Quinault spoke suddenly as though he'd woken from a doze. 'His parents are keen Party members, dedicated communists, which makes him a rebel in his own family, as well as against the regime. I knew them briefly, in the war. It was possible to work with them then, of course ... Hungary was on the side of the Nazis ... they were in exile here for a while. Yes. But now everything's changed and communism means something very different to Gyorgy from what it means to his parents. Yes. An interesting boy.' And now McGovern caught a glance from the old man. Perhaps this was some sort of message, a clue. But probably not; youth in rebellion against parents was hardly news. Hadn't his own father, after all, been a committed communist? Gyorgy Meszarov was probably simply in revolt against stifling Party dogma, Party duties. It gave McGovern a fellow feeling for the boy he hadn't even met.

'You should talk to him,' said Quinault, echoing McGovern's own thought – that he would speak to him, and soon. He laughed again. Sunk in his chair in the shadows, Quinault heaved his shoulders up and down. McGovern found the giggle disconcerting, especially as he had no idea of what the joke was supposed to be.

There was a knock on the door.

'Come!'

A young man who wore a short black gown over his tweed jacket stood in the doorway.

'Come in, come in, Watson. But don't shake your umbrella all over the floor like that.'

'Sorry, sir. I didn't realise ...'

'It's your tutorial time. No need to apologise.'

McGovern stood up. 'It's I should apologise. I've taken up too much of your time.'

'Not at all, Insp – Mr McGovern. Do come and see me again. Any time.'

chapter 12

MANFRED JARRELL HAD HAD plenty of time to reflect on Blackstone's phone call. He got a cup of tea in the canteen and sat brooding. What the dubious doctor had told Blackstone made no sense. The girl was already dead when she reached the hotel? How? Why? That a defrocked, so to speak, doctor had signed the death certificate was definitely suspicious, but it didn't prove the girl had been murdered and why should you believe anything a crook like Dr Swann said in the first place? Blackstone, however, had been in a state of great excitement.

Jarrell, by contrast, had mixed feelings about the whole enterprise. What was the point of reopening the case – which wasn't even, in any case, officially reopened? If it was to placate some journalist McGovern had got friendly with, well, there could be a point to that. If it was to form the spearhead of a campaign against police corruption, it was, in Jarrell's opinion, misguided. The police hadn't been called to the scene. They weren't necessarily to blame for that. It was a distraction. If Moules wanted to clean up C Division, he should start with the Vice Squad. There were ways of working that Moules thought needed to change. Well and good. Whether he'd succeed in changing them was another matter. It was of course essential to get convictions. It was how it was done that came into question.

Jarrell knew quite well what his colleagues thought of him. They liked the disagreeable but all too accurate comments he made about some of the high-ups. They liked his perceived lack of ambition. He wasn't a threat. He was an oddity, almost a mascot. Looks weird, but he knows a thing or two, was as near to a compliment as he'd get from them, but he was more than satisfied. He had the ultimate ascendancy: he didn't care what they thought of him. He gracefully accepted his role as resident eccentric and even hammed it up from time to time, effectively disguising his contempt.

Jarrell knew more than they realised about his colleagues' private lives, their foibles and obsessions, and sooner or later it would all come in useful. They by contrast knew little about his. He'd plodded away for six years, content to be McGovern's sidekick, happy to learn from the Scot and to keep away from the limelight. He'd rejected all suggestions that he seek promotion. This was put down either to misplaced loyalty to McGovern or to an irresponsible fear of assuming authority. The truth (as only McGovern knew) was that his mother had long been ill with multiple sclerosis. His father, incapable of caring for the woman he'd taken for granted and whom he'd married to serve him, became depressed and taciturn. Six months after his wife's death he'd succumbed to a fatal heart attack.

Jarrell had grieved, but now he was free. He could make his move. He abstemiously sipped his tea. He watched his colleagues as if from a distance. He stood outside their world. They knew that, but were quite unaware of the extent of his ambitions. He was more enthusiastic than McGovern about Moules' anti-corruption plan, which he saw as a plausible stepping stone to greater things. He was determined, however, not to be known to be associated with it. In the meantime, he was far from sure that the Argyle Street business was the right way to go about it.

He was not pleased to see Slater bearing down on him.

Slater reminded Jarrell of Cyclops, the one-eyed giant of ancient legend. Perhaps it was the way Slater charged noisily around, or his reputation as a bully. It was known that he'd had a very good war in the commandos and in recent months – or perhaps it was longer – he'd begun more and more to treat his work as if it were another combat mission. Jarrell wondered if anyone besides himself had noticed this change. When Jarrell had worked with him five years earlier he'd found him to be an easy-going copper and in fact rather lazy, preferring the pub to most other locations. Now he seemed supercharged with energy.

He came to a halt beside Jarrell's table. 'How many souls have you saved today?' His voice rose above the low-level buzz of the canteen. One popular joke about Jarrell was that he was an evangelical Christian. His colleagues firmly believed this and were under the delusion that it riled Jarrell to be ribbed about it, when in fact he was an atheist with no interest in religion whatsoever. However, he'd long ago stopped denying it as that only reaffirmed their conviction.

Pleased with his joke, Slater broke into thundering laughter. His laughter was not reassuring. Those who felt its force found it even more frightening than his anger. When he laughed he became the anarchic lord of misrule and there was always the uneasy feeling that it was going to get out of control. Moreover his mood changed so quickly that his merriment was never safe. Storm clouds of suspicion inevitably darkened his face again before long.

'What are you up to, then?'

'Just doing the rounds in Bloomsbury.'

'Keeping your cards close to your chest as usual. Make a first-class poker player you would – if it wasn't against the Bible.' This was the cue for another uproarious laugh. 'Doing the Lord's work. Hey – is Moulsey a God-botherer too? You and he should get along fine, then. Trying to lead us up the paths of righteousness. Oh my Lord! Whatever next! We'll all have to pull our socks up, won't we?'

It was not part of Jarrell's plan to be associated with Moules' clean-up drive. 'I have no idea what his plans are,' he said coldly. 'All mouth and no trousers, I suspect,' he added. He looked at his watch and stood up smartly. 'I'd better get going.'

He parked his car near the hotel. It was one of those December days when the cold slowed everything down to zero. The city itself seemed numb, its stony streets in hibernation. Jarrell's breath blew out in white clouds and dampened the scarf he'd wound round his face. He stuck his hands in his coat pockets and looked around at the bleak, blackened buildings. He paused on the pavement, thinking about the case. The woman was the weak link, blurting out the name of the doctor like that. So a doctor had been at the scene. Very convenient to have someone on hand to sign the death certificate with no questions asked. They didn't call the police. And the doctor lived nearby, only a few streets away. Might be a good idea to pop round to see him later on. It was too cold to linger.

The hotel passageway was at least warm. It smelled stale. A dark-haired woman appeared from a room to the right.

'Mrs Camenzuli?'

Jarrell's attitude to women was far different from Blackstone's. To Jarrell, Maria Camenzuli was simply another slovenly and most likely deceitful witness whose gender was irrelevant. However, he did notice a fading bruise round her eye.

He flashed his identity card. 'I'm just here to ask a few questions,' he began pleasantly.

'You speak to my husband.'

'He's at home, is he? Perhaps there's somewhere we can talk ...'

'I call him.'

The proprietor, when he appeared, was a type familiar to Jarrell: uncooperative, a man for whom the first line of defence would be attack. Jarrell had little sympathy for the unattractive specimens with whom he often had to deal. Even in the Branch, the types he came across were more usually seedy crackpots than dedicated subversives, or else, as he saw it, in the case of the Irish in particular, they were straightforward thugs, who liked to dress up their crimes with political justifications. McGovern, he believed, had always been too nice, too keen on understanding. Yet the Irish did at least bother to cook up a reason for their violence. Men like Camenzuli were just vicious for the sake of it.

Camenzuli reluctantly led the way down the stairs at the back of the house. The basement sitting room was hot and cluttered with furniture, ornaments and sporting publications.

The more Jarrell questioned the Maltese, the less he said. When his wife attempted an answer he shut her up with a glare. 'Why you come here?' he snarled. 'Case is closed.'

'You know that? You followed the case, then.'

'Of course we followed case. Not good for business when someone dies in hotel.'

'We have reason to suppose it may not have been an accident.'

'Of course it was accident.'

Maria Camenzuli glanced beseechingly at her husband. 'They—'

He turned on her savagely. *'Shut up!'*

'What is it, Mrs Camenzuli?' Jarrell leant forward. She shrank away, glanced again at her husband.

'You leave my wife alone.'

Sick of the man's stonewalling, Jarrell eventually stood up. 'You don't mind if I have a look around, do you?'

'You have search warrant?'

'It's not a case of searching the premises. I'd just like to see the staircase, where the girl fell down, you know.'

'You saw staircase already. When you come in. You got

eyes,' said Camenzuli rudely. But as Jarrell made for the stairs anyway, he followed him, angrily protesting there was nothing to see. He glared from the hallway as Jarrell climbed upwards, examined the banisters, looked at the tattered carpet at the top. Then the arrival of a guest, or potential guest, distracted him. A discussion ensued. Jarrell heard Camenzuli calling his wife, then heard footsteps downstairs into the back of the house.

Jarrell thought he'd have a quick look round some of the bedrooms. Locked doors of this type presented no challenge. Jarrell didn't expect to find anything, but it never hurt to have a look around.

The first bedroom he entered was furnished with a flimsy wooden bedstead covered with a rather thin counterpane. The wardrobe and chest of drawers were heavy and old-fashioned. The search was not arduous. He moved on to the next room. Jarrell felt under the mattress, seeing skeins and balls of dust, a few pennies and the odd bus ticket. The dust made him sneeze explosively. He looked for loose floorboards and for hollow spaces in the plastered walls; he opened rickety wardrobes. Signs of occupation were meagre too: here a glass of water in front of a fly-blown mirror; there a toothbrush by the basin; a pair of shoes, a girlie magazine.

Camenzuli started shouting again. Jarrell knew he couldn't push his luck further. He glanced round one last time. The visit, the questions, the search – a useless exercise. Then he noticed a fall of soot in the fireplace.

He knelt down, rolled back his jacket sleeve, undid his shirt-sleeve cuff and rolled that up as well, then cautiously stretched his hand up into the mouth of the chimney.

He drew out a package wrapped in newspaper. It was uneven and squashy. He pulled back the newspaper, and beneath several layers something pale blue became visible.

Jarrell's throat constricted. He was looking at a woman's handbag.

It was a cheap thing, made of imitation leather. The shiny blue had cracked at the edges. The clasp was loose. Inside there was a little diary, some loose change, a lipstick, a handkerchief.

He came out onto the landing. Camenzuli glared up at him. He stood and looked down at his adversary from the top of the stairs. There was now no sign of the potential guest.

'You come down now. I not give permission—'

Jarrell descended slowly. 'I wonder if you can explain how this came to be hidden in the chimney of the back bedroom?'

When he reached the hall Jarrell opened the bag and took out the diary, leafed through it.

'What is? Someone left behind – is nothing.'

Jarrell smiled. 'A diary inside the bag identifies the owner as Valerie Jarvis.'

Mrs Camenzuli started to cry. Her husband watched Jarrell, but said not a word, his beady eyes fixed on the cheap pale blue handbag. All three of them stared at it, as if it were a ticking bomb.

chapter 13

IT WAS NOT UNTIL the next day that Jarrell was free to visit Dr Swann. He waited by the basement door, but there was no answer to the bell. He waited, rang again, waited. The door, tucked under the steps leading to the front door above, was protected from view and he had no hesitation in picking the lock.

Letters and a newspaper lay fanned out on the mat. He stood still and tense, then stooped to pick them up. He stopped to listen in the dark passageway; sniffed an odd smell he couldn't identify.

'Anyone at home?'

But he knew that only the silence would answer him. He advanced and opened the door on the left.

An old man lay back in a leather chair set at an angle to its twin. The room itself was pleasantly warm after the icy street and smelled of something medical.

For a second Jarrell thought the man was sleeping, but almost at once he knew he was staring at a corpse. Whatever had been the cause of his death, his distorted expression did not suggest a peaceful end. Jarrell noted that the dead man's spruce style of clothing – the bow tie in particular – could not hide the shabbiness of the clothes themselves: frayed cuffs, trousers almost threadbare in places. The left shirt cuff was undone. Jarrell pushed up the sleeve and saw needle marks. As he moved around the body he trod on something and, bending down, retrieved the syringe. He looked at it and then replaced it where it had fallen.

It might not be murder. In fact, an overdose seemed the more likely cause of death. Yet it seemed strange that no sooner had the dead man's name cropped up in the investigation of a death that was now regarded as suspicious, than the man himself had died an unexpected – an unnatural – death.

He looked round the room. It would require fingerprinting, but he should at least investigate the desk and the papers lying around on it. It looked as though someone had disturbed them, had been searching for something. He put on his leather gloves. They made his fingers clumsy, but would have to do.

Among the papers on the desk Jarrell found a couple of letters from charities that the doctor had evidently contacted for help and as Jarrell looked through the papers, both on top and in the desk drawers, it became clear that the dead man was in serious financial trouble. There were letters relating to the doctor's tenancy; he was in arrears with the rent. But it was fanciful to think of his landlord murdering him for that. Perhaps a deliberate overdose had been the way out.

Jarrell made a superficial first search of the front room. He returned to the corridor and the back of the house, where he found a single bedroom and behind that a kitchen and scullery. There was no bathroom. The lavatory was outside the back door.

The bedroom contained nothing personal apart from a framed photograph of a woman in old-fashioned dress, possibly the dead man's mother. In the chest of drawers, there were handkerchiefs and underwear, neatly folded, woollen cardigans and socks. The kitchen was equally neat and spare, just a wooden draining board and butler sink, a gas stove, a small, scrubbed wooden table and a cupboard containing a few tins, a packet of sugar, a jar of marmalade and a pat of butter, or probably marge, on a plate.

He returned to the front room and took from a saucer on the mantelpiece the set of keys he had noticed earlier. There were five keys, a yale and mortice lock, presumably for the front door, and three smaller ones. One was of a type to open the filing cabinet in the corner.

This contained a few more letters and bills. There was also a sheaf of publicity photographs of some of the boxers Swann had, presumably, tended at one time or another. There were also before and after photographs of the men whose faces Swann must have altered. It surprised Jarrell that the photographs had even been taken, let alone kept, but they didn't seem relevant now – unless, it occurred to him, a visitor had filched the one that could lead to his recognition. A crook of that type, however, Jarrell thought, would probably have used a rougher method than lethal injection to kill the doctor.

A second, rather battered key with a round shank and a circular head with a hole in the middle looked as though it might fit the old mahogany medicine cupboard that stood against the wall. It did. The twin doors creaked open to reveal rows of drugs in carefully labelled compartments: morphine, digitalis, phenobarbitone. Several were empty. Had there been a theft? That would point to murder. Or had the old man simply run out of supplies?

The fifth key fitted the back-door lock. Jarrell opened it, but did not step out into the cramped concrete yard.

He let himself out of the flat and locked the door. He ran up the steps and looked up and down the empty street. He didn't think anyone had seen him, but you could never be sure. Not that it mattered.

The sky hung in a heavy sulphur-coloured mass just above the rooftops. It would soon snow.

chapter 14

THE WEDDING-CAKE HOTEL WHERE Blackstone was lodging in Eastbourne stared out to sea with majestic complacency. Its guests, some of whom were permanent residents, included several wealthy widows lucky enough to have so far escaped the ministrations of Dr John Bodkin Adams.

It hadn't snowed here, but when Blackstone ventured outside, the bleak vista of the windswept front was deserted. No question of a stroll. You were bowled along by the wind in one direction or struggled against it in the other. Waves crashed up against the shore and spat foam up onto the pavement. The seaside in winter was altogether too elemental. Blackstone retreated speedily indoors.

He had done his duty. He'd interviewed the doctor. He'd scooped his rivals. Bodkin Adams was almost certainly about to be arrested, but Blackstone had found him astonishingly calm. He had, for example, said carelessly of one of the elderly ladies who had died under his care and left him a substantial legacy, that he was only surprised she hadn't left him more.

The man's bland effrontery had astonished even the cynical Blackstone, although the journalist knew he should not have been surprised. It was extraordinary how many individuals believed they'd get away with breaking the law. Grotesque and awful crimes were passed off with lame excuses, violence was justified with self-righteous indignation. In a way the eternal optimism of the criminal was endearing. He – and sometimes it was a she – looked on the bright side, expected something to turn up, hoped for the best, met the starkest of evidence with determined denial; or, in the case of John Christie, the mass murderer, seemed gratified by the attendant notoriety. Certainly, Bodkin Adams was serenely insistent he'd done nothing wrong – and perhaps he was as blameless as he claimed to be. Sometimes, Blackstone thought, it was too easy to take the cynical view, to assume the worst of human beings. Yet he hadn't liked the man. He'd recoiled from the doctor's oily air of righteousness and found his quiet voice chilling.

Even more sinister to Blackstone was the loyalty of Bodkin Adams' patients. The few, at least, that he'd managed to talk to wouldn't hear a bad word about their physician. The manner in which the police had victimised him was disgraceful, they said.

Blackstone had woven their support and the support the doctor clearly had from local dignitaries and high-ups into a piece he felt would delight the Little Man. It had all the ingredients, in particular the agreeable horror of its central character: the doctor, the man you could trust, turning his expertise into the art of killing rather than curing. Blackstone, needless to say, made no direct accusation. It was all done with the subtlest of suggestion. He'd done his job, but the case and its quiet horror still didn't engage him. It might end up being the scandal of the decade, but he didn't care. He couldn't wait to get away and to continue instead his quest for the reason for Valerie's death.

Bodkin Adams was arrested. Then he was released on bail. There was a lull in the proceedings and Blackstone was free to take a taxi all the way along the coast.

By the time he arrived in Portsmouth Blackstone had prepared himself for what might be a difficult encounter – if it took place at all. You always had to be prepared to draw a blank. He registered at the station hotel for the night. It was nothing like as grand as the one on Eastbourne esplanade. Next he visited the local library. There he trawled through the electoral register, beginning with a poorer part of town.

He consulted the phone book, then returned to the register and made a list of three Jarvises who didn't appear in the phone book. Valerie's parents were poor; they most likely didn't have a telephone. There were not too many Jarvises and he had to start somewhere. He chose one. It was a semi-detached house in a run-down suburb. He drew a blank. No-one was at home. Wearily, he found a bus that returned him to the centre and set off again, this time for an even shabbier part of Portsmouth, near the docks.

The district had been badly bombed. In fact, the whole of Portsmouth had been pummelled by the Germans. He saw some signs of rebuilding – a new town centre, new housing, new shops – but as he approached the district of pygmy terraces, pinched dwellings with front doors directly on the street, he saw acres of rubble and damaged houses still boarded up.

Number 15 had escaped the bombs. He banged on the door. As he waited, he rehearsed what he should say, the questions he should ask, but foremost in his mind was the need to break the news of Valerie's death.

The woman who answered the door looked nothing like Valerie. Perhaps she was anaemic, for she was pale and looked tired. She was neatly dressed with wispy hair in a roll and wore National Health glasses. She gazed at him palely, sad already, as if fearful that an unexpected visitor could only mean bad news.

Blackstone presented his card and stood there humbly, unthreatening, hesitant. 'I'm sorry to bother you, but I wondered ... I'd very much like to talk to you ...'

'You're from the papers ...?' She looked at him doubtfully.

'It's about your daughter, Mrs Jarvis.'

'Val ...?' It was a shock, he could see that, because now she had the frozen look of someone assimilating unexpected news. 'Oh ... I ...' She looked at him blankly.

'I'd like to talk to you about Valerie. I won't take up much of your time. I have some news of her, you see.'

She still stared and then mechanically moved aside and he stepped into the parlour that opened directly from the street.

'It's not good news, Mrs Jarvis, but it might in some sense be a relief to know ...'

She sat very still with her hands clasped together over her apron as Blackstone broke the news. She stared at him with her pale eyes, enlarged by her lenses, and didn't react at all.

'I'm very sorry to have to tell you this,' he said; and in truth, he was. No longer distracted by the scandal and rumour surrounding Bodkin Adams, he had felt depressed all day. Now this dull parlour with its heavy three-piece suite and the central table – all the furniture crowded together – made him feel worse. The only decoration was a framed collage of a pierrot made out of what looked like sweet papers in blue, silver and red against a black background. He stared at it fixedly, willing the woman to talk.

Eventually she did. 'I hadn't seen Val in a long time. She never paid us a visit and she wasn't much of a hand at writing. I don't know ...' She lapsed into a dispirited silence. Gradually Blackstone coaxed the story out of her.

A girl who left home at sixteen, who ran off with a foreign sailor from the docks. Thought she'd fallen in love and was going to get married.

'She was full of dreams, was Valerie, thought Prince

Charming was coming round the corner of this street any moment.'

'She was the romantic type, was she?'

Mrs Jarvis talked on in her flat, dismal voice as she told the familiar story. 'She'd believe anything. He spun her a yarn. Her father tracked her down in London and threatened the man with the police. He tried to bring her back, but she wasn't having it. But then the seaman went off back to where he come from, on his ship, I suppose, and that was when she wrote the letter, asking for money. My husband went back up there, but she wasn't where she'd been before, he asked other people in the house, it was all flats and bedsits, but nobody knew – or else they wouldn't say. And that's the last we heard of her. It killed my husband.' Her pale voice drained the events of emotion. She sat expressionless, her hands still folded in her lap.

No-one seemed to care that Valerie was dead, not even her mother. He didn't know what else to say. There was nothing further to ask. He didn't know what he was doing in this dismal room; didn't know why he'd come.

Well – he'd felt her family should know and even that he could share his sadness with them. Now her mother's flat indifference made the journey seem pointless. Then Mrs Jarvis spoke again.

'I tell a lie – she did get in touch – once. It was after Arthur passed away, though. Sent a postcard saying she was going to get married, said she was well and happy and we shouldn't worry about her no more.'

'Was there an address?'

Mrs Jarvis shook her head.

Well and happy – married. Blackstone's mouth was dry. He swallowed. 'Do you still have it – the postcard?'

She looked at him dully. 'Oh ... I'm not sure ...' She showed no sign of moving.

'D'you think you possibly might have it somewhere?'

'You want me to look?' The request seemed to surprise her.

'That would be very helpful. If you don't mind.'

'Well ... I don't know ...' But she rose and looked vaguely around. 'I suppose ...' She opened each drawer of the sideboard in turn and after a few moments, retrieved it. 'Here you are.'

The words, written in round, careful writing, were more or less as Mrs Jarvis had remembered them. What interested Blackstone was the card itself. It was a publicity card for the California Club. A palm tree, a beach and some swimmers advertised the place, with an address near Leicester Square.

'I expect you were pleased,' he said. 'Must have set your mind at rest.'

She shrugged and gazed at him with her pale, enlarged eyes. 'She didn't think about us. Just another fairy story like as not.'

Her words upset and angered Blackstone. No-one had cared for Valerie, not even her mother. It didn't even seem to matter that the girl was dead.

'What am I supposed to do now, then?' Blackstone hated her flat, anaemic voice. 'I got no money to bury her.'

'I suppose that's up to you, Mrs Jarvis. You could get a death grant, you know,' he said. 'You'll surely want to see her buried properly.'

He was in a sour mood all the way back in the train to London, took a taxi back to his flat from the station and had a final look at the Bodkin Adams interview. Then he had a kip and after that he decided to eat at the nearby Cumberland Hotel.

He looked round the bar with its dark wood panelling, pink mirrors and square-cut 1930s sofas and chairs, all orange and brown and beige. He ordered a whisky, but this evening the alcohol merely deepened his melancholy. Perhaps it was a mistake to have come here. This was where he'd met her that time. Sonia had arranged the rendezvous, but the location had been his choice.

She'd worn a blue dress and a much shorter and less fashionable coat. With this combination and those clunky high-heeled shoes she looked like a little girl dressed up in her mother's clothes. But when she shrugged off her coat that décolletage was something else. And that smile.

Yes, she really did look like Marilyn Monroe. The voice spoilt the illusion a bit. Monroe's soft breathy vowels caressed you as she spoke, but Valerie's was a flat, rather common south coast twang. Yet the way she talked drew him to her. A girl like her must – surely – know her way about, but she seemed naive, even innocent. She didn't touch alcohol, she said, but he drank almost a whole bottle of wine, followed up by a couple of brandies. When he invited her back to his flat for a coffee she seemed pleased and surprised – as if the outcome of this meeting hadn't been known from the beginning, as if this was just a first date that had gone unexpectedly well, as if she was thrilled to have met such a sympathetic beau.

He'd been no good at all in the bedroom – too much alcohol, probably – but she'd been sweet about that too. It had only occurred to him afterwards that she might have been relieved. She'd coaxed and then comforted him and managed to make him feel less embarrassed, even suggested it was her fault. And they'd talked. He told her about his work at the paper and she seemed genuinely interested. She in turn had described the dreariness of life in Portsmouth and how she didn't get on with her mother and how she'd come to London to see the bright lights.

In the morning he'd escorted her downstairs and hailed her a taxi. He gallantly handed her into it, crushing an extra five pound note into her hand.

'You can always get in touch with me through Sonia,' she said.

But he hadn't. It wasn't exactly shame for his feeble performance, nor the shadowy consciousness that he'd be exploiting her. He probably wasn't exploiting her; she probably enjoyed the life. But there was something about her that made him feel sad and to wish that life were different, that things didn't have to be like this, that somewhere they could have met in a different way. It wasn't that he wished she was an innocent sixteen-year-old again, but rather that he longed to be young and innocent himself, wanted for a crazy moment to recover all those illusions he'd so readily jettisoned along the way.

So he hadn't got in touch with Valerie again. And Sonia hadn't said anything either. She usually followed up on the arrangements she made. But this time she didn't and the weeks and months slipped past. For a while Blackstone was seeing the woman who wrote the *Chronicle* agony column, and after that a girl who worked in the canteen, and he more or less – almost – forgot about Valerie.

Until Rob Crowther at the mortuary pulled out the drawer. The shock of it; he'd thought he was going to be sick, shaking all over, fumbling for a cigarette. 'Steady on, old man,' Crowther had said. 'Didn't know you knew her. I'm sorry. Rotten luck.'

Blackstone ordered a brandy with his coffee at the end of the meal. The caffeine and alcohol were poison, really, and didn't promise a good night's sleep, but he lingered in the half-filled dining room with the clatter of plates and the buzz of voices for company.

Most likely, he thought, it was that ferret of a hotel manager who'd done her in. Nasty piece of work. He'd done his research on Camenzuli – Maltese Mike as he was known in the underworld; dug up all the previous on the nasty little low-life. But motive, that wasn't so easy. Whoever it was Camenzuli was working for – he must have been working for someone – might have told him what to do. The important thing was to find out who that was, but Blackstone had so far drawn a blank.

Marriage and happiness – the endlessly recurring dream. There must have been a man, though, to foster the illusion.

Blackstone wondered who that man could have been. Could have been anyone. Could have been Sonny Marsden. Could have been one of Sonia's clients, introduced to Valerie in the way he himself had been.

She had been so young, twenty or twenty-one at most. Her warm flesh had been so alive. And then to see her laid out in the mortuary ... a tag from some old play – Shakespeare? – was haunting him.

Cover her face – mine eyes dazzle – she died young.

chapter 15

CHARLES HALLAM WAS GRIPPED with cold, his whole body pinched together, stiff and hampered with it. Sweaters, scarves and duffel coat couldn't protect against the chill. He'd woken at the blackest point of the night from a nightmare in which a deeply buried event had burst from the mausoleum of his unconscious. Something that had happened a long time ago was happening again. He stared down at the broken body on the flagstones below. This time the man he'd pushed off the terrace, his mother's hated admirer, wasn't properly dead, but struggled to his feet and with blood running down his face began to climb the steps before Charles was propelled back to consciousness on a wave of terror.

He'd lain for a long time in the dark, unable to shake off the fear – and the sickening uncertainty: that he now no longer knew, and perhaps had never known, if he had acted deliberately to kill or if it had been a fatal accident.

He had to forget again.

The wind skinned his face as he biked in from his digs in Park Town. The colleges huddled dark as the sky. There'd been no sun for two weeks. He left his bike outside Balliol. He was due to meet Fergus Berriman in the Cadena, the idea being to proceed from there to the Free Hungary meeting, to be followed by a rally. Oxford politics, when it meant pompous posturing at the Union by middle-aged twenty-year-olds planning to become prime minister, had always bored Charles rigid, but since the arrival of the Hungarians, things had improved.

He thought if he browsed through the bookshops along the Broad, he might forget the nightmare, but first he wandered into Elliston and Cavell's, the stuffy department store on the corner. It was the last week of term and there were parties. Even the postgraduates held parties at this time of year, although most were dreary affairs in suburban digs with beer and Algerian wine. There was always a single light bulb that hung from the ceiling and shed a deadening glare on proceedings. Such festivities made a dispiriting contrast to champagne at Christ Church. All the more reason to cut a dash of some kind, to at least be striking, to mark his distance from them. He thought he might buy a new shirt, but first he paused by the scent counter. He liked to wear scent himself, partly in order to shock, and had run out of Chanel's Cuir de Russie, a current favourite. He gazed dully at the array of bottles and sprayed his wrist with Lanvin's Arpège. At once he wished he hadn't, for it had been his mother's favourite. Scent was memory itself, and memory intensified absence. His eyes filled with tears and he turned quickly away.

The cold outside air made him gasp. The tears stung his eyes. He walked along the Broad crushing all thoughts, all memories.

The dusty gloom of Thornton's second-hand bookshop steadied him. After a while he was thinking about the Romans, then Quinault, and from there his thoughts moved to Reggie. So she was having an affair and her boyfriend knew Quinault, but it seemed strange that she should have been so interested in the Professor. Gossip was vulgar, of course, particularly when it was about the famous. Charles regarded it as totally beneath him to be interested in celebrity gossip of any sort. It was the sort of thing his stepmother, Brenda, liked to talk about.

Reggie's interest in Quinault was a different matter. It flattered Charles to have been let in on her secret and Turbeville's connection with the Professor shed a new light on the old man. The student view of the dons was of an archaic and dried-up species, an evolutionary curiosity, inhabiting college corridors like lizards rustling through ancient ruins, oblivious to modish undergraduate obsessions such as jazz and existentialism.

Charles, on the other hand, having now passed into a new Oxford with a different perspective, had begun to understand how very modern some of the lizards were. It was the undergraduates who were parochial and frivolous. Their tutors had a far wider view of the world, a far greater grasp of the meaning of power. Quinault was no longer some out-of-touch old buffer with a musty and possibly dubious interest in the early Roman emperors, but an actor in the modern world of power and politics.

More changed, however, than Charles' view of Quinault, was his vision of himself. *Then*, before Schools and the – he had to admit – rather wonderful moment of his Congratulatory First (he had walked into the room for his viva and instead of asking questions the examiners had stood up and each shook his hand) he had taken himself and his peers for the life and soul of the party, the stars in the firmament. Now he was no longer the effortless success, but found himself on the lowest rung of a ladder he wasn't sure he wanted to climb. That he was there at all must mean he had ambitions, a fact that had previously escaped him. You couldn't go on just being wonderful – and wonderfully clever – for ever. You had to scrabble around in the dirt like everyone else. It bored him.

He tried to remember what Reggie had said about the relationship between the Professor and her lover. Charles did not see why it worried her; there was nothing so very odd in the visit of a politician to his former tutor; but Reggie must be jealous or insecure and he'd promised to help her. He really had no idea how, or what more he could discover. Poor Reggie, madly in love: it didn't quite fit with his picture of her. He enjoyed the interest she showed in him and that, twice his age, she'd made him her friend. It was flattering and enhanced his sense of sophistication. To him she was a glamorous figure, but he'd seldom wondered about her inner life.

Even when she'd managed to get him into her bed before his sixteenth birthday, he simply hadn't noticed that she was infatuated with him. The experience had been interesting, if not overwhelmingly pleasurable, but his interest had concerned himself and his own reactions.

He was so accustomed to being desired that in a strange way, it cut him off from the feelings of others. Yet he was not vain. He took his looks for granted. So far as he was concerned, there was nothing unusual about them. It was even rather a bore at times, so that – rather like Penny and her friends, although he didn't know this – he would complain that his would-be lovers 'only wanted one thing' and were uninterested in him 'as a person'. Fergus' response to this had merely been that he should be so lucky and had he ever considered that his looks might be more interesting than his so-called personality.

He approached the corner of Cornmarket. The smell of roasting coffee – better, to be honest, than the drink itself – wafted from the Cadena. Fergus Berriman was seated at the back of the café. He was the only postgraduate Charles found at all sympathetic. This was because he was not like the others. While Charles was younger than the rest, Berriman was older. He came into the ambiguous Oxford category of 'perennial student'. His research – into the work of the Latin poet Lucretius – had lingered on for some years; he wrote for *Isis* and published poetry in obscure little London magazines and had been a communist until, like many others, he'd left the Party after Khrushchev's denunciation of Stalin.

Fergus was already going bald and had fierce horn-rimmed glasses. He never wore a coat, seemed not to possess one, but his tweed jacket was invariably buttoned up over his portly form and completed with a red scarf that swathed his neck.

'Have you heard the latest? Imre Nagy's been arrested in Budapest. They've taken him to Moscow.'

'I hadn't heard.'

'It's appalling. I don't know what to think – I still can't believe communists would do a thing like that.'

Charles hoped Fergus was not going to wrestle with his conscience over coffee. He'd followed through his friend's eyes the upheaval among the British communists, as the Party was split between those who left and those who stayed. Fergus had often said 'I come from a Party family, you know,' as if it were some alternative form of aristocratic descent, but now his family and many others were riven with conflict. He and his mother had renounced their membership, while his father had stayed 'in'.

'You know ... the Soviet troops going in like that – some of them are just peasants, or they come from places like Uzbekistan – some of them even wanted to side with the students, but – God, what a mess.'

Until the Khrushchev revelations Fergus had always seemed aggressively sure of his political views. But perhaps that had been precisely because he had always had inward doubts. Fergus did protest too much sometimes.

'You're so cynical and blasé, you don't understand,' he said. 'I'm not even on speaking terms with Dad any more, but at least I'm here, not there. At home, I mean. He won't speak to my mother either and she has to go on living in the same house with him.'

'You should be an anarchist, like me.'

'Anarchism's a bourgeois deviation,' said Fergus, retreating into the jargon of the Party heritage he had renounced.

'Anyway you're the opposite of an anarchist. You're just bloody *bourgeois.*'

Suddenly it seemed absurd and they started to laugh.

'Drink up. We'll be late.'

'I wanted a bun. I'm hungry. I didn't have any breakfast.'

'No bun. We haven't time.'

The Free Hungary meeting took place in a small hall in Lincoln College. This college had been at the forefront in helping the Hungarians. A group of Lincoln students had started a petition of protest that had reached the national dailies, and three of them had even set off on a mission to take penicillin to the freedom fighters in Budapest, flouting the rule that forbade students to leave Oxford in term time without permission.

The abrupt passage from frozen outdoor chill to fusty interior charged Charles with tension and heightened his awareness of everything around him as if his nerves were exposed. He was sweating, yet he was shaking as well. The buzz of voices, the crowded panelled room and the smell of damp wool and cigarette smoke combined in a wired-up atmosphere of expectation. Something momentous might actually happen. It was like going to meet someone with whom you were in love.

A very young-looking bespectacled undergraduate called the meeting to order. As his words fell on the unusually silent and respectful audience, Charles was still scanning the room, and became aware that a whole cohort of actual Hungarians were crowded at the right side of the hall. One was holding a red, white and green flag. These must be the refugee students who were now settled at a hostel in Headington. They looked, really, like students anywhere, but shabbier and to Charles more romantic. One in particular stood out. He was wearing an off-white Aran sweater – surely an item from the clothes collected for the new arrivals. His dark hair fell over his forehead, and his jagged profile and the intense manner in which he was gazing at the speaker had something grand and noble about it, or so it seemed to Charles. He was standing next to two young women, one of whom wore a peasant kerchief, the other a black beret.

Two of the Lincoln protest leaders spoke, each briefly, to an audience eager to be urged on to action against the international outrage. 'Tens of thousands of students and workers have died!'

Charles steadily watched the Hungarian who'd caught his attention.

'This grotesque invasion must be condemned by all liberals, libertarians – and *socialists* – above all, socialists who care for freedom and democracy—'

A communist tried to heckle, but was shouted down.

When a Hungarian rose to speak the room was silent as it had not been until now. The fidgeting and shuffling and muttered asides ceased. Bluish smoke floated across the hall.

He was a round-faced and rather unattractive youth in an old leather jacket, but he spoke well in fluent English, with quiet passion. As Charles listened the events ceased to be just another absorbing yet abstract item of international news. This boy had lost his brother in the fighting. His parents had been arrested. He himself had only just escaped conscription into the Soviet army.

The quiet words gave Charles some glimmering of what had actually happened, what it meant in terms of actual lives, of fate. Perhaps after all it was worse than Suez. The testimony from the four Hungarians who spoke, three well, one in halting English, moved him far more than he would have expected. He even had a lump in his throat. Yet, absorbed though he was, his gaze remained on the dark Hungarian and finally he caught his eye. The Hungarian stared back. Charles held his gaze. He was sure he wasn't mistaken.

The meeting ended with a rallying call to the march the following day. As the audience banged against chairs and surged raggedly from the hall, Charles eased his way past the loiterers and caught up with the Hungarian he'd noticed earlier.

'I don't suppose you have a light?'

It was a hackneyed ploy. The Hungarian gazed at him sombrely. 'Of course.'

They walked across the quad side by side. Charles looked back a little guiltily, but Fergus had stayed behind to argue with the communist heckler.

'When did you get here?'

'Last week. Before that I was in Austria. You English have been very kind, but I think I only just begin to know – only now am I understanding what has happened. I think I am still shocked, you know.'

'You speak very good English – all of you.'

The Hungarian laughed. 'In school we must learn Russian – our second language. But it is a form of resistance that we instead in our free time learn English, you know.'

'Well, that's good news, because I don't speak Hungarian.' He nearly mentioned that he spoke Russian, but at the last moment thought that might make his new friend suspicious. 'So I shouldn't have been able to talk to you otherwise,' he lied. 'I'm Charles Hallam, by the way.'

'My name is Ferenczy Andras. In Hungary we say the last name first. You should call me Andras.'

'I write for the local paper, the *Oxford Mail*.' This was not a complete lie. Following a group visit to the Soviet Union in his second year, together with others whose National Service had consisted of the Russian course organised by the Navy, he'd got an article on Russian student life published in the local paper. 'It would be terrific if I could interview you – you could talk about your experiences – if you felt like it ...'

'Yes ... that would be – that is – provided my identity ...

you see my parents are still there ... reprisals ...'

'Of course. What about a coffee? If you've the time.'

Again the Hungarian hesitated. Then he smiled. 'I find my friend. You don't mind? He can come too?'

Actually Charles did mind, but he could hardly object. The friend's rosy cheeks, round brown eyes and friendly smile made a striking contrast to Andras' brooding gloom. He seemed in excellent spirits. 'Meszarov Gyorgy.'

Charles led them to the coffee bar in the High.

'Good coffee,' said Gyorgy. 'Not like in the hostel.' He smiled. 'But bad coffee is not our big worry just now.'

'You're staying at the hostel then – most of the Hungarian students are there, aren't they?'

'No. Andras is in the hostel. But I am one of the lucky ones. I am placed with family. If that is lucky. I am not sure.' He turned and spoke to his companion in Hungarian. Andras smiled and shrugged.

'Oh?'

'Professor Quinault. Is asking questions. And his wife, she seems ... she does not like me, perhaps.'

'Professor *Quinault*? He's my supervisor. I'm a D.Phil. student. Postgraduate.'

'D.Phil.?'

Charles started on a laborious explanation of the British research system, but soon felt he was boring his audience and instead turned the conversation and focused on them. It was disappointing that Gyorgy seemed the friendlier and more outgoing of the two, lively and ready for a laugh despite the traumatic escape from his homeland and the uncertainty of his future. Andras looked down into his coffee and smoked. He had beautiful hands with long fingers.

'Let's meet again, shall we? I can show you round Oxford a bit, if you'd like.'

'Oh, yes.' Gyorgy was all enthusiasm. 'That is very nice

indeed. You come to the hostel, I am always there, but Andras does not like it there, so he use my room at the Professor's house.'

Andras looked into the distance. But then he said: 'Better to come to the house. The hostel is so noisy. If you want to talk, write article, that is much better. So you should come to the house. I hate the hostel.'

chapter 16

BLACKSTONE COULD JUST ABOUT remember how once waking up had meant springing out of bed and getting down to business. These days the return to consciousness was slow and painful. He groaned, rolled over and squinted at his watch, groped for his fags and lit a cigarette as he stumbled to the window.

He pulled the curtains apart and looked down at the street far below. At mid-morning London was chilly under a white sky. The pavements were crowded with Christmas shoppers like scurrying ants. How he hated Christmas – the cheap tinsel, the garish lights and decorations, the droning canned music, and worst of all, the mad compulsion to spend money. How much better London had been in the blackout.

He washed and dressed and descended in the smoothly purring lift. He walked to the nearby Maison Lyons for coffee, but the very thought of eggs made him feel sick. He lit up, breathed in and felt better. The second cigarette of the day was the one that really made the difference. The first was just resuscitation.

Years of smoking and alcohol had played havoc with his digestion and somewhere in the back of his mind he knew about the diseases that were waiting, but he'd crushed that dread firmly into the mental cupboard that contained all his nightmares, all the unspeakable horrors of life. He was a hard-bitten reporter. Dead bodies were his living, no gruesome mutilation he hadn't seen. But there were other, worse threats menacing him, to be at all costs never thought about at all, those diseased bodies his father had been so fond of describing.

He drank two strong cups of coffee with plenty of sugar and smoked as he turned the pages of *The Times*. He scanned the deaths column on the front page and the sport at the back. Anything else was for later.

He'd decided to pay another visit to North Kensington. He was curious to know why Sonia had pushed him in that direction. She must have heard something. She was a reliable source of information.

He took the tube to Holland Park and walked along Ladbroke Grove. The residential streets were eerily quiet. The stucco barracks, walls darkened with soot, stared down emptily. Railings were broken or gone, windows blank or draped with dingy muslin, and the Greek columns and heavy porticos were a baroque monument to a failed grandeur that had perhaps never existed, save in the mind of some long-dead property developer.

There was a chip shop in the Golborne Road. It was shut. Blackstone stood back and looked up at the façade of the house next door. Curtains half dragged across; loose pointing, blackened bricks. He pressed the bottom bell.

He waited for a long time. Why did residents always take so long to answer the door in this part of the world? At last it was opened.

She was wrapped in a dressing gown that had once been white, but her smile lit up the grey day. What a vivid flower on this dung heap.

'Is Dr Jones at home?'

'He is. Is he expecting you?' The Irish accent was of a piece with her black curly hair and blue eyes.

'No. But I hope I can see him. If he can spare me a few

minutes. The name's Gerry Blackstone.'

'Pleased to meet you. I'm Rita. Come in, will you please.' She was so friendly he could hardly stop himself from planting a kiss on her rosy cheek. What vitality! And she had none of that air of sullen suspicion he was used to in this part of London.

'Rita!' At the deep-throated roar from inside the cavernous building, the girl jumped. 'What the hell you doing out there? In this frigging freezing—'

'I'd better get back inside ...' With an apologetic smile at Blackstone she scampered away into the gloom.

The journalist advanced into the passage. The brown varnished wallpaper was peeling away. The place smelled rank and gamey, of leaking gas, paraffin, fried onions. He walked to the back of the house where, in a room overlooking a small garden, he knew he'd find his friend. Dr Darcy Jones.

The grizzled old West Indian sat very upright in a cane armchair. He wore an ancient but well-preserved lounge suit. His eyes, behind old-fashioned round spectacles, were light coloured, as was his skin. A stick rested at the side of his chair.

'Good morning, my friend. We haven't seen you for a while. I'm glad of a visit. Sit down. Would you like something to drink? Some tea or coffee? Rita is an obliging girl. She won't mind.' The old man rang a small brass bell that stood on the octagonal table beside his chair. 'I wish Carl treated her better. Mind you, he doesn't beat her or anything of that kind, but he shouts all the time. Shouts at me too. A real shouter. Always been a shouter. In the meantime, how can I help you? I assume there's a reason for your visit.'

'It's about Sonny Marsden, Dr Jones.'

Darcy Jones had lived in England for a long time, many years before the first post-war West Indians arrived on the *Windrush*. He was from a different generation, a different background, an old intellectual, a Marxist, indeed. He'd written books, mixed with radicals in the 1930s, but now, aged and ailing, he was living out his life in his chair, surrounded by his books, still writing, but forgotten.

He suffered from arthritis, asthma and weak kidneys, and in old age his mind, undamaged, had turned to local matters. What he didn't know about North Kensington and Paddington was not worth knowing.

'Sonny Marsden? I hardly think there is anything new I can tell you, my boy. You're acquainted with the man. His activities are an open secret.'

'Would he commit a murder?'

Dr Jones stared at the reporter. 'He's hot-tempered. Like my son. They get so riled up, these young men. I say to him, keep calm, you'll achieve more that way, but they don't seem capable of listening.'

'There's a girl been murdered. She used to be Marsden's girlfriend, or so I heard.'

There was a knock on the door of the room. Rita entered.

'Would you be so kind as to make us some tea, dear?'

'Sure, darling. What's this, though, about a murder?'

Blackstone thought he'd never seen such blue eyes. 'She was called Valerie – did you know a Valerie at all?'

Rita shook her head. And she smiled, apologetic, as though she'd have been so much happier to be able to oblige.

'A looker. Blonde. Like Marilyn Monroe.'

'Ah …' Now she hesitated. 'To be sure …' but she looked doubtful. 'I'll be thinking while I'm making the tea – I'll ask Carl.'

Dr Jones sighed. 'She's a good girl. I'm afraid she's wasted on my son. And to think I named him after the great Karl Marx himself. But that's another story. Tell me, though, why are you so interested in this other young woman?'

'I'm a crime reporter.'

Dr Jones stared at Blackstone. He stroked his goatee beard.

'These crimes are personal tragedies, I understand that. But you turn them into gruesome entertainments. Isn't that so? And you ignore the systematic crimes of society. Why aren't you or one of your colleagues looking into the crimes the system perpetrates on its people? Look around here, for a start. Much of the property is actually owned by the Church, would you believe. And yet in this one London borough you'll find more crimes of injustice than you could report in a year – in these rotting houses.'

'I know. It's a standing joke, isn't it? The Church Commissioners – landlords to the biggest brothel in Europe.' Blackstone fished for his cigarettes as he took a turn about the cluttered room; so many books, in shelves and piled on the floor. Wooden shutters divided the room; beyond them in the front room was the old man's bedroom. Blackstone knew that, because on his previous visit the old man had had bronchitis and had been propped up in bed. He seemed better today.

'Sit down, Mr Blackstone, you're just like those boys, my son and his friends, always so restless. Let me tell you what you should write about in your paper. The degeneration of this city. How this slum came to exist. How Thomas Cubitt, the Victorian philanthropist, bought hundred-year leases from the great aristocratic families who owned London and how he built these houses for the rich, for rich, bourgeois families with many children and many servants. I've studied the history of the area. They did not anticipate the future well, those Victorians. It turned out differently from their expectations. Married couples had fewer children. There were fewer servants after the so-called Great War. Better-off families moved to the suburbs. Then, after the recent war, respectable working-class tenants moved into council housing. And now those hundred-year leases are coming to an end. The great families are selling off their land and the leaseholders are trying to get rid of the tail end of their leases. And you see the result. There's sub-letting, illegal tenancies, it's worth no-one's while to do the repairs, and on the other hand there are new owners who will get evictions by fair means or foul.'

That had been a feature of the Christie case: Christie and his wife – who at length became one of his victims – had hated the West Indians and their landlord had deliberately moved several immigrants into the house where they lived with the idea of annoying them so that they moved out.

'It certainly is something the *Chronicle* should take up,' conceded Blackstone. An investigative team; he might mention it to the Little Man. 'But I specialise in murders,' he added.

'Specialise!' Dr Jones drew his lips down in distaste.

Rita returned with the tea. She'd asked Carl about Valerie, 'but there was never a girl with such film-star looks down in these parts. They'd all be remembering a girl like that.'

Blackstone watched her pour the tea and present a cup to Dr Jones. She was gentle and solicitous. She patted the cushions at Dr Jones' back and the old man patted her hand and smiled up at her as he thanked her.

Blackstone envied him for having such a lovely creature to minister to his needs – how different from his own uncared-for existence. When she passed him his cup he thanked her with a smile as engaging as he could muster. She tidied up a few of the papers lying on the ground. Blackstone wished she'd stay, yet was impatient for her to go, as he wanted to continue his talk with the old man.

After she'd shut the door behind her, Dr Jones said: 'Carl's up in court again next week. This time I fear it'll be a prison sentence.'

'I'm sorry to hear that.' He waited a moment. 'You see, someone suggested Marsden might have had something to do with this girl's death – the story I'm investigating. As a matter of fact, I knew the girl.'

The pale old eyes observed him. 'You are a sentimentalist at heart – all you gutter journalists.'

'That's a bit unfair.' But maybe, conceded Blackstone silently, maybe there was a grain of truth in the old man's words. Had he really cared about Valerie? And had she been telling the truth, or was hers just another sob story to ease the money out of his pocket?

'Sonny Marsden's a pimp. He's had connections with many young women. But if Carl recalled nothing, then it is probably not true. In which case you have to ask yourself why someone told you that.'

Blackstone hadn't quite thought of it as deliberately misleading. Sonia didn't give much away; the information she passed along was always calculated. But she never misled people. Someone, perhaps, had misled *her*. But that only raised a further question: why? And who?

'Men like Sonny Marsden give us all a bad name. It's a slur on the whole community. And you and your brethren writing up all the scandals in your gutter press, you do us no favours. There are many Jamaicans, Trinidadians and all the rest who work hard over here, send money back, hope to bring their wives and children, lead respectable lives. Sonny Marsden's brother is one such, I believe. Why don't you write about that side of things? How they had dreams, dreams that were disappointed. They come here thinking the streets are paved with diamonds and all they find is pavements of broken glass.

'This country is anti-coloured people,' continued Dr Jones. 'There is so much prejudice here. Everyone – even men such as Sonny Marsden – was so proud of being British before they came here. But now they're disillusioned. And disillusionment leads to cynicism and either apathy or anger. And you could be in a position to do something to counteract the trend. You could write about what is really going on instead of salacious tales of gangs and prostitution.'

'I'm a crime reporter,' repeated Blackstone. He knew Jones was right, but there was nothing he could do about it. He wrote about what people wanted to hear. The Little Man insisted on that.

He stayed, knowing Dr Jones was lonely, and the conversation moved back to the safer territory of the Church Commissioners and their negligence. Religion was one of Dr Jones' bugbears. He was an atheist and the hypocrisy of his pious landlords gave him a perverse satisfaction.

Rita returned to collect the tea tray.

'Wait!' He'd almost forgotten. He took out the postcard of the California Club. 'D'you know anything about this place, by any chance?'

Rita held it, frowning. She shook her head. But then: 'I tell a lie. I did have a friend worked there ... I think that was the name ... yes. Dawn. She's not there any more, though. She went to a much grander place, that big club in Soho.'

He retrieved the card. He was no further forward, but the California Club's address was on the card anyway. He needed to pay a visit.

First, though, he decided on a return trip to the Premier Club. Instead of Johnnie Hay it was his sidekick in charge, one of those pale, thin and insubstantial individuals, of indeterminate age, whose lives seem dedicated to acting as the shadow of a more enterprising boss.

'He's in his office – wouldn't want to be disturbed,' muttered the man, who, Blackstone realised, was only about nineteen years of age.

'He won't mind seeing me.' And Blackstone moved past him towards the cubby hole at the back that passed for an office.

Hay was seated at an empty desk. He was smoking a cheroot and gazing blankly into space.

'Sorry to disturb you, Johnnie ...'

The owner responded with his thin-lipped, yet engaging, melancholy smile. Always emollient. He was not a man to express any annoyance he might have felt at being thus interrupted.

'Not at all, old chap – just waiting for a phone call. What can I do for you?'

'Just wondered if you had any news. Anything interesting.'

'About that girl you were sweet on? Or just generally?'

'Either – both.'

Hay smiled and shook his head. 'Why aren't you down in Eastbourne, Blackie? That's where you should be. John Bodkin Adams. That's going to be a bigger story than some girl falling down the stairs will ever be.'

'I've been down. Got an interview. It'll be in the paper tomorrow. And I'll be going back soon enough. I tell you, though – Bodkin Adams has friends in high places. And I've talked to some medical friends of mine. The British Medical Association is petrified. The NHS is virtually broke. The commission that reported on it said it's massively underfunded. They're desperate for cash. So the last thing they want is a gigantic scandal about a respected GP who turns out to be a mass murderer.'

Johnnie Hay whistled quietly. 'You don't say,' he murmured and puffed at his cheroot.

Blackstone didn't want to talk about Eastbourne. 'Anyway,' he said firmly, 'in the meantime, I wondered if you'd heard anything ...'

'About the girl?' Hay shook his head. 'No.' He was still smoking his eternal cheroot. It had gone out several times and each time he relit it with a series of little puffs like an expiring toy train. It was a form of punctuation, interrupting his words. It gave them more emphasis and yet somehow hedged the whole conversation about with uncertainties. 'And tell you what, old cock. I'd leave well alone if I were you. It ain't worth the trouble.'

chapter 17

QUINAULT'S HOUSE WAS SET back from the road, brooding behind the shrubs of its neglected garden. Old man's beard lolled over thrusting curtains of ivy. Rhododendrons and castor oil plants loomed on either side of the path. In the daylong twilight a fine sweat of drizzle veiled the Gothic hulk, so that it appeared to be actually dissolving in the liquid air.

Charles left his bike by the gate. The words 'The Grange' could just be seen incised into the mossy wood. Andras had invited him, but now he was here he looked up at the place uneasily. From the beginning Charles had been sure the looks he'd exchanged with the Hungarian were unambiguous, but now he wasn't so certain. He could not fathom Andras. They'd met in a pub. Andras hadn't said much, but then as they were about to part inconclusively he'd surprised Charles by issuing a definite invitation to Quinault's house. At that point Charles was beginning to doubt if Andras was worth the effort, but he couldn't pass up the invitation. Apart from the possibility of seduction, it was also, of course, a chance to perhaps gain more information about the Professor to pass on to Reggie, whose interest in Quinault he'd more or less forgotten, but now conveniently remembered.

The prospect of visiting Quinault's house presented itself as vaguely illicit. It was in some unspecified way risky. It crossed a border. Charles embraced risk; while still at school he'd got away with many misdemeanours, had often sailed close to the wind then and since. He couldn't possibly pass up this latest unexpected opportunity to play with fire by trespassing on Quinault territory. He'd probably find nothing interesting, but any little scrap of information would please Reggie and he was keen to keep in with her. Her hints about the don's influence in places far beyond Oxford and the visit of the MP, Turbeville, had aroused Charles' curiosity, not something easily achieved, so the prospect of exploring the hideous Gothic monstrosity of a house appealed to him.

Now he was here, however, he felt nervous and shivery. In fact he felt rather odd. He wondered if he might be getting flu. But he braced himself and walked up the drive to the massive pseudo-medieval door. When he pulled the large metal handle a bell clanged far too loudly. He waited for so long that he began to half hope Andras wasn't there. He was about to turn away, but then the door did open.

'So – you are here.' Andras stared at him. They stood there awkwardly. Charles wondered if Andras was regretting the invitation.

It was almost as cold in the house as outside. The hall was panelled in dark wood, the wooden staircase turned halfway up and disappeared into the gloom.

'It is good of you to come.'

Charles frowned. 'Why good? I wanted to.'

Andras was taller than Charles and as he strode ahead his way of walking was thrilling, manly and yet at the same time there was something subtly feminine about his movement. Charles began to be interested again.

'Gyorgy's room is on first floor.'

They were going straight up to the bedroom, then. Not that that meant anything. North Oxford was bed-sitter land.

Everyone entertained friends in the rooms with a divan and a gas ring.

There was a short corridor at the top of the stairs. Andras pushed open the first door and Charles followed him into a bleak room encumbered with dark furniture and a hospital-type metal-framed single bed. Andras bent down and switched on a single-bar electric fire. There was a smell of scorched dust as the element warmed up.

'So. You came,' repeated Andras.

'Yes. I came.' Now that Charles was here he definitely wasn't sure he wanted to be. He was distracted by thoughts of Professor Quinault and frustrated not to be downstairs, poking around and discovering the old man's secrets. He sat down on the bed, feeling tired. He was definitely sickening for something. He felt very peculiar.

Andras advanced and stood over him. Then he sat down too, close to Charles, and put an arm round him. It was a stiff, jerky movement and perversely Charles edged away, his coquettish glance a cover for his paralysing ambivalence.

The Hungarian stood up again and moved to the window, from where he looked moodily out over the back garden. After a moment he turned to Charles.

'Is so cold ...'

'It's bloody freezing in here,' agreed Charles, but he was thinking that Andras must be used to the cold; it was surely much colder in Hungary than in England.

'Madame Quinault does not like fire on too much.'

'I thought you said she's out all day.' Charles was shivering, but it was a reaction to the situation more than the temperature. Although, perhaps, he was running a temperature; his tense mood was becoming stranger and stranger. 'She won't know if you turn on the fire. And – for Christ's sake, it's *cold*!'

'She is out. She goes out always. This is good, that she is not there, because she does not like us. Well, she does not like that I am here. They had an argument. They do not think I understand so good English. It was not necessary, she thought, to offer a room to Hungarian.'

'Lots of dons have.'

'This is what Professor Quinault say. It looks bad not to do this. But his wife is thinking only of money.'

'They're not poor.'

'They argue always about money.'

'They must be incredibly mean if you're not supposed to have the fire on in the middle of winter. He *is* out, isn't he? The Professor.'

'Of course. He always out also.'

Charles knew that would be the answer. Quinault spent ninety per cent of his time in college. Not that there was anything unusual about that: many of the dons, whether bachelors or husbands, seemed to prefer to live their lives in college. 'Don't they mind that you're here instead of Gyorgy?'

Andras didn't reply. He continued to stare out of the window. After a while he said, 'Is too difficult. Everything is difficult.'

'It must be bloody being a refugee.' Charles took out his Balkan Sobranies and offered them to Andras.

'These are like Russian cigarettes.' Andras looked at Charles suspiciously, but he took one anyway.

'Tell me about it – how you got away. What it was like.'

'You have seen pictures.'

Charles had certainly seen photos of the streets of Budapest strewn with glass and buildings reduced to rubble and smoke, but it had seemed unreal. 'Were you actually fighting?' He watched the Hungarian, who was now seated on an upright chair smoking, his shoulders slumped, his legs apart, his hands resting on his thighs, his gaze on the linoleum floor.

'I was at the university for a time. Some soldiers, they change sides. Joined us. From them we had guns. The worst thing was – Russians withdrew. In the first days we hoped – all seemed possible – but then they returned. With tanks. And deep down we knew would happen like this.'

'It must have been pretty awful.' Charles felt his words to be insultingly inadequate, but he was distracted by the ambiguity of the situation and why he was here. He felt he was in a false position. It seemed vulgar and callous to be even considering making a pass at someone who'd barely escaped with his life. He also no longer felt sure whether his presence was on Andras' account or to gain access to Quinault's private life.

'You are not truly interested.'

'Of course I am. How can you say that?' Charles touched the Hungarian's arm, but his hand was shaken off.

'For you British it is new drama. Big excitement. In hostel there is excitement too. Everyone talking, talking, sometimes hearing of people we know. From new refugees coming. Here at least I don't think about that. There is no point thinking.'

'You don't want to talk about it, then?'

Andras continued to stare at the floor. 'No.' He brooded, but after a moment's silence he continued. 'What else is to think about? The fighting – is still going on, now. While we sit here. It say on the wireless there are pockets of resistance – that is the phrase? My friend was shot, others arrested. Secret police came to my parents. Arrests were happening every day. We were hiding. There were rumours – if we were captured we would be sent to Russian army and so we knew we had to try to get away. We had to get to a part near the frontier where there were swamps. Less Russians there. When we got close there was storm but we can't stop, we have to wade through – mud and water. It was deeper than we thought – I cannot swim, I was scared, I was almost drowning. And there were Russians, they were near. They send up flares and we heard machine-gun fire. We are going on for many hours. One time there is a bit of drier land – we rested for an hour, then went on – two or three hours more, hoping we are now in land between the frontiers. We saw the Austrian flag – that was strange moment. Too exhausted to feel ... even pleased.'

As if the outburst had relieved his feelings, Andras squared his shoulders and stood up. 'Well, I am here now.'

It was so cold. Charles thought he was getting a sore throat. 'Why don't we go for a walk? We could go to a pub I know. It's a walk to get there. Across Port Meadow.'

'If you like. Yes. Perhaps is best.'

But as he followed Andras downstairs, Charles remembered his promise to Reggie. 'Why don't you show me his library first? Isn't that where he has his collection?' It seemed wrong and forbidden. 'Have you seen it?'

Andras shook his head.

'He's very proud of his collection. It's famous, you know.'

'If you want. Is down here I think.' He led the way along another panelled corridor.

'I'm not really supposed to be here.' It felt exciting and dangerous to be prowling round the Professor's house. It was all part of his weird mood.

'Why not?'

'I don't know. I'm his student ... I suppose I should only be here if he'd invited me.' He had no idea how he'd explain his presence if Quinault found him. There was nothing wrong in befriending one of the refugees – apart from his real motivation.

'But I invite you here,' said Andras.

Dusty tapestry curtains were half drawn across a French window so that the library was in semi-darkness. Its walls were lined with books from floor to ceiling on three sides. Along the fourth, glass cabinets enclosed The Collection: the Greek and Roman figurines, pots and metal pieces that Quinault cherished.

Charles peered at the objects behind glass. He wondered

if he dared open one of the cabinet doors in order to actually touch the objects. He pulled at one of the little metal handles, but the cabinet was locked.

'What are these things?' Andras stood behind him, close to him, also staring at the statuettes.

'They are very rare and valuable,' said Charles, wondering exactly how much they were worth.

'I do not like these things. In museum with light is okay, but in this room with many books and it is all so … there is so much, you know, on the table, the books – I don't know the word …'

'Dust?'

'I don't know, anyway, it is dark, the house is all dark.'

'It's pretty creepy. Yet you'd rather be here than at the hostel?' Charles still didn't understand about the substitution and his words were intended as a question, but Andras didn't reply.

Charles turned away from the cabinets. The whole idea of collecting things repelled him. He edged his way round the table and as he did so he glanced at the papers and books with which it was littered. The papers seemed to consist of pages and pages of notes in Quinault's minute, neat, yet illegible handwriting. This was his opportunity.

'There are many rooms in this house. It is empty so much, and strange. So many rooms and no-one in them.'

But Charles was no longer listening. He switched on the table lamp and leant forward, peering at the papers piled and strewn over the table. They were not after all only Quinault's notes. There was a pale blue envelope, the address handwritten. There were several cuttings from newspapers. One from the local paper was headed: 'Road proposal for Christ Church Meadow philistine, says Warden'. He looked more closely. As he did so he noticed a letter on cream-coloured paper, headed with a portcullis. From an MP by the look of it. He picked it up.

It was handwritten in jagged script. 'Dear Professor Quinault, I shall be passing through Oxford next week and if convenient I should very much appreciate an opportunity to review our arrangement ...' It was signed Rodney Turbeville.

A pile in the centre of the table consisted of what were apparently notes on Quinault's academic work. Quinault had used a very soft pencil and the tiny characters were blurred to the point of illegibility. Some were written in classical Greek.

The third pile, on the left, consisted of material relating to Hungary and the uprising: cuttings, especially from letters columns, relating to the various funds set up for the arriving students. There was a list of Hungarian names and Quinault had scribbled notes alongside them. So he was interested in the Hungarians, which Charles found odd – even suspicious – in itself. What reason had Quinault to be so interested in them? Charles was about to draw his new friend's attention to the list, but thought better of it. Andras was still staring at the figurines.

All this interested Charles, but he was frustrated since he did not know what he was looking for – although the letter would interest Reggie. 'Review our arrangement'. That might mean anything.

It was excitingly illicit to look through a person's belongings in this way. Charles warmed to his task. He no longer felt uneasy. His feverishness, which came and went in waves, had lent him a brittle kind of energy. A desk stood to the side of the table. He opened the shallow top drawer. It contained pens, pencils and stamps. Below it were deeper drawers to the left and right. He opened the drawer on the right. It took him a second's disbelief before he understood that he was staring at bundles of used banknotes, each wad secured with a rubber band.

Andras had said the Quinaults were always quarrelling about money. And here was tons of it ...

'Well, well, well. Look at this.'

Andras wasn't interested. 'I think we go now. It's – somehow horrible in here.'

'You must see this.'

Andras stared at the stash of notes. 'We go,' he repeated. 'If someone find us ...'

Charles laughed. 'There's no-one here. We've got the place to ourselves.'

The doorbell rang.

'Oh, God.' Charles closed the drawer. He was suddenly sweating, although the room was freezing.

They reached the hall. As they did so, the front door opened. Andras must have left it unlocked. The man who stood there was tall and quite imposing in his overcoat and plaid scarf. He removed his hat. 'Good morning. I'm looking for Gyorgy Meszarov. I believe he's staying here?'

Charles glanced at Andras, who was staring speechlessly at the stranger. Charles could tell he was scared, and there was something rather too authoritative about the tall man. Charles felt certain he was a policeman. He had that particular kind of presence that couldn't be mistaken: a certainty about his right to be there.

'Who are you?' he asked, sounding bolder than he felt.

'I'm checking on the welfare of the recent Hungarian arrivals. It's a routine visit.' He produced some kind of identification card, but it had disappeared again before Charles could read it.

The stranger looked at Andras. 'Gyorgy Meszarov? Settled in all right? Everything satisfactory?'

Andras nodded. Charles couldn't understand why he didn't tell the policeman that he wasn't Gyorgy. 'Everything is fine. We have to go now.'

He made a move in the direction of the front door, but the stranger put up a hand in an attempt to stay him.

'We're on our way out,' echoed Charles. He was suddenly

very anxious to get away. He wasn't supposed to be here. There was something about finding all that money that made him feel guilty, which was absurd, as if merely looking at it was some kind of theft.

The policeman gazed thoughtfully at Charles. 'And you are …?'

As if it was any of his business; but Charles said: 'I'm Professor Quinault's research student. I came to see him about my work, but he's out.'

'That's a pity. I was hoping to have a word with him too.'

Before Charles could stop them, the words flew out of his mouth. 'Is it because of all the cash lying around in his library? You're a policeman, aren't you? I hope Professor Quinault hasn't been breaking the law.'

What mad impulse had made him say that? Was it to cause trouble?

The stranger focused on Charles with increased interest. Andras looked from one to the other. He pulled at Charles' sleeve. 'I think we go.'

'Yes.' Charles now wanted to get away even more than Andras did.

'Wait a moment. What's this about cash?'

Charles had to put a bold face on it. 'I just thought you ought to know.'

'Are you implying there's something suspicious about it?'

Seizing the opportunity, Andras shifted past the policeman and made a bolt for the front door, slamming it behind him.

'I'd better have your name.'

'Do I have to tell you? Look, I've got to go. My friend's upset.'

The policeman continued to stare at Charles. 'You've volunteered information about something you seem to find suspicious.'

'I'm sorry – I have to …' Charles gestured in the direction

of the departed Andras.

'Are you making an allegation about the Professor?'

'No, it's just that – I don't know why I said that ...'

'I might need to talk to you again about this. Where can I find you?'

The policeman spoke in such a way that Charles couldn't stop himself from replying. 'Charles Hallam. Magdalen College.' He moved determinedly towards the door. 'I have to see he's all right.'

'I may be in touch, Mr Hallam.'

Charles was panicking as he ran towards the gate. He stepped out onto the pavement and with relief saw Andras loitering further along the road. When the Hungarian saw him, he slowly walked back.

'Why you say that about money?' Andras was shaking. 'Now will be trouble. He was policeman, no?'

'Why didn't you tell him you're not Gyorgy?'

'I don't like he come asking questions.'

'I'm sure it's only some routine check.' But he cursed himself for having mentioned the money. He had felt so odd all day. It was as if nothing was quite real. A crazy impulse – and now Jesus Christ knew what trouble it was going to cause. But he said carelessly: 'He seemed more interested in the Professor than you.'

That would be something to report back to Reggie. If only he hadn't given the man his name. One should avoid the police at all costs. Charles' sexual adventures had led him into plenty of dubious situations and he now regretted drawing attention to himself in that stupid way. Nothing to be done about it now, though.

'Are we going on this walk, then?' he said. 'I'll wheel my bike part of the way. Or no – I'll leave it. I can get it later.'

'Someone will take it.'

'If they do I'll borrow someone else's. It's like that here, kind of group ownership, sort of.'

The cold bit into him. 'It is the year's midnight and the day's,' he muttered.

'What?'

'It's a poem.' His voice sank to an inaudible murmur: 'The world's whole sap is sunk ... I am every dead thing in whom love wrought new alchemy.'

chapter 18

THE QUEEN'S HEAD WAS even emptier than usual, a single solitary drinker leaning against the bar. Blackstone read the *Evening News* from cover to cover. Twenty minutes had passed before Jarrell, hatless and with raincoat flapping about him, strode into the bar. He greeted Blackstone, ordered lemonade and brought it to the table. Before he even sat down he said: 'There's been a development. I found her handbag. In the hotel. It was hidden up a chimney. We took the couple in for questioning. And now, believe it or not, he's admitted it.'

'Admitted what?'

'Admitted he pushed her and that's why she fell down the stairs.'

'He's *confessed*? Camenzuli?'

Jarrell nodded.

'What were they doing at the top of the stairs?'

Jarrell sat down. His movements, always jerky and angular, agitated still further Blackstone's now-disturbed state. Jarrell seemed always impatient and in a hurry. That, Blackstone felt, was not how detectives should be. They should be methodical, their every move considered, which was more McGovern's style.

'I thought the wife would crack. We split them up, obviously, when we hauled them in. She was beside herself. Hysterical.

Terrified. I thought she'd tell us everything, I thought it would all come pouring out. I didn't think there'd be a problem. But nothing doing. Couldn't get anything out of her. Nothing coherent anyway. Just floods of tears and she knew nothing about anything. I think she was more frightened of him than us – her husband, I mean. And there wasn't much to go on. The handbag seemed incriminating at first, when we found it, but anyone could have hidden it.'

'The very fact that it was hidden, though—' began Blackstone.

'Well, yes. Was there a reason it wasn't in the ambulance when the body was removed? I began to think it might have been a deliberate attempt to make sure she wasn't identified – or not identified quickly. But then I also suspected it might have been hidden on purpose to incriminate the couple. A plant. It wasn't that carefully hidden. There was soot in the grate – that was what drew my attention in the first place.'

'A policeman would notice that, I suppose,' said Blackstone, 'but perhaps not a layman.'

'Well, eventually we decided to let her go. We released her on police bail. We concentrated on Camenzuli. A tough nut to crack. And we didn't crack him. He was rock solid. He stuck to his story. The girl arrived on her own. She said she'd be joined by someone. She asked for a room, she went upstairs. She went into the room. Later she came out again, tripped and fell down the stairs. He even suggested she'd hidden the bag herself. We held him in the cells overnight. In the morning his wife came to see him with some cigarettes and a change of underwear. Later that morning we started in on him again. I wasn't hopeful at all. But blow me down, he said he had something to tell us. Quite calm. Just said he wanted to make a statement.'

'And his story?'

'He claims she arrived with a man. They went upstairs. The

girl seemed reluctant, but she went. Quite soon they heard raised voices, the girl was almost screaming. She came out onto the landing. The man was in the bedroom doorway. The Maltese went up and told them to keep quiet or else leave, both of them. The bloke ran downstairs and left. The girl was hysterical, became abusive. Camenzuli tried to restrain her, she reacted violently, there was a struggle and she fell down the stairs.'

Blackstone frowned. He pulled out his cigarettes. 'Manslaughter? He'll argue it was an accident, surely.'

'He made no bones about it. He hit her deliberately to shut her up. He pushed her as well and that's how she fell down the stairs. There's to be another autopsy anyway now. We confronted his wife with the story. She corroborated it.'

'What did he have to say about the handbag?'

Jarrell shrugged. 'He claimed the girl must have put it there herself. That's obviously nonsense. We didn't get to the bottom of that.'

Blackstone thought the whole thing very fishy. 'Are you happy with the confession?'

Jarrell shook his head. 'They shouldn't have let the wife in to see him. They were only together for a few minutes and an officer was present. But of course they spoke their own language. All I can think of is someone got to her overnight and told her to tell him that that's his story. He'll be paid. Besides, it's a weak case. He'll probably get off anyway. Might not even get to court.'

'So who benefits?'

'Whoever he's covering up for.'

'What's Moules's view?'

Jarrell frowned. 'Not sure. It means the case is reopened. I think he was hoping I'd turn up some stuff about the police. Other than that, I don't think he's that interested.'

Blackstone stamped his cigarette on the floor and fumbled

for his packet. 'Yes. Didn't McGovern sell it to him on the basis that it might open up the wider question of police methods?'

'That's right. The police weren't called to the scene originally. But that was down to the Maltese. He didn't inform them.'

'The hospital must have told them – when her body arrived. And there was an inquest, so ...'

Jarrell smiled. 'There's better ways of opening up that particular can of worms than this case. But I'm working on it. Keeping my ear to the ground.'

The handbag puzzled Blackstone. 'Why did they hang on to the handbag and then hide it? It would have made more sense just to get rid of it.'

'Yes,' agreed Jarrell. 'You'd have thought they'd throw it away – get rid of it completely instead of hiding it. Or why not just send it along with the girl's body? What was the point of concealing her identity?'

'You think it could have been left by someone else? Incriminating evidence planted deliberately?'

Jarrell sipped his drink. 'Possibly ... I really don't know. Maybe. It sort of corroborates the confession. Actually, it gave us the pretext for taking him for questioning in the first place. There was no guarantee we'd find it, though ...' His sentence faded away into a shrug.

'You don't believe his confession?'

'I don't know. It's semi-plausible. But his story changed so suddenly after his wife had been there.'

'There's also the doctor's story,' Blackstone reminded him. 'You haven't forgotten that, have you? That she was already a corpse when she arrived at the hotel.'

Jarrell hunched forward over his lemonade. 'Yes – the doctor. You go round to see him – he's quite friendly to begin with, you say. He drops this big hint about how she was dead on arrival. Then he goes off and gives himself some magic medicine and doesn't want to talk any more. He actually *said* she was dead on arrival.'

'Yes. I'm sure those were his words.'

'Seems unambiguous. But there's something else you don't know. He's dead too.'

'I hadn't heard that.' Blackstone's hand shook slightly as he twitched the ash off his cigarette. 'That's ... God ... the implications of it! That has to be ... he was murdered.'

'That's the thing. It's gone down as an overdose. But I looked very carefully at the old man. There he was, his sleeve unbuttoned, needle marks, the syringe on the floor where he'd let it drop from his nerveless fingers, as they say.' Jarrell was now talking with a kind of impatient humour. 'I thought it seemed a little staged. I had another look at him in the mortuary. I looked at his hands. And I think he was left-handed. The middle finger of his left hand was calloused and ink-stained, suggesting that was the hand he wrote with.' He gestured at Blackstone, whose cigarette was glued to his right-hand fingers when it wasn't stuck between his lips. 'But it was his left shirt sleeve that was unbuttoned and the syringe lay to the right of his chair – all as if he'd injected himself with his right hand. That would cast doubts on suicide, as well as on an overdose. There wasn't a suicide note, either.'

'As soon as the Camenzuli woman let slip his name someone paid him a visit. But how did that someone know I'd talked to him?'

'You look a bit shaken,' observed Jarrell. 'Take it easy.'

'It's a shock. It's almost as if it was somehow my fault. I get wind of his name. I pay him a visit. Next thing – he's dead.'

'I was shocked too. Believe me. I found the body. Went round to question him. And there he was. Dead. Someone must have found out that the Maltese woman had passed on his name.'

'Possibly. But hardly anyone knew. I knew ...'

'Well, someone was worried about him. After you'd seen him, it could be he got in touch with someone – perhaps he was alarmed, perhaps he was hoping for help of some kind – and that person, we don't know who, got scared too, went round and shut him up. That's my theory. He could have been a witness. Once we'd arrested the Maltese, someone must have got the wind up so they eliminated him. They could only have known you'd talked to him if he told them – that must have been what happened. And they wanted to be on the safe side. They were afraid he'd talk.'

'He wasn't that forthcoming when I saw him.'

'He mightn't have stood up to sustained pressure, though.'

'Who benefited by Valerie's death? That's the real question,' ruminated Blackstone. Perhaps no-one did. Perhaps it was, as the Maltese now admitted, essentially an accident, the unintended outcome of a stupid quarrel, the girl's death pointless.

That, however, wouldn't have made it necessary to get rid of Dr Swann – if Jarrell was right and that was not just another unrelated accident, a coincidence that it had happened when it had.

'There's something else,' said Blackstone. 'The girl wrote her mother a postcard to say she'd met a man and was getting married. Her mother said she was hopelessly romantic, always expecting a knight in shining armour to come along.'

Jarrell clasped his bony hands together. They made an unpleasant cracking noise. 'A man in the case. That's no surprise. She might have been deluded about the marriage part, but why get in touch with her mother if none of it was true?'

Blackstone nodded. Hadn't the postcard been a way of sending a message? See, I didn't go to the bad after all. At last I'm going to be the respectable girl you always wanted. You can be proud of me now. The sadness of it caught him unawares. 'We need to track down this boyfriend,' he said. 'I should have made that a priority, I should have been on to it as soon as I got back from the south coast, but ...' He'd done nothing about it, had given in to his reluctance. He didn't want to know about her love life, the men she'd known. His sentimentality had got the better of him.

'The problem is, we've charged a suspect, he's remanded in custody, though he could get bail at some point. Things will roll along for a bit. I've got other crimes to investigate. Bloody Moules keeps us at it. I'm not sure how much more manpower he'll want to devote to the girl.'

Blackstone looked at his companion. Jarrell's faded carroty hair and pallid, unhealthy complexion belied the energy he brought to his work. His greenish watery eyes and sharp nose, and his hunched, thin shoulders gave him the look of a rather peculiar bird. He reminded Blackstone of a heron that at the moment appeared to be looking into the middle distance and dreaming of fish. 'If you tell him about the syringe and being left-handed... That's good detective work. He'll listen to that.'

Jarrell stood up suddenly. 'You're right. The case against the Maltese is weak. I don't want to look like an idiot when they throw the case out or Camenzuli retracts his confession. I'll get him to let me widen the investigation.'

There seemed little more to say. Blackstone eked out the silence with his cigarette, smoking it down until it burnt his finger. 'Valerie was working at some dive in Soho, the California Club. I ought to go and have a look at it. Should have been there already, as soon as I got back from Eastbourne,' he repeated. But he'd put off going. He'd dreaded what he might discover, how sordid her life had been.

chapter 19

BLACKSTONE KNEW HE OUGHT to get back to the office to sort out a few final details of the Bodkin Adams interview. The lawyers had been through it with a fine-tooth comb. There must be nothing remotely libellous. He was proud of the interview. He was tempted to return to the noise and comfort of the great news machine that was the *Chronicle*, but he knew he must no longer put off a visit to the California Club and so he wandered down the streets of Fitzrovia in the general direction of Leicester Square.

It was just the sort of place he'd expected: a seedy little basement bar, customers sparse at this hour of the early evening when the pubs were open and tourists were enjoying an early meal in the restaurants of the district, or else queueing up for the cinema or en route to the theatre. Two slightly bedraggled hostesses sat on high stools at the bar. He took a seat in a corner and the darker of the two girls approached him.

It took him a while to turn the conversation in the direction he wanted. The requisite bottle of fizz had to be consumed. He had to flatter the girl – she said her name was Lauren – and gain her confidence. Girls like Lauren were careful not to drink too much; the idea was to loosen up the punter. And he was happy to appear to linger, ordering several brandies as well, and feeding her little sips as she sat on his knee.

If she knew of Valerie's fate, she didn't let on – but then she'd only started working at the California Club quite recently. Yes, there had been a girl of that name who'd worked at the club, but then she'd left to go to the new place up the road, ever so posh it was, the boss took a shine to her. Toni on the door probably knew more. He'd been working here quite a while.

Toni on the door swept his glistening black locks off his forehead. 'She's dead. You know that, don't you?'

Blackstone nodded.

'We was friendly, like. She went off to work at the big new place, the Ambassadors. Then she met some geezer. She was going to go off with him, she told me. Thought he was going to solve all her problems. Starry-eyed she was, an' all that. Couldn't see it myself. Anyway, it didn't go down well with the boss, that didn't. She hadn't worked off her contract. Well – there was more to it ...'

'You met him, then? The boyfriend?'

'Nah. To be honest I thought she might've made it all up. Except it caused trouble with the boss. Perhaps she made that up, too. Could have been some other reason. Ta.' Toni accepted Blackstone's offered cigarette.

Blackstone's throat tightened. He inhaled some smoke the wrong way and started to cough uncontrollably.

'You okay, mate?' Blackstone's cough could be alarming.

Blackstone nodded speechlessly. When he'd finally caught his breath, he wheezed: 'Know where I could get hold of him – the boyfriend? What was his name again?'

Toni eyed him warily. 'Don't remember the name. Why d'you want to get hold of him anyway? She's dead, ain't she?'

Blackstone produced a banknote. 'Purely personal. I'd just like to meet him. I was fond of the girl.'

'Ta.' Toni trousered the note. 'Well, it's up to you, mate. Lives down Bethnal Green way, I believe. She used to meet 'im at the Italian caff. That's all I know.'

Blackstone was almost sure it wasn't, but he thanked the boy.

'Don't go letting on I talked to you, mind. Boss doesn't like it when strangers come round asking questions.'

'The boss?'

'Vince Mallory. You've heard of him, I should think.'

'I do indeed know Mallory,' said Blackstone smoothly. 'Met him when I was working the East End. Decent bloke.'

Toni gave him a very straight look. 'You can say that again, mate.'

Blackstone took a taxi to Fleet Street. He added some final finishing touches to the Bodkin Adams interview – he was a perfectionist when it came to writing, even if the subject bored him. He then decided to walk up to Holborn and take the tube to Marble Arch. However, as he plodded along the street, quiet at this time of mid-evening, he sensed he was being followed and hailed a taxi to take him back to his flat. He looked round as he paid off the driver and another taxi chugged past.

In the morning he found a letter on the doormat. Hand delivered; there wasn't a stamp – or a name or an address on the envelope for that matter. The message on the single sheet inside had been constructed from letters cut out from newsprint. It was quite artistic, with its different fonts.

NEXT TIME IT WON'T BE A LETTER

He didn't think there'd be any fingerprints.

chapter 20

McGOVERN STOOD IN QUINAULT'S hall, digesting the encounter with the two youths. Their agitation had taken him by surprise. He hadn't dealt with it well. Yet now he looked round with a surge of anticipation. Because what an opportunity this was! He had the place to himself and while he had no good reason to search the house and certainly no search warrant, he was accustomed to such situations. Should Quinault or the wife come home unexpectedly he'd have some explaining to do, so he needed to act. Perhaps Gyorgy Meszarov *had* been billeted with the Professor for some special reason. The Hungarian had certainly been anxious to get away, so perhaps he had something to hide.

It was the words of the young man who badly needed a haircut, however, that propelled McGregor down the passage to the library. What an extraordinary thing to have said. The careless, deadpan way he'd spoken – with a flash of malice, McGovern felt. He was up to no good, McGovern was sure. A strange young man. He might even have interrupted a plan by the two of them to steal the money – if it existed.

Whatever their motive, the young man's words acted as a shot of adrenalin. The first thing McGovern did in the library was to examine the French windows and unlock them, in case he needed to make a rapid departure unseen. He wore gloves as he began to search the room, beginning with the desk. It was not long before he had opened the drawers of the desk and discovered the money the long-haired one had spoken of.

He hadn't definitely expected to find it. The mischief-maker might have been lying – presumably for the hell of it – or at least exaggerating. But now here were three thousand pounds – he counted – stacked in an unlocked drawer. He contemplated it.

He opened the next drawer down to find household bills and bank statements. Everything was in place. There were no big bills. The Professor's bank account was in the black and he appeared not to have withdrawn any large sums from it.

McGovern turned to the papers on the table. Quinault seemed to be doing some research of his own on the Hungarians. A list of names had some notes scribbled in the margins; but the notes were in an unfamiliar script. After a moment, McGovern recognised it as classical Greek. Frustrated, he turned over the material relating to the new road scheme.

He looked round the room and gazed at the objects behind glass along one wall. He was about to look more closely when he heard the unmistakeable sound of the front door being opened. He slipped out by the window into the garden and waited.

If he leaned forward he could see into the room, but it would be risky. He could hear noises, but not well enough to guess what the old man was doing. However, then he heard his voice. He must be on the telephone. The voice ceased. McGovern decided to take the risk. He peered through the window. He could just make out that the Professor was removing the money and placing it in a bag or case of some kind.

There was no knowing how long Quinault would remain in the house, but McGovern decided to wait and then to follow him. He needed to know where the old man was taking the money. He stepped carefully towards the corner of the house.

Fortunately his footsteps made no sound on the path, which was simply damp, beaten-down earth. He eased his way along the side of the house. The shrubs and the ivy that tumbled over the partition fence protected him, he hoped, from the sight of any neighbours who might be looking out of a side window.

He reached the front of the house and waited. When he heard the front door open and then bang shut he flattened himself against the wall. Quinault walked slowly away. He was carrying a small attaché case. He stopped to examine an object by the gate and then walked on.

McGovern followed him at a distance. The Professor crossed the road and made for a bus stop on the other side of the road. McGovern hung back. He had no cover. Then a bus bore down towards the stop and Quinault hailed it. So that was the end of that.

Except that the object that had caught Quinault's attention by the gate was a bike. McGovern seized it as the bus moved off and soon was sailing along in its wake.

The bus deposited Quinault at the railway station. By now McGovern was committed to his impulse. It had become an intuition. Quinault made for the London platform. McGovern hastily bought a ticket and followed him. He knew that his target might leave the train at some intermediate station and all he could do was peer out of his window each time the train stopped at a station. The train stopped at Didcot, then at Reading. Quinault remained on the train.

As McGovern left Paddington station, he felt confident that his quarry had not seen him, was unaware of his cat-like presence. Often, when you followed a suspect, they knew all along that you were there. Because they were expecting you, were on the look-out, knew they were suspect. Quinault, though, had no reason to think he would be followed.

McGovern followed Quinault onto a bus and unexpectedly the old man climbed the stairs to the upper deck. He disembarked just before Edgware Road and made for an area of residential side streets where forbidding yet expensive-looking terraces and mansion blocks suggested faceless wealth. The area was more than respectable, but less than fashionable. Above all it was anonymous. Quinault disappeared into a blank-fronted block of flats.

The lobby was empty. The modern lift indicator showed it was stationed on the second floor. McGovern climbed the stairs. The carpeted corridor gave access to two flats.

McGovern looked round, then walked back downstairs. Outside, he looked for an inconspicuous position from which to wait and watch. The only convenient point was a bench placed at one side of the small formal garden in front of the building. He sat down and opened his newspaper. The cold bit into him, but he didn't have to wait long. Less than fifteen minutes later, Quinault appeared on the shallow steps. He paused and looked around before walking off.

Once again, McGovern followed him onto a bus. After a short ride this one deposited them both near Bond Street. Quinault walked past fashionable dress shops, then the auctioneers Sotheby's, before disappearing into a side alley. By the time McGovern reached the turning, Quinault was nowhere to be seen. McGovern stepped into the icy shade of the narrow passageway. There were buildings with entrances on one side, a high wall on the other. He walked the length of the dead end and back, but the entrances were anonymous. Rows of bells had, in some cases, names beside them. They might be jewellers, or antique or fine arts dealers. Quinault must have disappeared into one of them, because otherwise McGovern would have seen him emerging from the passage again, but there was no way of knowing which one.

McGovern looked up and down Bond Street with a sense of anti-climax. The chase had excited him, but now he was brought up short. He had an intuition that Quinault had reached his destination, whatever it was, and he felt disinclined to hang about in the street indefinitely awaiting his re-emergence. So now he was at a loose end. He was in London, when he should have been in Oxford, and he had nothing to do for the rest of the day. He walked slowly towards Marble Arch. The impulsive chase began to seem a little crazy.

It was the sight of the money that had impelled him. Such a large sum was suspicious. And that block of flats; just the sort of anonymous place where a spy would feel secure. Russian or Hungarian, a spy would blend in with the tourists and the cosmopolitan birds of passage living in the dull, expensive rented apartments all around that part of London.

The buildings off Bond Street were equally anonymous and might house any kind of enterprise, legal or illegal. At one time there'd been an East German spy who'd lived in a flat above one of the most expensive boutiques in the area.

Now he was in London there must be someone he could talk to. Not Moules, for a start. McGovern felt sure his unorthodox behaviour would horrify Moules, even if it could be finessed into a shot in the dark, a brilliant hunch. A contact at MI5? No: he was on bad enough terms with them already. Jarrell? No: he had other fish to fry.

Blackstone. Blackstone knew about crime. Blackstone knew about the Met. Blackstone was a wily bird. Blackstone had given him his home number. It's hopeless trying me at the office, he'd said, you'll never reach me there.

'You're in luck. Last week I was in Eastbourne. You couldn't have got hold of me at all.' The journalist seemed rather proud of the fact. 'Now I'm having a well-earned rest. My day off. Matter of fact I was asleep when you rang. This is my breakfast. I come here most mornings – when I'm at home, that is.'

McGovern looked round the familiar interior of Maison Lyons, a bit like a cinema with art deco zigzags and an abstract design on the carpet. He ordered a lamb cutlet – his lunch – while Blackstone was putting away eggs and bacon. While they ate, McGovern told the journalist all that had happened at Quinault's house.

'I wouldn't have picked you as an impulsive sort of bloke,' commented Blackstone, on hearing McGovern's account.

'It was the cash. And all in a drawer that wasn't even locked.'

'Might have forgotten to lock it. Might have remembered he'd forgotten to lock it or come back to make sure.'

'No. He came in to remove it. But the money itself. Three thousand pounds is a large sum.'

Blackstone drank some coffee. 'What couldn't a man do with three thousand pounds, indeed? Buy a house.'

'He's got a house.'

'Perhaps he's, you know, keeping it under the mattress. He doesn't trust the bank. Or the wife.'

'Men like Quinault don't keep money under the mattress. And he has a bank account.'

'Paying off spies? Something like that? Is that what you're thinking? Then why come to me? That's not my speciality.'

'I thought you might know of other reasons a man might have so much cash. You could give me a new angle on it. Although I'm not ruling out espionage. I followed him to a block of flats. Balmoral Mansions. Impersonal. The sort of place you find all kinds of people who want to keep quiet about their activities.'

Blackstone set down his knife and fork. 'Balmoral Mansions? I know someone who lives there. And you're right about keeping quiet. I don't suppose you know the number? Of the flat, I mean. And which entrance? There's more than one.'

'It was the entrance at the front. And I don't know the

number, but he took the lift to the second floor.'

McGovern offered Blackstone a cigarette, which he accepted. 'I'll make some enquiries,' he said finally.

chapter 21

IT WAS THE BEGINNING of a new week. Jarrell decided to pay one of his informers a visit. Sammy Parker resided in a grim Farringdon Road tenement located opposite the hostel for homeless men and near the postal sorting office. Jarrell mounted the stone stairs. They were roofed over, but open at the sides so that the wind blew along the third-floor access balcony, cutting through his thin raincoat like a knife.

Jarrell knocked on the door at the end.

'Detective Sergeant Jarrell!' Sammy Parker looked nervous, although he spoke with a pleasant smile.

'Hello, Sammy, keeping well I hope. Got a moment? This a convenient time?'

Their relationship was still at the honeymoon stage. It dated from soon after Jarrell had returned to general detective work. Jarrell had caught Sammy Parker trying to burgle a watchmaker's shop late one evening. He had soon guessed that his captive was a man who might prove useful and had decided to take an interest in his new acquaintance.

He now followed Sammy into a sitting room filled with the fug produced by cigarettes and a smoking coal fire. After the freezing fog outside, it was too hot. There was also a smell that cut the cigarette fumes with a whiff of old cabbage or worse, cats perhaps. A boxing flyer was propped on the mantelpiece.

Jarrell did not want to sit down on the vast, sagging settee. It was none too clean and covered with cat hair. So he stood with his back to the window and watched his host with a certain affectionate contempt. Sammy Parker was small, lithe and cheery and a bit too ingratiating. The weakness in his character, as Jarrell had quickly discovered, was that he didn't like to displease or disappoint those with whom he came in contact. He didn't know how to say no, whether to fellow thieves, women or the police. Since he moved in rather disreputable circles, this had got him into a lot of trouble.

'Fancy a cup of tea? I'm having one meself.'

'Thanks. I will.'

While Parker was in the kitchen, Jarrell took a look around, but found nothing to interest him. When the tea arrived he regretted accepting it, for his cup showed the remains of a lipstick stain and the orange brew was sickly with too much sterilised milk.

'Michael Camenzuli,' he said. 'Tell me about him.'

'You ain't come across Maltese Mike before?'

'I worked in the Branch until recently, remember?'

'I heard he's in trouble.' Sammy didn't seem too upset. 'Nasty bit of work. A knife man.'

'He's put his hand up for a girl who fell down the stairs at his hotel and broke her neck.'

'That so?' Sammy put his head on one side in an enquiring fashion, but something about the informant's expression caused Jarrell to believe he knew this already.

'Why would he do that – if it wasn't him who pushed her?'

Sammy's laugh was a catarrhal wheeze. 'You asking me, mate? How should I know?' He took a gulp of tea. 'Mind you, he'd do anything for money.'

'Such as?'

'He's a fucking grass, that's what he is.' This came strangely from a man who was at this moment passing information to a police officer, but Parker appeared not to notice the inconsistency. 'Yeah, do anything for money would Maltese Mike. Got a gambling habit, see. Sell his soul to a copper, he would. Or anyone else, the devil included. People think 'e was involved with the Messina gang, but 'e weren't, not really. Hung about on the fringes, but 'is real ambition was to be a boxer. Bantamweight. Was with Vince Mallory for a while. But that wasn't going anywhere. He had too much of a temper and he couldn't lose the knife habit. Knives and boxing don't mix, that was Mallory's view. Got done for carving someone up and Mallory didn't like that. But they say he done Mallory a good turn of some kind or other and that's how he's ended up running that hotel.'

'You mean Mallory owns the property?'

Sammy shrugged.

Jarrell nodded towards the leaflet on the mantelpiece. 'You follow boxing yourself, I see. That's one of Mallory's fights, isn't it? Camenzuli – Maltese Mike – he's still doing favours for him?'

'Dunno. Doubt it. Mind you, 'e's in with a lot of people. No-one trusts him, but they all use him.'

'He runs with the hare and hunts with the hounds, eh?'

'You could put it like that.'

'Any particular hound?'

Sammy ignored the question and instead asked one of his own. 'What about this girl, then?'

'Why would the Maltese confess to pushing her down the stairs?'

''Cos he done it? Like I said, 'e 'as a temper.' Parker grinned. 'Who was the girl, then?'

'She'd worked at Mallory's club.'

'Well, there you go, then.'

'You're not telling me Mallory had anything to do with it.

I don't buy that. He's a successful businessman.'

Parker laughed aloud at this naivety. 'Wasn't always quite so legit. Wasn't like he is now. Don't tell me you don't know nothing about Vince Mallory. Seems he was in the army. In Germany at the end of the war. Involved in the black market out there, I reckon. Him even *being* in the army was a miracle, I'd have had him down as a deserter. Amazing he didn't skive off out of that somehow or other.'

Jarrell, too, was astonished Mallory hadn't managed to avoid conscription. However, he reflected that even the most crooked individuals sometimes accidentally found themselves going straight.

'Got into the black market back here, they say. But then he got into boxing. When he was operating down the East End, he had problems. Enemies, rivals. He needed protection. Jack Spot come round, offered to help him out, but Mallory said no. Offices got smashed up. He still said no. Got roughed up himself – in spite of his bodyguard, I believe he had protection from Harry Evans at the time. Remember Evans? Good boxer, he was. Anyway, so eventually Mallory thought, if I'm going to get protection, I'll get it from the top. And he got it from Detective Superintendent Gorch. Nobody could touch him after that.'

'Gorch?' That was a shock. Jarrell had respected Gorch. But he didn't show his dismay, merely said in a neutral tone: 'Is that so?'

Parker grinned some more. 'You didn't know?' He eyed Jarrell, sensing discomfort. 'Thought Gorch wore a halo, did you? Anyway, Mallory don't get on so well with your current lot. Inspector Slater in particular.'

'I'm aware of that.' Jarrell frowned. 'But why would Mallory want to get rid of this girl?'

'I'm not saying he did.'

Now that Mallory had opened that glitzy club in Soho, the

Ambassadors, he was a fashionable figure and almost respectable. He'd made strippers glamorous. He'd made sexiness smart. Jarrell filed these thoughts away for future study. In the meantime: 'So all you've told me is, Camenzuli might do Mallory a favour. Or be leaned on to do him a favour.'

'Say that again.'

'But that doesn't explain why this particular favour.'

'True,' agreed Parker obligingly. 'It don't.'

Jarrell let the silence settle. Then: 'Anything else?'

'Can't help you about the girl, I'm afraid.'

'Why doesn't Mallory get on with Detective Inspector Slater?'

Sammy laughed. 'You're asking me that? Old enemies, ain't they? Slater knows he's a crook. Or used to be. They say he's trying to get him on immoral earnings. Close the Ambassadors on some trumped-up charge of being a brothel. Running a disorderly house or something.'

Jarrell looked at his creature. He was holding something back. 'I think you know more than you're letting on.'

'Strewth, nah, Inspector. I wouldn't do that.'

'It's Sergeant, Parker. But I've another question. Know anything about a Doctor Swann? Died of an overdose the other day.'

Sammy looked thoughtful. 'I had heard ... poor old sod,' he began cautiously. 'Course, he worked for Mallory too at one time.'

'I know. Funny how Mallory's name keeps cropping up all over the place.'

'It is, Sergeant Jarrell.'

'Have a think about it. Anything you might hear in that direction. I'll call again in a couple of days.' He slid a note into Parker's waiting hand as he left.

The pub where Slater and his crowd often drank was not far from Parker's dismal buildings. Jarrell decided to look in and see if Slater was there. He walked through the back streets, wondering how much he'd learned that was useful. Not much – other than about Gorch. That was a shock, and an unwelcome one. But it was interesting that Mallory's name kept coming up. He'd have to find out more about him – have to pay him a visit, perhaps – but now he found himself thinking about Slater rather than the boxing promoter. The change he'd noticed in the man was subtle, but these days the Inspector seemed driven, which he hadn't been in the past. He hadn't won further promotion. That might be the problem.

The Crown had the special tangible atmosphere of a bar patronised by the law. It was the same with the pub the Pentonville screws drank at in the Caledonian Road: an ambience secretive, edgy and bombastic all at once.

He withstood the usual jokes about his non-drinking. He good-humouredly accepted soda water and the ribaldry that came with it. He just wished pubs served coffee as cafés did in France – that had been a revelation on his first, recent, trip to Paris with his fiancée.

He leant against the bar and listened to his colleagues. There was a lot of animosity towards Moules, coupled with rose-tinted memories of the Gorch era. The former Superintendent's name revived the discomfort he'd felt at what Parker had told him. He didn't want to dwell on the new and unwelcome knowledge that Gorch might have been as crooked as the rest of them, so he decided to throw a little firework into the conversation and see what happened.

'Anyone been to that strip club in Soho? The Ambassadors? Quite fancy a visit myself.'

There was a little silence. Slater, red in the face already – he must have been drinking for a while – slammed his empty jar on the counter, signalled for more. 'What you bringing that up for, Jarrell? It's none of your fucking business. We're trying to get him on immoral earnings. So what?' When Slater laughed he always sounded angry. 'Where have you been, Professor? You've spent too long doing fuck all in the fucking Branch.'

So much for the illusion that these ex-members of the Flying Squad regarded him with cheery acceptance. He'd always recognised a vein of potential hostility beneath the bonhomie, but of late it had seemed surreptitiously to swell as Slater grew louder and chronically angrier.

'There's a lot I don't know,' said Jarrell quietly and hoped it would be enough. The tension relaxed. Slater shouted again for another round.

'No – my round,' said Jarrell. Then, having drunk up his soda water, he slipped away as quietly as he could and walked back in the direction of Argyle Street. As he strode along he pondered on Slater's sudden rage. A decision formed in his mind. He must slide his way into Slater's confidence. Through such an intimacy he would discover what was really going on. He must know more about Mallory.

chapter 22

JARRELL BELIEVED IN HIS own ability. In his book, that wasn't arrogance. He was just smarter than Slater and the others – including McGovern. He had no time for the bribery and graft that went on. He was 100 per cent behind Moules' efforts to clean up the CID. McGovern was unaware how grateful his former Sergeant had been to be pushed into helping the Superintendent with his anti-corruption crusade. Sooner or later it would dawn on Jarrell's colleagues that he was the one who was going places and they would begin to fear and hate him. But you had to be hated by someone to get anywhere in this job.

He was doubtful that the Argyle Street business would forward the anti-corruption cause, as it had revealed little evidence of police wrongdoing. Yet its curious connections intrigued him: Camenzuli's link with Mallory, and Mallory's with Slater.

Leaden drops of rain fell on his shoulders as he approached the Camenzuli hotel. By the time he reached it, the rain was sharp and hard.

He peered through the glass door. A 'No Vacancies' notice swung against it. The hall light was dim. He pushed the door, but it had been locked. His hand hovered over the bell, but he thought better of it. Instead he worked on the lock and soon he was inside.

It was unnaturally quiet for a hotel. Hotels were usually quiet places, but this one seemed as deserted as the *Marie Celeste*. The heating system sighed as if gently sleeping. The upper floors were in darkness. He doubted there were any guests at all. Maria Camenzuli was all alone in her basement. As he crept towards the back of the house he heard the wireless – music and voices. No doubt she needed that to keep her company, to stave off the loneliness and fear.

He crept down the basement stairs. The door into her sitting room was partly open. Now he moved noisily, pushed the door wide.

Maria Camenzuli screamed when she saw him standing in the doorway. She cringed back in her chair. Her knitting sank to the floor.

'Did I frighten you?' He smiled menacingly. 'No need to be alarmed. You remember me, don't you?'

She gasped for breath, pushing herself far back in her chair as if she was hoping to disappear through it. Her eyes were huge.

'Mind if I sit down?' Jarrell sat down on the chair that faced her without waiting for an answer. 'I'm the detective who was here before. When we arrested you and your husband. You haven't forgotten, have you?'

Dumbly, she shook her head.

'Your husband's been charged. You must be worried. Worried sick, I'd say.'

She stared.

'He's made a confession. He says he pushed that girl down the stairs. Now I wonder what made him do that.'

Jarrell paused. He watched her. She was shaking, mesmerised by his presence. 'You visited him, didn't you. You passed on the message to say he should confess. It'd be worth his while in the end. They'd see you both right. That's what happened, isn't it? So who told you to pass that message on, Mrs Camenzuli?'

Her eyes were huge. She was too frightened to speak.

He raised his voice. '*Who told you?*'

She shook her head, or perhaps she was just shaking with fear. Her head jerked to and fro.

'You will tell me, Maria.'

He stared at her. She *had* to tell him. But after a few seconds of silence he knew she wasn't going to. She was more frightened of someone else than of him.

He waited. She stuck it out through the silence and eventually he decided to try a different line of attack. 'Okay,' he said, 'but whoever approached you, or whatever the reason, the fact is, it didn't happen like that, did it? Your husband didn't push the girl down the stairs. So if you want to help him, you'd better tell me what really happened. You want to help him, don't you?'

She still stared and it suddenly occurred to Jarrell that perhaps she was not that keen on helping her husband. It could be she preferred him inside; but now he had no choice but to press on. 'I heard she was dead when she arrived. Is that right? So who brought her here?'

The woman was shaking her head again. She was beginning to annoy him. He leaned forward and spoke quietly, forcefully. 'You're saying she wasn't dead? But she was dead, wasn't she? Or did your husband kill her?'

She shook her head.

'Tell me what happened, Maria.'

He watched his victim. Her hands moved as if she were washing them. Was that what they meant by 'wringing your hands'? He'd never seen anyone do that before. 'You must tell me, Maria. Or I might have to hurt you.'

'No – please ...'

'Then tell me what happened.'

She looked at him beseechingly. Her jaw trembled. She started to cry. Finally she whispered: 'Man brought her. '

'What did he look like?'

'I not see him. My husband upstairs. I am down here. When I am went upstairs only the doctor.'

'But your husband described to you what happened. And now the doctor is dead. Did you know that?'

Now her look was pure terror. She clasped her hands over her mouth.

'Someone didn't want the doctor around any more. Because he was a witness. Witnesses can be dangerous. Someone called round to see the doctor, and when that person left, the doctor was dead. You wouldn't want that to happen to you, would you? Because you're a witness, too. And all alone on your own here now.' Jarrell stared at his victim. He let his words sink in. 'Tell me what really happened.'

'I not know. Not know nothing.'

Jarrell brought his chair closer to her, so that their knees were almost touching. He leaned forward and placed his hands on the arms of her chair. Now he was leaning right over her. 'You do know. I know you know. And you're going to tell me. Because if you don't ...' and he leaned away from her as abruptly as he'd moved forward.

But Maria Camenzuli only shook her head, tears seeping down. She made a gurgling noise as she tried to sniff them back.

He'd terrorised her. It hadn't been difficult. She hardly knew what she was saying. But it was only a start. And he hadn't got what he wanted.

'I'll be back tomorrow.'

He stood over her, gaunt and disproportionate in the hot little room. The gas fire hissed. There was a fusty smell he hadn't noticed before, of cooking and polish and old textiles, but what might have been – had been – the comforting fug of the fire and the easy chairs and the rosy light was claustrophobic and ghastly.

'Don't see me out. I'll find my way.'

Outside, Jarrell looked up and down the street. It was still raining. He stood on the pavement and then walked back up to the hotel. The building was now in total darkness. He peered through the glass door. The rain trickled down inside his collar. He shivered and turned away.

chapter 23

AT FIRST THEY'D MET at hotels, a different one each time, but in recent months they'd used the flat Rodney leased in Pimlico. Regine interpreted the change as an important step forward, although in fact the flat was no less impersonal than the hotels. Also, she didn't have a key. Rodney always arrived first. Yet he took a risk in inviting her at all. Neighbours might notice her. Other MPs lived in the block. That he was prepared to take that risk said something.

Suppose his wife turned up unexpectedly. Oh, she'd never do that, Rodney said carelessly. But the fantasy alarmed Regine, at least at first. Later she thought that if his wife *did* find them together, would it be such a bad thing? At least then the situation would be out in the open. So hoped Regine, the romantic optimist. Regine the realist knew that married men were not so easily detached from their wives. She knew this, not from experience, for this was her first venture into double adultery, but from her observation of her friends – and enemies: the poetess Edith Fanshawe, for example, whose affair with a married man had been leading nowhere before she ensnared her banker.

Regine wasn't even sure she wanted to detach him; nothing so rational; nothing so calculated. It was just that when they were apart she longed and longed to be in bed with him. It hadn't started like that. To begin with it had been at least partly about getting a foothold in the political world, for William's sake as much as her own. For might not William himself become a politician? Look at Harold Macmillan – he'd been a publisher too, and now there was talk of his becoming prime minister. To be a political hostess: it was a rather intoxicating thought. Now, though, everything had changed, for she'd fallen in love.

On this December evening Rodney had had to leave abruptly, called to the House by the division bell. That there was a parliamentary division bell in the flat would be a valuable selling point, as Rodney had pointed out. The thought that he might sell the flat had unsettled Regine. Surely they would meet here into the indefinite future.

Left alone, she lay in bed and didn't know why she felt close to tears. Then she thought of him as he entered the House of Commons, rapid, eager, the very picture of the public servant, the man in charge, when half an hour ago he'd been at her mercy and she at his. She was encouraged by that. She, after all, knew things about him no member of the public knew – nor, he assured her, his wife.

She slid out of the warm cocoon of sheets and eiderdown and dressed slowly. She felt tired now. She sat at the dressing table to comb her hair and reconstruct her make-up, applying violet eye shadow and dark lipstick. The memory of love began to fade as gloomy thoughts crept in. She thought again of what he'd said, what he hadn't said and the hidden messages in his careless words about his wife. Oh, she can open a fête with the best of them, but she doesn't understand that politics means compromise. To her it's all clear and simple and straightforward. The Tory Party is always right and that's the end of it. She doesn't understand you have to make choices. She doesn't understand my misgivings over Suez, she sees things in black and white, but you, you see how difficult it is, don't you, Reggie

... You take an interest in these things. Lettice doesn't have an enquiring mind.

It was encouraging to hear him thus dismiss his wife to her. Yet for all Regine knew, he might at other times and in her absence dismiss her just as casually. But no – of course he didn't say similar things about her. For no-one knew about her – at least she hoped they didn't.

Now she was ready to leave. But here she was alone in the flat. It was an opportunity. She was not due home just yet. William was at an old boys' dinner and she'd asked nanny to stay late to put the twins to bed. She laid her fur coat aside, draped over the sofa. (The violet mohair was too conspicuous for visits to the flat.)

She was not a systematic person, but now she did her best to make a thorough search. There were few clues to the politician's tastes and interests. Copies of Hansard were ranked in chronological order on the bookshelves, together with a few thrillers of the kind that dealt with wartime heroics, alongside back numbers of the *Economist* and the *Spectator*. The familiar cliché of a Modigliani reproduction adorned one sitting-room wall. The twisted, elongated face looked, to Regine, like that of a discontented mistress.

She looked in the drawers of the console table and in the desk in the sitting room and the nearly empty ones in the tiny cabin kitchen. There was hardly even any food, just some coffee, some tea, biscuits, a few tins and in the fridge a jar of caviar. On the other hand, the drinks cupboard was well stocked.

The impersonality of it depressed her. This was hardly the entry into Rodney's life she'd hoped for.

She returned to the bedroom. She had carefully stripped the bed and remade it minus the sheets. These were put in the linen basket, to be removed and washed, Rodney said, in the morning. The bed was smooth and innocent now beneath its white counterpane.

She turned her attention to the dressing-table drawers. Here there were a few signs of Lettice. What an affected name that was, but Lettice came from the old Tory aristocracy and hers was a traditional family name, Rodney had told her. And it was not Lettice herself who threatened Regine but that family, that ancient, aristocratic family. Rodney would never dare to offend his in-laws by destroying his marriage. His father-in-law was in the House of Lords and a powerful figure in what Rodney always referred to as 'the Party', as though it were the only one.

Rodney was torn; Regine believed that. He was mad about her. But ...

The madness of love did not last for ever.

Regine sat at the dressing table again. She removed the pretty lid from the box of Coty face powder, covered with a design of powder puffs on a bronze ground, and saw that the box was almost empty. What did that mean? That Lettice came to London often or hardly ever? Impossible to tell.

The longer she lingered in the flat the worse she felt. Her search had been pointless and had merely depressed her.

She reached for her coat. Just as she did so the telephone rang. The coat slid to the floor as she looked around for the instrument. Better to ignore it, but the temptation was too great. Heart pounding, she lifted the handset.

'Abbey 4850,' she said. Nerves made her almost swallow the words.

'Is Mr Turbeville there?'

A woman's voice. Regine's heart seemed to be bouncing in her throat and choking her. But it wasn't Lettice. The accent was wrong.

'I'm afraid he's not. I ...' She had a brainwave. 'This is his secretary. Would you like to leave a message?'

'Please tell him Sonia called.'

The telephone clicked at the other end. The line purred.

Regine took a taxi home to Kensington. The house was warm and glowed with soft light. The twins were asleep already. There was white wine in the fridge, left from yesterday. She poured herself a glass, took it to the drawing room and tried to feel pleased with the new colour scheme. They'd decided on Morris curtains rather than wallpaper, which, she thought, would have made the room too dark; instead she'd had the walls painted subtle celadon green. She'd taken much trouble to make the room aesthetically perfect, but this evening the weight of its beautiful Hepplewhite furniture, and two really quite valuable paintings on the walls, oppressed her.

It was inexcusable. Her previous husband had had unpleasant sexual habits and smoked a smelly pipe. He was irritable and he wasn't good-looking. To be honest, money had been the main thing; and anyway it had been during the war, when everything was difficult and provisional and rash decisions were understandable.

William was so different. Regine could hardly understand how she had ever got into this position. It was wicked to have even thought of being unfaithful to such a decent man. Good-looking too, tall, blond, so English and rather bashful with it. It was his innocence as much as anything that had first attracted her. He was several years younger than she and at first she'd thought she would teach the shy boy (well, he was thirty, but seemed so much younger) all about love.

It hadn't quite worked. Whether it was because he was so involved in his publishing firm, or whether his particular kind of decency had an inhibiting effect, but she had come to see that there were certain acts that shocked him and that he did not wish to explore. A sort of prudery, perhaps, or maybe he wanted to keep her on some kind of pedestal, although they'd been married now for five years. It wasn't that he wasn't keen on love-making; on the contrary, he was enthusiastic. It was just that ... but she was too tired to think about it.

Oh, what is the matter with me? Why am I never satisfied with my lot? She looked at herself in the mirror, sat down again, turned on the wireless, then turned it off. This restlessness was terrible.

A woman called Sonia rang and wanted to speak to you.

Of course she could never tell him. That would be tantamount to asking the fatal question: who is she? Who are you seeing apart from me? I thought at least you'd be faithful to your mistress, if not to your wife.

If only, if only: she longed to return to the safety of her peaceful marriage. How good, how benevolent it seemed, now that she was separated from it. For she had been happy, hadn't she, with William, happy enough at any rate, until Rodney had appeared.

She forced herself to calm down. She made herself scrambled eggs and toast and ate them at the kitchen table.

Later she went upstairs, undressed for bed and lay in the purity of the lovely white room. She tried to read her book, a peculiar novel by this new writer, Iris Murdoch. Everyone was talking about it, but it was too eccentric to grab her imagination. She let it fall from her hands and stared at the wall.

She must have dozed off, for she was startled to hear William bounding up the stairs as he called her name. He sat on the edge of the bed, flushed from the evening's drinking.

'How was the dinner?'

'Bloody Quinault was there,' he said. 'That was a surprise. He's always made a point of being educated at a grammar school. I suppose someone brought him. Typical really. He has a finger in every pie.'

chapter 24

THE AMBASSADORS CLUB FORCED itself garishly on the street, shoved between the cramped terrace houses and dark, traditional restaurants on each side of it in one of Soho's central areas, demanding attention. Its façade, decorated with neon, made a bold statement. It was the future.

Beer crates clanked on the pavement. A car hooted its horn. Soho had its sleeves rolled up, preparing for the evening's entertainment.

Jarrell stood outside and looked up at it. Then he mounted the steps. At mid-morning the interior smelled of dust and soapsuds. A hoover buzzed in the basement. The foyer's red carpet, mirrors and photographs of leggy girls in ostrich feathers, ogling ridiculously into the camera, looked tired at this hour. The weedy-looking waiter who was overseeing the drinks delivery glanced at Jarrell's identity card indifferently. 'I'll say you're here.' Jarrell waited in the foyer.

It was some minutes before he was summoned upstairs, not by the waiter, but by a young woman in a tight pencil skirt and red sweater. The lift took them to the top floor. Mallory was standing in the doorway. He was a big man and looked as if he might have once been a boxer himself. His bespoke suit emulated the impeccable conservatism of the bent copper or big-time gangster. A man less confident than Jarrell might have felt shabby and lean in his presence. Jarrell did not.

The office was decked out in black leather and mahogany to create a club-like atmosphere that to Jarrell felt excessively masculine. Photographs of boxing stars decorated the bookcases that lined one wall.

Mallory's wide, flattish face was dominated by the blue eyes. The retroussé nose appeared too small for the pale expanse, as did the rosebud mouth, which now twisted into a strangely feminine dismissive moue as a big hand came out. 'What can I do for you?' Jarrell's fingers were crushed.

'I'd like a word about Valerie Jarvis. She worked for you until recently.'

Mallory's bright blue eyes trained themselves on Jarrell. 'Terrible thing. Tragic accident. I hadn't seen her for a while, but I heard.' He gestured towards a drinks trolley adjacent to his desk. 'Whisky?'

Jarrell shook his head.

'Coffee then. I'll ask Julie ...' He spoke through the intercom.

'As it happens, sir, it seems it wasn't an accident after all. The proprietor pushed her down the stairs. He's confessed.'

'Is that so?' Mallory picked up a cigar box and offered it to Jarrell, who refused. 'You don't smoke? These are excellent.' Mallory selected one himself and began the ritual of lighting it.

'Camenzuli. Known as Maltese Mike. Worked for you at one time, I believe.'

Mallory didn't say a word. His cigar was taking up all his attention.

Julie in the red sweater appeared with a coffee tray. She poured a stream of liquorice black into white china cups. Foamy milk followed in Jarrell's cup.

Mallory took his coffee black. 'Good stuff,' he said. 'Italian. Espresso. From down the road. Camenzuli. I may have had dealings with him in the past. But it would be a while ago.'

'You should remember. He trained with you. Bantamweight. Didn't make the grade. Vicious temper.'

Mallory smiled. 'There were quite a few of them. Wanted to fight for all the wrong reasons.'

'But you don't remember him?'

'It rings a bell, but ...'

'His story is there was an altercation. He lost his temper and struck the blow that sent her down the stairs to her death. Does that seem plausible to you?'

'If you don't mind my asking, what's the problem if he's confessed? You don't need my help.'

'On the contrary, Mr Mallory. It could be helpful to know a bit more about your relationship with the Maltese. And with the victim. For instance, why she stopped working for you.'

'Can't see how that'll help you.'

'We need to build up a picture ...'

'Her heart wasn't in it. She'd met someone,' he said. 'She began to get sloppy. Kept showing up late. I had to let her go. Pity. She was a looker. Very popular.'

'But it was all quite amicable, was it? You parted on good terms?'

'I ain't going to lose sleep over a stripper.'

'Not even when her life comes to a sudden end?'

'That's a different matter. She'd left. Nothing to do with me what happened when she wasn't working for me no more.' His eyes narrowed. 'Terrible tragedy of course, but ...' The sentence faded into a shrug.

'No-one said her death had anything to do with you, Mr Mallory. What gives you that idea?'

Mallory occupied himself with his cigar.

'I heard you weren't too pleased she left.'

'That's the trouble with you coppers. You spend too much time listening to idle gossip,' said Mallory with a flinty smile.

The façade was impregnable – although it was not exactly genial.

'Camenzuli's been charged, but I'm not convinced and nor's my guvnor. We're wondering who put him up to it.'

The smile was fixed tighter. 'You know, Detective Sergeant Jarrell, I can't see what this has to do with me. Very sad about poor little Valerie, but you've lost me now.'

'You and the Maltese go back a long way, I've heard.'

'Like I said, you coppers shouldn't listen to idle gossip.'

'Were you annoyed when the girl left, or by the way she left?'

'I didn't give a sodding toss. There ain't exactly a shortage.'

Jarrell stood up. 'I won't keep you. There's just one thing, though. Someone else you knew was present when Valerie Jarvis died. A certain Doctor Swann. And the funny thing is, he's also departed this world.'

Mallory didn't turn a hair. 'I'd heard,' he said blandly. 'I was sorry to hear it.' The eyes seemed bluer than ever. 'But I hadn't seen the old geezer for a very long time. And now I think we've finished this little conversation. I'm sure you've got work to do.'

chapter 25

JARRELL COULD NO LONGER postpone a visit to Pentonville prison. He disliked prisons. Prisons were places where everyone, including visitors, was guilty: family, lawyers, police, all were subject to the power of the guards. The screw in the lodge behind the vast old-fashioned gate looked at him with resentful suspicion. Jarrell stepped through the door cut in the huge portcullis and stood in a dark cobbled entrance.

The screw glared at Jarrell. His grotesquely exaggerated bunch of keys rattled. 'We've had no notice of this visit.'

There was an argument, but more for form's sake than anything else and eventually Jarrell was allowed in. He was led across a bleak yard and through echoing halls and passages. The vast cheerlessness and Dickensian ugliness of the place struck him as inefficient and counterproductive. The prison system, like the police, needed to be modernised.

He waited in the legal visit room. When Camenzuli arrived he looked even smaller than he had in his hotel.

'You gotta cigarette?'

'I don't smoke.'

A look of intense disgust darkened Camenzuli's face. For a second Jarrell thought he was going to leave.

They were up close across the little table. Maltese Mike

hadn't shaved for a while; the black stubble was like a rash all over his face.

'Where's my wife? She not been to see me.'

'That's a lie. Your wife has been to see you. And after her visit you made a false confession. So what I want to know is why you made that false confession. You know that's an offence in itself, don't you? Wasting police time at the very least. Possibly perverting the course of justice.'

Maltese Mike wasn't impressed. 'I don't have to say nothing.'

'You didn't push the girl down the stairs, did you?'

'I tell you what happen. Why you don't want to think that? Why you don't believe me?'

'Because it is not true, Mr Camenzuli. So I want to know who put you up to it in the first place.'

The Maltese glared.

'I suppose whoever put you up to it told you it was a weak story. Be whittled down. You'll get bail. Clever brief could persuade a jury it was an accident after all. Probably never come to court anyway.'

Camenzuli squinted suspiciously.

'That's all very well,' continued Jarrell. 'But the thing is, they could be wrong. It could get worse rather than better. A clever brief could just as easily make it look more like actual murder. You've got form, Mr Camenzuli. You're known to be a violent man. What's more, a malicious man. And can you prove you didn't strike that girl down deliberately? No. You can't. *I* know you didn't. But a jury might think otherwise.' He stopped, to let it sink in. Maltese Mike looked unimpressed.

'How much were you offered? What was your price? A tidy sum, I bet. Well, then, you see, there you'd be sitting in prison and Maria would get that money, wouldn't she? And who's to say she won't just make off with it? You can't be sure she'll stick around until you've done your time.'

'You—' The Maltese half rose. He clenched his hands. His black eyes were pinpoints of hatred. He spat. A blob landed full in Jarrell's face.

Jarrell fished a handkerchief out of an inner pocket and wiped the spittle away.

'That's not really an answer, is it?' He sat and waited. He could almost see Camenzuli's thought processes as he stared at the table. But he didn't speak.

'Okay. Forget it. It's your lookout.'

Jarrell returned to the station. Moules seemed satisfied with the confession and as the case hadn't, after all, revealed wrongdoing on the part of the police, so far as the Superintendent was concerned, that was the end of that. Moules was interested in police malpractice, not in some girl who was no better than she should be getting slapped around by a small-time crook. Certainly, the case was questionable. Why had the police not been involved at all, for example? But Jarrell had looked into that, and it turned out to have been a misunderstanding. That was the official story, at any rate. In addition, there was now a plausible suspect. Jarrell had other work to do, lots of it. Yet while the Superintendent might accept the result, Jarrell did not.

At lunchtime the police station was quiet. A couple of depressed individuals, a man and a woman of indeterminate age, waited listlessly on a bench. Jarrell knew some of his colleagues would be at the pub, but he had no intention of joining them there.

It was a surprise to find Slater in a back office, poring over some papers. This was a piece of luck.

'Hullo, me old darling.'

'Where is everyone?'

'The usual. I ain't had any dinner, though. Ambushed by bloody Moules. Asking questions about my bloody expenses. Strewth! Look at this.' And he gestured towards the expenses sheet in front of him. 'Saying I gotta check the figures. I've had enough of it. Why don't you come for a bite? I'm bloody starving.' Slater's face was as flushed as usual, but it was a bit early even for him to have been drinking already.

Jarrell could hardly refuse the surprise invitation. And indeed, while it was unwelcome, it was also an opportunity. He'd hoped for a quiet hour looking over another case, but a chat with Slater over a meal might be more useful.

At the Bloomsbury Dining Rooms Slater ordered roast beef for both of them. 'This is on me.' Slater winked and Jarrell understood that this was a free lunch, the result of some arrangement between policeman and proprietor. They sat in a booth surrounded by panels of dark varnished wood. As he ate, Slater leaned forward and stared at his companion. There was something slightly disturbing about him today.

'I'm in trouble with bloody Moules again. The Tony Marx case. He reckons I got the wrong bloke, but I can't break his alibi anyway. You're his blue-eyed boy, ain't you, you got any idea why he's got it in for me?'

Here was another surprise, but Jarrell didn't show it. He sliced a soggy roast potato and carefully placed a piece on his fork. 'You're mistaken.' He chewed and swallowed. 'I'm no particular favourite of his. And I don't know why you think he's against you in any way.' He knew he sounded pedantic and repressive, perhaps not entirely convincing. He watched Slater surreptitiously, pretending to be more interested in his lunch than he actually was.

'Don't tell me he ain't set on some clean-up campaign. Everyone knows that after what he got up to in Birmingham.'

Jarrell smiled. 'I think the Superintendent may be exaggerating the extent of his success in Birmingham.'

'Eh?' Slater frowned. 'How d'you know?'

'Don't you think it's human nature for people to boast a bit – to make out their achievements were greater than was actually the case?'

Slater liked that. He laughed. 'Now *that's* a policeman speaking. You're a right one, Professor. I've often wondered what brought you into the force, you don't seem like a proper copper to me, but there you have it – never believe a word anyone says.'

Jarrell looked modestly at his plate.

'So what's Moules' plan?' persisted Slater. 'He wants my guts for garters, that's what I think. Got it in for me, he has.' And he slammed his knife and fork together, his laughter replaced by brooding resentment.

'What makes you say that?'

'Oh don't come that with me. You know as well as I do.'

'I'm sure you're wrong,' said Jarrell firmly.

'Then why all this about Tony Marx? It's one bleeding case, that's all. Look – time for a pint. Or – I got something better back at the station.' He laughed again. 'Oh no, I forgot, you don't drink, bloody poofter.'

'I'd like a coffee here, though.' Jarrell didn't want to let go of Slater just yet. 'So, Tony Marx, that's going nowhere. What makes you so sure it's the suspect with the alibi?'

Slater shrugged. 'Got previous. Loads of it. And he knew Marx down Bethnal Green way. He's a violent man.'

The explanation didn't impress Jarrell, but he continued: 'And just remind me. What's his alibi?'

'He was at the cinema. Went to the cinema with his brother and brother's girlfriend.'

'The film?'

'*The Ten Commandments*. Cecil B. de Mille.'

'Thou shalt not kill. How appropriate.'

Slater glared.

'Seriously. He could describe the plot?'

'Yes. And the bloke at the box office remembers him. And the usherette.'

'Isn't that rather odd?'

'What's odd?'

'Them remembering him. New film. Big crowd. Queues at the box office.'

'We've interviewed them. Can't be budged.'

Jarrell smiled. 'And they have the ticket stubs too?'

Slater nodded.

'The sort of thing you'd normally throw away,' pointed out Jarrell.

'Don't need you to tell me that. Marx was a villain anyway. And it's not only that. Moules keeps nosing about – expenses, informants, you name it.'

Jarrell listened as Slater continued to grumble and it seemed to him that this was after all the lazy Slater of old. He didn't seem to have exerted himself excessively in tracking down Tony Marx's murderer. He'd just picked someone with a record more or less at random, without even bothering to construct a plausible cause for suspicion.

'What about that girl?' said Slater, abruptly changing the subject.

'What girl?'

'Argyle Street. The girl.'

'You know what happened. The hotel manager coughed.' Jarrell didn't want to discuss it, didn't want to share his doubts about the case.

'Don't see why Moules bloody reopened it in the first place. I heard that it was that bloody *Chronicle* man got hold of McGovern. Started nosing about and digging it all up again. What's the point? It was a bloody accident. Those bleeding news johnnies. I can't stand them. Someone ought to tell him to lay off.'

'It bothers you, does it?' Jarrell's green eyes watched his companion covertly from below his sandy lashes.

'No – course it don't *bother* me. Just a flipping waste of time, that's all. *Moules* bothers me.'

'The victim had worked for Vince Mallory,' ventured Jarrell.

Slater stared at him. 'Whoever you charged I reckon Mallory's behind it somewhere. And they say he don't like women – he's in the skin trade, but don't appreciate the female sex. That's a laugh.' And disconcertingly, Slater himself laughed, a laugh that grew, filling the room so that other diners looked up from their food. Then, as suddenly, he fell silent, brooding on dark thoughts of his own.

chapter 26

AS MCGOVERN WALKED BRISKLY away from Oxford railway station, crossed a bridge and turned into the quiet streets near the centre, the beauty of the mossy old buildings struck him as it had not done before. Even the dank and misty air was part of the city's pleasant atmosphere. He passed the New Theatre and the Ashmolean museum. By this time the mist was turning to drizzle. Shoals of cyclists whirred past him, as quiet and purposeful as fish in a stream.

After his meeting with Blackstone he had gone home to Bromley. The more he'd brooded over his argument with Lily, the more it had grown in his mind to a fearful obstacle, a blight on their future life together. Mike and Eveline – particularly Eveline – were turning Lily against him. Their influence was poisonous. They were bent on luring her into an alien artistic world in which he had no place. He allowed his suspicions free rein as he sat on the suburban train to Bromley. He anticipated finding Lily and her friends plotting against him in his own sitting room. He was going to have it out with her once and for all.

Lily was alone. The look of delight on her face at his unexpected return couldn't be faked. She'd hugged him, brought him a beer and asked about Oxford, pulling him down on the sofa and nestling against him.

There'd been no solution. They'd avoided the subject of children. But there had been a reconciliation, for the moment at least. He'd stayed the night. He woke next morning with new optimism. Things weren't as bad as he'd made them out to be.

He'd exaggerated. Of course Lily loved him; and she'd come round to the idea of children – of course she would.

He was returning to his work in Oxford with an enthusiasm he hadn't so far felt. He would talk to the students – it was his ostensible task anyway – and try to discover what the Hungarian billeted at the Grange had been so frightened of. It wasn't surprising that a boy who'd just experienced an uprising crushed by police and military should be wary of the forces of law and order, and he'd certainly been agitated. More peculiar was his friend's provocative behaviour and his brazen admission that he'd been rummaging around uninvited in the Professor's private affairs. There was certainly more than met the eye there.

Simon Holt was waiting for McGovern at the hostel. A firm handshake; spectacles with tortoiseshell frames; a tweed jacket; flannel bags. 'Sorry we haven't met sooner. I thought we'd catch up yesterday. Sally Mabledon said you would be here.'

'I was unexpectedly called back to London.'

'Well – good to meet you. Better late than never, I suppose. Let's go into the back office, shall we. You can make yourself at home there. It's where the files are kept.'

'I hope I'm not too much of an imposition. My understanding was I'd be stationed with the police.'

'The Superintendent had other views. He's not a fan of the probation service. I'm a probation officer, by the way. And very jealous of his position, is Superintendent Carter. He didn't take kindly to the thought of someone from the Met nosing into his affairs.' Too late, the probation officer seemed to become aware of how rude he sounded. 'As he sees it, of course. You're welcome, so far as we're concerned. But I think you'll find everything's in order.'

'I'll try not to get in your way. Mrs Mabledon has already shown me round. Best if I just get on with going through the records to see if—'

'Reds under the beds, eh. I don't think you'll find many of those here. Although there is one group I should draw your attention to. It's ironic in a way. Some of the first refugees were actually communists, fleeing the revolution. They thought the rebellion was about to succeed. A funny lot, as a matter of fact. You get a feeling some of them were government stooges, offspring of same, something of that kind. I thought you might find them of interest. Now they're here, though, they show no signs of wanting to go back. I think they're pleasantly surprised by life in England. They've heard terrible stories of capitalist exploitation. Some of them seem to have been told Charles Dickens was writing about the present day. Of course the reality turns out very different. That hasn't stopped some of them from arguing and picking fights with the others – taunting them sometimes.'

In the back office Holt took a sheaf of files from the cabinet and sat down on one of the easy chairs, with a gesture to suggest McGovern take the other one. 'Sally's not here today,' he explained. 'And I'll be on the phone to the Canadian High Commission for most of the time. It seems to have been chaos at the Austrian end. Many of them didn't have passports. So I suppose it's not surprising some wrong 'uns got through.'

'I don't know if there's another office I could use. I shall want to talk to them – some of them, anyway – individually and I thought the best way might be for you to let them know I'm here to support them, to hear of anything bothering them.'

'I don't think you'll find they'll complain about the way they've been treated.'

'I'm sure you've done everything possible. There's no

criticism of your arrangements. But if I just call each of them in for interview they might feel a wee bit uncomfortable, coming as they do from a police state. If it comes from them – if they come to me, that creates a better situation. I'm sure you see ...'

'Of course. I'll put a notice up on the board.'

'Thanks. That would be helpful.'

'There's a little room along the passage – it's used for storing papers.'

It was bare enough, with just a small table, a couple of bentwood chairs and wooden filing cabinets along one wall.

'Well – I'll leave you to get on with it, shall I?'

McGovern decided to look through all the files before concentrating on Meszarov to get a general idea of what to expect. He glanced over the meagre information provided for each refugee. He looked for the home town, education, parents' work, and how and when exactly they'd arrived in Austria and then Britain. He looked with special care at the group identified as sympathisers of the regime. Then there was a third group, the smallest, who weren't students. That was probably the group in which petty crooks were to be found; some at least were probably neither sympathetic nor hostile to the Hungarian regime, politically speaking, but had simply seized the opportunity to get away.

Gyorgy Meszarov's parents were academic mathematicians. He'd quite frankly stated that they were Communist Party members. Gyorgy himself was studying maths. Quinault had described them as committed communists, but it was impossible to know. They might be disillusioned now, but probably Party membership was a necessity for their posts at the University of Budapest.

He put the files aside and decided simply to wait. If no-one came to see him, he could hang about the hostel and surreptitiously watch the comings and goings of the students; and at some point track Meszarov down and have a proper talk with him in order to find out why he'd been billeted with Quinault: a student with communist parents placed with a man suspected (it seemed) of subversive activities or at least of unwelcome meddling.

After an hour he had had no visitors, so he took a break in order to stretch his legs. He paced up and down the hallway, smoking. There was a certain amount of activity; every few minutes another young lad passed through and some had gathered in what seemed to be a day room to the right of the reception area. Eventually he decided to take a look.

There were four men and a girl. The girl, with a thin face, wore a black beret. She was leaning against a young boy in a relaxed way, suggesting intimacy and familiarity. Her stare was not friendly.

A youth nearer the door looked up. 'You want?' he said. He stood up. The shabbiness of his clothes surprised McGovern – but of course he shouldn't have been surprised. The Hungarian's dark, unsmiling face was not hostile, but shadowed more with a deep watchfulness. It was a look neither of hope nor of expectation, a look of patience, endurance.

'Is news for us? Canada? You are social worker?'

The girl spoke up. 'You are the man we can talk to. I saw the notice.'

She stood up. She wore baggy dark blue trousers and a green sweater, but while her clothes were as shabby as those of the boy, she contrived an air of jaunty chic. 'I am Irén. You can talk to me if you wish.' It seemed more like a challenge than a friendly offer.

'With pleasure.'

She said something in Hungarian. The young men laughed.

In his chilly little interviewing room she turned her chair around and sat astride it. 'So. What should I talk about?'

McGovern smiled. 'It's up to you.' He waited. He looked at her more carefully now. She had very black eyes. Black curls sprouted from beneath her beret and framed her thin, sallow face. Her lips were thin too. She wore no lipstick, no make-up at all, but then she probably had none.

'You have met Andras. He told me.'

'Andras? No. Gyorgy Mezsarov. But barely – I hardly spoke to him.' McGovern concealed his surprise. 'He's a friend of yours?'

She shrugged. 'Well, we are all friends here ... well, not all, some of us. I came with others from Austria. With Gyorgy and Andras. Also with David and Ernö. We are all good friends – and Eva. Eva was staying with family, but they were not nice to her and she is back here now. You did not meet Gyorgy. Gyorgy is here. Andras take his place at the house.'

'Why was that? Do the people here know?'

'Andras is unhappy boy. He loves Gyorgy very much, perhaps too much. Gyorgy will go soon to Cambridge, he is offered place to study there. Mathematics. But Andras will go to Canada, where he has uncle. He does not want to go.'

'If he wishes to stay in England he can discuss that with the people here. They might be able to make alternative arrangements.'

Her thin mouth twisted into a little moue of disappointment – with him, with his words, with the hostel set-up? He wasn't sure.

'Why did they change places?'

'Gyorgy does not like being there, because the old man ask about his parents. Knew his parents. It has to do with the war.' She paused, screwed up her face in a frown. 'Gyorgy did not like all the questions he asked.'

'The Professor asked Gyorgy about his parents? What sort of questions?'

Irén stared at him. She disconcerted him. It was her knowing air and the feeling he had that she was playing a game with him. 'I don't know. Why? Does that interest you? You must talk to him. But he is not here – he goes out on bike every day. He is not like others here, always worried. He thinks it is great here. Well, is easy for him, he knows he will go soon to Cambridge. He is very happy about that. I love Gyorgy. He is great fun. But he is not interested in the revolution. His family is communist, you know. Many privileges. But Gyorgy thinks it will be better here. And he did not like having to be in youth movement and all those things.' She leaned forward. 'Shall I tell you story about this? He find some sunglasses. In old shop or something. These you can't obtain. So he wore them to a rally. For this he get in trouble, because sunglasses are bourgeois. Sunglasses you wear in Hollywood. Good communists should not wear these things.' She sat back in her chair again. 'Can I ask you for cigarette?'

'Of course. I'm sorry. I should have offered—'

She brushed the apology aside as she accepted the cigarette.

'So Andras has taken his place at Professor Quinault's house,' said McGovern. 'Officially?'

Irén didn't answer the question. Instead: 'Andras thought they could spend more time there together. He thinks Gyorgy will still be there sometimes. At least he wanted this to happen, I think.'

'And what about you, Irén? What are your plans? Are you destined for North America too?'

She smiled wickedly. 'Oh no. I should not like that. I have no family there. I shall stay here – I shall live in London. I have place in acting school. But now I think you are going to be very kind and take me for coffee in centre of Oxford. Tea and coffee are horrible here in hostel. And it is boring here too.'

'Another time perhaps. I need to talk to some of your friends here. Can you persuade one or two of them to have a chat with me? And Gyorgy, when he comes back. If you tell him I shall be here tomorrow morning, can he come and see me then?'

When she smiled she became attractive. 'If you say he must, then I will see he does.'

chapter 27

BLACKSTONE HAD INVITED SONIA to dinner at a discreet little place off Dover Street. Mayfair was a part of London he disliked. The wealth behind its stony façades sucked the air out of the streets.

He was careful to arrive early and was happy to wait, fortified by a double whisky. The softly lit restaurant, with its pink damask tablecloths and pink shaded table lamps, was rather too much like a boudoir for his taste, but perhaps women liked that. Sonia, of course, was not just 'women'. She liked anywhere expensive, however, and this restaurant certainly wasn't cheap.

He had no special plan. To question Sonia directly would be useless. Discretion was her watchword. They might begin with an exchange of views on Suez and Hungary, for Sonia had claims to education, and presented herself not simply as a woman of the world, but as a woman in the world, a serious person. Perhaps in a different century she would have shone as a salon hostess, or become the mistress of kings and archdukes with all their wealth and influence at her disposal. Yet those women, as far as Blackstone could remember, had traded on their erotic appeal, had risen from bed to bed. Sonia, by contrast, was a fixer, whose own sexual tastes and life remained a mystery.

She was, of course, or had been, married to Vince Mallory. She'd told Blackstone she'd met the boxing promoter when he was in Stockholm negotiating a big fight. That, and the fact that she had grown up in Malmö, was all Blackstone knew. The couple lived apart. There were no children, but Sonia was always clear she remained on good terms with her husband. Mallory was said to have a weakness for the boxers he steered to success, but that might be malicious rumour put about by his enemies.

What fascinated him about Sonia was the way she rose above the usual human desires. She had, or seemed to have, no vices, no obsessions, no weaknesses that Blackstone could see. He wasn't even sure how much she cared about money. Of course she liked it, who wouldn't, but it wasn't, he believed, straightforward greed that drove her. What did? He didn't know. Until Valerie's death had stirred his curiosity he hadn't especially cared to know either. She provided a service of which he'd availed himself from time to time and was an occasional source of useful information. Now, though, the memory of the girl he'd so briefly known lying glassily in the mortuary was causing him to ask questions, to wonder, to speculate as to what Sonia's place in the scheme of things might really be.

He stood up as Sonia crossed the room behind the waiter, who was slightly over-acting his role as he showed madam to her table with pantomimed obsequiousness. It was almost as if he knew what she was, knew that her classy sophistication was as much a mask as his exaggerated politesse.

Blackstone had made an effort to smarten himself up. He'd shaved, his tie and shirt were clean and his suit freshly pressed. He still didn't look good enough for her in her shellacked perfection; black this evening, as discreet as ever, the perfect suit, the perfect court shoes, with the perfect contrast of the perfect pale mink stole and everything topped by the perfect gamine cap of dark hair. Did she really do so well out of her business? She was only an upmarket madam, after all. But as she approached their table, walking with a slightly hesitant sideways movement, he was flattered she'd taken so much trouble.

They exchanged pleasantries; Hungary and Suez were indeed briefly mentioned. Then Sonia leaned forward and said, 'I can talk to you as an old friend, can't I, Gerry? If I ever want to get something into the papers I know who to come to. But I also know you can be discreet when it suits you.'

'I'm a journalist. I'm the soul of discretion, and most of all when printing a story might get me into trouble. Having said that, my job is to get a story.'

'Yes, but you said yourself, nine out of ten stories never get printed at all.'

'That could be – but what are you getting at?'

'Sometimes things – stories – need time to develop, to come to fruition.'

This was bait of some kind and he wondered what the trap was.

'This thing with the girl,' she went on, 'that's not going to be splashed all over the papers, is it?'

Blackstone watched her. She seemed calm enough. 'It hasn't aroused much interest so far,' he said cautiously. 'Would that worry you – if it did?'

'No ... no ... Mallory wouldn't be too pleased.' She always referred to her husband by his last name. Was it to distance herself from him? 'You understand. The Ambassadors is very chic just now, you know, and any kind of scandal could be damaging. Not that Mallory had anything to do with it, of course.'

If that was the case, why say it? wondered Blackstone, but Sonia continued quickly: 'Some sordid little story about a back-street hotel ... you can play it down, can't you?'

'I'll do my best.'

'I'm expanding the business too, making some changes.'

She smiled as she spoke, a long-lipped smile; she looked sad when she smiled. 'I'm going to host parties, special parties – you know, for adventurous couples and single people too. Things are going to change anyway, aren't they? Isn't there some talk of a change in the law?'

'You mean the Wolfenden Committee?'

'Is that what it's called?'

'The rumour is they're going to clear women off the streets and let up on poofs, but not poofs in *pissoirs*.'

'Charming. So there'll be competition from all the girls who'll be renting a room with a telephone and trying to turn themselves into call girls. Little tarts.' She frowned and her long lips twisted. 'I could wring their little necks.'

Her venom startled him. It wasn't like Sonia to display spite, or indeed any emotion, but he supposed she feared the loss of lucrative business.

'You wouldn't be in charge any more,' he ventured.

The spasm had passed. She was glassy cool again. 'I've never been ... *in charge* as you put it.'

'Could you start a club?'

His companion shook her head. 'Mallory owns clubs. As you know. I don't want to get involved in any of that. But times are changing. Britain is becoming a little bit more unbuttoned, don't you think?'

The waiter was hovering with his order pad and Sonia picked up the menu.

'Hors d'oeuvres, please, and grilled sole,' she said without hesitation.

Blackstone ordered lobster bisque and steak as the easy way out and thought how funny it was to be ordering steak, and how everyone had forgotten about rationing after a mere two years and yet how there still seemed something a little unreal about this new shiny society of television and teddy boys and teenagers and astonishingly full employment. And all in the middle of another shoddy little war. Yes, Britain was loosening up a little. But: 'Maybe,' he said; and then: 'So you want me to try to shut down the Argyle Street story.'

'I just wondered, Gerry,' and she created a little diversion by extracting her cigarette case from her bag, then putting a cigarette to her lips, leaning forward so that he could light it. 'I just wondered whether it's a good idea to get too excited about ... you know – that poor girl.' She blew out a plume of smoke, her gaze off in the corner. 'Don't you think that kind of scandal ... if it became one ... would be sort of turning the clock back? You know, those sordid *News of the World* stories. We don't want to go back to that sort of thing, do we? Turning sex into a dirty little hole-in-the-corner secret?'

Was she warning him off? Did she have the *power* to warn him off? The story definitely bothered her and he'd have to find out why; but perhaps not by asking overt questions.

'Sex is always good for a column or two, but Bodkin Adams is the big story now,' he said soothingly. 'That and the international scene, of course.' It was he who'd got Valerie's story into NIBs in the first place in the vague hope it would lead to more information. Now he regretted it. The idea of her wasted life all over the front pages upset him. Camenzuli's arrest had already reached an inside page and there was always the possibility that it would blow up into a sleazy scandal. Sonia's reasons for wanting it buried were no doubt very different from his and he would – eventually – discover what they were.

The first course arrived. The waiter bent solicitously over Sonia as he arranged her plate.

Blackstone took a spoonful of soup. It tasted good: salty, creamy lobster flavour, but with a hint of sharpness.

He made a sideways move. 'Before we leave the subject, there is just one more thing about poor Valerie. I wondered why you were under the impression she knew Sonny Marsden.'

Sonia poked at the clusters of salad on her plate. 'Call this hors d'oeuvres? Not half what you'd get in Sweden.' Disdainfully, she lifted a forkful of Russian salad and chewed it without enthusiasm. 'Did I say that?' she said vaguely. 'Oh it must have been just something I heard. And girls like her, well, you know ... a lot of the girls like the West Indians.'

'I'm not sure what you mean when you say girls like her.' He spoke stiffly.

She looked at him curiously. 'I'm sorry if I misled you.'

'The question is, Sonia dear, *why* you misled me.'

'Gerry! Don't be angry. It was just a possibility, that's all.'

He decided not to pursue it – for the moment. He spooned up his soup. When it was finished he wiped his mouth and smiled. He reached for his cigarettes. That was enough about Valerie for now. He'd learn nothing more from Sonia. 'I heard a rumour myself about a client of yours,' he said.

'Oh?'

'I know. You're discretion personified. I was just rather amused, though, that you have eminent Oxford professors crossing your threshold.'

From the way her eyes flickered – so slightly – he knew he'd hit the mark.

But: 'I don't know where you can have heard that.' She seemed almost bored.

Something clicked. Of course. He couldn't believe he'd never thought of it before. If Sonia had visitors seeking her services who were eminent in one way or another, then there would be ample opportunities for her to blackmail them.

Blackmail! Why had he never thought of that?

'Special Branch are interested in him.'

She raised her eyebrows. Otherwise her mask was perfection. But his words had hit home. She was thinking about it. He'd leave it to sink to the bottom of her mind and see what happened.

'And you're interested in that?'

'I could be,' he said.

'You know I never discuss clients.'

'Of course not, Sonia,' he replied smoothly. 'And I'm not asking you to. But I suppose you have quite a few distinguished visitors and not necessarily of the kind one might expect.'

'You're fishing, Gerry.' Momentarily, she was almost flirtatious.

'No, darling, I'm just interested in you. Everything about you. You're such a mysterious woman, you know that, don't you?'

She looked away and for a moment her mouth quivered slightly. He almost thought she was close to tears, but that would be unheard of and perhaps he'd been mistaken, for when she looked at him again there was no hint of emotion. 'There's nothing much to know about me, Gerry, and it's kind of you to take an interest, but I'm not in the least interesting. Or mysterious.'

The waiter brought the main course. Sonia picked delicately at her fish, lifting the flesh off its bones. 'But you know, people are so amazingly stupid, just begging to be exploited. Masochists. Not that I exploit them any more than a dominatrix exploits the men she thrashes. She's just giving them what they want. And that's what I do too.'

He found her contempt rather chilling and had nothing to say in return. They ate in silence. Only when she had finished – but her plate was left half full – did she speak again. She looked at him solemnly, almost tragically. 'You know,' she said, 'if I ever ...'

'Ever?' He smoked, watched and waited.

She seemed to be lost in thought. But all she said was: 'Oh ... nothing.' Then she changed her mind. 'As a matter of fact, Gerry, I did a rather silly thing the other day. I left a message for a client. I rang his flat. Some woman answered. His secretary, she said. I left my name. That was stupid of me, wasn't it? I don't know what possessed me. But I don't suppose it matters, really.'

Blackstone wondered why she'd mentioned it and if it was a tiny chink in the armour. He smoked and waited for her to say more.

After a contemplative pause as they looked at the menu and chose dessert, she began again: 'If I ever needed a lawyer, Gerry, is there someone – I mean who would you recommend?'

'A lawyer, Sonia? What have you been up to?'

She smiled. 'Absolutely nothing, darling. It's purely hypothetical.'

'I'm sure your husband knows the best lawyers going.'

'No, that wouldn't ...'

Suppose Sonia *did* dabble in blackmail. The threat of getting a story into the papers would be enough to make a public figure cough up. Perhaps that was the reason for Quinault's visit to her flat. To pass on to her some of the money McGovern had seen at the house. But even a blackmailer might face threats in return.

part two

chapter 28

THE DROWNES' PARTY ON New Year's Day was an institution. Regine dressed carefully – as if she did not always dress carefully – or rather, she dressed lovingly, for she cared more about clothes than about most things. Today she chose the deep blue grosgrain William had bought her for Christmas.

The rooms through which she moved to greet her guests were as beautifully arranged as she was. Even the canapés were artistically planned, and the hired waitress who presented them wore a parlourmaid's uniform.

Regine slipped among her guests and not for the first time wondered if New Year's Day really was the best time for a party. For one thing, hangovers, of which there were clearly many, due to the celebrations of the night before, did not discourage her more determined guests from starting again. Some people – writers in particular – never knew when to stop. There, for example, was Norbert Price, the well-known novelist, slavering over Edith Fanshawe, the poetess. She was now, of course, and had been for some time, also Lady Pearson, the banker's wife, as in a game of Happy Families, but in whichever role, she now recoiled from Norbert with a look of fastidious horror. Regine, who had many reasons for disliking Edith, knew she must rescue her.

'Norbert, darling, you're looking a little tired. Why don't

you sit down? Edith and I have so much to talk about. We need to catch up, don't we, darling?'

Norbert Price subsided onto a nearby sofa, but pulled at the hand of his hostess. 'Reggie ... lovelier than ever ... what have you been doooo-ing with your ravishing self?' He pulled so hard that she almost fell, ending up in a sitting position beside him. He leaned forward, pretending to straighten the front of her dress, but in fact to fumble at her breast. She moved to put herself beyond reach, but it wouldn't do to rebuff him too obviously. He was a Drownes' author, after all.

'How is your new novel coming along? We're all so looking forward to it.' This was a coded way of saying that it was very late.

'Isz ... going to be my ... masterpiece, Reggie my angel.' He spoke with the exaggerated precision of the drunk. 'Masterpiece,' he repeated. It was unclear whether he meant it or was engaged in self-mockery, which in turn might be a sort of double bluff; or whether he was too drunk to know what he was saying.

'That's marvellous, Norbert. William's very excited ...' Out of the corner of her eye she noticed that Edith the poetess was now in conversation with the other Edith, Edith Blake, Regine's enemy, the sidelined doyenne of Drownes'. She snatched up Norbert's glass. 'Let me get you a refill,' and she slipped away, left the glass on a bookshelf and changed direction, closing in on the two women.

'Happy New Year!'

'And to you too, Regine.' Edith Blake never called her Reggie. Never ever. For the first two or three years it had even been 'Mrs Drownes'. 'I was just complimenting Lady Pearson on her recent *slim volume,*' she said archly. 'I was saying I feel her work has deepened so much in recent years.'

'Since my marriage,' began the second Edith.

'Since your marriage?' Regine wanted to say something

filthy, because Sir Avery Pearson was so extremely rich and, reputedly, impotent, freeing his wife to take up with various literary types whose circles she continued to frequent. In addition, she was under no obligation to produce a child, since Sir Avery had sons by his previous marriage, before old age had curtailed his activities in that direction. Regine almost envied Edith. She had done so well for herself and was such a cold bitch. 'Yes, your recent poems have been really beautiful,' she said. 'I see what Edith means – something so *spiritual* about them.'

This seemed to be accepted at face value. Actually, Reggie had thought them little more than a pastiche of T.S. Eliot. William hadn't been too happy either, although they had sold quite well – for poetry.

Reggie continued sweetly: 'Sadly, poetry seems to be going a little out of fashion. William is quite worried – the reading public is changing, standards dropping, he thinks. All down to this awful commercial TV. People just want to watch quiz programmes and tired old music-hall routines repackaged for the box. People perhaps don't appreciate any more the – the *quiet quality* of your work, they want something ... I won't say cruder ... more ... they want their culture in primary colours. If you know what I mean.' As she dropped her words of poison her plaintive expression conveyed a sensitive appreciation of the beauty and importance of Edith's work, but also the tragic possibility that it might soon no longer sell, at which point Drownes' would be regretfully obliged to cease its publication.

'Oh I don't think there's *any danger* of Lady Pearson's gems going *out of fashion,*' said Edith Blake repressively.

Regine stifled the irritation she felt at this evidence of Edith Blake's craven devotion to the poetess. It was a veritable schoolgirl 'pash'. Edith Blake was one of those women who seemed never to have quite grown up emotionally. She usually dressed in spare tweed suits, but sometimes veered off into girlish dirndl skirts and childish cardigans. Her round, pink face was unlined, so that she seemed altogether younger than her fifty years, and she walked, not awkwardly, but in the way a little girl might walk, occasionally even breaking into a kind of skip. She seemed more hoydenish than lesbian, but Regine had dark suspicions about her relationship with her secretary, although that was more likely an intense schoolgirl friendship than an erotic liaison. It was very hard to couple the word 'erotic' with Edith Blake.

'Oh, there's Rodney Turbeville.' Lady Pearson had looked away for a moment. 'I must have a word with him. My husband is very keen to talk to him about the Oxford road programme. His old college ...' She moved off.

Regine managed not to turn round. Rodney had spent Christmas with his wife's family in the north of England. She hadn't expected him back so soon, had hoped but hadn't expected he'd be at the party. His sudden appearance brought on all the feverish symptoms of forbidden love, a surge of optimism and a kind of surrender in anticipation. He must care, then. He'd had to come. He'd had to see her.

'I'm sure you know Drownes' is hoping that Sir Avery is going to invest some of his money in the firm.' Edith Blake smiled killingly at Regine.

Actually, Regine didn't know. She hoped she concealed her shock. 'Of course.'

'So we need to be very tactful ...'

Regine managed to say calmly, 'Drownes' has always supported her.' But she seethed inwardly. How could William not have told her? 'I must say hello to Turbeville in a minute.'

'I'm sure you must.' Was there an innuendo in Edith's words, her smile?

'William's hoping he'll finish his biography of Disraeli soon.'

Regine couldn't wait to get away from Edith Blake, but

instead of approaching her lover she passed into the second drawing room and the drinks table, feeling she needed a drink herself. There she encountered Norbert Price again. He seemed to have recovered a little and was talking to a man she had never seen before.

'Hope you don't mind. I cleared it with your hubby – brought a mate of mine along. Gerry Blackstone.'

The stranger was dressed in the untidy manner favoured by journalists and he was not bad-looking, in the pale, unhealthy way that seemed the fate of many writers. 'I hope you don't mind,' and his smile was rather charming. 'At least I didn't gatecrash. Not quite, anyway.'

'Of course not. I'm delighted.'

'Gerry's the chief crime reporter for the *Chronicle*,' said Norbert.

'Oh! That is exciting.'

A crime reporter! Not part of the usual literary crowd then. An exotic. Possibly an interesting addition to her coterie. Regine was delighted. 'You must see life in the raw. I suppose you're covering the Bodkin Adams case.'

He was, indeed, and his stories about that and other investigations were amusing and outrageous, but she didn't forget about Turbeville. He mustn't leave before she'd had an opportunity to speak to him. It was Blackstone who created the opportunity.

'I don't suppose you'd introduce me to – isn't that Professor Quinault – talking to the MP – Rodney Turbeville, I think?' he said. 'I understand the Professor is quite involved with the Hungarian refugees in Oxford and I just wanted ...'

'Of course.'

Edith Fanshawe had moved on and Turbeville and the Professor stood by the French window. They seemed to be talking about something rather serious, judging from Rodney's expression. Impossible to read the older man. His face was all gnarled and knobbly, like the joint of a tree.

'I think we've met.' Turbeville nodded at Blackstone. 'The Royal Commission on Newspapers?'

'Yes – I apologise if I'm interrupting you, but I believe you're very involved with the Hungarians, Professor, and I wanted ...'

'Would you mind if we went outside for a moment?' Turbeville smiled at Regine. 'It's rather hot in here. And I'm dying to see your garden.'

'And it's so mild suddenly.' Regine smiled coolly and led him through the back room and down the steps outside.

'Good Christmas?' He smiled in that heartbreakingly tender way of his as he lit a cigarette. 'I'm dying to kiss you.'

'Darling – we can't – not here.'

'You're driving me wild, though. You do know that, don't you.'

'I missed you. Did you miss me?'

'Of course I did, darling.'

'Did you? Really?'

'We must meet soon. Next week's a bit difficult, but after that ...'

A date was fixed and Regine asked: 'What were you talking to Quinault about? You looked terribly serious.'

'Oh, he was quizzing me about the bloody Oxford road scheme. And before that, the fat lady writer was giving me the third degree about it too. '

Fat lady writer! The description delighted Regine. 'Don't be cruel. She has become a little plump since she married her rich banker, but she's a well-known poetess, you know.'

'Lady poetesses give me the pip.' He stubbed out his half-smoked cigarette. 'Look – we'd better get back inside.' And as they parted he murmured: 'Dinner then, on the tenth. Our usual place – in Duke Street Mews.'

It was a small club with a restaurant near St James' Square. Regine was not hungry and toyed with the chicken and mushroom vol-au-vent, but the wine was good and she drank more than usual.

''Fraid I have to get back to the House quite soon, old girl, but why don't we go and sit in the car for a bit. Eh?'

There was always the car when they didn't have time to go to the flat. It was parked at the far end of the Mews. Regine thought it was terribly risky. Rodney said no policeman ever came down to the end – but imagine the scandal if one did.

They were in the back seat and Rodney was pressing as ever. 'God, all these clothes you women wear. This skirt … and God, Reggie, you're so …'

His weight pushed her sideways, her shoulder and neck against the window. But she had her ways, and made it easy for him, although she was too tense herself, imagining the policeman's face in the window, to fully enjoy the forceful need that drove him into her.

His breathing ebbed back to normal. 'God, Reggie, you're a wicked little thing. Drive a man wild … you little devil …'

The risky situation excited him as much as it inhibited her. He loved risk. His gambling years and war exploits proved that. By comparison with guerrilla warfare alongside the Partisans in the Balkans, betraying your wife was quite a minor sort of risk. But there could perhaps be other risks, more unusual, more thrilling, like making love almost in public with the ever-present possibility of discovery.

'You enjoy doing it like this, darling, don't you?' she murmured.

He raised his head from her bosom. 'You mean you don't – it wasn't …'

'Of course not, darling, that's not what I meant at all. I just thought – I just wondered what other exciting places you might have ... and what exciting ladies ...'

He didn't rise to the bait. 'Sweetie.' He tightened his arms round her, 'It's you, not the places, lovely one. And you're the exciting lady ... as if you didn't know.'

chapter 29

'HAPPY NEW YEAR! Very mild for January – such a relief after last month. I thought we'd never see the sun again.'

Before McGovern had time to reply, the phone rang and Sally Mabledon's smile faded into a harassed frown. 'Yes – yes. No – but we sent the papers well before Christmas ... yes, but ... I know. I know ...' As the conversation continued she seemed to become visibly more untidy, her perm frizzed up, her cheeks hot and shiny. She banged the handset down with a big breath. 'This Canadian scheme! There are so many problems. Badly organised.'

'You got my request, did you? Gyorgy Meszarov?'

'Yes, indeed, Inspector. He promised he'd be waiting for you in the day room.'

In the bleak day room Irén was holding court again on the sofa, surrounded by – McGovern thought – the same three boys he'd found her with before.

'Gyorgy Meszarov?'

The boy who jumped to his feet was a rosy-cheeked picture of health. Brown curly hair sprang over his forehead and his brown eyes danced with vitality. He held out his hand. 'Happy to meet you, sir.'

'Can we talk? In my office?'

McGovern had expected Meszarov to show suspicion similar to that of Andras, but he seated himself in the little office with complete composure. 'Why you want to see me?' he asked at once, but the question came with no sense of fear.

'You were supposed to be billeted with Professor Quinault. But you're here and it's Andras Ferenczy living at the Professor's house. I talked with your friend Irén before Christmas. She said the Professor asked you too many questions.'

How fresh-faced and open Gyorgy Meszarov was! He seemed untouched – though he surely couldn't be – by what he'd been through.

'Did she tell you my parents are enthusiastic communists?' He spoke with a wry smile. 'I am fond of them. It was very difficult – that I decide to leave. They believe in it all, but I could not. I don't like when Professor asks all these questions about them. I am very awkward with this. I ask why he want to know all this and he say it is just they were friends in the war, but I don't believe him. He knows much about them. They came here to escape the Horthy regime in my country. You know about this? The pre-war Hungarian government, fascist. Horthy support the Germans in the war. The Professor says he worked with them then. Undercover work, he calls this. I do not know. They have never talked about this. I think it is trap to make me talk about them. But why he want to do this?'

'I can understand you must have felt uneasy. But why did your friend Andras have to take your place?'

'He want to. He is unhappy. Hates being here – noise, talk – I don't know why, but he thinks he will be better there. So ...' Gyorgy completed the sentence with a shrug and a smile.

'The Professor didn't object?'

'What can he say?'

McGovern held out his cigarette case and Gyorgy accepted a cigarette gracefully. When it was lit he leant back in his chair and inhaled with evident enjoyment. 'I have no money for cigarettes here. That is also difficult.' He laughed. 'Now I am – what – angry – because no cigarettes. Before was being shot at and have to leave country.'

There was a knock at the door. Before McGovern could answer, it opened. 'You remember me?' The young woman with the black eyes and dark curls stood with her hand on the doorknob.

'Irén. Of course I remember you. How are you? What can I do for you?'

'I am fine. I am soon going to London.'

She'd found some lipstick and the red gash against her white skin made her look more than ever the bohemian student, today wearing a big black sweater and jeans. 'You like my jeans? They gave me here. In Hungary so hard to get. Impossible. Apparatchiks say jeans are capitalist plot to draw youth away from socialism. Like sunglasses.' She laughed.

'You're looking very well.'

'Thank you. But I am here about Andras. Has Gyorgy told you about Andras?'

Gyorgy spoke to her in Hungarian. He turned to McGovern. 'I was—'

Irén cut across him. 'Gyorgy and I, we are worried. Andras is frightened. He had visitors. Two men came and threatened him.'

'What sort of men?'

'They were men like you.' Irén looked at him, as if he ought to know what kind of men.

'I'm not sure what you mean. You mean they were British?'

'I think you are not welfare officer.' Her black eyes challenged him.

McGovern ignored this. 'The men were like – what?'

Gyorgy looked for somewhere to stub out his cigarette.

'Hungarians. Perhaps they think Andras is me. Andras say nothing, but—'

'What kind of threats?'

'They say he will be in trouble if he does not do what they say.'

'What did they want him to do?'

'I think spy on us. Inform.'

'You're sure they were Hungarian?' As soon as he'd spoken, McGovern realised how stupid that sounded.

'There are some here who support the government. We all know that. But these men – it was different, I think.'

'Why are you telling me about this?'

'You say you are here to help, that you have to know everything is in order.'

'Andras should speak to Mr Holt or Mrs Mabledon.'

'He is scared. He is even afraid of being sent back to Hungary.'

'They'll not send him back.'

'Perhaps, but he is scared.'

McGovern silently considered the possibilities: Hungarians from the Embassy, Hungarian communists, British freelancers up to something – or nothing: just a frightened refugee, a misunderstanding.

Finally he said: 'He can come and talk to me here if he thinks that would help.'

'I think he is too frightened. He does not like to come here. And now he does not like the house, either.'

'No-one can help him if he doesn't talk to anyone.'

Gyorgy nodded. 'I will say he must talk to you. And to people here.'

'I will speak to them, too. But, Gyorgy, what about you? Do you feel safe? If these men discover they spoke to Andras, not you – are you frightened they'll come after you?'

Gyorgy stood up. 'Thank you. But is okay. I know when I

come here that there is this risk. In Cambridge will be better, but they know I am here, in England. More likely my parents will be in trouble. That is bad too. But that is the way it is. And they have influence. Perhaps they will not be too much blame.' He spoke with resigned dignity, which contained its own kind of optimism. 'And will be all right for me here. Thank you, anyway.'

He left the room, but Irén did not follow him. 'You have not yet invited me to have coffee.' She smiled at him.

'Another time.'

'Oh, you are *mean*!'

McGovern wondered why she bothered to flirt with him, but flirtation was probably simply her way of relating to the men who crossed her path.

'I will see you soon again, I hope. And you will try to help Andras.'

'I will.' McGovern stood by the door and watched her prance away down the passage, her confidence seeming undented by his rebuff. He glanced at his watch. Twelve. He could plausibly go and get something to eat, but first he looked in on Sally Mabledon. She was at her desk, typing. Holt was standing by the window. It was the first time McGovern had seen him since before Christmas. Poor Sally Mabledon seemed to do all the work.

'I see you were busy this morning,' commented Holt.

'The girl Irén wanted to talk to me. She's worried about her friend, Andras Ferenczy. He exchanged places with the other boy I saw, Meszarov. Meszarov didn't like staying at Professor Quinault's.'

'Gyorgy is off to Cambridge very soon. As for Irén,' Holt exchanged a look with Sally Mabledon, 'rather attention-seeking, I'm afraid. Got an eye for the men.'

'I see.'

'Andras isn't happy,' conceded Sally Mabledon. 'We know

that. But he can always come back to the hostel. And we're sorting out his situation as fast as we can. He has an uncle in Winnipeg, a priest. He'll be living with him. It's a good university there.'

McGovern hesitated. He was on the point of telling them about Andras' anonymous visitors, but changed his mind. They would not be able to deal with it. He would have to ring London and talk to someone. So he restricted himself to: 'I'm sure you're doing your best.'

The telephone rang. Holt stayed put. Sally Mabledon answered it.

McGovern went in search of lunch. On second thoughts, he wondered if perhaps he should have told them about Andras' visitors, but it would have served little purpose. He needed at least to speak to Andras Ferenczy first. What did the boy do with himself all day? He wasn't at the hostel. Perhaps he just moped about at Quinault's. McGovern knew he'd have to visit Quinault's house again. Or perhaps – whatever the Hungarians believed – the strangers had more to do with Quinault than with either of them.

chapter 30

THE OPPORTUNITY TO CONFRONT Quinault came sooner than expected. McGovern decided to treat himself to lunch at the Mitre, a traditional, old-fashioned inn on the High Street. There he could think in peace. Steak and kidney pudding, followed by apple tart and custard, were welcome. He ordered coffee in the lounge. This, with Persian carpets and deep sofas, was more like a club than a hotel.

It was only as he took a copy of *The Times* from its rack that he noticed Professor Quinault seated by the window with – he assumed – a fellow academic. A piece of luck.

Quinault saw him. He waved – it seemed like a kind of summons.

McGovern walked over. 'How are you, sir?' Quinault made no attempt to introduce his companion.

'I'm glad to see you, McGovern. I was going to get in touch. There was a small matter ... I don't suppose you could come round to my rooms in College? This afternoon? That's extremely kind. Around three o'clock? Very good. I'll see you then.'

McGovern watched Quinault from behind his paper. The coffee arrived. It was elaborately served in a silver pot, but didn't taste any better for it, being both weak and bitter.

The Professor and his companion left together. McGovern stared ahead and tried to decide what to do. He had time to go in search of Andras now, knowing that Quinault was not at home. It was only one-thirty – a quick taxi to the Woodstock Road and back would get him to Corpus Christi by three.

The boy might not be at home. Mrs Quinault might be.

Then there was Andras' English friend. McGovern had forgotten about him, but it was the friend who had talked about the money in Quinault's library.

Why had he mentioned the money? A mischief-maker? His behaviour, when you thought about it, had been outrageous – to riffle through the desk drawers of a distinguished academic who was also his tutor.

It might be worth following up. He was a student at Magdalen College, just down the road.

He paid for his meal, walked down the High Street and found the Magdalen College lodge. The porter was obliging.

'Mr Hallam, sir? Oh no, he doesn't live in college. He's not an undergraduate. He has digs in Park Town. I can give you his address ...'

'Thank you.'

By now it was after two, which didn't give him quite enough time either to search out Mr Hallam or to go looking for Andras Ferenczy, so McGovern loitered past the shop windows on the High Street. Most displayed men's tailoring, college insignia and evening wear, outposts of Jermyn Street. He went to the bank, still killing time until it was reasonable to make for Quinault's college rooms.

Again, he walked round the silent quad and up the worn steps. Again, he stepped into the dim, ancient study and was greeted by the crumpled figure.

'A glass of sherry, I think.'

McGovern raised his hand in refusal.

'I insist. I insist.' The words were accompanied by a suppressed titter. In fact, thought McGovern, Quinault seemed to be sharing a private joke with himself a lot of the time, privy to some amusing knowledge unknown to others.

'So how do your investigations progress?'

'I've not encountered anything suspicious.'

'Is that so? Is that so?' Quinault bent forward and poked the fire. 'My scout doesn't know how to lay a fire properly. Would you believe it? Been doing it all his life and still gets it wrong.' He flung some coal on the faltering flames. Smoke billowed forward.

McGovern coughed. 'How is your particular student? The one you have staying with you.'

'Oh …' Quinault screwed up his face to a look of vague confusion. 'I haven't seen him for some time. He's hardly ever there, it seems. And neither am I.' Again, the sound that was not quite a suppressed giggle. Then his expression changed abruptly. He peered at McGovern. 'Why? Have you any special interest in him? Any reason to suppose that … there's some problem, anything amiss?'

'I just wondered. Well – frankly, I did wonder why you specially asked to have Gyorgy Meszarov billeted on you.'

Quinault, having dealt with the fire, leaned back and looked at his visitor. The silence became uncomfortable, at least to McGovern.

'Your question concerning the Hungarian student is rather impertinent. But I shall answer it. I knew his parents during the war. Did I not tell you already? They were communists, but we found them useful at the time.'

McGovern said: 'Out of friendship to them you thought you should keep an eye on their son. To see what he might be up to. And yet you told me you have nothing to do with … all that any more. In which case it seems odd you asked him so many intrusive questions that he felt he had to get away and sent his friend to stay with you instead.'

Quinault silently stared at him. McGovern found it hard to read his expression in the dim light.

'I invited you here,' said Quinault finally, 'because I was curious to know – I'm out of touch, you understand, I lead a quiet life here, cut off from the great world – my former colleagues don't always keep me informed. Of what's going on.' He giggled again. 'And why should they, you ask. Why indeed!' His voice dropped to an expiring sigh. Another pause. 'I was just interested to know on whose orders you followed me – you remember the occasion? Or whether that was just your own initiative.'

McGovern swallowed. Quinault spoke again.

'You're not going to deny it, I trust.'

McGovern decided he was. 'You're mistaken,' he said. 'Why would I follow you? When was this supposed to have happened?'

'I was not particularly impressed by your skill – or lack of it. I saw you at once. At Paddington I deliberately sat upstairs in the bus, in order to make it easier for you.'

McGovern was angry and nettled, furious with himself for having been spotted by Quinault and with Quinault for taunting him with it. He tried to sound as much in control as he could, but he was seething with humiliation. No matter that targets often knew they were being followed. Quinault wouldn't have been expecting it. 'So your reason for asking me to come here today was to accuse me of following you to London,' he said. 'But what reason would I have to do that?'

Quinault spoke sharply. 'You should be in a position to tell me that, I think. And why should my interest in Gyorgy mean that I still have any connections with the service?'

'The kind of questions you asked Meszarov made him feel very suspicious and uncomfortable.'

Again came Quinault's shrill chuckle. 'Foolish boy. I knew his parents. Perfectly natural to ask after them. Old friends in the war. Only too glad to hear they're flourishing under the new regime,' he added, with what McGovern took to be malevolent irony. 'If the boy didn't like it … having offered hospitality to a student I could hardly refuse a substitute.'

'Wasn't it rather embarrassing?' McGovern stood up. He wanted to get away. He'd lost face, but so had Quinault.

'Not as embarrassing as your lamentable lack of skills as a shadow. And now, if you'll excuse me I have rather a lot of work to do.'

chapter 31

BETTY'S, ON THE HIGH, had until recently been an old-fashioned tea shop. The stick-back chairs and wooden tables remained, but the arrival of the Gaggia machine and Pyrex cups had converted it into a coffee bar. Charles had told Andras he'd be in the upstairs room, but he wondered if Andras would remember that. It might be a better idea to take a seat downstairs and then be sure of seeing the Hungarian when he entered, but he went upstairs anyway, in case Andras had arrived before him, although Charles was early.

At once he saw Penny at a table in the corner. Otherwise the upstairs room was empty.

'Haven't seen you for ages. Not since Julian's party – before Christmas. I was going to get in touch ...'

She smiled. 'I'm very well.' But she looked anxiously beyond him at the stairs.

'I'm meeting a friend,' he said, 'but I'm early.'

'I'm meeting Alistair. But I'm early too.' She laughed the way the girl undergraduates laughed, eager and yet somehow apologetic, as if they didn't quite have the right to be at this ancient university. 'The waitress hasn't been up,' she said.

'I'll go down and get you a coffee,' he offered.

'Oh, thank you. Cappuccino, please.'

Charles returned with the coffees. 'They're not downstairs either,' he said.

'Did you have a nice Christmas?' Penny enquired brightly.

'No, actually. You know my mother died just before Christmas last year. We all tried desperately not to mention it. A ghastly veil was drawn over the subject.'

Penny put a hand to her mouth. He knew he'd embarrassed her and wished he hadn't mentioned his mother.

'Sorry – I'm being boring.'

'No you're not. Christmas can be awfully sad if people ... anyway I think it's a bit overrated, don't you? Christmas, I mean. I was stuck with my family too. I missed Alistair. They kept on asking about him.' She still kept her eye on the stairs.

Charles looked at his watch. By now Andras was late. He might not turn up.

From below came the sound of voices. Penny jumped up. 'I think that might be them. It sounds as though they've decided to sit downstairs. I'll go and see.'

'I'll wait here.'

He was glad Penny had left. He wanted to be on his own when Andras arrived – if he arrived.

On the first day after his return to Oxford Charles had waited outside the Quinault house, lurking on the other side of the road until Andras came out, and then had crossed over to intercept him. It was difficult to know if the Hungarian had been pleased to see him, but they'd started off along the road together and had ended up walking all the way into town. They'd parted by Balliol and Andras had promised to meet Charles here – now – this afternoon.

Charles was beginning to think Andras wouldn't come, but then the Hungarian loomed into view at the top of the stairs. He surged clumsily across the empty café, noisily pushing aside the stick-back chairs in his way. His presence confused Charles. Perhaps he didn't fancy him after all; he was drawn to the sharp planes of the melancholy face shaded by ragged black hair, while at the same time the clumsiness irritated him.

Having moved so roughly across the room, Andras sat down as carefully as a girl.

'You see I am here.'

'I didn't think you wouldn't be,' Charles lied. 'D'you want some coffee? You might have to go back downstairs. The waitress doesn't come up here very often.'

Andras shook his head. 'Not matter.' He pulled out a packet of cigarettes.

'What have you been up to?'

'Up to?'

'Doing – what have you been doing since I saw you?'

Andras smoked. He coughed. He rubbed his hand over his face. He looked round at the nearly empty room. Finally he said: 'Something happen.' He glanced sideways at Charles. His eyes were dark and pained.

'What d'you mean? What sort of thing?'

'Two men. They come to see me.' Haltingly, he described the visitors. 'They asked me questions – about my friends. About my family in Hungary. And about other Hungarian students here. Was very difficult.'

'What sort of questions?'

'Just – informations.'

'Like the policeman who was in the house – at the Professor's?'

'Yes … no. They spoke very good English. Perfect English. But I am sure were Hungarian … I was more frightened. There are two of them. And they say if I not have these informations they will – I don't know what they will do. Something.'

'They threatened you?'

Andras nodded.

A rather unexpected wave of concern washed through Charles, a physical sensation that was a kind of dread, as though he himself were threatened.

Charles put a hand on the Hungarian's arm. 'I'm sorry. What are you going to do? Have you told the police?'

Andras shook his head. 'No – no,' he muttered.

'But ...' Then Charles remembered that Andras had been living in a police state. 'Is there someone at the hostel you could talk to?'

Andras huddled into his jacket.

'Look – there must be someone. Gyorgy – your friend at the hostel.'

Andras lifted his hand as if to ward off a threat. He sighed deeply. 'I think they think I *am* Gyorgy. Is Gyorgy was to stay there at the beginning. I not say who I really am.'

'Then you shouldn't be so scared, if it wasn't you they really wanted. But you ought to tell him, oughtn't you?'

Andras shook his head. 'No. It is – the way they talk – they think I am Gyorgy and perhaps think Gyorgy is *on their side* ... is hard to explain. I have say to Irén and Gyorgy about the men, but not – not the way it seemed they think Gyorgy – the way there is something not right, that ... I can't explain.' Andras screwed out his cigarette barely smoked.

'You don't mean you're suspicious of Gyorgy?'

'Yes. No. I don't know.' Andras looked utterly miserable. 'I don't really think that. I trust him. And yet ...' His voice trailed away. He was holding back tears.

Charles squirmed with a mixture of embarrassment, worry and powerlessness. 'God, I'm sorry.' But how incredibly feeble that sounded. 'You know, you really should tell the people at the hostel.'

Andras shook his head, but didn't answer. After a silence that Charles forced himself not to break, the Hungarian said: 'I can't go back now.'

'To *Budapest*?'

'To Professor's house.'

'Ah.' Charles felt slightly sick. 'You could come back to my place,' he said carelessly.

'There was that other policeman who came. You remember? Who was he?'

'Do you mean – you think he was connected with the two men?'

Andras shrugged.

'Christ – I'd forgotten all about him. He asked for my address. You know, I'd *completely* forgotten. But I just gave him the name of my college.' Charles put his hand on Andras' shoulder. 'You're not worried, are you ...?'

'I should be worried I think.'

'*He* wasn't Hungarian, he was English – well, Scottish, actually. He was interested in the Professor, not you.'

'But that is also ... I don't like that. Let us walk. I must think ...' He stood up, scraping his chair back roughly.

Charles followed Andras downstairs. The lower room, deserted earlier, had filled up and as he edged his way between tables he saw Penny and Alistair with Julian and two others at a corner table. Penny waved.

'Wait a minute – Andras – some friends of mine ...'

He worried he'd lose Andras if he loitered, but he couldn't resist the glamour of being seen in the company of a Hungarian. And in fact Andras followed him meekly enough.

So chairs were moved to make room for them in the circle of four men with Penny and a second girl, whom Charles recognised immediately as Venetia Templeton, a current Oxford star: one of those girls who got written about in *Isis* and *Cherwell*, the student mags, especially after she'd starred in a student production of *The Tempest*. He introduced Andras and the interest level rose exponentially. Andras, too, seemed lifted out of his withdrawal by their interest. One of the men began to question him about the uprising. Alistair fetched more coffees.

Charles watched the girl who wasn't Penny. Venetia

Templeton was small and neat and precise. Unlike Penny, she had hair beautifully cut in a russet bob, an almost 1920s look. She wore jeans and a black cashmere sweater and no make-up. Very French. For her part she mostly listened to the men's intense conversation, her head slightly on one side like a bird, her delicate eyebrows sometimes raised in amusement, her dusty pink lips on the verge of smiling, but from time to time she made a remark that they all found very witty, although really it was the way she spoke, her green eyes and sprightly manner. She was not flirtatious and yet something about the way she sat there compelled them to focus on her, in spite of the distraction of Andras, as if they were interested in her reactions to Andras more than in Andras himself. Alistair seemed particularly smitten. Penny was valiantly trying to keep her end up, smiling and laughing with the men, but she looked uncomfortable.

Charles wondered how he could ever have been attracted to Alistair, who was certainly good-looking in an ever so English way, clean-jawed with short curly hair and blue eyes, but Andras was so much more interesting.

'Shall we go?' he muttered. Andras nodded.

Outside in the dark Andras just stood there as though he did not know what to do next.

'Have you got a bike?'

'No.'

'I'll leave mine here then. The one I left at your place disappeared, but I've got another one now.' Charles steered his companion across the road as purposefully as he could past the Camera and in the general direction of Park Town. There was bustle in the twilight of the late afternoon as students wheeled home from lectures and tutorials to prepare for whatever lay ahead in the evening.

The house in Park Town belonged to the widow of a Professor, but she didn't behave like a widow. She was quite young – years younger than the Professor, he'd been told – and seemed to have several gentleman friends. She did tutoring for St Anne's College, but seemed uninterested in either a career or children.

This was the first time in the four months he'd lived there that Charles had brought someone home. He didn't think Mrs Hewitt was the sort of person who would mind and perhaps she wouldn't draw any conclusions. She might not even notice. Nevertheless, he was relieved to find the house in darkness.

Charles' bed-sitting room was icy cold. In the glare of the overhead light it looked forbidding, but once he'd lit the gas fire and turned on the floor lamp and the reading lamp on the desk it felt more welcoming. Charles set the kettle on the gas ring, which was in a cupboard by the chimneypiece. 'Coffee?'

Andras stood by the door. He had the look of a man who has slept for twenty years and then woken to find himself in utterly unfamiliar surroundings.

'Or would you like something stronger? I've some whisky somewhere.'

Andras moved trance-like towards the linen-covered divan and sank onto it.

'I think whisky, don't you?' said Charles. 'Give me your coat. The room's warming up now.'

Andras did as he was told. Handed a glass of whisky, he drank. He stared up at Charles, who was standing in front of him. He looked angry, the mood seemed unpropitious, yet Charles knew this *was* the moment, and he was adept at seizing the moment. He knelt down between Andras' legs, moved his hands hypnotically up the hard thighs and then upwards to his waist. He undid the button at the waist of Andras' trousers, conscious of the rough, grey cloth. The tranced passivity of this stranger excited him. He would wake the sleeping animal, provoking it to violence.

It worked. The Hungarian's hands on Charles' head forced him roughly downwards.

~

Charles woke up. It was pitch dark. He was lying on the floor. The cold must have woken him. It must be the middle of the night. Andras snored on the bed. Charles ached all over. He hadn't bargained for quite such clumsy desperation, it had come out of the blue, as if Andras was fighting against his own desire and was angry with Charles for arousing it. If that was totalitarian sex, no wonder Andras wanted to get away.

It seemed important to know what time it was, but Charles had no idea where his watch was. He didn't remember getting undressed. It seemed even more important to have a piss. He got up painfully. He had no dressing gown so he put on his coat to go to the bathroom on the next floor down, tiptoeing in order not to wake Mrs Hewitt. He washed himself. He looked at himself in the mirror. His lip was swollen where Andras had bitten him. He managed a smile. 'You've only yourself to blame, dearie.'

He climbed the stairs, clinging to the rickety banister, and stumbled back into his room. The eiderdown had slid to the floor. Charles wrapped himself in it and his coat and settled down in the easy chair.

Hours later, he woke again. Daylight seeped through the curtains. He forced himself out of his cocoon to light the gas fire. He shivered, his fingers clumsy with the matches. He crouched near the hissing tongues of flame until his skin began to burn. He gathered up yesterday's clothes, which were strewn around the floor, and put them on again. He returned to the bathroom, washed his face and shaved in an effort to look more respectable and minimise the swollen lip.

He made coffee in an elaborate glass percolator constructed

of two balloon glasses connected by a glass pipe, a cherished item purchased in Paris on his first – and only – visit, before his first year at Oxford. The fragile parcel had been brought home with difficulty and every time he used it, which was often, he wondered if it had been worth the effort.

While it was brewing he went out in search of milk. The frosty air revived him. He began to think of the encounter in a more satirical light, working it into an irony-laden anecdote with which to entertain Fergus. At the corner shop he bought *The Times* and some sticky buns along with the milk.

Andras was pulling on his trousers in the twilit room. Charles opened the curtains.

'Good morning.' He kissed Andras lightly on the cheek.

Andras didn't respond. 'I have drink too much.' He rubbed his face with his hands.

'We didn't drink much, did we?' Charles didn't remember anything about drinking and at the moment didn't think he had a hangover. But there was the empty whisky bottle on the floor. It had been nearly full. So he'd probably feel terrible later. Unless Andras had drunk the lot.

'I go,' said Andras. His voice was hoarse. But he accepted a cup of coffee. 'Why we did this? Was wrong.'

'What d'you mean, wrong?' Charles stared at him. He made no attempt to touch him, instead returned to the armchair and waited for more.

'I go back to Professor house now.'

'You're not worried about the police any more?'

'It looks strange I not go back.'

'That's true. But you said you couldn't go back.'

Andras was hunched over his coffee cup and saucer, which he held uncomfortably between his knees. 'I have to go.'

'I'm sorry. I didn't mean to make things worse.'

Now Andras placed the cup and saucer on the floor. He looked up, looked at Charles for the first time as if he actually saw him. 'Things are a mess. I am not ... my ...'

'Why did you say it's wrong? Is it forbidden in Hungary?'

'No ... yes ...' Andras smiled. 'It is not legal here, I think, but people do it – in Hungary is more dangerous, even if is not exactly illegal.'

'It's quite risky here.'

'I am Roman Catholic. '

'*Catholic*?' This disturbed Charles far more than if Andras had confessed to being, after all, a paid-up communist.

'You have heard of Cardinal Mindszenty?'

'Vaguely.'

'He was found guilty of treason because he opposed the communists. I am not really good Catholic, but it is a question of freedom, political question.'

Charles suddenly felt immensely tired. His life was at such a great distance from this man.

'Charles – perhaps you can help me, tell me what I should do.'

'I think you have to tell the people at the hostel. Or go to the police. The police here are not like in Hungary. Or get hold of the detective who came to the house.'

The events of the night felt more and more unreal. All remnants, even all memory, of lust had disappeared as if their violent contortions had been a dream. Now Charles felt only pity, and he hated to pity people. Pity was a huge turn-off. He much preferred the strong, unemotional types.

'Perhaps I can stay here with you – for a time.'

Yesterday Charles would have welcomed that, but now it was the last thing he wanted. Anyway, it was impossible. He doubted if Mrs Hewitt, however easy-going, would welcome an extra lodger.

'Or is better if I go to London. There no-one will find me. For that I need money. Perhaps you could lend me—'

Charles laughed, but he was beginning to feel angry. This

was ridiculous. One minute Andras was moving in, the next he wanted to be paid for sex. Of course, it wasn't like that, but Charles, bruised and stiff, suddenly wished Andras would just go away. It was all too much.

'Look,' he said, 'I have to go out now. You can stay here for the time being if you want, or go back to Quinault's. Either way, I'll meet you ... where ...? I'll meet you in Blackwell's bookshop in the Broad. Broad Street. You know where that is? It's less conspicuous than the Cadena or Betty's,' although as he spoke, he wondered why that should matter. 'I'll meet you in the classics department. Say, at four. And you can tell me what you want me to do – how I can help you, if I can. But for now, you *have* to go up to the hostel and tell them what happened. They'll help you. They'll find somewhere else for you to stay.'

He ruffled Andras' hair with a carelessness he didn't feel. Andras looked up at him for a moment. He gripped Charles' arm. 'I'm sorry.'

'There's nothing to be sorry for,' said Charles. 'Remember – Blackwell's, the classics department. Four o'clock.' Then he gathered up his books and notes and left, feeling quite urgently now the need to get away.

chapter 32

BODKIN ADAMS WAS COMMITTED for trial. Blackstone would be back in Eastbourne in the coming weeks to scavenge for more lurid information about the doctor. Now, though, he could concentrate on Valerie.

His meetings with Jarrell at the Queen's Head had become a regular event. On this particular Monday lunchtime it was Blackstone who was late after an evening's heavy drinking in Fleet Street. McGovern, as well as Jarrell, awaited him.

They shook hands. 'The Bodkin Adams trial will go ahead, then,' commented McGovern.

'His lawyers were hoping it wouldn't.'

'A lot more than meets the eye, I'd say,' said McGovern.

'We've only heard the beginning. Thank Christ I can forget about it for a bit. Depressing, that's what it is. Gullible, lonely old women with too much money and no reason for living and that slimy doctor. And Oxford? You finished with that yet?'

'Not exactly.'

'You know you followed your Professor to that mansion block in Bayswater?' said Blackstone.

McGovern nodded.

'Well, I know Balmoral Mansions well. There's a woman lives there, she runs a kind of call-girl racket – that's not what she calls it, but ... I knew Valerie worked for her at one time. When you said your Professor went to the second floor, I wondered. *Her* flat's on the second floor. Before I said anything to you I wanted to check on the other flat on that floor. That could have been the one your bloke was making for. But it's untenanted at the moment. So I reckon it was Sonia's flat—'

'Well,' interrupted McGovern, 'you don't know for sure no-one's there. It may be officially empty, but in use for some purpose or other. Are you thinking of espionage? It's possible it could even be a safe house. However, for that sort of purpose there'd normally be a cover story. An officially empty flat where people came and went would be too suspicious.'

'This woman has a wide variety of clients. Well-known names. You know the sort of thing. She's given me useful information from time to time and it's occurred to me blackmail could be a nice little sideline for her. Don't know why the penny didn't drop sooner. Obviously, it'd have to be done carefully, I mean she wouldn't want to upset her regular customers. But – I thought that could be the reason your Professor had all that money. He was paying her off.'

McGovern appeared to consider it. 'That's a nice wee theory, but it was *too much* money. Unless Quinault has some monster of a secret, it's just too much.'

'An appalling secret, such as being a Soviet spy,' insinuated Blackstone.

'Surely even a blackmailing madam would report that to the authorities,' protested Jarrell.

'You never know. She might prefer to keep it to herself. For future use,' said McGovern. 'Anyway, it's a strange coincidence. I'm interested. The possibilities are – well – interesting. I'll think about it.'

Blackstone watched McGovern and could see he was a bit stunned. 'I thought you'd be interested,' he said craftily. 'Because it creates a link – not a strong one, it's true, but a link all the same – between what you're up to in Oxford and the Argyle Street hotel business.'

'How so?' McGovern stared blankly at him.

'The woman I mentioned is married to Vince Mallory. And Valerie worked for him. And it's beginning to seem as if Mallory might be behind what happened.'

McGovern didn't show it, but Blackstone knew he was interested. He'd seen that withdrawn expression on his face before. It meant he was thinking.

'I have a proposition. An evening out, the three of us, with the womenfolk. A night on the town. At Vince Mallory's smart club in Soho. Don't look so surprised. I told you the girl was working for him there before she died. She'd taken a step up in the world – well, in that world.'

Jarrell jumped at the proposal. 'Observe him on his own terrain.'

'You've already done that,' said McGovern. 'You went to see him at the club.' He lit a cigarette. Blackstone had noticed he smoked only moderately and usually when at a loss for words, or when he was thinking about something. Eventually he said: 'It's not the kind of thing my wife would enjoy.'

'Sweet-talk her. Glamorous night out. Up the West End.'

'You don't know her, Blackstone.' McGovern smiled.

'Explore the terrain. Observe. You know what I'm talking about. We'll get a feel of what's going on. Talk to some of the girls, possibly. Look, I went down to Eastbourne. I poked around. Found out far more than I would have sitting up here in London.'

'That's different.'

'It's a good idea, sir,' said Jarrell. 'Come on. It can't do any harm. If your wife doesn't fancy it – well, you'll be off the leash.'

McGovern shrugged. 'You're right. It could be useful.' He didn't sound convinced.

They met in the bar of the Regent Palace Hotel. There was the usual slight awkwardness at the start of such an evening: a group of work colleagues gathered for a social occasion. The men squared their shoulders, smoked and tried to look at ease. The women had never even met before, yet were expected to chat to one another – about children, domestic matters, possibly holidays, as if there were nothing more, as if they existed only in relation to the men who had brought them along, with pride or resignation as the case might be.

The three women this evening did not fit the stereotype. Jarrell's fiancée, Anita, was a fierce-looking brunette, bright and confident, Blackstone thought. She was a solicitor's clerk, she told him, with ambitions to become a solicitor herself. Well, that was something: an ambitious woman and, while you couldn't call her beautiful, she was at least striking-looking. It surprised him that that scarecrow Jarrell had landed a bird like that. He'd assumed she'd be a mousy little thing, like so many policemen's wives. Then there was the lovely Lily McGovern. Thought highly of herself, she did, but Blackstone suspected her air of gracious reserve was in part the result of being half-Indian in a family of wealthy white Scots; a bit of a misfit. Her mother had run off with an Indian – that was the story, Blackstone had heard. So Lily's head, held proudly on her beautiful long neck, had a touch of defiance about it.

Rita, of course, was different; Rita, the little Irish girl from Golborne Road, who spent her life looking after Dr Jones and being shouted at by his son.

That Mr Blackstone – Gerry now – should have invited her out at all was extraordinary, Rita felt. He'd simply turned up on the doorstep. As she discovered later, he'd heard that Carl was inside again – got it from Sonny Marsden, he told her. The cheek of it! The minute Carl's back was turned! Mind you, she was glad they'd banged him up. She wouldn't be staying with Carl at all if it wasn't for Dr Jones. She was worried about him. She couldn't leave him. Carl cared bugger all about his dad, but someone had to look after the old man.

Doubts about Blackstone's motives weren't going to stop her enjoying herself this evening. You look lovely, Gerry had said when she opened the door to him. Her friend had got her a deep green satin dress – second-hand, but good as new. Expensive, it was, properly lined with silk and ever so soft to the touch. You know one or two of the girls at the club, don't you, sweetheart, Gerry had said. Be good to have a chat with them if you get half a chance. They'd be dancers and that, though, so it wasn't very likely. But she'd give it a go. And whatever happened, she was determined to have a great old evening. It wasn't often she got a chance to go up west.

To McGovern's amazement, Lily had been enthusiastic. 'Let's see how the other half lives. We're too serious, don't you think? I'd like to have a bit of vulgar fun for a change.'

In dark red velvet she looked lovelier than he'd ever seen her. 'I'm so proud of you,' he'd murmured and kissed her.

'Are you?' There was a wistful note to her reply.

After a round of drinks the party walked off into Soho. Vince Mallory's club was a garish break in the shabby Frith Street façade. Red neon snaked the name across the front: 'The Ambassadors'. Life-size photographs of women dressed in nothing but ostrich feathers flanked the door. The red-carpeted foyer glittered with mirrors to create an illusion of space. The new arrivals had their coats lifted from them and placed behind the counter by a girl in a black waistcoat and no trousers. The music sounded faintly up here, but as they descended the brightly lit stairs it swelled pleasantly, bearing them towards the cabaret in waves of syncopated sweetness: strings rather than big brass or jazz, with a little breath of romance in the hothouse atmosphere.

Rita clasped Blackstone's arm and smiled up at him. The lipstick printed against her rosy face was too harsh for his taste, but the black round her blue eyes was perfect, creating a suggestive shadow that softened and saddened them.

'You're a lovely girl, d'you know that?'

'Don't be silly.' But he knew she was pleased. She was already so obviously enjoying herself. He wished he were young and open like her. Then things would be so simple.

They were shown to a good table, not too near the band. They had a clear view of their fellow guests and of the raised performance space and the dance floor. A waiter brought bowls of crisps, cheese straws and cubes of cheese and pineapple on toothpicks. Champagne foamed from the bottle.

'This is on me, remember. Or rather, on the *Chronicle*.' Blackstone had made that clear from the start. 'Now let's spot some celebrities.'

Lily raised her glass. 'Thank you, Gerry.' She drank, then turned to her husband. 'Let's dance.'

McGovern made a token protest, but followed her readily enough. They joined the half-dozen other couples that circled sedately round the piste. Blackstone watched them. McGovern's dancing was minimalist, but smooth, and he and Lily moved together in sinuous harmony. You could tell, thought Blackstone, from the way a couple danced, how well they were suited, in bed and in life. If the way McGovern and Lily danced was anything to go by, theirs should be a marriage made in heaven. She was a beautiful woman. The pile of hair on top of her head and the red dress that glided against her body set off her pale skin wonderfully. You'd never have guessed she was half-Indian.

McGovern and Lily sat down again. The troupe of dancers, all long legs and sequins, pranced onto the stage and performed a slick routine to a scattering of applause. They were followed by a crooner, who was little more than a poor replica of Elvis

Presley, but Blackstone didn't mind. He was looking for well-known faces. You never knew when gossip might come in useful.

Rita watched in total absorption. He whispered to her: 'After this – go to the ladies and then see if you can get backstage and talk to some of the girls. You might know some of them, mightn't you?'

'I don't know about that. And what am I to be asking?'

'I told you. Ask after a girl called Valerie.'

'Your long-lost love, is it? The one like Marilyn Monroe?' She was half teasing him, half annoyed. However, at the next intermission, she obediently disappeared behind the scenes.

It was only when he looked around, now the music had given way to a buzz of talk, that Blackstone noticed the table at the opposite side of the room to theirs. It was Mallory's table, must be, for there was Mallory himself. Blackstone hadn't noticed him before. He must have only just entered. Two women and a man had seated themselves with the club owner. Blackstone recognised Stanley Coleman, the property developer, and a dark, striking woman. The second woman was Sonia.

That was a surprise. Sonia was rarely seen in the company of her husband. That she was here now underlined the importance of Mallory's guest. Stanley Coleman in cahoots with Mallory, the boxing promoter and strip-club owner: that was really something. The property tycoon had made a fortune post-war, of course, he was one of the richest men in Britain. There'd never been any suggestion it wasn't all above board, but he'd have to have a long spoon to sup with Mallory.

As Blackstone watched, Mallory rose. He was an imposing man, his wide chest filling out his mohair suit, his thick hair plastered back, effeminately long, yet strictly controlled. He edged round his table and now was walking straight over in Blackstone's direction, his hand outstretched well before he reached them.

'I heard you were expected this evening. Good to see you here. How d'you like the place?'

Blackstone struggled to his feet. 'I'm impressed. Very successful ...'

He introduced his companions without their official titles. They were just Mr and Mrs McGovern and Mr Jarrell and Miss Finch. Mallory's gaze swept over them and fixed on Jarrell. His smile was hard as nails. It was a smile that had atrophied onto his face, a smile for all occasions, the same smile for greeting an old friend or for watching an enemy knocked to a pulp, for chatting up a rent boy or for kicking out an informer.

Mallory stayed to talk, without sitting down. Then: 'Champagne's on the house,' he said, and he turned away with a parting salute. Blackstone watched him as he returned to his own party, slipping gracefully between the tables, so delicately and fastidiously for such a large man.

'You know him, then?'

'I thought I told you – when I worked in the East End.'

'He knew who we were,' commented Jarrell. 'He recognised me, anyway.'

'That's hardly surprising,' said Anita Finch. 'It was only last week you paid him a visit.'

Lily looked anxiously at her husband. 'It doesn't matter you being seen here?'

Blackstone leaned forward. 'Everyone comes here. MPs, government ministers, famous actors, film stars, the lot. Look, there's Gilbert Harding over there.' He nodded his head in the direction of the TV personality.

McGovern wasn't listening. He was staring across at the promoter's table. 'Who's the woman sitting next to him?'

'Why?' Blackstone scrutinised his companion, who looked as if he'd seen a ghost. 'She's his wife.' He lowered his voice. 'She's also the woman I told you about – the one who was visited by your Oxford prof.'

McGovern stared. Sonia was talking to the man Blackstone had identified as Stanley Coleman.

'Excuse me a moment.' McGovern stood up. His movement was clumsy and he almost knocked over a chair. Sonia, distracted from her conversation, turned to look. Then she also stood up, appeared to excuse herself and glided from the room. McGovern watched her departure. He slowly turned and sat down again.

'What's the matter, darling?' Lily's smile was teasing. 'You look so serious suddenly.'

'I recognised her.'

chapter 33

WILLIAM DROWNES HAD CAUGHT sight of his wife talking to Turbeville in the garden at the New Year party. He'd had an uneasy feeling about Regine for several months and because of something about the way the two of them stood facing each other, suspicion at that moment became certainty. His wife was unfaithful. He minded desperately. He'd never thought of himself as a jealous man, but then he'd never had reason to be jealous. Now he was astonished by how painful it was. A torrent of different disagreeable feelings tormented him. He was shocked, angry, wounded and disgusted by her disloyalty and her careless indifference as to how it would look. It reflected not just on him, but on Drownes'. She had let the side down.

In the following days he came to suspect that Edith Blake knew too. Now poor slighted, sidelined Edith became his ally. Nothing was said. Nor had William any thought of confrontation, much less divorce. Quite apart from the firm, there were the twins to consider. Most painful of all, he still loved Regine. He wanted not to love her any more, but he found himself incapable of disengaging himself from all the habits of admiration, affection and even awe built up over the past six years.

The liaison, however, as Edith Blake subtly hinted, could be turned to good effect. Surely Mrs Drownes' friendship with the

MP could be used to persuade him to complete his biography of Benjamin Disraeli, Victorian Prime Minister, one-nation conservative, Queen Victoria's favourite. Everyone knew he'd been working on it for three years. Now that he was a minister he had less time, of course, but surely Mrs Drownes was capable of deploying her charm. It would be the book of the year; and quite apart from the book, to land an author who was also in the government was a catch in itself. And with Sir Avery's money, they could afford to make a splash. Drownes' had big ideas for 1957.

More surprising than Regine's behaviour was that of Lady Pearson, the other Edith. William was both alarmed and flattered when she hinted that a closer relationship would be welcome. He desperately hoped he could make his wife jealous. But if Reggie noticed, she showed no sign.

'I need to talk to you.' There was urgency in Rodney's voice.

This time they were not to meet at his flat or at 'their' restaurant. They were apparently not to make love at all. They met at Kew Gardens on a sad, cold February afternoon. They dropped their pennies in the slot and walked through the turnstile. Turbeville pulled his hat down and thrust her arm through his. Then he changed his mind and his arm went round her waist.

'You know I'm mad about you, don't you?'

Regine ducked her face away so that he did not see her sad little smile. They walked at a stately pace, despite the cold, along the broad avenue. They seemed to be entirely on their own. The gardens were deserted.

'Couldn't wait to see you. Wish it could have been sooner – but now I'm at Transport ... I'd have happily stayed at the Home Office, y'know. The Hungarian chaps deserve all we can do for them. I really felt I was doing some good there. I told Harold. Begged him to let me stay. But you know how it is – new top chap has to make his mark on his cabinet – obligatory reshuffle …'

'Will he make a good prime minister?'

'Couldn't be worse than Eden, I tell you that much – anyway, this bloody Oxford road scheme. You would not believe the viciousness – some of those old dons – have they got the knives out! I'm only surprised there hasn't been a murder. And your friend, Quinault, he's one of the worst.'

'My friend, darling? I thought he was *your* friend. You said you thought the world of him.'

'Thought the world of him? Did I say that? Well … he's a clever old bastard. Involved in all sorts of hush-hush stuff in the war, you know. The trouble is, like a lot of them, he's a bit too clever by half. He's ruthless, too. For some reason I don't entirely understand, he was absolutely gung-ho to get the relief road running through Christ Church Meadow.'

'That lovely meadow …?'

'Well, something has to be done about the traffic. Magdalen Bridge is practically impassable at all times of day. And the Littlemore link road is a big question mark too. Years of indecision. For every scheme there's some vested interests against it. One of the colleges always has an objection. To cut through the Meadow would be in many ways the best solution. Cut the Gordian knot, you know. But it's bloody controversial. Raise a lot of hackles, and … I sometimes think Quinault's so keen on it just to do down some enemy or other. The politics of it all is absolutely – Machiavelli's hair would have stood on end. Labyrinthine. The Vatican couldn't do better – or do I mean worse? Quinault's been on and on at me about it. Old reptile. I wish I knew why the road's so important to him. He's a bit too keen on interfering with the Hungarian arrivals, too. I mentioned it to Duncan—'

'Duncan?'

'You know, sweetie, my replacement at the H.O. *He* doesn't give a toss about the refugees. Cold fish, if ever there was one. And not one to risk crossing MI5 if there's anything going on there.' Unexpectedly, he laughed. 'But anyway, I have some news for Quinault about Christ Church Meadow. Christ Church just withdrew consent. It was so simple in the end. The Gordian knot cut after all. The meadow belongs to them and they just weren't having it.'

'That must be a relief.' She looked up at him. 'Does that mean you'll have more time? You know Drownes' is terribly keen on the Disraeli biography. William would absolutely love to publish it. You do know that?'

'More time? I doubt it. The Oxford road scheme was the least of my worries – well, not exactly, but as soon as one thing's sorted out something else comes along. That's politics. Building a better Britain! Trouble is, the boat's holed beneath the water line. Britain, the great post-imperialist nation! More like the *Titanic* in slow motion.'

Reggie didn't think this was what Rodney had met her to discuss.

'The thing is, Reggie, there's a hell of a lot of pressure on at the moment ...'

Now she was alarmed. She huddled into her violet coat. To feel cold was to feel unloved. Untended. She needed attention. She could only flower when a lover's attention beamed on her, opening her petals, exposing her heart.

'It's a wonderful subject,' she said obstinately. 'Surely the Prime Minister has the same ideals – a one-nation Tory – it's a book for the times ...'

Perhaps she'd said the wrong thing, for Turbeville's laugh sounded an impatient note. 'Oh, Macmillan's a wily old fox. Don't be taken in by the performance. He can out-act Laurence Olivier any day.'

They walked on. Where paths crossed, Turbeville stopped. 'Isn't there a tea room somewhere? Over there?'

As they walked in the direction of the Orangery, Turbeville conceded: 'Well, it would be good to get it finished. You're right. It is timely. Good old Dizzy.' Silence.

It wasn't until they were settled opposite each other at a spindly tea table, that he continued: 'Lettice thinks I don't spend enough time with her and the kids.'

So it was what she had feared. He wanted to end it. Reggie braced herself.

'She must know you have to be in the House and that as a minister your work is relentless,' she said calmly. 'She comes from a political family, after all. And there's your constituency.'

'The thing is – I've been meaning to talk to you about this for ages, but it's so – so humiliating. You see, I've not always, well, I think I told you a bit about my – you know, colourful past. Things haven't always been easy with Lettice. All her back problems – and the pregnancies. And of course she's utterly conventional. In a way ...' and now he was almost talking to himself, the words were familiar. If she hadn't heard them herself at first hand, she had friends who had and there was nothing new, after all. He'd just wring his hands for a bit and then everything would go on as usual. Either that or – but she couldn't bear the alternative.

Turbeville continued to talk in an undertone. 'She's conventional so she expects me to have mistresses, that's how men are ... and so forth ...'

Regine said quickly: 'I do understand. If you think we should see less of each other for a while, I'd perfectly see – I know how difficult it is ...' Reggie knew how to save face, although this was only an opening gambit.

Turbeville gripped her hand across the table. 'That's not what I want. It's not that straightforward. You and me – that's one thing. But before I met you there were times ... when I was still gambling a lot, you know, I got in with a crowd who – well, there were parties. There was this woman who organised parties – there'd be lots of girls – now it turns out someone took photographs ... the fact is, I'm being blackmailed.'

chapter 34

BLACKWELL'S BOOKSHOP SPREAD through a warren of low-ceilinged rooms. Charles loitered at the tables where new books were set out, but made sure to reach the classics section well before 4 p.m. He was again deliberately early so as to exclude the possibility of a misunderstanding about the time. He half suspected – and more than half hoped – Andras wouldn't turn up. He didn't look forward to seeing him again after the night they'd spent together, so clumsy both physically and emotionally. He didn't want the responsibility of the Hungarian's distress. He didn't want to feel guilty. He didn't want to feel sorry for Andras. For Charles, pity was always messily mixed up with contempt. He felt responsible for Andras, felt he had some sort of obligation to help, but at the same time he knew there was little he could do. And that made him feel impotent and angry.

So he arrived early. Then, should Andras fail to keep the appointment, Charles could not blame his own lateness. He would know then that the Hungarian had decided not to see him and he would not need to feel guilty. He'd be able to tell himself he'd done what he could.

He waited, and while he did so, continued to prowl the bookshelves. The very situation of being in a bookshop offered infinite possibilities. Each volume opened a door and beckoned him along a different path. He bought books lavishly, but too often they then lay unread or merely dipped into, and instead of providing nourishment the end effect was like eating too many sweets from a box of chocolates.

He wandered up and down the shelves. He became immersed in a new translation of Juvenal, his favourite classical author. The next time he looked at his watch he saw that it was twenty to five. Andras was forty minutes late; he wasn't coming. Now that his half-wish had been granted, Charles was – contrarily – disturbed and even disappointed. Andras had been agitated. Something might have happened to him. He might have fled to London to escape the strangers who had tracked him down and started to ask questions. The mysterious visitors could even have kidnapped him. Or, as a Catholic, he might have found refuge in one of the many religious foundations in the city. He might even have *confessed*. That could get Charles into trouble.

Even to think of the Catholic dimension unnerved and irritated Charles. Only an idiot could go on practising a religion that went against your every normal and natural desire. Charles hated the Christianity that saturated the university. Religiosity swamped the place from every direction. He'd even encountered a Jesuit who'd tried to seduce him on the grounds that sodomy was only a little sin of the body. The hypocrisy of it was both disgusting and comical.

He wished he could forget Andras, but he couldn't, because he knew that Andras had been genuinely frightened. It was real – it wasn't like his own life, sliding idly along from one indifferent experience to the next. Andras was skating on very thin ice. He might actually have fallen through into the freezing water beneath.

Yet realistically, there was absolutely nothing Charles could do. He considered going round to the Quinault residence, but that would never do. He could bike up the hill to the hostel at Headington to see if Andras was there. But Andras disliked the hostel and anyway, the moral and physical effort demanded was beyond Charles in his present mood. The flu he'd thought he was sickening for before hadn't materialised, but now he felt he might be getting it after all.

The most likely explanation was that Andras simply did not want to see Charles again. The whole thing had been a mess, an experiment neither wanted to repeat. You could hardly blame Andras. Charles felt exactly the same.

Partly relieved, Charles was at the same time annoyed to now be at a loose end with no plans for the evening. He decided to pay a call on Fergus Berriman on the off-chance. His friend's digs were near his own, so he wouldn't have gone much out of his way if Fergus was out.

Fergus was at home. He was by himself and was toasting crumpets in front of the gas fire.

'I'm glad you dropped round.'

'Haven't seen you for ages.'

There was a lot to discuss. The topics hardly varied: the Communist Party, the Hungarians, Harold Macmillan, Suez and – a new and dramatic piece of gossip – the three Oxford students who had run away to join the Hungarian revolution. One was the granddaughter of a senior Labour Party figure.

Charles envied them. He'd have liked to cut a dash in a similar dramatic and glamorous way.

'You're too lazy to do anything like that. It's hard work being a militant. But in my view the three of them are just adventurists. They've romanticised the uprising. It is a counter-revolution ...'

'You're talking as if you're still in the CP.'

'No I'm not! Mind you, I'm not sure it was the right thing to do, leave I mean ... but anyway, two wrongs don't make a right. The Soviet intervention was wrong, misguided, a bad error, but the uprising was doomed from the start and you can bet the CIA was in there somewhere.'

Charles feared Fergus was about to embark on a lengthy investigation both of the strategic failures of the uprising and of his own conscience. To see off this possibility he said quickly: 'I met up with those Hungarians again. The ones I talked to before Christmas. You know, at that meeting.'

Fergus took no notice. 'To get a perspective on the Party – now that I've left – I've embarked on a novel about it. One can't understand the deformations of revolutionary consciousness without an analysis of the unconscious motivations underlying action.'

'God! Are you going to go all Freudian now? Doesn't sound like a bestseller to me, with all those long words. Shouldn't you actually *meet* some of the refugees? I got off with one of them if you want to know. I can introduce you if you like. I know a lot more about totalitarian bloody consciousness after one night than you'd find out in a lifetime. He could tell you quite a lot about deformations of consciousness.'

'Sex as the royal road to knowledge. Also very Freudian.'

'He's a tortured Catholic. He's billeted with Quinault.'

'That would be enough to make anyone tortured.'

'He said some sinister Hungarians came round to see him.'

'What?' Fergus stared at him. 'What d'you mean?'

'These men came round. Andras was terrified. I think he may have … I dunno, run away somewhere.'

'The attentions of the police are a perennial hazard for revolutionaries.'

'Don't be so bloody pompous.' Berriman's highfalutin words jolted Charles into beginning to feel once more rather alarmed for Andras. It was hardly a matter for jokes or irony. 'Well, no, actually that's a really *frivolous* remark. You're always accusing me of being frivolous, but—'

'You're right. Sorry. That is a bit sinister.'

'He might really be in danger. But I couldn't persuade him

to go to the police or tell the welfare people. And when I was there with him – at Quinault's house – another policeman turned up on the doorstep. I think he was some kind of detective, pretending to be a welfare officer. Said he wanted to talk to Quinault as well as Andras.'

'How very odd. Mind you, Quinault's a thoroughly sinister character in my view.'

'Well, yes, because I tell you what else happened. Andras was showing me the old man's collection, you know, all those Roman things, and I poked around in his study a bit. And you'll never guess what I found – I found a drawer with an enormous sum of money in it – a whole drawer full of cash. And I told the detective about the money.'

'Told the detective – welfare officer, whoever he was? Why on *earth* did you do that? You want to be careful, Charles. Quinault's your supervisor.'

'Well, I thought I ought to. I wasn't feeling very well.'

'You can't afford to get on the wrong side of Quinault. He has a reputation, you know.'

'What sort of reputation?'

'He pursues vendettas. He bears a grudge. He hounds his enemies. Of course Oxford's the ideal environment for that sort of thing. The knives are always out in some neck of the woods or other. To mix metaphors.'

'I don't know why I told him. The man who came round, I mean.'

'Just wanting to shock as usual, I suppose. So exactly what happened?'

Charles described the occasion as he remembered it, and the more he described it the more it worried him. Eventually Fergus said: 'Well, there's nothing to be done about it now. And I suppose you may have been right in a way. But you'd better watch your step. Are you aware Quinault's speaking on Roman domestic deities this evening? At the Ashmolean. I was thinking of piling along. Might be a good idea if you came too. Make sure he sees you. It'll show a proper respect.'

~

'The slides were the most interesting bit.'

They emerged from the museum to find that it had started to rain.

'I like the Roman attitude to religion,' said Charles. 'They didn't take it seriously. And at the same time they were so superstitious.'

'What is there to like about that?'

'They knew it was all irrational and ridiculous. Everyone had to make obeisance to the Roman deities as a recognition of Roman worldly power. It had nothing to do with God or faith at all. That's what organised religion is. It's all about power. All the rest is just hypocrisy. Though I suppose their gods stood in for aspects of nature, a form of animism. It does make a kind of sense to worship nature.'

Fergus looked sceptical. 'The trouble is, I just don't find religion very interesting. The opium of the people and all that.'

'That's why it *is* interesting. Like any other form of addiction.'

'Look, why don't we bike over to Walton Street for fish and chips?'

Charles had no appetite. 'You've just eaten those crumpets.'

'That was nearly three hours ago and I'm still hungry.' Fergus was always hungry.

As they waited in the queue Fergus said: 'You know Regine Drownes.'

'You know I do. You met us once, in the Mitre.'

'I wonder ... could I ask you a huge favour? You're one of her little favourites, are you? God knows why. You never write anything.'

'I don't have to.'

'Women like that always seem to have a penchant for pansies.'

'If you're going to ask a favour, it might be better not to be insulting.'

'Insulting? You used to spend your whole time prancing around Oxford and boasting you'd fucked half the university. The male half.'

For once Charles actually laughed. 'Especially the really butch ones. Giving them a surprise. Those were the days! But of course if you want me to introduce you or call on her in London or something I'm happy to oblige.'

'I need to promote myself a bit more if I'm to go in seriously for a literary career.'

'I'm going down this weekend. I'll arrange something.'

They parted company. Charles biked the short distance to Park Town. Head down, for it was now raining hard, he propped his bike against the side wall before walking round to the front door. As he fumbled for his key, he was nearly knocked sideways as the figure huddled unnoticed on the steps rose up and grabbed him.

'Charles! You're ...' The words were stifled in sobs.

For a split second's shock he thought it was Andras. Then: 'Penny. For Christ's sake. What on earth—'

'Oh Charles, I'm so glad you've come back.'

'Come inside.'

In the hall Penny was shaking. Her teeth chattered. Her hair and coat dripped on the floor. He pushed her up the curving stairs with the graceful, rickety banister and with his arm round her shoulders propelled her into his room.

'Sit down.' He gestured at the unmade divan. He lit the

gas fire. He was wet enough himself. He hung his coat over the back of a chair.

Penny huddled on the divan in her outdoor clothes, still crying.

'Here, give me those … I'll make some tea – or look – what about some whisky?' But the empty bottle lay on the floor. He put the kettle on the gas ring. 'Or coffee? Hell, there's no milk.'

He sat down beside Penny and proffered the cup of milkless tea. Her sobs developed into a paroxysm of coughing.

'What's the matter? Penny …' He put his arm round her, but she pulled away from him.

'I – I'm …' But as soon as she started to speak, sobs choked her again.

'Calm down. Take it easy.'

Gradually the tears subsided.

'Tell me what's the matter. What's happened?'

'I'm going to have a baby.' Somehow, saying it so starkly dried up the tears, at least for the moment. She looked owlishly at him, her face all blotched and red. A little string of snot hung from her nose.

'Here …' Repelled by her defenceless state he pulled out his hanky and pushed it into her hand. It was a disaster, of course, but he had no idea how to react or what to say. He knew this sort of thing happened. In some other universe.

Penny blew her nose. 'Charles, what am I going to do?'

'Is it Alistair's?'

He jumped back as she shouted: 'Of *course* it's Alistair's! Who else do you think?'

'Shssh! Does he know?'

'No! That's the thing. He said …' and now the sobs started again – 'I can't tell him. We're not going out any more. He ended it. He's fallen in love with Venetia Templeton.'

The divan shook with her sobs. She was almost howling.

It was horrible. Charles put his hand cautiously on her arm. 'Penny – just tell me – surely—'

'Surely *what*? Everyone knows. The whole of St Hilda's—'

'Knows about the ... that you're ...?'

'*No*. About Venetia, you fool.' Anger seemed to give her strength. 'He's gone off with Venetia.' She blew her nose again, mopped her eyes.

'But he – he can't do that. You must tell him. He'll have to marry you, won't he?'

'He won't. I can't make him. Anyway, I don't *want* to get married. I'll be sent down either way. Girl undergraduates aren't allowed to be married. You must know that.'

Charles had no idea about any of it.

'Isn't there anything you can ... *do*?'

'I've tried. Drank a lot of gin and had a hot bath.' Now she was almost laughing. 'Jumped down some stairs over and over again. Went for a bumpy bike ride across Port Meadow. It's *still there*.'

He feared she was about to tip over into hysteria. Vulgar phrases floated into his mind – up the duff, bun in the oven ... and he remembered his stepmother Brenda saying something about a girl who came into the hospital bleeding to death ... 'Abortion's illegal, you know,' said Penny in a hard voice. 'I'll be sent down. I'll be an unmarried mother. What'll I say to Mummy? She'll be so ...' She banged her fist on the divan. 'And Daddy. It's my fault. All my fault. I shouldn't have – Daddy talked to me about men. He said I had to be careful not – not to arouse them too much. He said there came a point when they couldn't go back. It was beyond their control.'

This didn't entirely fit with Charles' much more extensive experience of male arousal, although the Andras episode could certainly have been deployed in support of the view advanced by Penny's father. This was hardly the moment for a discussion, however, because she was about to start crying again. She *was* hysterical. He began to panic, but with desperation came an idea, although he hadn't even thought of it until the words came out of his mouth.

'I'll talk to my father. You know he's a doctor. He'll know what to do.'

It was a spur-of-the-moment thought. He himself was surprised by it, but he'd said it instinctively, probably to stop her from completely losing control.

'What can he do? He can't do anything, can he?'

'He might be able to.'

'Charles, it's illegal.'

'My stepmother was a nurse, you know, before they married. She said something – sometimes it's allowed. I was going to London this weekend anyway. I'll talk to him, I'll think up some story.'

'But …' She blew her nose. 'I don't see how it'll work.'

'I'll just say it's a friend who's in trouble.'

'He might ring up the college.'

'He won't do that. He's not that sort of person. Anyway, I'll try. Look – it's getting late. It's nearly half past ten. If you're not back by eleven you'll be in more trouble. You could stay here, of course …'

'That would be worse. If anyone found out – your landlady.'

'She couldn't care less.'

'I'll be all right. I've got my bike.'

'I'll ride back with you.' His relief that she was leaving prompted the chivalrous gesture.

'Don't be silly.'

He followed her downstairs. 'It'll be okay,' he said. 'Chin up.'

Penny wheeled her bike to the gate and cycled away down the dark, silent road.

chapter 35

As soon as McGovern had seen Balmoral Mansions, it had occurred to him that the faceless block would make an ideal location for an espionage hideout. Now it seemed he might have been right.

He rode upwards in the mahogany-lined lift and rang the door bell. 'Mrs Mallory?'

An elderly woman dressed in black answered the door. She looked flintily at McGovern. 'Mrs Mallory is not expecting a visitor this afternoon.'

He produced his card. 'I think she'll see me.'

He waited in the peach-coloured lounge. What a difference from where he'd first met her in the ruins of Berlin. In those days he'd been naive. At first he'd liked her. Frankly, he'd been attracted to her. He'd also been sorry for her, believing her to be the victim both of the war and of a cruel father. Only gradually had he understood her complicity in the old man's schemes. She'd searched the Berlin bomb sites for orphaned children to be offered to men like Miles Kingdom, Quinault's friend. McGovern had heard that Kingdom's death and the revelations about him had upset Quinault to the extent that he'd travelled to East Berlin himself, renewing old espionage contacts in a fruitless effort to clear Kingdom's name. Perhaps – very likely

– Quinault had encountered her there. And now, five years later, they were still in touch.

She stood in the doorway and from the way her expression changed he understood that she hadn't recognised his name. That wasn't surprising, as he'd gone under a different one then. She recognised *him*, though. And she was literally speechless.

'You're looking very well, Frieda.'

She recovered and stepped forward. 'It's Sonia.'

'Don't pretend you don't remember me.'

She gestured towards the sofa. He looked at her and her gaze dropped away. 'I wondered if you'd catch up with me,' she said. 'After we ran into each other in Trafalgar Square last spring. Do you remember?'

'Of course.' He hadn't done anything about it at the time. He'd been too busy with the impending Khrushchev visit. At least, that was his excuse, but more to the point was that he didn't want to rake up the past and especially that part of it, didn't want to dwell on how he'd been taken in and even half seduced by her sad plight.

'And now you have – caught up with me.'

'It would seem so.'

The maid entered with a tray.

'You'll have tea?' McGovern watched Sonia's elegant movements as she arranged teacups and lifted the pot. 'Or would you like something stronger, perhaps?'

McGovern shook his head. 'Thank you. This is fine.' He waited just long enough to heighten her unease – not that it showed, her preoccupation with the tea concealed it, but he was sure she was nervous; she must be.

'I saw you the other evening at the Ambassadors Club,' he said. 'It was quite a surprise to see you there. Your husband's doing very well. And you're looking so well. It must be a very interesting story.'

She gazed at her long, pale nails. 'It's a *long* story. I don't know about interesting – quite boring, actually.'

'Boring? I shouldn't have thought so. Getting away from East Berlin can't have been that easy.'

'That was not so difficult. You know that. I just crossed over into the West. That was the easy part. It was more difficult to persuade them I was a genuine refugee. But I had a stroke of luck when I met Mallory. He was over there on business, to organise an international boxing match. I met him in a bar. We got talking. I was able to help him in various ways. One thing led to another and now I am here and am married to him, so I am a British citizen. Really it is a straightforward story, not interesting at all.' There was the slightest tinge of triumph in her voice as she tapped her cigarette against the glass table. Her bracelets made a clicking sound.

McGovern leaned forward to light the cigarette. 'I'm not here to talk about the past. Well, not exactly. At the time I never thought of your relationship with Miles Kingdom as anything other than you providing him with what he wanted. But perhaps it was more than that. You – and your father – could have helped in other ways.'

'I'm sorry. I don't know what you mean.'

'Your father was well in with the East German Communist Party. But only for his own ends. He was an opportunist, one of those Nazi supporters who managed to get in with the new regime. So you, or you and your father, could have provided Kingdom with contacts. You knew about Kingdom's work in the intelligence services, I take it.'

She shook her head. 'I never concerned myself with anything like that.'

'It's strange then, isn't it, that someone who knew Kingdom very well, who was also in the secret services and still has contacts, has been in touch with you. You know Professor Quinault, don't you?'

She smiled. 'I run a dating agency. I introduce people. I have clients.' She looked at him, faintly smiling, slightly mocking. Then she looked modestly down at the hand that played with her cigarette.

'Am I supposed to believe that, Frieda? It seems rather too much of a coincidence. Quinault was Kingdom's friend, and now we find that he's been using the services of the very same woman who knew Kingdom, one of the most important British agents operating in Berlin at the end of the war.'

McGovern knew there had to be a security connection. He watched her closely. She appeared at ease, but it was a pretence. She sat upright, *too* still. There was none of the easy relaxation of a woman on firm ground, with nothing to fear.

She had plenty to fear. He knew of her criminal past. It was doubtful that any sort of case could be brought against her, in fact there was zero chance, and perhaps she knew that. Yet the truth could damage her in other ways.

'Does your husband know all about your past?'

She didn't answer.

'Do you still have links to East Germany? That could be very useful.' It could be useful, for example, to Quinault as a lever to regain influence – if that was what he wanted – with the secret services. 'Quinault must know that you knew his great friend, Miles Kingdom.'

She jumped up and walked about the room. 'This is stupid. You are so wrong. He comes here for the same reason as the other men who come here.'

'So you admit you know him and that he comes here. But I should be careful what you say about that too, Frieda. You could be suspected of running a disorderly house.'

She sat down again. 'My husband won't like it if he hears you've been threatening me.'

'Your husband's a well-known businessman, a successful businessman, isn't he? Are you suggesting he'd step outside the law and interfere with legitimate police enquiries?'

She sat down again, lifted the teapot and poured herself a second cup.

'I'd just like some cooperation, Frieda. I'd like to know more about you and the Professor.'

Perhaps Blackstone was right and she was blackmailing Quinault. Perhaps she knew something about *his* murky past in the secret service. Or perhaps it was after all just that Quinault didn't want his wife to know what he got up to at Balmoral Mansions.

She smoked, gazing downwards, in silence. The cigarette was finished before she spoke again. 'There's nothing to know.'

'How did you meet him?'

'A friend introduced him.'

'Who was this friend?'

'He was recommended.'

McGovern hesitated. Perhaps it was a mistake, but he decided to show her his hand. 'I have reason to believe that Professor Quinault has paid you large sums of money.'

Her laugh surprised him. There was an edge to it that he couldn't put his finger on. It suggested ... irony? Triumph? It somehow made the idea more plausible that, after all, the money in Quinault's attaché case had been destined for her. Perhaps Blackstone's blackmail angle was not so far-fetched. 'Why is that amusing?'

She had recaptured her poise. 'You are amusing,' she said. He remembered – and quite vividly – that way she had of playing the part of a knowing woman of the world, running rings round a naive detective who was out of his depth.

'I'm glad you think so.' His cold anger strengthened him, but he was up against a blank wall. He had no real evidence. So Quinault had paid her a visit. He couldn't prove the relationship was other than a sordid business arrangement. The blackmail line was pure speculation. As was the espionage angle. And Berlin was too far in the past to truly threaten her.

The money in Quinault's library was the only suspicious fact. Only by questioning Quinault would he discover more about that. Yet he continued.

'It's interesting, isn't it? One of your clients, if that's the right word, is or was a secret agent. And you left East Germany, East Berlin, only a few years ago. You were still there in 1951 when I met you. And we all know it's the espionage capital of the world. Your father had connections—'

'My father's dead now. He died in prison. And I knew nothing.'

'You could return now as Mrs Mallory, a British citizen.' But even as he spoke, he knew that of course it was all pure speculation.

'Please do not imagine that I have any interest in spying. Or in East Berlin – or Germany. That is the last place I should ever wish to visit, ever again.'

He could well believe that, at least. He could also think of circumstances in which she could be put under pressure to return, but since he had nothing concrete to go on he decided to put espionage aside for the moment. 'There's another matter. A murder case. A young girl. You knew her, I think. You'd employed her.'

'I don't employ anyone.'

'Your husband employed her.'

This mention of her husband brought about an odd change. It was now the other Frieda who leaned towards him, soft, vulnerable and pleading. 'What happened to her had nothing to do with Mallory.'

'I didn't say it had,' he answered, startled. He leaned back, watching her. There was something bothering her in relation to Mallory. As if her words belied themselves. As if the girl's death *did* have something to do with Mallory. 'And yet,' he persisted, 'it did, didn't it? In the sense that she worked for him and then left. And shortly afterwards died in what now seem to be suspicious circumstances.'

'I really know nothing about it. I hadn't seen her for a long time. And Mallory and I lead separate lives. I don't know why you're asking me about her. Some man has been charged, I think.'

'You knew that? You've been following the case, then.'

'Not really.' She played with her bracelets.

'Frieda—'

'Please call me Sonia.'

'It's not important, is it, whether I call you Frieda or Sonia? You're the same person.'

'Actually, I'm not, Chief Inspector McGovern. I'm a very different person.'

He ignored that. 'You knew the girl. What was she like?'

She shrugged. 'She was a fool. Mallory was right to get rid of her.'

'Get rid of her?'

She glanced at him. 'Sack her is what I mean, of course.' She was upset now, was regretting the words she'd used.

'You're quick to defend your husband,' he said, 'but no-one's accused him of anything.'

'Naturally I defend him. I owe him a lot.'

'And what about Professor Quinault? I wonder what he owes you. Or you him.'

Sonia lit another cigarette. 'I don't think this conversation is getting us anywhere, is it.'

'Are you telling me to leave?'

How blank her smile was. She raised her eyebrows. 'I'm not telling you anything.'

'No. I'm aware of that.'

'I didn't mean—'

He stood up. 'I know what you mean. I apologise for taking up your time. And thank you for the tea. But you know I'll be back, don't you?'

The Queen's Head was not so far from this end of Bayswater and he decided to walk there. He crossed the Edgware Road and followed New Cavendish Street into the hinterland of Marylebone. All the while he quietly seethed with tension. He wished he hadn't recognised Frieda in the Ambassadors. Naturally he'd been curious, first when he'd caught sight of her in Trafalgar Square the previous spring and then when he'd seen her again in the unlikely setting of her husband's club; but the truth was, he wanted nothing more to do with her.

He resented being dragged back into an ugly past. MI5 were no doubt simply using him in some scheme of their own with Quinault. He didn't care about their little games. He wanted no part of it.

Yet there was all that money in Quinault's desk drawer.

Blackstone was waiting for him in the melancholic atmosphere of the pub and for some reason McGovern found his presence soothing. Blackstone was easy-going. He wasn't judgemental. Perhaps it was down to cynicism, but at least he wasn't abrasive or demanding.

'Enjoyed the Ambassadors, did you? It's a pretty awful place really, but I suppose it's the way we're all going. A bit of glitter on poor old England, the old tart. 'Fraid I drank too much. Wasn't feeling too clever the next day. Same again, thanks,' he added, as McGovern gestured at his glass.

'So how d'you get on with Mrs Mallory?' he asked as McGovern set down the tankards.

'I didn't get much out of her. Didn't handle it too well, I'm afraid.'

'She's a tough nut to crack.'

'She insisted Quinault's nothing but a client.'

'I thought you knew about her murky past in Germany.

That's what you told me at the club, after you'd recognised her.'

'It's a long time ago. It's all speculation – her and Quinault.'

'What about ... Argyle Street?'

McGovern shook his head. 'I did get the idea she was trying to protect her husband. She was very touchy when I mentioned him. Quite defensive.'

Blackstone became more animated. 'Yeah. I bet Mallory's involved somehow or other. I wondered if Sonia might be covering up for him. That would explain why she sent me on a wild goose chase after Sonny Marsden in Notting Hill – trying to protect Mallory by sending me off in the wrong direction. But anyway, Rita unearthed a few titbits of gossip at the club. Met a girl she knew when she went round the back. Might get some more information there. I'm meeting up with them tomorrow morning.'

'She wasn't cooperative. It maybe was not such a good idea to pay her a visit at all at this stage. Showed my hand a wee bit too early.'

'Does the spy angle really add up? There's no sort of evidence she's been in touch with the East Germans, is there? There's not much she could tell them if she was, I should have thought.'

'The link with Quinault is odd, though,' insisted McGovern.

'I still think she's blackmailing him,' said Blackstone. 'That's the only thing that can explain the money. I'm going to poke around a bit and see what else I can find out about her other clients. And you can push the Professor some more, can't you? '

'It's tricky.' McGovern stared ahead. 'But I have to go back up to Oxford tomorrow, in any case. One of the refugees is missing.'

chapter 36

MAISON LYONS WAS BLACKSTONE'S home from home. He'd long since ceased to notice the surroundings. The waitresses knew him and he didn't object to starting the day with a bit of flirtation; when, that is, he wasn't too hung over.

He'd dressed rather more carefully than usual. He hadn't seen Rita since he'd driven her back to Notting Dale from Mallory's club, driving cautiously on account of the amount of liquor he'd consumed. Fortunately, they'd arrived safely, although he had been pretty drunk. He had kissed Rita on the cheek with paternal solicitude. It was not the time to take things further, but she'd agreed to meet him here at Maison Lyons today and to bring her friend from the Ambassadors.

He ordered coffee and waited. While he waited he read *The Times*. 'Top People read *The Times*' was the newspaper's new slogan. Top People – who were they, Blackstone wondered. Top People were to be seen at the Ambassadors; Top People visited Sonia; Top People made a mess of Suez; Top People denounced juvenile delinquents and feckless council tenants, yet turned a blind eye to whatever Sonny Marsden and Vince Mallory were up to. Top People had been too stupid to believe that Burgess and Maclean could possibly have been Soviet agents. Top People were the upper crust of a cesspit.

But there were the girls he was waiting for, advancing

between the tables like a couple of film stars! Rita was the looker, of course. Her friend was too lanky and anaemic to appeal to Blackstone and wore an unflattering pale pink coat. He stood up, courtly. He liked to treat women with respect.

'This is my friend, Gerry. Gerry, this is Dawn.' Good girl. He'd told her not to say anything about his being a crime reporter.

'Pleased to meet you,' simpered Dawn.

The waitress hovered, gave him a sly wink.

'Coffee for the young ladies, please, Beryl. I'll have another cup myself. Or do you prefer tea?'

The girls chose coffee. It was more sophisticated. They talked about the Ambassadors. It was a marvellous place to work, Dawn told him. She was ever so lucky. She might be able to put in a word for Rita, if Rita was interested.

Blackstone didn't think that was a good idea at all, but he listened, prepared to spend time putting the girl at ease before he started asking questions. He might not even have to ask questions; what he needed to know might all emerge naturally as she talked about her work and the girls and the boss.

Mr Mallory, Dawn told him, was a very good boss. The dancing was very artistic. He was strict, of course, you had to be on time and work hard at the routines. You could be fined for lateness. That was what happened with Valerie. She met a young man and her time-keeping began to slip. Mr Mallory didn't want her to leave. He didn't like the young man, though. Some of the girls thought he was jealous, but that wasn't it. In the end things got quite bad and he gave her her cards. She was in a state then, her bloke hadn't any money, there were all sorts of rumours.

Blackstone listened. With Rita sitting next to him he didn't want to display emotion, but the story disturbed him. 'What sort of rumours?'

Dawn shook her head.

'Do you know why the boss was so angry? What was it about?'

Dawn picked at one of her pink nails. After a while she said: 'People said Val talked too much.'

'Talked too much? What about?'

Dawn shrugged unhappily. 'Her boyfriend?' She didn't seem convinced. She said hesitantly, 'He was a bad lot, supposed to be.'

'Who was her boyfriend?'

'Archie Le Saux, he was called. They said he was no good. Come from a bad family or something.'

'Archie Le Saux!' Blackstone felt sick. The Le Saux clan – a bad family! That was a massive understatement. They were notorious down the East End. His hand shook as he lit another cigarette. Dawn was looking uneasy now.

'I hope I didn't say the wrong thing. It weren't no secret.'

Blackstone couldn't understand why, if it wasn't a secret, he hadn't known about it. He spoke reassuring words, but it was obvious she felt she'd said too much, as if it were a secret after all. She moved around uneasily in her chair. 'Look – thanks ever so for the coffee, but I've got my rehearsal now.'

Blackstone watched her departing figure blankly. He couldn't believe it. Valerie, mixed up with Maurice Le Saux's nephew. That just wasn't possible.

'Are you all right, Gerry?' Rita put a hand on his arm.

He finished his fag, stubbed it out and pulled himself together. 'Yeah, yeah, I'm fine. What about a taxi back to North Ken?'

'Don't be daft. What's the Central Line for? Or I could get a bus.'

Blackstone insisted and in the padded depths of the cab his arm was soon round her soft, plump waist and his mouth seeking hers.

'I like you, Gerry.'

He loved the way she was so open and natural and straightforward. That was how Valerie had been. Only different. Valerie had been a romantic who lacked confidence, an unpromising combination; Rita by contrast was an optimist, and pragmatic too, for now she pulled back from him.

'You know Carl only got six months. He'll be out in four.'

'Mmm. No, I didn't know.' He stroked her hair. 'Carl's no good to you, darling.'

'The trouble is, there's the old man. Who's going to look after him, if I ... if I'm not there?'

'A lot can happen in six months. Don't worry. We'll sort it all out.'

Yes, Rita was a sweetie. She was a comfort to a man.

But Valerie: Valerie with Archie Le Saux. The boyfriend she was going to marry; the knight in shining armour.

He walked back from Rita's up to Bayswater and turned into Kensington Gardens. The wind had cleansed the bleached sky; new acid-green grass and even some snowdrops poked through the mud. A flock of birds seemed hurled like a fistful of confetti from the hand of God, whirled into a ball of netting that then unfurled across the sky. But his mood only darkened.

He spent the day looking up background material on Bodkin Adams in the Newspaper Library far out in north London at Colindale, a dismal region of flimsy factories, automobile concessions and dingy housing. He found it impossible to concentrate and eventually gave up and took the tube back to central London. He left the underground at Holborn and walked down Kingsway. The roar of the traffic, newsvendors shouting the evening headlines, the lights spiked out against the darkness of shabby streets – he took it all for granted, and barely noticed the newsreel movie of city life unfurling endlessly day after day. Yes, it was like walking through a newsreel, life as a newsreel. There was always news, the endless traffic rolling off the presses, great waves of it, and he was tossed along in it too, along with all the flotsam and jetsam eaten up by the juggernaut of passing time measured out in the latest scoop, the latest *story*. Events piled up, each new event burying the previous one; what was it Macmillan had said? 'Events, dear boy, events.' That's what got you in the end.

He was in search of a colleague and turned into Ye Old Cock Tavern, where he was most likely to be found. He saw his mates at once, round a crowded table. Sam White, wire spectacles askew, hair falling over his forehead, was at the centre of the conversation. Blackstone fetched a beer and joined them.

Suez. The argument never ended. The *Chronicle* had supported the war from the outset. That didn't mean the paper's journalists agreed with the line. Some did, some didn't. Blackstone personally despised Fleet Street jingoism, but he was fatalistic about world affairs. All he felt certain of was that it would turn out badly, in the short term and in the long term as well. And then there was Hungary.

'Suez gave them cover. That's why they went in, when we were all looking the other way.'

'We have to show the bloody Yanks they don't rule the world.'

'Fact is, they do.'

'Nasser was a fool to block the canal. He had to go.'

'So Hungarian students are slaughtered.'

'Don't be a bleeding pessimist. The Russians have had it in the long run.'

'For Christ's sake, man, are you serious? Imre Nagy's in Moscow. Their army's enormous. Twice the size of the Yanks'. And communist regimes all over the bloody globe. They're in charge. Absolutely.'

'And we're Airstrip One – basically we're just a silo full of nuclear bombs.'

Blackstone manoeuvred himself so that he was seated by White. 'What's this I hear,' he muttered, 'about Stanley Coleman chumming up with Vince Mallory?'

White was the city and financial correspondent. His bent spectacles gave him a slightly squiffy look. 'Who told you that?'

'I saw them together at Mallory's new club.'

'Stanley Coleman?' White thought about it. 'Never. Coleman's one of the richest men in Britain. He owns more of Britain than the bloody Queen. He's richer than the Duke of Westminster.'

'Well, there he was at Mallory's table.'

White shook his head. 'Everyone goes to the Ambassadors, it's the with-it place, isn't it? Been there myself.'

'Yes, but not as Mallory's special guest, I imagine.' While half listening to the Suez–Hungary argument that circled round and round, never getting anywhere, Blackstone tried to imagine in what circumstances Coleman could be relevant.

Suppose Mallory was hoping for some sort of financing from the property tycoon. Mallory was said to be very rich himself and he certainly had the Rolls and the Aston Martin and the huge pile out in Epping somewhere to prove it. But you never knew. He might be under-capitalised. He had to pay a lot of people.

If that were the case, he wouldn't want bad publicity about a girl dying in suspicious circumstances. Besides, Stanley Coleman was Jewish. Mallory wouldn't want unpleasant rumours getting out about his wife's secret past in Germany, either. McGovern had told him her father had been a Nazi who'd then managed to get on the right side of the communists. That wouldn't go down well at Coleman's HQ.

Yet – was it Mallory he should be thinking about? More

urgent was to find Archie Le Saux. That's who he should have been thinking about. Was thinking about. He should have followed it up when he'd first heard word of a boyfriend from Toni at the California Club, but it hadn't seemed important. No: that was untrue. He'd known it was important, all right. He should have got on to that lead at once, but he hadn't wanted to. He hadn't wanted to know about a boyfriend. But now he had to; which meant he had to find Archie Le Saux.

He slipped away. In the smoky darkness of the foggy street the pedestrians passed like wraiths, each going he knew not where on the treadmill of life. He felt desperately tired and so weary, endlessly burdened by the dismal ugliness of it all.

There was an envelope lying on the hall floor. No stamp. Printed on the sheet of paper inside were simply the words: FINAL WARNING.

chapter 37

CHARLES WAITED UNTIL BRENDA, his stepmother, was in the basement kitchen washing up, before speaking to his father. In the drawing room his mother's chaise longue still flaunted its arabesques at an angle to the chimney piece, but Brenda had placed a Pierrot doll cushion on it. She had also introduced Murano glass ornaments representing Pinocchio and other Disney characters along the chimney ledge. A large, new, walnut-encased television had replaced his mother's rosewood bureau.

'There's something I need to talk to you about, Dad.'

Dr Hallam glanced warily at his only son.

Charles carried his confession off with a convincing mixture of regret and self-blame, tinged with just a tiny suggestion that Penny was perhaps a bit reckless. He summoned public-school understatement to the words 'Of course, I'd do the decent thing', spoken with stiff upper lip fully in place.

'I'm disappointed to hear a well-brought up, well-educated girl should have ... well, ensnared you in that way,' said Dr Hallam. He seemed stiff with embarrassment and awkwardness.

It really hadn't been like that, Charles hurried to insist. It had all been his fault. He'd got carried away ... he had taken precautions, but ...

Charles tried to gauge his father's response. Yes – more than anything else he was embarrassed. He seemed irritated rather than angry: a messy business, but these things happened. 'You should have been more careful. You're not really in a position to get married, but I suppose in the circumstances, as you're prepared to stand by her—'

He shouldn't have said he'd stand by her! That had been the wrong approach. 'She doesn't want to get married,' he said, feeling he sounded slightly hysterical. That wasn't it at all. He'd offered to marry her, but she'd refused. She wanted to finish her degree – was desperate to stay at Oxford – her whole future at stake. Also (and it was important to get this point across, although it wasn't true) if *he* got married it might mean the end of his D.Phil. Professor Quinault would take a very dim view.

'Penny's in a terrible state. She's really quite suicidal – she'd do absolutely anything rather than bring shame on her family and ruin her future. I'm terribly worried about her.'

Charles watched the play of expression on his father's face. 'It'll ruin both our careers.'

Dr Hallam walked up and down, poured himself, unusually, a whisky. Finally: 'You say the girl's mental state …? Well … there are circumstances … if she really is distraught … It is a serious matter, but I'll see what I can do. She'll have to see a psychiatrist, though. But for God's sake be more careful in future.'

As his father spoke Charles noted a subtle shift of mood. Social embarrassment and a dislike of upsetting the conventions were displaced by the worldly understanding that existed between men. Charles got the message that he'd been a bloody fool. However, sheltered girls sometimes went off the rails when offered the freedom of student life and shotgun marriages were not always the happiest. Moreover, a young man's career was not to be put in jeopardy by an accident of this kind.

Above all, however, and more important than any other

consideration, Charles recognised his father's unspoken, but heartfelt and exhilarating sense of relief, because now he could hope his son was not after all, as he'd feared for so long, a homosexual and a pervert. It had been, thank God, just a phase.

Charles described his success to Fergus as they approached Regine's Kensington villa. 'Penny will have an abortion and Dad won't worry so much about me being queer – for a while, anyway.'

'And to think I thought it was chivalry on your part. No doubt you have an ulterior motive for introducing me to Mrs Drownes as well.'

'Not at all. That is pure kindness.'

'You seem really close to her, but she's so much older than you. Does she prey on young men? Doesn't she realise she won't get anywhere with you?'

'No, it's – she confides in me. I don't know many of her friends, so I'm not in a position to gossip.'

Charles had occasionally wondered himself about the bond that held them together. Yet he knew, really. It was Freddie, of course. In a peculiar way he'd become a kind of substitute for Freddie. This he did not bother to explain; it would have involved too long a story.

It was one of Regine's young authors' afternoons, but Charles could not help noticing how distracted she seemed. Her interest in Fergus' articles for *Isis* and his poetry, published in a 'little magazine', quickly flagged. The other guests drifted away. Regine murmured to Charles: 'Darling – stay for a little longer, could you?'

Fergus took the hint. 'I'm afraid I must be off, Mrs Drownes. So delightful to have met you ...'

Regine drew Charles down on the sofa beside her.

'You seem a bit ... is something the matter?'

'I'm sorry I couldn't concentrate on your friend. I'm sure he'll go places. He has that look of steely determination about him.' Her laugh was halfway between mocking and sympathetic. 'But I'm so worried I can't think and there's no-one I can talk to – I've got to tell someone. Rodney's in a fearful state about it.'

~

Oxford was mistier than ever. Damp seeped into mossy grey buildings. Rain-washed streets dissolved into blurry distance. On Sunday morning one church bell after another rang with plaintive, unbearable insistence. For ever afterwards the plangent call to worship from all over the city was to be the sound that – wherever he was – returned Charles to that Oxford time and the dank melancholy of long-drawn-out Sundays.

He seldom bothered to read the *Oxford Mail*. He was therefore unprepared for the news Fergus imparted to him when they met for coffee in Betty's.

'You see this? One of the refugees drowned.' Fergus folded the paper back at the relevant page. 'An early morning runner saw the body floating in the Cherwell.'

Charles took the newspaper. He read the item with the stifling dull stupefaction of shock.

'The body of Andras Ferenczy ... whether an accident or suicide ...'

Andras had been worried – no, more than worried, he'd been frightened. The men who came to see him ...

Fergus was staring at him. 'It wasn't the one—'

Charles nodded. 'I was supposed to meet him. He didn't show up. It was the evening we went to hear Quinault ...'

'Christ. I'm sorry.'

'I bet it *was* suicide. God, I feel …' But he didn't know what he felt. 'I should have done something.'

'What could you have done?'

'I should have talked to his friends … but I hardly knew them … I only met them once.'

'You're not Florence Nightingale. You can't save everyone.'

'Apparently not.'

'Are you upset?' enquired Fergus, looking curiously at his friend.

'Of course I'm upset.' Charles moved sharply and sent his coffee cup hurtling to the floor. It didn't break, but left a puddle of liquid, some of which sprayed onto his trousers. 'Oh, damn.' He mopped at the mess with a paper napkin. 'I don't know what the hell I feel.'

'You need to talk to someone.'

'I certainly do.'

Unfortunately, there wasn't anyone – apart from Fergus, of course. It was out of the question to bike up to Headington now. He couldn't easily talk to Andras' Hungarian friends and he absolutely couldn't talk to the people in charge. He couldn't tell them he'd had an illegal sexual relationship with the drowned refugee. It wouldn't bring back Andras and might even get Charles himself reported to the police.

It preyed on Charles' mind that he might have in some way contributed to the fatal impulse. It *must* have been suicide. Andras had been in such a state. As he thought back to their night together, he recognised in retrospect some kind of desperation in the way Andras had behaved.

Perhaps it had been the prospect of living with his uncle, the priest in Winnipeg, that had driven Andras to take his own life. Charles preferred to think that. He didn't want to feel guilty.

Charles had always taken it for granted that he loved the

beauty of the university city. Today, as he moved restlessly around the narrow, secretive side streets, its hoary ancient colleges began to repel him. He bought coffee beans at the coffee shop in St Michael's Street. He went into the grocer's, Grimbly Hughes, in Cornmarket and sat on a high cane chair while a white-coated assistant fetched cheese, butter and tins of baked beans. He crossed the road and made for the covered market and Palms, where you could get salami and Parma ham. He visited the bread stall.

It was all pointless because he wasn't hungry. He couldn't think why he'd bought so much stuff. He biked back to Park Town with the parcels in his basket. He ran upstairs and then, in his room, had no idea what to do.

He lay on his divan and tried to read Donne's poetry.

He took some codeine and fell asleep.

chapter 38

HOUSES HUDDLED TOGETHER in the cramped East End streets, their pinched terraces unchanged since Dickens' time. Here and there monumental flats rose from what had been a bomb site, without making any impression on the general air of smallness and of buildings shabby beyond decay, of things hanging together by a thread. It was the raw new blocks that looked out of place.

Men and women in dark garments made their way along pavements hampered by market stalls. Buses swept by in clouds of dust and exhaust. Bicycles jangled and wove between lorries. A pony-drawn rag-and-bone cart limped along, the man's plaintive cry piercing the noise of traffic.

The Bethnal Green Road was wide enough, yet crammed with sluggishly moving vehicles until it widened out by the Green itself, where the buses swept round to the stop. Blackstone looked about in search of the Italian café. He saw it at once. Its fare was advertised in coarse red and black capitals on its windows. Inside, the white-tiled walls were clean and the signora was friendly.

Blackstone's arrival caused little interest. There were few customers during this slack period between breakfast and midday dinner. The signora wiped her hands on a cloth and stood over him solicitously. He ordered coffee and a cheese sandwich.

The tea urn hissed behind the counter. Blackstone watched his fellow diners surreptitiously. A workman in dusty overalls in the corner was clearly just that: a labourer. Three youths with Elvis Presley quiffs at the centre table wore distant memories of teddy-boy gear. They muttered to one another. One boy jiggled his leg compulsively. Blackstone considered asking them if they knew Archie Le Saux, but before he'd made up his mind a fourth young man entered the café.

There was a break in the atmosphere. The three youths stopped talking. The signora stiffened as she stood at her station. Even the urn held its breath.

The tension cut across the fug of steam and lethargy, but passed almost before you clocked it. Blackstone watched the young man slouch across to a table in the corner. Slight and girlish, he had blond hair, a lock of which fell in romantic fashion across his forehead. His blue eyes were reddened with fatigue. He lifted a languid hand in the direction of the signora. No words were exchanged, but moments later she brought him a mug of tea.

The three youths scraped back their chairs and left. The labourer was poring over *Titbits*. The signora disappeared behind the scenes.

Blackstone watched the young man pour a stream of sugar into his mug. He didn't stir it. Blackstone judged him somewhere between boy and man, as if he'd got mislaid in the middle. His jeans and leather jacket suggested a claim to some sort of outlaw status, which his slumped posture contradicted. He fished a tobacco pouch from his pocket and made a roll-up.

Blackstone edged his chair close. 'Trouble you for a light?'

When the boy smiled he looked suddenly angelic. He passed some matches across to the adjacent table.

'I'm looking for Archie Le Saux – told he comes in here most mornings.'

The smile disappeared. The boy stared.

'Wondered if you might be him, as a matter of fact.'

'And if I am?'

'Can I get you anything?' Blackstone extracted a banknote and waved it vaguely in the direction of the counter. Le Saux shook his head. 'Well ...' Blackstone left the money under his plate.

'Why you come looking for me?'

'I'd like to talk about Valerie.'

The bloodshot eyes were watchful.

Blackstone let the silence drift on a while. 'Tragic end for a lovely girl like that.'

'You knew 'er, did you?' Le Saux's voice was sarcastic.

'Yes, as a matter of fact I did.'

Le Saux looked at him with slightly more interest.

'Needed someone to look after her, I thought.'

Blackstone hadn't expected his words to have quite the effect they achieved, for he saw that Le Saux was close to tears.

'Terrible, what happened, shocking accident,' said Blackstone softly.

Le Saux squinted against the cigarette smoke. 'Weren't no bloody accident.'

'No?' Blackstone waited. Le Saux had sunk back into his torpor. 'I was fond of Valerie,' said Blackstone, trying to coax a response. 'Couldn't believe it when I heard.'

Le Saux slouched in his chair. He wasn't looking at Blackstone. 'I know you ain't the bloody Bill,' he muttered, 'but who the sodding hell are you?' Then he seemed to lose interest and sat staring at the blank, steamed-up window.

Blackstone was beginning to think it could be a big story, but he'd have to be very patient, treading on eggshells. He was conflicted too, because he didn't want Valerie to become a big story. He waited, smoking, outwardly casual, but seething within. He ordered more coffee from the signora. The workman left. Two more came in.

'I'm here to help you, Archie,' said Blackstone. 'It must be tough, being your uncle's nephew. Have to do as you're told. Your mother's so ill. Your uncle doesn't want her upset. Very fond of his sister, I believe. I suppose you have to keep quiet, do you, take it on the chin? Shut up about what happened to your girlfriend.'

Le Saux became more animated. 'It's not his fault. It's down to Mallory.'

Blackstone smoked.

'He didn't like me. And when Mallory doesn't like someone or something ...' His voice faded and Blackstone wondered if he was coming down off something, although he had no idea what. Le Saux's attention came and went in waves. And he should have been more suspicious than he actually seemed to be of this stranger who was asking him questions. 'But why'd he have to sack her?'

'He didn't like you? Was he jealous? I've heard he wasn't interested in girls.'

'Mallory likes power. Likes people being in his power. And if they try to get away he don't forgive them. I'm lucky I only got a smack in the jaw.'

'He didn't like it on account of your uncle?'

'He didn't like what happened.' Le Saux's voice faded again. He began obsessively to pull out more strands of tobacco from the packet. He carefully laid out a cigarette paper and assembled the strands on it, licked the edge, lit up again. 'Who are you, anyway? Why am I talking to you?'

'Because we cared about Valerie.'

The boy's eyelids drooped. He seemed to have lost interest.

'What did Mallory do?'

'Mallory don't like my fucking uncle and that's the truth.'

'Enemies from way back, eh? I remember that. Used to work round here myself.' At once he wished he could have bitten it back; the wrong thing to have said. If the boy knew he was a reporter ... but luckily Le Saux wasn't alert enough to pick up on it.

'Mallory thinks he's better'n the rest of us. But he ain't.'

Blackstone agreed soothingly.

'Didn't think I was good enough for one of his girls.'

'Mmm. Because ...?'

'Work for my uncle, don't I? Ducking and diving. I'm the errand boy.' There was bitterness in his voice.

'So you were warned off, is that it?'

Le Saux didn't reply, overtaken by another wave of lethargy. This time his silence seemed set to continue indefinitely. He simply wasn't listening; he wasn't even there. Blackstone stood up. He left the note lying under his plate. 'I'd like to talk to you again.'

'Yeah? I'm always around.'

A February sun washed the dirty London sky with the sweetness of winter sunshine in mild weather. Blackstone barely noticed.

He could not accept that that wastrel had been loved by Valerie. A petty criminal, for that he surely was if he worked (a euphemism) for his uncle – his uncle's errand boy, he'd said – had been Valerie's knight in shining armour. The idea of Archie Le Saux as the love of Valerie's life was unbearable. He rejected it out of hand. It could not be true. Yet apparently it was.

Le Saux had as good as accused Mallory. Could *that* be true? Mallory had a past, but not that kind of past. The way he'd toughed it out against Jack Spot, for example. Hadn't resorted to violence himself in spite of all the provocation, but had faced him down and then done the clever thing and got police protection. Mallory was a businessman – a crooked one, true, but a businessman, not a murderer. Too clever to need to resort to murder. Yet everyone was pointing the finger at Mallory.

Le Saux was in a bad way. Blackstone was sure it was

about more than the girl's death. Sure, he'd lost his girlfriend in horrible circumstances, but his state expressed something beyond grief ... resignation, perhaps. More than that. Surrender. He was someone who'd given up. He'd thrown in the towel. Blackstone had sat in the café with him for less than half an hour, but he'd felt that aura coming off him, of a man who had given up hope. The question was: why?

chapter 39

THE BAR AT PADDINGTON STATION was as anonymous as the Queen's Head, but for the opposite reason: it was always crowded with transient travellers. The only problem was you had to shout to get yourself heard. However, Jarrell and Blackstone managed to find a secluded corner.

'Isn't McGovern coming?'

'Yes. That's why we're here. He said he'd be late. Off the Oxford train.'

'I'd forgotten. I'll forget my own name next.'

'You do look a bit rough.'

'I'm fine. Just a bit tired, that's all.' Blackstone passed his hand over his face. He felt all of his forty-two years today. 'I got another threatening letter,' he said. 'At least they're still stuck at square one. No shit through the letter box. Or bombs. Just another anonymous message with stuck-on letters. How worried should I be?'

'You should take it seriously.'

'How do I do that? Leave home? Call the whole thing off?' Blackstone looked round him. In this crowded bar the two of them were as if sealed off septically in their separate conspiratorial capsule from the rowdy talk, the yellow lighting, the whole scene as brown-varnished as some fake old master. It all seemed unreal, he remembered Le Saux, he felt giddy, the lights pulsed and danced …

'Are you okay?' Jarrell's gaunt face loomed over him.

'Felt a bit faint – all right now.'

'Are you sure?'

'Get me another, would you, old man? Same again, Bell's. Be right as rain then.' His fag had smouldered to nothing in the ash tray. He lit a fresh one. Whisky in hand, he felt better, and catching sight of McGovern's tall figure, he waved. 'Here he is.'

McGovern looked oddly diabolical this evening. He was wearing a different hat, more of a fedora. And the Black Watch scarf round his neck was quite dashing. He carried a beer to their table. The three men, so like all the others in the crowded saloon, might have been chatting about the races or football through the smoke and noise. They might have stopped off for a pint after work, missed their usual train, or stayed on in the hope of chatting up the secretary. But they were different. They worked in secret.

'It was just girls' gossip,' said Blackstone, reporting on his encounter with Dawn. 'But I caught up with the boyfriend. He's in a bad way. My guess is drugs. Anyway, he more than hinted that Mallory was behind it all.'

'You're suggesting Mallory *killed* her? What was the motive, then? Jealousy? Was he smitten? I thought he was supposed to be – perhaps he fancied the boyfriend.'

Blackstone shook his head. 'Anything like that, I think the boyfriend would have told me.'

'You're probably right,' said Jarrell. 'More likely something to do with whatever was going on with Mallory and Le Saux. The uncle, that is.' Blackstone shifted in his seat. 'I'd forgotten those two had a history. Completely forgotten. It went back a long way, of course.'

Jarrell's beaky nose looked longer than ever. 'The Super's

disappointed. He was hoping for some dirt on CID. That's why he okayed reopening the case in the first place.'

Blackstone wiped his sweaty brow with his handkerchief. 'Sonia really pulled the wool over my eyes with that story about Sonny Marsden. How did it take us so long to get almost nowhere?'

'Moules called me in today. He wants a result. He says we should question Camenzuli again. We've got to break him, he said. He thinks the first confession was real. Or even if it wasn't, it'll do.'

McGovern frowned. 'I thought he was against all that sort of thing. Phoney confessions.'

'He didn't actually *say* it'd do. Not in so many words. But he's lost interest now there's no corruption angle. He just wants it out of the way. I said I'd interview the Maltese tomorrow.'

'Sonia tried to send me in the wrong direction,' said Blackstone. 'That suggests it does have something to do with Mallory. She's covering up for him in some way.'

'It was sheer luck I followed Quinault to her flat. I didn't know it was her flat then, of course. Just chance that was where he was going.'

chapter 40

JARRELL STRODE BEHIND THE warder along the prison corridors. He'd had a brainwave.

Camenzuli was waiting for them, seated behind the little table in the interview room. He'd grown a thin moustache now. It drew attention to his crooked mouth and made him look angrier than ever.

'Your wife hasn't been to see you lately, or so we hear. Any idea why?'

The prisoner scowled.

'Mallory's wife knew your wife, isn't that right?' continued Jarrell. 'I think it was Mrs Mallory who talked to your wife and told her to get you to confess to something you didn't do. A false confession – that's a serious matter.' He paused to let it sink in. Then he coaxed: 'But you can put things right now and we'll see what we can do for you. Get you a lawyer who'll apply for bail. Get you out of here. So I'd like you to tell me what she told you. And then you'll retract your confession – your second confession – and tell me what actually happened at the hotel.'

'You better ask my wife.'

Jarrell grinned. 'I'm asking you.'

'I tell you what happened already.'

'Well, in that case why should I ask your wife? To corroborate?'

'She not been to see me.'

'Disappeared, has she?' Jarrell smirked at his victim. 'Just as I predicted. Someone's paid her off and she's done a runner.'

Camenzuli's face reddened dangerously. 'What you mean?'

'Gone off with the money. The payment.'

'You find her. Then I talk.'

'It has to be the other way round, I'm afraid. You tell me what happened and then I'll track down your wife.'

Camenzuli spat out the story in gobs of venom. His fury extended to the whole world, or at least to his whole world, as he described the visit from his wife and what Mrs Mallory had told her he should say. Camenzuli hissed with spiteful eagerness. She'd promised to get him off if he confessed.

'It was Mrs Mallory who told your wife to come here with the message that you were to confess?'

'She say it all be all right later on.'

'So what's the real story? Let's hear it.' Jarrell leaned back in his chair. 'Was the girl dead when she arrived?'

Camenzuli shook his head.

'Then why did the doctor say that?'

'I don't know nothing. Perhaps he just mean as good as. The man she came with was in a rage. It was him said they had to call the doctor pronto.'

'What man? Who was the man with her?'

The stuffy interview room seethed with the impotent rage of the prisoner. Camenzuli could contain himself no longer. 'I'm not talking no more,' he shouted and shook with fury as he leaned towards Jarrell. 'You find my wife,' he shouted. 'You find what she done with the money.' As if it had only just dawned on him that he wasn't going to get the reward.

'Who was this man?'

Camenzuli stood up and glared at the screw. 'Want to leave now.'

Jarrell scraped his chair back. Another warder escorted him back through the long passages and locked metal doors. He was relieved to be out in the open air again. The air was foggy and yellow in the Caledonian Road, but it was better than the stale prison atmosphere. He leapt on a bus as it drew away from the stop and it swung him down to King's Cross.

He walked up Argyle Street again and stopped in front of the Camenzulis' hotel. The sign on the door still said No Vacancies. The curtains were still drawn across the ground-floor windows.

He rang the bell, but there was no answer. He rattled the door handle and tried to open the door, but it was locked. This time he didn't bother to force the lock because he was almost certain the hotel was empty.

He stepped back and looked up at the house on the right. The bells studding the door frame suggested multi-occupation. Curtains limp with dirt languished against grimy windows. The basement area was clogged with overflowing dustbins. Jarrell pressed a bell at random. At first, nothing happened. Then he heard shuffling footsteps.

'Yes?' A young woman in a flowered cotton overall stared at him listlessly.

Jarrell lifted his hat. 'I'm sorry to disturb you, but I wondered if you'd seen the lady next door recently, the lady who runs the hotel?'

He marvelled that a young woman could already seem so weary of life. Her wan, pretty face was almost expressionless. However, she roused herself sufficiently to say: 'You looking for a room? There's another hotel further up.'

'I'm looking for Mrs Camenzuli. Have you seen her lately?'

The girl shook her head, as if surprised Jarrell didn't know. 'She's gone away. Closed the hotel. I 'eard she was going back to Malta.'

A child started to howl from within the house. The young woman turned away. 'Shut up, Eddy,' she shouted, but without conviction.

'Who told you that?'

'*Eddy!*' The girl was distracted. 'Dunno – just 'eard – at the shop. And then I saw her. She left with a lady. In a taxi.'

'What did the lady look like?'

'I dunno ... dressed smart, she was.' The child was still howling. 'Look, I have to go.'

Jarrell turned away. The door rattled shut behind him.

If the presence of the police in his office annoyed Mallory, he concealed it, was geniality itself. As on Jarrell's previous visit, whisky, cigars and coffee were offered. This time Jarrell declined all three.

'We're continuing our enquiries into the case of Valerie Jarvis.'

Mallory's smile was fixed to his face as usual. 'Surprised to hear that. I thought someone had been charged.'

'So you haven't heard he's retracted his confession?'

'No, I hadn't heard that.' Impossible to tell if it was true.

Jarrell smiled pleasantly. 'I'm afraid it may be rather serious, in the sense that it now appears as though it was your wife who persuaded Camenzuli to confess in the first place.' He watched Mallory, whose expression never changed.

'I'm surprised to hear that. Frankly, I think it's unlikely.'

'However, that's what the suspect says.'

'Changes his story rather a lot, don't he?'

'Indeed, sir, he does. In this case, though, there's corroboration of a sort as your wife seems to have helped Mrs Camenzuli return to Malta.'

'Can't say I see how that corroborates anything.'

'A man was present when Valerie died. Another man. Not Maltese Mike. Not the doctor. Do you have any idea who that man might have been?'

'Of course not. I wasn't there.'

'Weren't you? I rather thought you might have been.'

Mallory's eyes were chips of iceberg. 'I could take exception to that remark.'

'Okay. But you were angry at the way things had turned out with Miss Jarvis.'

'Of course I was angry. Would you want to see your best dancer take up with a louse like Archie Le Saux?'

Jarrell leaned forward a little. 'What's wrong with Archie Le Saux?'

'What's wrong with him? He should be inside and you know it. But you all cover up for each other, dontcha?'

Jarrell scrutinised Mallory's face, wide, pale, granite-like.

'I don't know quite what you mean, Mr Mallory.'

'And I don't quite understand the reason for this visit,' said Mallory, 'but it's obvious you think I had something to do with Valerie's death. And you're making allegations about my wife that I don't like.'

'It's only fair to tell you that a number of individuals have suggested your involvement in some way.'

Mallory's smile made his eyes even colder. 'Is that so?'

'It's suggested your wife was covering up for you and that in pursuance of that she persuaded Camenzuli to confess to having killed the girl.'

'My wife gets some funny ideas sometimes, but that's a new one on me.' He stood up. 'She and I go our own ways. In the sense that she doesn't interfere in my business and I don't interfere in hers. The idea that she might have done as you said – well, it just don't wash. I can look after myself and she knows that. And now, look, I don't want to seem inhospitable, but I'm a busy man. And I'm not the sort of man to do coppers' work for them. But you want to think a bit more careful about Archie Le Saux. You know who 'is uncle is. You know what they're like. Archie's a vicious piece of work and you know it. You've been looking in the wrong direction, Sergeant.'

'Are you suggesting Archie Le Saux murdered his girlfriend?'

'Even Archie wouldn't do a thing like that. Well – not when it was Valerie. You've heard about love, Sergeant? He went crazy when he found out what had happened. Went around snivelling all over the show. Hadn't the guts to do what he shoulda done – which is strange, when you come to think about it. But the agony was – it saved his bacon, didn't it? The irony of it – enough to make a corpse laugh. You've all been a bit slow on this one, ain't you? Haven't put two and two together. Sad to say it, but you're the last to know.'

chapter 41

JARRELL WENT BACK TO the station. As he arrived he encountered Slater and some of his cronies on the way out to the pub. He could have gone with them, but he reckoned the opportunity of searching their offices outweighed the usefulness of listening to them when they let their hair down.

It was an exceptionally quiet evening. Apart from the Sergeant at the front desk, there was only a lonely WPC typing letters. He found an excuse to send her down to the stacks in the basement to look for a file.

'Yes, sir.' Annabel was pretty, pert, popular and naive. No question or doubt seemed ever to cross her mind. Life was as plain and smooth as bread and butter.

Of course it was risky. And might prove fruitless. Jarrell himself wrote nothing down. That is to say, he wrote the necessary official notes and records of interviews, but he tried to keep his secret and most useful information nowhere but in his head. He hoped Slater was less careful.

Slater was certainly not meticulous. The Inspector's desk drawers were in extreme disorder: a whisky flask alongside cough sweets, illegible notes on the backs of old envelopes, loose change, banknotes, newspapers, paper clips, old bills and assorted business cards, pens and pencils, even a screwdriver.

Jarrell persisted and in the wide, flat top drawer found something worth looking at.

The manilla folder held notes about the Tony Marx case. Among them were notes about a witness who'd withdrawn his evidence.

He looked at his watch. It was past eight in the evening. The witness worked at a Soho restaurant. This would be their busiest time. He would follow it up in the morning. He slipped back to the main office and by the time Annabel reappeared he was studying a traffic report.

'I couldn't find the file you asked for, sir.'

'Oh – well, never mind.' Jarrell wasn't surprised, as the file didn't actually exist. 'Sorry I sent you downstairs for nothing.' He pulled his raincoat off its peg. 'You're working late.'

'I'm supposed to finish typing up this report for Inspector Slater.'

'He won't be coming back this evening.'

'Are you sure?' The girl spoke doubtfully. 'He said—'

Jarrell had feared the Inspector might return, but: 'He won't come back now.' He noticed Annabel looked relieved. 'Were you supposed to finish the report?'

'Yes ... but it's not that. I didn't want to be here on my own.' She flushed and turned away awkwardly.

'An empty office in the evening can be quite eerie,' agreed Jarrell encouragingly.

'I didn't mind if it was empty.' The girl laughed, but uncomfortably. Then she spoke in a rush. 'I didn't want to be here alone if he came back.'

'Why was that?'

'I know it's stupid, but he makes me nervous. I know it's silly.'

'I've noticed Mrs Ellis usually sends one of the older women down when he has some typing or dictation.'

'That's because he can't keep his hands to himself.' Now

Annabel was emboldened. 'Well, it's not exactly that. Having your bottom slapped is one thing, but he chases you into a corner. Once he pushed me up against the wall. I thought he was going to – I didn't know what he was going to do.'

'You should have complained.'

'Superintendent Gorch said it was all just fun. We shouldn't take it seriously. Anyway ... you know ... you have to expect ... it's just that he's such a big man ...'

'He is a big man. I'd be nervous.'

'Yes.' Annabel smiled at him gratefully.

Jarrell hesitated. 'Well, you don't want to stick around here any longer. Fancy a coffee on the way home? You can tell me more about it.'

chapter 42

THE NEXT MORNING JARRELL was to investigate a robbery from a souvenir shop near Tottenham Court Road underground station. The case did not interest him. After he'd taken statements, looked over the premises and arranged a visit from the fingerprinting squad, Jarrell left the main street and walked south into Soho. He continued until he came to the alley where Tony Marx had been killed all those months ago. The back doors of cafés and restaurants opened on to it. Dustbins dotted its length. Suspect liquids trickled towards the gutter. He looked up and down and then walked round into Frith Street.

There had always been Italian cafés in Soho, but now they were changing. A monster steel Gaggia machine stood behind the counter of the Palermo. In other respects it remained a traditional Italian café serving simple dishes as well as coffee and snacks. Jarrell seated himself near the back and when the waitress appeared he ordered coffee – cappuccino indeed, barely a novelty any longer – showed his police card and asked if Alfredo Signorelli the cook was around.

The girl looked startled, but did as asked. When she returned she glanced at the three other customers and lowered her voice. 'He says, do you mind to go round to the back? He will meet you by the back door.'

So Jarrell swallowed his coffee and returned to the alley. A slender young man was already waiting, cigarette in hand. He leaned against the wall and watched Jarrell approach. He had a long, medieval face and a resigned nobility of expression.

'You're not the one was here before, then.' He seemed surprised.

'That was Inspector Slater, wasn't it?'

The chef shrugged. 'Don't remember the name.'

'I believe you witnessed the murder of Tony Marx and made a statement, which you later retracted.'

Signorelli stared at the ground.

'Were you leaned on – threatened?'

'I made a mistake,' murmured Signorelli.

'I've seen a copy of the original statement you made. In that statement you said you clearly saw what happened. You stated you were out here, you were smoking a cigarette, just like you are now, you don't like to smoke in the kitchen, you said, some cooks do, but you don't approve, so you were out here, having a fag and the fight blew up out of nowhere, two men came pounding round the corner and one of them stabbed the other in front of your eyes.'

Signorelli's eyes scoured the ground as though looking for escape, as if he might vanish through the asphalt.

'You said you recognised both men.'

'I made a mistake. That's all.'

'What – you mean you recognised Marx, but not the man who killed him?'

Signorelli was silent.

'At the time you said you saw him quite clearly. You made no bones about it. So I'm thinking that someone threatened you into withdrawing your statement. Look – fair enough. No-one can force you to give evidence. I'm not trying to persuade you or lean on you in any way. I just want you to confirm to me – off the record – that it was the man you originally said it was.

It's not my case. You won't be in court. This is about something else.'

Signorelli looked sideways at Jarrell. 'How do I know—'

'Look – I'm not taking notes. I'm on my own. No-one to back me up. Like I said, it's off the record.' And Jarrell produced a banknote.

'I know the man. He was always hanging around here and the Ambassadors up the street. He was going with one of the girls, people said. I even knew his name. It was Archie Le Saux.'

'Archie Le Saux.' Jarrell drew a deep breath. After a pause: 'So why did you change your mind?'

'You're a policeman. You know the family – I didn't. I'm a respectable man. I didn't expect what happened. They waited for me one night. I got beaten up bad. They told me I hadn't seen nothing. So that's my story now.' As soon as he'd spoken, Jarrell could see he regretted it. But it was too late now. He had spoken.

It took Jarrell all afternoon to complete his report on the souvenir shop robbery, to organise the fingerprinting and report to Moules. He then spent half an hour on the telephone trying to track down Blackstone. All efforts having failed, he walked down to the press room at Scotland Yard and there he ran him to ground.

He signalled to him across the room, hoping no-one else would notice, eased his way to the door and into the passage and waited. When Blackstone joined him, he said: 'Can we talk somewhere? I've some new information.'

They walked up the windy sweep of Whitehall away from the bars frequented by their own kind, passed under Admiralty Arch and eventually found a small pub in Duke Street, St James'.

This was a different world, a world of fine arts galleries and gentlemen's clubs. Here they were completely anonymous.

Blackstone listened carefully to Jarrell's account of his meeting with Alfredo Signorelli.

'The Le Saux gang are notorious. No surprise there.'

'The strange thing is, though, we've heard nothing about it. Slater never said a word. He's never mentioned Le Saux.'

'You think the other suspect is some sort of red herring?'

'Well – it's an excuse for him not getting a result.'

'The waiter was threatened by some of Maurice Le Saux's lot, though?'

'He's a chef, not a waiter. But yes. And more than threatened. Roughed up. Quite badly he said.'

'That surely doesn't surprise you.'

'You'd think Slater would be only too keen to nail Le Saux's nephew. Open-and-shut case.'

'And Maurice Le Saux would do anything to stop it. The boy's the son of Maurice Le Saux's sister. They say he adores her. She's ill, an invalid. Maurice Le Saux would never want her upset in any way. Though if I were her I'd be pretty upset to have a son like Archie Le Saux.'

An awful possibility was forcing itself to the forefront of Blackstone's mind. 'Valerie was his girlfriend. She *must* have known. She must *surely* have known her boyfriend – what he'd done.' He simply couldn't say the word 'murder'. He couldn't bear to believe that Valerie knew her lover was a murderer.

He looked round, as if noticing his surroundings for the first time. The place was warmly lit and darkly panelled and its customers were sleek as hell, Jermyn Street types in their coats with velvet collars and their contemptuously perfect vowels. They had lots of inherited money and they married girls like the one who leaned on the bar with her fur coat half off her shoulders and a shining sweep of dark hair against her porcelain face.

While Valerie ...

Jarrell nudged him back to the present. 'You told us Archie Le Saux said Mallory had killed the girl. Or suggested that.'

'Well—' Blackstone coughed explosively into his whisky.

'That cough of yours isn't getting any better. You need to see a doctor, if you ask me.'

'I'm all right. I'm not asking you. What Archie Le Saux actually suggested, if I remember right, was that it was Mallory's *fault*. He didn't actually accuse him.'

'Nor did Camenzuli. He just said another man was present and then blew a gasket and refused to say anything more.'

'He implicated Mrs Mallory, though.'

'Now that his wife's disappeared.'

The girl in the fur coat, followed by her escort, passed close by their table so that they caught a whiff of her rich, expensive scent.

'You can't believe anything Camenzuli says.' Jarrell sipped his tonic water. 'But I'm thinking that once the chef, Signorelli, withdrew his evidence, where else could Slater go? Valerie Jarvis must have known what had happened, what her boyfriend had done. What he was accused of, anyway. She might not have believed it, but she must have been aware – perhaps Mallory was angry about that, wanted her to come forward, talk to the police—'

Blackstone spoke almost under his breath. 'Yes, Slater must have been desperate for a witness, for evidence. Once Signorelli was frightened off. He'd have naturally thought of the girlfriend. He'd have been desperate to get her to tell him the truth. And Sonia must have known something about that. I have to see Sonia.' He rose from the table and made a phone call from the phone at the back of the room.

'I can't stay long, Gerry.'

'Nice of you to come – spur of the moment idea.'

Sonia had dressed casually, casually for her, at least. It was just a drink, after all. She had wrapped herself in a voluminous white coat that opened to reveal a simple black skirt and sweater.

'What did you think of the Ambassadors?' Her legs crossed, cigarette in hand, she made a good job of seeming completely at ease.

'He's done very well. Quite the place to be seen. Congratulations in order.'

'Why did you bring the policeman with you?'

'He was interested to see the club. Just curiosity.'

Even at this time in the early evening, the cocktail hour – not that people drank cocktails much, these days – the atmosphere in the Cumberland lounge was muted and soothing. You have all the time in the world, the solid fittings and dim lights seemed to say. But Blackstone did not have all the time in the world. He wanted the truth about Valerie.

He smiled at Sonia. 'I was surprised to see you there. You live pretty much separate lives, or so I thought.'

'That's true.' She spoke languidly. 'But he wanted me to meet Stanley Coleman. If Coleman's going to do business with Mallory, he's the sort of man who'd want it to be all kosher, Mallory the upright married man and all that.'

'Kosher indeed. But actually it's not the Ambassadors I wanted to talk about. It's Valerie.'

'My poor Gerry! You're not still eating your heart out over that, are you?' Her tone was light, but she looked away from him, smoke drifting between them.

'No, it was never a big thing.' Blackstone smiled. 'But the thing is, you see, when I first mentioned it you seemed to know nothing about it, couldn't even remember when you'd last seen the girl, even her name escaped you, but now I discover your husband employed her and there was some kind of row when she left. It makes it seem as if you might have been less than frank with me, Sonia. And I thought we were good friends.'

It was killing her to smile, but she managed it. 'We are, Gerry. Of course we are.'

'Then why didn't you tell me what happened?'

'I don't *know* what happened.'

Her voice was strained. She cleared her throat. Perhaps now she was telling the truth.

Blackstone snapped his fingers at the waiter and asked for another double whisky. He poured Sonia a second cup of tea. 'Were you afraid of what might have happened? Because Mallory was involved in some way? Wasn't that why you asked me – that time we had dinner – about keeping things out of the news, or getting them in?'

'Did I say that?'

'Maybe Mallory took a fancy to the girl. That would be a bit of a turn-up for the book, but then again perhaps he swings both ways, so maybe he didn't want her to leave ... and when she still tried to, things got nasty and he went a bit too far.'

She shook her head.

'Or perhaps you were jealous. Valerie was gaining too much influence.'

'Don't be silly, darling. She was a stupid little thing. She never – well, I'm sorry, Gerry, I know you were a bit sentimental about her, but honestly ...'

She crossed and uncrossed her beautiful legs and looked round for the waiter.

'I'll have to be going soon, darling.'

'You got to hear about it, but you didn't really know what had happened. You were afraid your husband had something to do with it. So you sent me off on a wild goose chase down Notting Dale after Sonny Marsden.'

'That's nonsense, Gerry.'

'You persuaded Maltese Mike's wife to visit him and tell him what he had to do – and then the bent doctor, who did know what had happened, conveniently died …'

Sonia stood up. 'Darling, now you're really being ridiculous. And anyway, I have to go.'

She walked away across the lounge with that hesitant, drifting walk of hers. He stood looking after her. That walk was so much less decisive than she was. She swayed from side to side, but it was not erotic. The way people walked could tell you a lot about them. But the meaning of Sonia's walk was hard to decipher.

chapter 43

BLACKSTONE WAS WOKEN BY the front doorbell. Or rather, as the first thing he saw was the window, bright sunshine cruelly impacting his headache, his first thought was that the doorbell must have rung. He turned over towards the still sleeping Rita and touched her shoulder and her hair, not wishing to awake her.

Slowly, he eased into a sitting position, suppressing groans, planted his feet on the ground, his stomach aching, rested awhile, then equally slowly and even more furtively, stood up and reached for his dressing gown, a schoolboy's woollen effort with piping round the collar. He approached his front door with caution. There had been no follow-up to the threatening letters.

However, for all he knew, the little package that had dropped through the letter box, alongside the newspapers, might be a bomb. He stared at it for a long time. It hadn't been delivered by the postman. It was too early for that. He pushed it gingerly with his foot. There was something about it that looked not quite right.

Eventually he fetched a bucket from the kitchen, filled it with water from the bathroom taps, placed it in the hall and dropped the package into it.

Nothing happened. He wasn't sure if anything was meant

to happen; whether it should fizzle, or somehow explode in the water, or just die. He left the bucket and its contents in the hall. Then he called the police.

chapter 44

JARRELL TELEPHONED TO REPORT the new situation just as McGovern was about to set off for what he hoped was a final Oxford visit. So he made a detour on his way to Paddington to call on Sonia Mallory.

'Mrs Mallory doesn't receive visitors at this hour of the morning,' said Mrs Smith repressively. She was fully prepared to face the world and she was stubborn, but after an initially firm defence, she yielded to McGovern's calm insistence. They both knew she could refuse to let him in, but: 'It is important for me to have a word with Mrs Mallory. It's in her own interest. I'll not stay long.'

He had to wait a while. Sonia never saw a visitor, client, friend or detective other than properly dressed and made up.

'I'm sorry to disturb you so early. Thank you for agreeing to see me.'

This morning there was no offer of coffee or tea or something stronger. She simply sat down and waited for him to speak.

McGovern came straight to the point. 'It's about Professor Quinault again, I'm afraid, and your relationship with him. It seems just too coincidental for you and he simply to have been what you say you were. You knew his friend and colleague, Kingdom, in Berlin. Perhaps he knew quite a lot about you from that time. I know I've asked you this before, but I ask you now to tell me the truth. It has nothing to do with any attempt to make trouble for you. It is simply my job to investigate the Professor. So let's start with how you and he met – over here or back there, in Berlin.'

When she looked at him, serious and sincere, it seemed, she suddenly reminded him of the girl he'd known as Frieda five – six – years ago in Berlin. Her calculation had been well disguised then, but even when he'd understood how cold she was, he'd still pitied her a little. He even pitied her now. She'd found success and security of a kind, but he couldn't believe it was the life that the young woman he'd known would have chosen.

'What would have happened if you'd stayed in Germany?' It wasn't at all the question he'd intended.

She looked at him blankly. 'Is this what you've come to talk about at this hour in the morning?'

He shook his head. 'I just wondered.'

'If you really want to know – my father was in trouble with the authorities, the communists found him out in the end, they'd have come down hard on me too. Prison, hard labour, probably.'

'Was it there you met Quinault?'

'Oh no.' He marvelled at how controlled she was, her economy of gesture.

'So how ...?'

'I don't know how he tracked me down. But he did. It must have been after Kingdom killed himself. He blamed me partly, I think. I imagine he started to look for me in Germany and eventually he found me here. I thought I had covered my tracks rather successfully, but clearly not quite well enough.'

'So it wasn't that he wanted you for espionage purposes.'

'That's a ridiculous idea.'

'Revenge, then, for what happened to his friend, to Kingdom?'

'No ...'

'Gerry Blackstone thinks you've been blackmailing him. Perhaps on account of what he gets up to here in your flat.'

'You asked me that before, you remember.'

'You seemed to think it was very funny.'

Sonia frowned. 'I didn't want to talk about it then. Perhaps I should have. I'm really not sure why I didn't. I suppose ...'

'Suppose what?'

'Oh ... nothing. I'm not a blackmailer, Mr Detective. Far from it. But you know, you should really look into the Professor's passion for antiquities. He spends a lot of money on those little relics of the Roman Empire. They're very expensive, I believe, almost priceless, and hard to get hold of legally.'

'You mean—?'

'I mean the boot's entirely on the other foot, Chief Inspector McGovern. You got it right. But the wrong way round. That's why I found it so funny.'

chapter 45

'CHARLES! *CHARLES!*' Mrs Hewitt called up from the hall. 'There's someone to see you.'

He stood at the top of the stairs and pushed back his hair. The tall figure stood against the light from the open front door. It took him some seconds to recognise the detective.

'DCI McGovern. I wonder if I might have a few words.'

'Charles darling, what *have* you been up to!'

'You've no cause to be alarmed, madam. A routine enquiry.'

Charles tried to appear nonchalant, his descent of the staircase intended to look casual. Yet he was feeling slightly sick, partly on account of having been woken too suddenly, partly because of the only half-acknowledged fear that shadowed his erotic life and its risks; those dangers that had always excited him, but which now made him feel nervous. 'I hope it isn't about my bike,' he drawled, and lounged against the banister.

'Is there somewhere we can—'

'Let's go outside,' suggested Charles hastily. He could not bear the thought of this imposing policeman in his bed-sitting room. There was something too scarily intimate about the exposure of his books, the picture of Oscar Wilde and, as revealing, of Montgomery Clift, easily reinterpreted as a secret betrayed rather than as a camp joke.

In the hall he grabbed his duffel coat from its hook. 'We could walk down towards the Parks,' he said.

'As you wish. It's about Andras Ferenczy, the Hungarian student. You've heard, I expect. He drowned.'

'It was in the *Oxford Mail*.'

'I met you with him.'

The fresh air had woken Charles up. He was beginning to feel prepared to approach this encounter as a challenge. 'For about five seconds,' he said.

'It wasn't too short a time to pass on some information about the Professor.'

'I hope it was useful. Is that what this is about?'

'It was a strange thing to do – to pass on that information. I'm interested to know what you were up to. But I also wanted to ask you about Ferenczy. I'm back here to help sort it out. It's the Oxford police's problem, essentially, but I've a responsibility too, so ...'

'How did you find out where I live?'

'You gave your address as Magdalen College. I asked at the porter's lodge.'

'Of course.'

'Ferenczy. Did you know him well?'

'How could I? He'd only been here for a few weeks.'

'But you struck up a friendship with him.'

'Well ... I met him at a meeting, that's all. You know, about Hungary and Suez and everything.' Caginess was the best course. 'Well, actually it wasn't about Suez. Just Hungary.'

Now the detective was explaining that anything Charles could say about the Hungarian's state of mind would help to determine whether the drowning might have been suicide or was accidental. He hadn't been drinking. It wasn't clear what he was doing by the Cherwell on that particular evening. All that seemed certain was that he'd drowned the evening before his body was found.

Charles had already tried to work out which evening that was. He didn't think it could have been the evening Andras failed to keep the rendezvous at Blackwell's. That had been the evening Penny had told him about her pregnancy. He hadn't gone down to London until the following weekend and only on the following Monday had the body been discovered – or was it yesterday? Either way, it could not have been that evening. Charles knew he had no cause to feel guilty for not having rushed round Oxford in search of Andras when he didn't turn up, yet feel guilty he did.

'I asked you what state of mind he was in.' McGovern's voice cut through Charles' thoughts.

'Sorry – I was thinking about that, but ...' He was unsure how much to say. The whole thing was a minefield. 'I don't really know,' he said feebly.

'Students at the hostel who knew him told me he was depressed.'

A few moments ago, Charles had felt enlivened by the thought of sparring with the forces of the law, but now he was in retreat again. 'Probably ... possibly,' he said warily.

'One of them suggested he might be troubled by feelings for his own sex,' said McGovern ponderously.

'Really?' Charles gazed far away into the middle distance, where the Banbury and Woodstock roads forked. 'Oh look, we've reached the Parks – we could wander in if you like.'

'There's a bench. We can sit down.'

Here and there a student wandered down a path or across the grass. A little wind got up and scurried a few dead leaves along the gravel. Charles suddenly felt immensely listless and dreary. 'God, it's depressing.'

McGovern leaned forward and looked closely at him. 'You mean it's depressing that he'd made a huge effort to flee his native country after a failed attempt to change things over there – and then, having got here, couldn't carry on?'

'Yes, that's more or less what I meant.'

'Unless, of course, it was an accident.'

'That'd be as bad, in a different way.'

McGovern produced a cigarette case. 'Smoke?'

'Thanks.'

'Mr Hallam – I don't know how well you knew Ferenczy. Is there anything – anything – more you can tell me? About your relationship with him? About how he was feeling?'

'I'm afraid not.'

'The Oxford police are in charge of the case and they're fairly convinced he killed himself. Everything his Hungarian friends at the hostel said points in that direction. There isn't a note – so far. It'll be necessary to search the house. His room at least. The Professor will probably not like that.'

'I shouldn't think he would.'

'About Professor Quinault. Is there anything more you can tell me about him? Why were you looking through his belongings? You had no right to do that, had you? What were you up to? Was there something about the Professor you felt was suspicious?'

Charles felt the man's gaze. This was the moment. He should speak. 'No,' he said, 'there wasn't. Not then. But there is now.' He paused – partly because he was on the brink, but still uncertain. It was the right thing to do, but was it *really* what Reggie had wanted when she told him?

He took a deep breath and began. 'I know someone in London – someone well known, who's – well, being blackmailed. At least, my friend is having an affair with him. They're both married, you see. And it's Professor Quinault who's blackmailing him. I know it sounds—'

'Why did your friend tell you this?'

'She couldn't go to the police herself. Her friend wouldn't let her. I think perhaps she sort of wanted me to.'

'She should have consulted her lawyer.'

'She can't do that. He's her husband's best friend. The lawyer, I mean.'

'The man being blackmailed is a public figure, you say?'

Charles nodded. Now he feared he'd said too much. 'She told me Professor Quinault needed a lot of money for his—'

'For his collection of Roman statuettes.' At last he understood. So that was what Sonia had meant when she mentioned them. It was the wrong way round, she'd said: because she wasn't blackmailing Quinault. He was blackmailing her. Although something had prevented her from saying it in so many words; some long-ago-developed defensive mechanism, to always say as little as possible.

McGovern stood up. He looked round the peaceful expanse of the Parks. He was so unprepared for this outcome that he was at a loss for words. 'Who'd have thought it?' he finally managed. '*He* was blackmailing *her!*'

'Sorry?' Charles looked at him, puzzled.

'Nothing. It's a surprise, that's all.' Unexpectedly, he smiled at the youth at his side. 'So I suppose in a way I've you to thank – for drawing my attention to the money. But I must warn you not to make a habit of riffling through other people's private papers.'

Charles smiled. 'I know,' he said. 'That's the sort of thing that only detectives are allowed to do.'

chapter 46

McGOVERN LEFT CHARLES HALLAM on the park bench and walked slowly away. Nothing had prepared him for what he'd just heard. In itself, Charles Hallam's startling information was useless, nothing but hearsay. But he had to pursue it.

He decided to return to Quinault's house. It was unorthodox. On the basis of some gossip imparted by a student he'd never get a warrant. Even to ask questions would be open to challenge.

He had to consider the possibility that Hallam had been acting out of malice. The death of the Hungarian student had upset him, perhaps. It was just a wild accusation. Or perhaps he bore some grudge against his Professor.

McGovern borrowed a parked bike from outside Somerville College. It was a woman's bike, but he didn't care. He left it in the drive of the Grange and knocked on the front door.

This time the front door was locked. He walked round to the back garden and tried the French windows. These were also locked, but he remembered how flimsy the lock was and prised it open without much difficulty.

He was once more in the Professor's study.

This time he made a much more careful search: of the desk and its drawers, of the cupboards beneath the glass cabinet and of the filing cabinets standing along the opposite wall. It was painstaking and wearisome, the sort of detailed work he was good at. He kept an ear open for the sound of either the Professor or his wife returning. He knew how he would explain his presence were they to turn up, and it no longer troubled him, because the pieces of the puzzle were slotting into place. He also now saw that the puzzle was different from what he'd expected or assumed.

Every so often he looked at his watch. It was nearly an hour before he found what he wanted.

A little notebook: it was written in Latin. McGovern had no Latin, but he did recognise Roman numerals and worked out that sums of money were set against Latinised names, with dates. At the back of the notebook a second set of notes appeared to record purchases of objects, some of which were recognisable as referring to the antiquities he collected: 'Minerva', for example.

It was simple and made perfect sense. Quinault obtained money for the artefacts he collected by means of blackmail. It might well be that the objects themselves were illegally obtained, looted from neglected sites in Asia Minor or the Middle East. That would make them very pricey. He slipped the notebook into his pocket.

The girl's bike was where he'd left it in the shrubbery. He biked into the centre of Oxford and made his way back to Corpus Christi.

There was an ambulance outside the college. A police car had parked further along the lane.

The porter's lodge was unattended. Policemen hurried in and out. Cyclists, one with a scholar's gown billowing out like a witch, skidded along the lane. Several groups of two or three undergraduates loitered in the quad. He asked one of the young men what had happened.

'One of the Fellows has died.'

At the police station, Detective Sergeant Venables was redder-faced and more distracted than ever.

'Two unexpected deaths like this in the past week! What a kerfuffle! Of course, in the Professor's case, there's nothing suspicious.'

McGovern could not deceive himself; he was bitterly disappointed. He'd been cheated. It was a shameful thought, but it was so. He was furious. The old bastard had had the temerity to die on him.

'What happened?'

'Heart failure. Apparently he had a heart condition.'

'I'll be returning to London shortly. I don't think I'll be back. My work here is completed.'

Sergeant Venables looked, thought McGovern, both surprised and relieved. 'There weren't any problems?' It was only half a question.

'None relevant to the inquiry. Obviously Ferenczy's death was tragic.'

'Yes. Yes, of course.' Venables looked solemn. 'You were informed, I take it, that we did find a suicide note?'

'No.'

'Apologies – apologies. An oversight. One of his friends found it.'

'Thank you for letting me know.'

Outside the police station McGovern stood, looked round. He still had the borrowed bicycle and decided to ride up to Headington before he left town.

Sally Mabledon was as usual entrenched behind piles of paperwork. She seemed genuinely pleased to see him.

'I've come to say goodbye,' he said, 'my work here's finished now.'

'Right.' She looked slightly puzzled. 'Was it – had it to do with poor Andras, then?'

'No. I wondered if Irén was around?'

'Probably. Have you looked in the common room?'

Irén was seated cross-legged on a sagging sofa, holding court to two new admirers. She leapt up when she saw McGovern.

'Oh, you are back! I thought you would come again, after Andras—'

'I think it's time I invited you for that coffee, isn't it?'

This time he left the bike behind. They took a bus into the centre.

'There's a coffee bar on Broad Street,' he suggested.

'I know. The Cadena. A famous poet sits there. W.H. Auden, he is called.'

They walked through from the High Street and past the Sheldonian. Irén peered through the window. 'Oh, I think he is not there today. Never mind. At last, a really good cup of coffee. Thank you.'

He smiled. She wore her black beret at a rakish angle. He admired her vivacity. To have come through the turmoil of the crushed revolution and still to be so full of life was admirable.

'You can have a bun too, if you like.'

'Oh please! I love these British buns. They are rather horrible, but I like them.'

'Or have a brandy snap.'

'What is a brandy snap?'

He ordered one.

'So what will you do, Irén?'

Her smile, so mischievous, suggested more than words could. 'I shall do many things.' She was so full of hope for the future. McGovern envied her cruel capacity to go forward ruthlessly, to leave disaster behind.

'I wanted to ask you about Andras. I was very sorry he drowned. He wasn't like you, was he? He couldn't leave the past behind. Or perhaps he was just too burdened by his doubts and his unhappiness. The police told me he did leave a note, so it seems clear it was suicide. I wanted to ask about the note. The Sergeant said one of his friends had found it. Is that right?'

'I found it. At least ...' and she looked up at him from under her short black lashes, 'it was not exactly a suicide note, but it was something he wrote in a notebook about how unhappy he was. So it was *like* a suicide note. And I thought it is better it is suicide, otherwise it is worse for his family – I suppose they will be told this has happened.'

'I don't understand. Wouldn't they prefer it to be just a terrible accident? Not that anything could be much comfort. But suicide—'

'They will never think it is an accident.'

'Are you saying it might not be an accident or suicide, after all?'

'I don't know, but you see in his notebook there was more. He did not say all the truth – to me, I mean – about the men. You remember the men who came to see him? I told you? They wanted him to spy for them, if he does this they will see he stays in this country, does not go to Canada. He would stay here with Gyorgy. They even said they will arrange for him to go to Cambridge with Gyorgy.'

'I too found out more about those men.' He had telephoned a contact. 'They are Hungarians, but they work for us, for the British. They have lived here a long time, well, since the war. They fled the communist regime. They'd been supporters of Horthy, of the fascists. But now they are working for us. However, what I don't know is how they were trying to use him, or what they thought they'd get out of him.' He found it all immensely depressing.

'Well, he does not know what to believe. He is so – he is in big conflict. So in the end, I think he did drown himself. He couldn't swim, you know.'

'What other explanation is there, unless it was an accident?'

'Could these men have done this? Pushed him in?'

'But if what Andras wrote was true, they wanted him to spy for them, Irén. They were hardly going to murder him.'

'Well – you are right. They would not do this. Yet you do not know what they might do. But I think we have to believe – I think it is better – that he drowned himself.'

'Yes. I think we probably do.'

chapter 47

ARCHIE LE SAUX WAS ARRESTED. The suspect put up no defence at all. He made no attempt to deny that he'd stabbed Tony Marx, although he wouldn't admit that it was on his uncle's orders. Jarrell, watching him, saw that some central spring was broken. He offered a few excuses: that Tony Marx had double-crossed his uncle; that he hadn't meant actually to kill Marx, only wound him; and that Marx had a knife, so he'd acted essentially in self-defence. But it was all without conviction. He seemed hardly to care what happened.

'So your uncle threatened Signorelli, the witness.'

Le Saux drew his hand across his eyes. 'I'm tired,' he said.

'Just a few more questions.' Jarrell wanted to be as brisk as possible. 'We have to talk about Valerie.'

Le Saux sat low in his chair. His eyes seemed half closed.

'What happened?'

Le Saux shifted around in his chair. 'I don't want to talk about that,' he muttered.

'Why not?'

'My uncle shouldn't'a done that. Then he wouldn't'a got onto Val.'

'Who wouldn't?'

'The copper, of course. The one in charge of the case.'

There was silence in the room.

'Inspector Slater?'

'Yeah – 'course.'

Le Saux was charged with the murder of Tony Marx. Now Jarrell was seated with McGovern in the Superintendent's office for the debriefing. Jarrell cleared his throat. To accuse a fellow officer was a serious matter.

'Le Saux still maintains that Mallory was really to blame for what happened. He sacked Valerie Jarvis because he was furious to find Valerie was in love with him – with Le Saux, that is. Not because of Valerie, but because he thought it reflected badly on the Ambassadors.'

'Slater, meanwhile, was furious that Maurice Le Saux, the uncle, had frightened Signorelli off. But then he saw a different opportunity. Valerie Jarvis had been sacked and her boyfriend was in a bad way. Now she hadn't any money. Her lover was a wanted man. Le Saux swears she believed him innocent. But Slater didn't know that. It may not be true, anyway. Slater got hold of the girl. He tried to get her to talk, took her to the hotel. He could do what he liked with her there, I assume. Camenzuli was his grass. His creature, really. Things got a bit rough and – well, he killed her.'

'So the doctor got it wrong when he said she was dead on arrival.' McGovern frowned. 'Why did he say that?'

'I don't know. And he can't tell us.'

'That information came from your reporter friend, didn't it?' Moules' spectacles glittered. 'Perhaps he misunderstood. Unless Camenzuli corroborates Le Saux's story we won't get far with this. We can't charge an officer on the basis of some rigmarole by a man we've just charged with murder.'

'Camenzuli will corroborate,' stated Jarrell confidently.

'Mind you, we'll still get him on another charge – accessory after the fact – perverting the course of justice.'

'And what about Mrs Camenzuli, who seems to have disappeared?'

'We believe it was Mrs Mallory. She was afraid her husband was guilty of Valerie's murder. She heard about the row when Valerie was sacked and jumped to the conclusion that Mallory had done it. She cast around for an alternative suspect. And lo and behold! Good news – the Maltese was arrested and once he was inside Mrs Mallory persuaded his wife to get her husband to confess.'

'That seems implausible to me,' said Moules. He was fidgeting with his desk accessories more than ever.

'With respect, sir, I haven't finished. The question is why Slater needed Valerie's evidence, why he needed her to tell him Archie had killed Tony Marx when there was the evidence of the chef, Signorelli. Did he perhaps need more evidence because Signorelli's wasn't definite enough? But it seemed to be extremely clear.

'Yet Slater went round to the girl's flat – room, I think it was, really – and the landlady said she'd left with him. Not exactly arrested, but she didn't want to go. Under some sort of duress. That's Archie Le Saux's story, anyway. Le Saux recognised Slater from the landlady's description. The next thing was, Valerie Jarvis was dead.

'Camenzuli knew what had happened at the hotel, of course, because he was there. And no need to call the police because a policeman was there already: Slater. Of course, Slater didn't let on he'd been there himself, but he was able to play it all down. The investigation wasn't taken seriously.

'On the other hand, Archie Le Saux also knew, or at least guessed, what had happened. So Archie told his uncle. And then all Maurice Le Saux had to do was make it clear to Slater that his nephew was not going to be arrested. Slater buried the evidence – though I must say he didn't bury it very deep – and cooked up another suspect, a suspect who turned out to have a very strong alibi. That may have suited Slater too, because by now the whole case was a mess. If he managed to frame someone it might all come apart in court – or earlier. It was better simply not to solve the crime, to kick it into the long grass. Difficult in the short run, but in the long run he hoped it would just go away – like the death of Valerie Jarvis promised to do.'

There was silence in the room. McGovern pictured the scene in the hotel. Why had Slater taken her there? Did he not want to question her at the station? Because whatever happened, Camenzuli would never talk?

Moules passed his hand across his forehead. 'I am simply astonished,' he said eventually, 'that Slater thought he could get away with it. But how very stupid of him to have killed the girl.'

McGovern met Blackstone in the Queen's Head, just as he had that first time, in November, months ago. The press of recent events was difficult to assimilate. He needed time to sort through facts and separate them from surmise and fiction. It was not a bad idea to mull things over with Blackstone.

Blackstone looked stunned when he heard Le Saux's story. 'To be honest,' he said, 'it hurts my professional pride. I'm usually pretty quick to hear the rumours. That story must have been buzzing around the underworld like nobody's business.'

'Maybe not. Maurice Le Saux would want it kept quiet.'

'To think – we were the last to know. How bloody humiliating. I need another drink.' It was McGovern's round. When he returned with a whisky and a beer, Blackstone said: 'I always knew Slater was a bit crazy.'

'We haven't got him yet. Jarrell's interviewing Camenzuli again tomorrow.'

'It breaks my heart. It makes me sick to think of it. He just batted her away like a fly. Snuffed out her life. She was just a young girl. With her whole life before her.'

chapter 48

BLACKSTONE TURNED OUT OF the lift towards his front door. He must have forgotten to double-lock it, because it opened before he'd turned the second key, but he was too tired and preoccupied to worry about that. It was a relief to have had it from Jarrell that Camenzuli had finally told the truth. He had described Slater's arrival with the frightened girl. He'd described how Slater took her upstairs and how from the sound of it he'd tried to terrify her into giving him the evidence that would convict her lover, Le Saux. Finally, he'd described how the two had struggled on the landing, how Slater had his hands round the girl's neck and then how the girl's broken body lay at the bottom of the stairs.

The television was on. Blackstone could hear it murmuring away. He must have left that on too. And the light in the lounge.

He made first for the kitchen where the whisky was kept. He was too exhausted to see Rita tonight. He poured himself a double and carried it towards the lounge.

A man rose from the sofa where he'd been waiting. He was tall, he was broad.

'Good God. Slater! What the hell are you doing here?'

'Whaddya think, me old darling? I'm waiting for you.'

chapter 49

McGOVERN RECEIVED A CALL from Detective Sergeant Venables. 'I just thought you ought to know,' huffed Venables down the long-distance line. 'The post-mortem wasn't quite so clear cut. In fact, the inquest returned an open verdict. The Professor had a congestive heart condition. He took digitalis, or had in the past. There was an excess of digitalis in the body. He probably died from digitalis toxicity.'

Venables' bald account was another indigestible fact to come to terms with. McGovern didn't know what to make of it, but it preoccupied him as he took a cab to visit Sonia Mallory. A cab was justified in the pouring rain; and he was also in a hurry. Lily wanted him home early on this particular evening.

As he waited for the woman he'd known as Frieda he looked round the peach-coloured drawing room and it suddenly seemed stale and cheap. Yet in its cheapness he found a sadness in spite of himself. How human beings strove to make something of their lives and in such unpromising circumstances. Frieda had clawed her way out of East Berlin and out of post-war Germany and here she was today, doing her best to put a glossy sheen on her sordid occupation. Then he remembered how she'd exploited others – children – to save her own skin and her situation lost its poignancy.

She looked as calm as ever. She played the hostess, but he refused her offer of a drink.

'This is a formal visit. I was sent to Oxford to monitor Professor Quinault's activities. Now he's dead, I wanted to tie up the loose ends.'

'Of course.' She was demurely dressed today in a white peter pan blouse and grey skirt.

'Why didn't you tell me you were being blackmailed by the old man? That would have been helpful. After all, I knew all about your past, so what had you to lose?'

'I didn't know where it might lead. I couldn't afford a court appearance. Mallory would have been annoyed. Bad publicity. I'd no idea where it might end. I preferred to keep quiet and pay. But it was becoming more and more difficult. One of my clients, an MP – a government minister, in fact – was having the same trouble. I got in touch with him. We met. He didn't know about Germany, at least I thought he didn't. I believe Quinault may have dropped some hints about my past, though. From something the MP said ... but anyway, whatever my past might have been it didn't bother him, because he was getting desperate. I had an idea as to how we might resolve it.'

'What sort of idea was that?'

'Well, I wanted to persuade him to go to the police. My name couldn't be brought into it, but I thought he should call Quinault's bluff. After all, he hadn't done anything illegal. But he said that wasn't possible. We tried to think of another way ... in the end, though, nothing came of it. I didn't see him again.'

'You tried very hard to prevent us from finding out what happened to Valerie Jarvis. You were afraid your husband had killed her. Wasn't that it?'

The room was so quiet. Little sound came from the outside world, veiled by the net curtains that shrouded the window. Had she felt safe here, relatively safe, at least, until Quinault had turned up and Valerie had died?

Sonia looked at her pale fingernails. She drew a cigarette from the packet on the glass table. 'He was angry,' she said in a low voice. 'It wasn't so much Valerie leaving in itself as her leaving with Le Saux. He couldn't stand Archie. He knows the boy's uncle from way back. They never got on. Old enemies, in fact, he told me. Mallory wanted him to do something about Archie. There were all these rumours flying around. Everyone *knew* it was Archie who'd done Tony Marx. I thought Mallory might have tried to get Valerie to go to the police – because she must have known – and he'd lost his temper and hit her and ... it would have been an accident, but I was afraid. I don't see Mallory often. We don't discuss these things.'

These things! As if murder were an everyday occurrence. McGovern watched her and waited for her to continue. But she simply sat and smoked in silence and eventually he prompted her. 'I know all about your past in Germany,' he said. 'You've no reason to lie to me. You may as well tell me everything that happened now that Archie's been charged. We have his version of events. But he's not the most reliable witness, especially against a police officer. You could be helpful to us if your story supports his.'

He could not imagine her giving evidence in court, but he had no alternative but to wait, bringing his silent, patient pressure to bear on her resolve, if resolve it was. She kept silent, so he tried again. 'Why did you – how did you – persuade Camenzuli to say he pushed Valerie down the stairs?'

She didn't look at him. She seldom looked at him.

'That was a bit desperate.'

'It worked, didn't it? I rescued Maria – really. She wasn't capable of carrying on the hotel on her own. I promised there'd be money. Her husband would probably get off anyway. People are so greedy. He fell for it. And, to tell you the truth, Maria was quite glad he was inside. And I helped her. I did pay her handsomely. So that she could go back to Malta. That was what she really wanted.'

Was this the truth? In preparation for this encounter McGovern had considered numerous angles. 'She was also a liability,' he countered. 'You never knew what she might say next. Likewise Dr Swann. There are doubts he died of an overdose. Or committed suicide. It's gone down as accidental death, but the case could always be reopened.'

'Yes – I heard poor Dr Swann had passed away.'

'Some drugs went missing from his flat.'

Sonia stood up and stalked over to the window. She lifted aside the net curtain and looked out for a moment. 'He was always a rather soft touch for his regular clients.'

'It seemed as if some morphine had gone. And other drugs – digitalis, for example. Not the sort of drug an addict would be looking for.'

She continued to look out of the window.

'Professor Quinault probably died from an excess of digitalis.'

Sonia sat down opposite him again. 'I hope you're not trying to blame me for Professor Quinault's heart condition.'

'You knew he had a heart condition?'

'Of course. I read the papers. I read his obituary.'

'Had Quinault not died, we would have pursued the charge of blackmail. It would have been difficult. Victims like yourself, or like the politician you mentioned, are reluctant to appear in court. Even if the blackmailer is convicted, the victims have also been found guilty in the public eye of whatever they had done. The sexual misdemeanours of a politician – it's very damaging. Your past – very damaging to your husband, as well as to you.'

She was silent.

'I returned to Oxford – one last time. I spoke to the porter at Corpus Christi. It was too late, of course. He couldn't remember who had passed in and out of the college on the day Quinault died. Undergraduates, messengers, visitors, tourists. I was at the college myself that day. The ambulance had got there before me. There was a lot of toing and froing. The porter was distracted. Anyone could have come in or out. And beforehand – there's no security. Anyone can just walk in and roam around the colleges. I wondered, though, what you were doing on that particular day. Three weeks ago. Tuesday the twenty-third.'

Sonia's calm was unruffled. Suspects often blustered when questioned about an alibi. They took offence and yet often at the same time looked furtive and evasive, even when perfectly innocent. Not Sonia. 'I expect I was here. I usually am. I could easily check. And Mrs Smith would vouch for me. She would confirm that I was here.'

He knew it was only a wild supposition. He had no evidence at all. 'In the end,' he said, 'you realised your fears about your husband were baseless. You learned that Slater had killed Miss Jarvis. So all your efforts had been a waste of time and effort. Apart, of course, from Quinault's timely death.'

McGovern unlocked his front door. Lily called from the kitchen. She had opened a bottle of wine and two glasses stood on the table. This was unusual.

'Is this a celebration?'

'Our exhibition has got a brilliant write-up in *Fine Arts Review*. And someone came to see it from the Institute of Contemporary Arts. The ICA! Isn't that amazing? They may even transfer it to their gallery in Dover Street. Can you imagine! That would be simply wonderful.'

'That really is something to celebrate!' McGovern took the corkscrew she proffered him. 'I wish I could say the same. The German woman – you remember? She's dangerous. I've only just begun to understand how dangerous. I've a very strong suspicion that she murdered two men she thought were a threat to her, or to her husband, but I haven't a shred of evidence. There's not a thing I can do about it. Not a thing.'

'You also solved two murders.'

'It was the journalist who solved them – with Jarrell's help.'

'Don't be like that. But listen – I have another piece of news. Something else to celebrate.'

'The good news about your exhibition.'

'But something else, as well.' She looked at him as he poured the wine. He couldn't read her expression. She raised her glass. They drank. 'Give me a hug,' she said.

McGovern encircled her waist. 'What is it?'

'I saw the doctor today.' She paused.

He caught his breath in anxiety. Surely she wasn't ill.

'It's what you wanted.'

He didn't believe it. 'But—'

'I know. But nothing's foolproof, is it? Perhaps the Pope stuck a pin through it.'

'Oh, Lily.' He held her tightly, not knowing what to say or even how to feel.

She looked up into his face. 'You're happy, aren't you, Jack? I did so want you to be pleased.'

'Of course I'm pleased, I'm so happy,' he muttered.

'Then I'm happy too.'

He stroked her hair and kissed her cheek and of course he was happy. Yet as they drank to the future, seated on opposite sides of the kitchen table, an unexpected sadness tinged his joy. It was a bittersweet celebration, because he knew that for her it was also a kind of defeat, and he almost wished he hadn't got his way, that he hadn't won. She would, of course, love his child, their children. Yet those children might in the end push her art into second place and that would mean that the thing he wanted most in life involved, for her, a kind of renunciation.

chapter 50

REGINE HAD INVITED CHARLES to the party she was organising at the Ambassadors Club. She'd told him he was welcome to bring a friend, so Charles had Fergus in tow. Fergus would now have a second opportunity to impress Mrs Drownes and the party might also, Charles suggested, provide a scene for the novel Fergus was writing.

Fergus dismissed this idea. 'It's about the decline of the Communist Party, not some sleazy thriller.'

Besides the Drownes themselves, guests included the currently rather notorious 'angry young man' Tom Harrison, a minor writer, who arrived with a bold-looking girlfriend dressed as an existentialist all in black. Sir Avery and Lady Pearson were also of the party. The guest of honour, however, was Regine's latest 'discovery', the crime reporter, Gerry Blackstone. The evening, in fact, was to celebrate his recovery after he'd been so nearly slaughtered by a detective who'd gone spectacularly mad.

The scandal had wiped everything else off the front pages. Blackstone should have died. He would have died if his girlfriend hadn't turned up in the nick of time. The policeman, Detective Inspector Slater, had sent the journalist anonymous letters and even a bomb before the actual attack, when he had left the reporter for dead. He hadn't even bothered to cover his tracks. His fury that Blackstone had uncovered the truth about the death of Valerie Jarvis had finally sent him over the edge.

The girlfriend had been worried when Blackstone didn't answer the phone and arrived at his flat to find the front door open and Blackstone lying in a pool of blood on the sitting-room floor. She'd called an ambulance and staunched the blood from the wound in his chest. Somehow the bullet had missed the vital organs, but he'd taken months to recover.

Charles assumed that the pretty young woman Blackstone had with him was the heroine of the story. 'Young enough to be his daughter,' muttered Fergus.

'You look super in a dinner jacket,' said Regine to Charles. 'You're looking terribly well. Is it because we've seen the last of that creepy old Professor Quinault? Or were you sorry to lose him?'

'Sorry to lose him? *No!* It's the best thing that's happened to me since ...' He couldn't think of anything. 'You know, I'm not really surprised he was a blackmailer. There was something repellent about him. He was so bitchy about everyone too. And he loathed women. Thought female classicists were the dregs of the earth. That new novelist – Iris Murdoch? – all he had to say about her was, poor woman, she knows no Greek.'

'I tried one of her books, but I didn't really enjoy it.'

Charles lowered his voice, although William Drownes was at the other end of the table. 'Your friend must be relieved. About Quinault.'

Regine took a quick gulp of champagne. 'Yes ... well ... yes, a tremendous relief. Now I suppose we'll go on as before.' She gazed down into her glass. 'Sometimes I don't think I *can* go on indefinitely like this ... things not changing ... ever.'

'Oh Reggie.' He squeezed her arm, but had no idea what to say.

'I'm just being morbid. Come and dance.'

He enjoyed the feeling that the guests seated at the tables

arranged round the floor were watching him as he circled with Regine, and that they made a striking couple, she with her red hair and elegant black dress, he in black tie, which was always so flattering.

Later he found himself in conversation with the crime reporter. 'I'm dying to hear more about Bodkin Adams. What a name for a murderer for a start! Quite Dickensian.'

Blackstone was smoking as though his life depended on it. 'But he ain't a murderer, is he? He's been acquitted.'

'I was utterly amazed! Could that possibly have been the right verdict?'

'Personally I doubt it. He had some very powerful friends. But don't quote me on that.'

The reporter's words shocked Charles, despite his blasé cynicism. They also exhilarated him, since here was someone other than himself who suspected that the myths everyone lived by might be just myths or even downright lies: the justice system not impeccable, the powerful dishonest and the political system corrupt. British complacency and conservatism might, after all, be nothing more than a flimsy façade. Fergus, of course, believed those things too, but he was a communist, even if he'd left 'the Party'. Perhaps Charles' disdain for the status quo meant that he was becoming a communist too.

'We're honoured,' muttered Blackstone. 'Here comes Mallory.'

Charles looked at the man who now loomed over their table. He first greeted Regine, but of course it was the presence of the crime reporter that had drawn him over.

He pulled up a chair between Blackstone and Charles. 'I never know, Blackie, whether we're friends or enemies. But at least one way or another, we've seen off Slater. And now he's safely in Broadmoor. Not fit to plead, eh? That was a let-out for the Met, weren't it? They wouldn't have wanted one of their own to be the centrepiece of a damaging show trial. God knows what might have come creeping out from the woodwork if it had come to court.' The gravelly voice was ripe with irony.

'Unfortunately true,' agreed Blackstone.

'Not happy about the Bodkin Adams verdict either, I'm guessing.'

Charles was aware of the bulk of the promoter next to him. The cigar he was smoking sent a waft of masculinity in his direction. The broad shoulders were not just the result of the padding of the smooth, dark suit. And soon Mallory turned his full attention onto Charles.

'Who's this? You haven't introduced us.'

'Friend of Mrs Drownes. Oxford graduate. Researches ancient Rome.'

'A college boy, eh?' The iceberg eyes pierced Charles like a laser. Charles flinched psychologically from Mallory's overwhelming presence. Yet he reacted physically in a manner outside his control, responding in the most languidly suggestive way. He was incapable of not playing up to the promoter's gaze. It was an irresistible force field of intent, to which his responses were automatic, without his even being aware of the way in which his sullen eyelids lowered, nor of the half-smile that sent a reply far different from the decisive 'No' he had in mind.

'Ancient Rome. That's interesting.'

'I'm afraid it isn't, really. Nothing about catamites and slave boys, or Christians mauled by lions, or anything like that, unfortunately.'

'Unfortunate if you've a taste for that sort of thing. I'd like to hear more about it.'

Charles smiled enigmatically. Of course he had no intention of having anything to do with this frightful and rather terrifyingly outsize bit of rough. Yet every movement, every glance, sent a different message.

'About the Romans?'

'About you. Saw you dancing with the redhead. You dance well. Well as any gigolo.'

'I'd probably quite like to be a gigolo. An easy life, wouldn't you think? Lying on the beach all day and dancing all night?'

'I thought you were brainy. Life of the mind and all that.'

'Well … I'm supposed to become a Fellow of the College – you know, to lecture at Oxford. But I did the Naval Russian course for National Service. It's partly a kind of training for the secret services and I'm not sure I wouldn't rather do that instead.'

'Would you?' Mallory smiled wolfishly. 'Looking for a life of adventure, then.' He handed Charles a card he'd extracted from an inner pocket. 'Come and see me. Next Monday, if that suits you.'

'Very kind of you, sir, but I'm supposed to go back to Oxford.'

Mallory got to his feet. He placed a forceful hand on Charles' shoulder. 'Another time then, my son.'

chapter 51

THE SUN HAD FALLEN behind the buildings. The High was in shadow. As Penny winged past Queens on her bike, the melancholy yet jaunty lilt of the Tommy Steele hit 'I never felt more like singing the blues' floated out from the quad into the empty street.

Had Oxford in the end been what she'd wanted? It had been worth it, hadn't it?

All the brilliance of the sunny day had been gathering towards this evening. She shot down to Magdalen Bridge, screeched to a halt and wheeled her bike through the entrance and into the quad. She felt brave enough to face Alistair's party on her own. Venetia was engaged to a Viscount from Christ Church, but there was no getting back with Alistair. She was no longer smitten. And she could never have told him about the operation.

In the end, it had been Charles' stepmother who'd escorted her to the psychiatrist's consulting room and then to the clinic. Brenda had seen her through. It was hard to understand why Charles disliked her, for she'd been so kind, especially afterwards. She'd seen Penny off to the station and when they parted she'd said: 'I know how painful it is, dear, and you probably think you'll never be happy again. But you will. Believe me. You have your whole future before you.'

The future was beginning now.